Political Affairs

A Contemporary Romance Novel

The Capitol Series
Book 1

Carolina Guzman

Copyright © 2023 by Carolina Guzman

All rights reserved. No part of this publication may be reproduced, stored or transmitted in any form or by any means, electronic, mechanical, photocopying, recording, scanning, or otherwise without written permission from the publisher. It is illegal to copy this book, post it to a website, or distribute it by any other means without permission.

Description: First Edition | Romance, 2023 | Series: The Capitol Series | Carolina Guzman Publisher |

Identifiers: ISBN 979-8-9894486-0-9 (ebook) | ISBN 979-8-9894486-1-6 (paperback) | ASIN B0CLKZZ8NJ (Amazon Kindle)

This is a work of fiction. Names, characters and incidents portrayed in it are the work of the author's imagination. Any resemblance to actual persons, living or dead, events or localities is entirely coincidental

Illustration: Kimbo Castillo - @comethaze93

Editor: Brandi Zelenka - @MyNotesInTheMargin

❦ Created with Vellum

The Capitol Series:
Political Affairs
Stringed Predicament - Coming Winter 2025

To 14 year-old me who saw this dream so far away and impossible. We did it pretty girl, we are finally following our dreams. It's going to be okay.

A Letter From The Author

Dear reader,

As I write this letter, I am finishing the final edits to get this baby to you. And while I am new to this, and this is my first work that it's ever published to a wider audience that is not just my computer notes or my secret journal, I want to give you a little background on why this work.

As you read in the dedication, this book is dedicated to 14 year old me, who had a pen, a journal and a dream. But most importantly is also dedicated to 26 year old me.

The idea of this book was born last year. May 2022 to be exact. The creation of this work came from a very dark period on my life that I have been battling since 2021. This book was a way for me to not only follow my long time dreams, but also to find happiness in my daily life. And while it may be a silly little romance book to some, for me, it was a beacon of light in my darkest of times.

I'm a very private person when it comes to my feelings, so this might be a shocker to my close friends/alpha readers who helped shape this book for the past year, but the reason this book was born it's because I was unhappy.

I was unhappy with my life, personally and professionally. While I am grateful to have a job that keeps a roof over my head, food on the table, and the bills paid, and while I am blessed enough to have a good livable wage job, I was still unhappy. Because truth to be told, the job I work doesn't fulfill me as a person, and I think it also influences the fact that I don't share, agree nor aligned —ideals, morals, and political beliefs wise— with the people I work with. But, in the society we live on, we cannot risk losing our stable job, with paid benefits and livable wages.

For the longest time, I chastised myself about this.

'At least you are fortunate and you have a job that pays the bills. Some are not as lucky',

'At least you don't live paycheck to paycheck',

'Your bills are paid, you have good benefits, what are you complaining about?'

These are some of the thoughts that have been invading my mind since 2021. So, I sat down and decided what I want to do with my life? What could I do fill up that space and void left in me after my 9am-5pm job? What could I do to bring a little happiness into my life? And so the idea of this book came to life. And I promised myself I was going to publish it, even if it meant self-publishing. So, I put pen to paper —or words to document— and started writing. And from this idea, came others. A series following the stories of characters in this book. And then some. After finishing this book, and sending it for feedback to my alpha readers, I picked up my fantasy book that I started to write ten years ago and finished it. And suddenly, the happiness was back in my life. I had a purpose. A reason to look forward to every day after 5pm.

I think in this society that we live on, we are conditioned, and it's ingrained in us, that if you have a stable job, you should be grateful and happy, because some are not as lucky. In consequence, we forget to follow our dreams, we forget to find things in our daily lives that brings us happiness. And so we become machines. We become products of the society that expect us to just work to survive.

However, I refuse to do that. I refused to be a product of the big machine. And so this book became my escape. My statement. My proof. My light at the end of the tunnel.

All this to say, to do what your heart desires. Even if the rest of the world thinks it's silly. If it makes you happy, if it brings you comfort, it's worth the shot.

And before you carry on, a few reminders:

Free Palestine

Free Congo

Free Sudan

Free Hawai'i

and last but not least FREE PUERTO RICO, THE OLDEST COLONY IN THE WORLD!

And another thing before you go:

While the main character's in the book are white af, there is a lot of diversity in my books. And it shall always be like that. From BIPOC characters, to LGBTQIA+, to Latine/Hispanic characters, because REPRESENTATION MATTERS!

Disclaimer and Warning

Disclaimer:

While I'm well aware the government as we know it doesn't work like how I wrote in this book —like at all, let's be real—, keep in mind this is a work of fiction and not real, so in my mind it does work like this. Keep that in mind when reading this. Not everything that happens here is how the government works in real life, but one could imagine how it would look like if it did worked for the people like it should.

Warning:

While this is a contemporary romance book and it doesn't have any major triggers, I did wrote about something that may trigger some. If you have experience the death of a parent, please keep in mind, in the book it's mentioned more than once the lost of a parent. As someone who experienced the death of a parent, in a way this was a closure for me and a way to deal with that lost.

xii *Disclaimer and Warning*

This book also contains adult material not suitable for minors. Read at your own risk.

Playlist

- Taylor Swift - Sparks Fly (Taylor's Version) **[Themed Song]**
- Taylor Swift - The Way I loved You (Taylor's Version)
- Taylor Swift - The Story of Us (Taylor's Version)
- Taylor Swift - Lover
- Demi Lovato - Two Pieces
- Demi Lovato - 4 EVER 4 ME
- Demi Lovato - Body Say
- Lewis Capaldi - Forget Me
- Lewis Capaldi - Pointless
- Lewis Capaldi - Heavenly State of Mind
- 5 Seconds of Summer - Kill My Time
- 5 Seconds of Summer - Lover of Mine
- Journey - Separate Ways (Worlds Apart)
- Passenger - Let Her Go
- Shania Twain - You're Still The One I Want
- Lauv - I Like Me Better
- Paravi - Angry

Prologue

Catherine - Freshman Orientation 2010

"Welcome, class of 2014, and welcome to the *Political Science* department!" a euphoric counselor said from the front of the auditorium. She was old in an *"I'm your grandma, and I'm going to bake your favorite cookies!"* way. She had round glasses and white hair with a couple of gray streaks. And while she was old, she stood with her back straight and a smile that adorned her wrinkled face. "Harvard University will become your home for the next four years of your undergrad. Should you decide to pursue graduate studies, we hope to keep you here. My name is Peggy, and I will be in charge of you today."

A boy sat down beside Catherine with a thud.

"Freshman orientation, the least of my favorite activities of orientation week," he voiced to no one in particular. "Devin Mack," he extended his hand to her. She turned to him. He had red hair, blue eyes, and a dimpled smile that could stop traffic. He looked athletic but not in an excessive way, the plaid shirt hugging his arms and showing his muscles under the shirt. He noticed her checking him out and gave her a mischievous smirk. She hesitantly shook his hand, frowning. His hand felt rough to the touch. Calloused.

"Catherine Babbitt," she said, her tone dismissive. Their class was big, and the faculty had too many departments. The chances of him being in any of her classes were slim.

"Kitty Cat," he replied, shaking her hand aggressively. She rolled her eyes. "Nice to meet you." She studied him. He was wearing ripped jeans, a band shirt, and Converse. "Good god, look at all the frat boy jerks and jocks. Future troublemakers," he continued, whistling. "I bet you twenty bucks, that one"—he pointed to a guy who was wearing slacks and a button-down shirt with its sleeves rolled up—"is the future president of Phi Delta, or whatever the fuck the frats are named here," he pointed out as if he knew from experience. She rolled her eyes.

"The counselor is talking," she said, shaking her head. Who was this guy who felt entitled to judge someone over their appearance? It baffled her how judgmental he was. Not only judgmental but placing stereotypes based on looks.

"Ah, you're one of those," he noted, propping his chin on his hand.

"One of those? What is that supposed to mean?" she asked him defensively. She tried keeping her anger from showing on her face but failed. He was pissing her off, going back to the stereotypes, and judging someone based on looks.

"Overachiever who never gets bad grades—a goody two shoes. One of those." He shrugged. She scoffed.

"For your information…" she replied as he placed a finger on her lips.

"Shhh, Miss Kitty Cat, the counselor is talking," he retorted. She jerked away from his hand. Furious. She was furious. She scanned the auditorium for a new chair, but the room was packed. She could either suck it up for the next hour or so, or she could stand on the walkways along the sides. She closed her eyes and took a deep breath. "Relax. It'll be over soon. These things don't last more than twenty-five minutes," Devin continued. She heard the distant voice of Peggy calling everyone to order.

"Alright, so we are going to divide into groups of two. You're going to pair with the person on your right, starting with those of you sitting in the walkways. So, for example, you"—Peggy explained, pointing to the guy sitting at the left corner of the front row—"will pair with her," she pointed to the girl to his right. "And you"—she said as she pointed to the next girl—"will pair with her, and so on— and you will introduce yourselves to each other."

Crap. Catherine thought. She ended up paired up with Mr. Band Shirts. She looked around anxiously to see if she could exchange partners, but everyone around her was already deep in conversation.

"Look at that Kitty Cat." He chuckled.

"Catherine. My name is Catherine," she corrected, crossing her arms, and glaring at him.

"Sure, Kitty Cat," he retorted. She rolled her eyes. "But we already did what she asked. So, where are you from?"

"I'm not going to tell you," she replied, busying herself by looking through the brochures for orientation day.

"Oh, come on, this is an exercise. We have to," he stated, wiggling his eyebrows, and giving her a devilish smirk.

"If I tell you, will you leave me alone?" she asked, not looking at him.

"Nope," he retorted, popping the '*p*' on the word. She rolled her eyes again.

"I am vastly annoyed by you," she grumbled.

"Vastly?" he repeated, whistling. "That's a big, formal word, Kitty Cat."

"Buffalo, Wyoming," she said, exasperated.

"Shut up, no way!" he exclaimed enthusiastically.

"What?" she asked, confused, turning to him.

"Hey neighbor, I'm from Story, Wyoming."

Double crap she thought to herself. Peggy's chirpy voice cut through her thoughts.

"Alrighty, everyone! Hope you got to know your neighbor because you might see them around for the next four years."

"Small world," Devin mused.

"Alrighty, we're going to take a two-hour recess so you can move around, familiarize yourselves with your surroundings, and have lunch. Afterwards, come back here so you can meet part of your faculty. Alright. Off you go."

"Thank God!" Devin said, standing up and stretching.

"Thank God, indeed," Catherine exclaimed, gathering her belongings. Hurriedly, she shrugged her backpack on her shoulders, ready to leave and put some distance between Band Shirts and her.

"Where are you going?" he asked, following her down the stairs and to the door.

"None of your business," she snapped, turning back to him, and shrugging unapologetically.

She turned and tripped. Devin reached for her, steadying her, an arm around her waist. He looked down at her and smiled, his dimples making an appearance.

"Feisty. I like you," he mumbled, leaving her in the middle of the hallway, staring at his receding back. "See you around, Kitty Cat," he expressed, looking over his shoulder at her with a mischievous look.

"Alright, alright, Mom, jeez!" Catherine said, shrugging off her mom's embrace, a little embarrassed. Catherine realized two things at that moment. One, she noticed, for the first time, the crow's feet around her blue eyes and the gray hairs adorning her beautiful black hair. The second, that she looked tired. While her mom, Leonora, was not as overbearing as some parents are to their only children, she had worked her ass off to get where she was. Raising her after her father died in a tragic accident at work, working three jobs, always making sure Catherine had everything she needed to succeed. Catherine wrapped her arms around Leonora's frail body and hugged her tightly.

"My little girl is so grown up," Leonora mumbled.

"Mom!" she exclaimed, shrugging off her embrace again, her face red with embarrassment. She looked to the opposite side of her dorm room, where her roommate, Emily, was sitting on her bed. Catherine shot her an apologetic look. Her mom coughed.

"Okay, I'm done," Leonora replied. "Remember, don't—"

"Don't open the door to strangers, don't accept drinks from anyone, and keep my pepper spray on hand. Yes, Mom. We have been through this ever since I got my acceptance letter," Catherine said, scrunching her nose in annoyance.

"I—" Leonora started to say, but Catherine interrupted her.

"Call me when you land. And for the love of God, cut down on the smoking. Those things are going to kill you," Catherine reprimanded, walking Leonora to the rental car. Her mom turned to look at her.

"Your dad would be very proud," she said, her voice breaking at the end.

"I know," Catherine replied in a whisper, hugging her.

Leonora got in the car and drove away. As she watched

her driving off, she thought about her dad. He died when she was seven after a tragic accident at work. She smiled a little, agreeing with her. He would have been proud of her and all her accomplishments. On her way back to her room, she thought about all the challenges she would face in her first year. She felt anxious, nervous, and giddy all at the same time. She went up the stairs and back up to her dorm room. She stood on top of the stairs, soaking in the feeling of change, of being far away from her mom.

"Would you look at that? A mysterious black cat is my neighbor," the voice of the annoying boy from the auditorium said. The feelings shattered. She rolled her eyes, annoyed. Devin was leaning against a door, his ankles crossed, hands inside the pockets of his jeans, and a smug look on his face.

"What are you doing here?" she asked, walking past him.

"What do you mean what am I doing here? I live across the hallway," he replied, pointing his thumb to the door behind him. She frowned, looking at the door he was pointing at. The door was right across from her dorm room. She groaned.

"Are you stalking me?" she asked, her hand on her doorknob.

"You aren't that important, Kitty Cat." He shrugged.

She scoffed. "You are so insufferable," she said, opening the door.

"And you are so uptight," he mumbled. She turned around, shocked, and saw him smirk as he closed the door to his dorm.

That night, she dreamed of the playful smirk adorning the face of her new neighbor.

Chapter One

Devin - First Day of Freshman Year

"*Carajo*," Devin turned to the voice of his roommate. He was packing his books and notebooks into his backpack. His roommate Kyle was a half-Puerto Rican who spoke Spanish and cursed too much. He had sandy blond, slightly curly hair, and blue eyes, and his tan skin paled as he looked at the clock on the nightstand. "Fuck," he cursed, passing a hand through his bed hair, slightly curlier than what it was the night before.

"Good morning," Devin chirped to his roommate. Kyle jumped from his bed.

"Why didn't you wake me up?" his roommate asked him, picking up a pair of jeans off the floor and putting them on.

"Kyle, I'm not your mom," Devin said. "We're adults, and you're responsible for waking up for class." He slid his backpack on and headed for the door. "I suggest you get an alarm clock. I'll see you tonight."

The door across the hall was opening, and he secretly hoped Catherine was responsible. A head full of black hair greeted him, emerald-green eyes piercing through him. Catherine rolled her eyes as she closed her door with a slam.

"Good morning sunshine. Ready for our first day?" he asked, leaning against his door, crossing his arms over his chest, and smirking at her. She mimicked his pose, leaning against her door. He felt the smirk grow on his face. She huffed.

"I'm grateful we don't have any classes together this semester," she said, heading to the stairs. She paused when her door opened, and her roommate came out.

"Babes, you forgot these," her roommate called from the door, dangling a lanyard with keys from her fingers. The lanyard was lilac with little pink tulips. A couple of keys and pepper spray dangling from the end.

Tulips and the color lilac.

He wondered if those two things were amongst the things she liked. Catherine turned to her roommate and grabbed the keys.

"Thanks." Catherine glared at him before she hurried down the stairs.

"I wouldn't be so sure about that," he teased, following after her. She seemed confused by his statement. "I saw the roster in one of my classes, and I'm pretty sure Catherine Babbitt was one of the names on it." She stopped at the top of the stairs at that. Her face adorned by a faint blush. He turned back to her and winked. "See you in class."

Later that afternoon, he walked to his *Introduction to Political Philosophy* class, large enough to take place in an amphitheater. Devin entered and sat in one of the back chairs, the ones in the front already full. Even the seats around him were occupied, but the one beside him was empty.

"Okay everyone, settle down," the professor called out.

"Jeez. Why is this class so full?" he muttered under his breath.

"Is this seat taken?" a soft female voice asked. He recognized it, like music to his ears. He had been dreaming about that sweet, melodic voice since this morning, looking forward to this class since he saw her name on the roster.

"Well, well, well. Look what the *kitty cat* dragged in. It is now," he purred, turning to her and smirking. Her eyes landed on him, opening up like two full moons. He smiled at her reaction. "I told you we had a class together." He shifted down the row, letting her take his original seat. She looked hesitant but sat down with a thud, sighing, and throwing her backpack on the floor.

"It's the professor," she said, taking out her notebook.

"Huh?" He followed her lead, taking his things out of his backpack.

"You asked why the class was so full. To answer your question, it's the professor. That's why the class is so full," she replied, turning to him. "He's one of the best."

"You heard my question?" he asked, confused. He thought no one heard him. She nodded. "Ah," he replied.

She threw her hair up in a ponytail, and her lavender perfume wafted in his direction. He inhaled slowly, breathing her in. He looked at her from the corner of his eye. She had put on a pair of glasses, round with a black frame. He turned his head slightly to get a better view of her. She had a long neck and sharp jaw, the skin smooth. A birthmark marked the skin between her neck and collarbone. She turned to look at him and caught him staring, boldly meeting his eyes. He smirked, turning back toward the front of the classroom. The class dragged on, and her scent remained. It was the only thing on his mind.

"Alright class, for your first assignment, which is due

next week, you are going to pick one political movement from the 1500s to the 1800s, and you will write a three-page essay on the philosophy and ideology of that movement," the professor announced from the front of the room. "If you have any questions, my office hours are on the syllabus. Drop by my office, and we can chat. Class dismissed."

Devin turned to his right, but Catherine was already packed and gone. He sighed, disappointed. He packed his stuff and left the classroom, though he didn't get very far.

"Oh, come on. Just tell me your name," a guy was saying to a female student in the hallway. His voice was pushy and arrogant, like the person he was talking to owed him something. Three guys were caging her in, her back against the wall. Devin turned the other way, minding his own business, trying to see if he could find Catherine.

"I don't want to. I'm not interested," the woman said. *Catherine.* He'd recognize that voice anywhere. He stopped in his tracks, turning around.

"Oh, come on, we're classmates. We'll be seeing each other a lot," the boy pressed.

"I said I'm not interested," Catherine snapped. Devin rolled his neck and approached the group.

"Come on, be a good girl and give me your name," the douchebag said, plucking at a piece of her hair and twirling it around his finger. She tried to move away from his hold. Something inside Devin sparked outrage, spitting fire into his veins. It ignited the innate instinct and need to protect her.

"What is this, high school? Is there a problem here?" he asked, glancing at Catherine. Luckily, he stood a good few inches taller than her aggressors. All three of them turned to him. "I suggest you leave her alone." Devin reached for her hand, entwining their fingers, and dragged her behind his back, her hand squeezing his in a silent thanks. He let go of her to cross his arms over his chest, taking a defiant stance and looking down at her aggressors.

"There wasn't one until you showed up," the douchebag scoffed as if Devin had interrupted an important moment.

"Listen, *bro*, I suggest you leave her alone. You can't go around bullying people. Grow the hell up," Devin said, leaning to the side and shielding her further when he noticed the idiot trying to peer behind him. He felt Catherine's hand grab the back of his shirt, fisting it tightly. He needed to get her out of their sight.

"Or what? Are you her knight in shining armor?" the douchebag asked, stepping forward, only a breath away from Devin's face.

"Just leave her alone," he said. "Are you okay?" he asked her once they were outside the building, not once letting go of her hand. She didn't seem to mind the contact either, since she made no move to pull away. He came to a stop in front of her. He crouched down until they were at eye level. She looked into his eyes, her pretty emerald eyes rimmed red. She looked down and nodded, like she was trying to convince herself that she was fine. "Hey, it's okay, he's gone," he reassured her, squeezing her hand. "Were you walking back to the dorm? I can walk you back if you want. I was headed there myself."

"Please, walk with me?" she asked, her words barely above a whisper.

"Of course." He let her go, but she grabbed his hand again. "Come on. Do you want to talk about it? You don't have to." She shook her head, so he gave her hand another reassuring squeeze. "I won't let anything happen to you, Kitty Cat."

They walked back to the dorm, only the reverberating

sounds of their steps on the gravel filling the silence. When they were at her door, Catherine let go of his hand.

"Thank you," she said softly. She looked up at him, her eyes traveling the planes of his face, studying him. While she was still upset from what happened, the color had returned to her face, tinting the apple of her cheeks with a slight blush. Or maybe it was the sun they walked under. Either way, she looked livelier now than she had twenty minutes before. She smiled a little and looked down. "I judged you too quickly. You didn't have to do that, but you did," he smiled down at her.

"Remember the homework," he said, walking to his dorm room. She nodded. "Go on in, Kitty Cat. I'll see you around." He only stepped into his room when he heard the lock turn on her door. That night he went to bed dreaming of pretty emerald eyes and black hair.

Midterms week, Freshman year

"Who are those slices for?" Kyle asked as Devin loaded a disposable plate with two slices of pizza and headed for the entrance. Devin ignored him and crossed the hallway to knock on Catherine's door.

"Did you leave your keys behind again, Emily?" she exclaimed from the other side. She froze, sizing him up with her gaze. Her eyes settled on the plate in his hand. "What are you doing here?"

"Eat," he said, thrusting the plate at her. He massaged his neck, looking around awkwardly. Maybe he intruded. He shouldn't have done this. What if she feels uncomfortable? Does she have any allergies? Is she lactose intolerant? "I know you're obsessing over assignments and probably haven't eaten anything today. No pressure on eating the pizza though. I just thought you should eat something."

"How do you... Never mind. Thanks," she said, her cheeks tinting a soft rosy color, and smiled while looking down at the plate in her hands. He nodded, turning to leave as she called out, "Hey, are you good at Econ? I'm having trouble with one of the exercises of the assignment." she hesitated. "If you're not busy of course."

"I'll be knocking on your door in half an hour," he called over his shoulder, stepping into his dorm.

"Oh, you have a crush," Kyle said as he walked in. Kyle's tone sounded a little off, but he decided not to dwell on it.

"Shut up," Devin mumbled, flipping off his roommate and grabbing a slice of pizza. He rifled through his backpack and looked for his Econ assignment. He and Catherine had the same professor but a different class.

"Why do you help her so much? It's not like she likes you," Kyle argued.

Devin shrugged. "I just like helping people."

"*Mentiroso*. You fucking liar. In the three weeks we've lived together, you haven't helped me once, even when I've asked." Kyle sounded offended.

"It's different with her. Her voice isn't as annoying as yours," Devin deadpanned.

He finished his slice of pizza and brushed his teeth. He gave himself a once-over in the mirror, splashing water on his face and fixing his hair, combing through it with his fingers. "I'll see you later."

He hurried across the hallway and knocked on her door.

"It's unlocked," she called from inside. Devin opened the door and let himself in.

"You shouldn't have your door unlocked like that. It's

dangerous," he chided. He spotted the plate with both slices of untouched pizza, her nose buried in her book. "You haven't eaten, either."

"Well, I need to finish all my homework so I can start the assignments due next week," she said, not looking up. He walked over to her, snatched the pencil from her hand, and closed her book. "Hey, I was..." she started to protest. He placed the plate in front of her.

"Eat. Coffee is not a meal. Eat, or I won't help you, Kitty Cat," he threatened. She gave him an annoyed glance, eyes squinting. "You want me to help you with the assignment? Then eat."

She huffed but didn't protest.

He looked around as she ate. The room looked like a typical dorm. Two single beds, two desks, and two small chest dressers. A mirror version of his dorm. Her bed was perfectly made, with little to no decorations on her side of the room. Her sheets were white, and there was one lilac-colored pillow. Her roommate's side was the complete opposite with bursts of color, fuzzy pillows, and decorations on her walls around the bed. One potted plant on her roommate's side of the window. There was a flyer on her nightstand about a campus meeting for volunteers at the local animal shelter. He smiled.

"I love what you've done with the place, Kitty Cat. Feels refreshing," he commented sarcastically.

"I didn't know I had an interior decorator here judging my room," she replied around a mouthful of cold pizza, her cheeks puffed full of food. He smirked, and she rolled her eyes. He was becoming addicted to her never-ending eye-rolling. It was turning into his favorite trait of hers. He would go as far as pissing her off, just to see her roll her eyes. He smiled, noting the little blob of sauce in the corner of her mouth. She wiped it away with her napkin.

"Is lilac your favorite color?" he asked, sitting at the foot of her bed.

"Yes, lilac and lavender shades," she replied, finishing her pizza. "I'm done."

"Okay, what do you have trouble with? Which exercise?" he inquired, moving to stand behind her. The lavender smell in her hair drove him crazy. He hadn't been able to get it off his mind since that first day of class. It was addictive and intoxicating.

"This one," she said, opening her book again. "I don't understand how to get the results." She pointed to an exercise. He nodded.

She listened with keen attention as he walked her through his notes, explaining to her as best as he could how to get the results. She tried it again, and he compared it with his results. He nodded, showing her the exercise, and letting her know she got it right. A sense of pride bloomed in his chest, and she offered him a grateful smile that reached her eyes and made them shine bright, the green in them becoming two shades lighter. He couldn't help but return her smile. Her eyes were on his notes again, her mind on numbers and graphs, determination on her features. Like she wanted to get it right. But his eyes and thoughts were all over her, her face, her eyes, her smell, and the little frown on her brow as she concentrated. He couldn't help but stare at her.

"Oh god, I'm going to fail this midterm so badly!" she exclaimed, dropping her forehead on top of the books on her desk. That snapped him from his thoughts. They'd been at it for a couple of hours, and she was still struggling to pick it up. He laughed.

"Not if I can prevent it," he said. "I'll tutor you regularly. We can meet up one day after class."

"Can you? I can't lose my scholarship."

"Of course, I can, Kitty Cat," he said. She smiled. "It doesn't bother you when I use the nickname."

"Not for the time being. We'll see later," she admitted.

"Am I not annoying anymore?" he asked, feigning shock.

"Oh, you are still annoying as hell," she shot back, rolling her eyes. He chuckled. There she was again, rolling those perfect emerald eyes at him. "Maybe less annoying." She offered him a little smile. "Thank you, by the way. For everything, I mean. Helping me that day after class and today. You didn't have to do any of it." She stared down at her fidgeting hands.

"He is an annoying asshole," he said. "If he ever gives you trouble, let me know, okay? Me and my boys will leave him a little gift at the frat house." She nodded, pondering.

"Who are your boys? Is it your roommate? Another classmate?" she asked, calling him out on his bullshit, like she could see right through him. She rolled her eyes again. He put his hands up in surrender.

"Alright, you caught me, Kitty Cat, it's just me. No boys," he chuckled. She laughed at him. "Still meant what I said, if he ever makes you feel uncomfortable again, let me know, okay?" She nodded, looking at him, a spark of something flashing in her eyes. Trust. She was starting to trust him.

"Am I interrupting something?" someone asked from behind them. They both turned toward the voice. "Should I come back later or…?"

"No, no it's fine. This is Devin. He's a classmate of mine. He was helping me with the Econ homework. He also lives across the hallway," Catherine explained.

"Ah, I see. I'm Emily, Catherine's roommate. Nice to

meet you," she said, extending her hand to him. He shook it. She was a petite, Asian girl, with a bob haircut and bangs that framed her chiseled high cheekbones. She had round glasses like Catherine and a couple of freckles raining on her cheeks. She had some colorful, flamboyant clothing on, just like her side of the room. A notepad and clipboard in her arms.

"Okay, I'll head out now. Let me know which day works better for you so we can start on those tutoring sessions. We don't want you to fall in the bad graces of the scholarship gods," Devin teased. Catherine laughed, the sound of it so contagious that he found himself laughing too. "Relax a little, Kitty Cat. And for fuck's sake, lock this door," he added, glancing pointedly at both of them. She walked to the door and shoved him out. "Good night, Kitty Cat."

"Good night, Satan," she returned.

"Satan?" he asked curiously.

"Devin, devil. Only one letter changes. Same thing," she said. He suppressed a laugh and nodded, crossing the hall. *He secretly loved the nickname.*

"Good one," he said as he started to close his dorm door, only shutting it once he heard the lock of her door.

Chapter Two

Catherine - Spring, Freshman Year

"Kitty Cat, stop stressing over it. You will do fine. It's not like the presentation plays a role in you passing the class," Devin said, looking at her flashcards.

"It does play a role, Satan. It counts for fifteen percent of our grade," Catherine argued. "What if I freeze—or worse, say it all wrong?"

Devin laughed, his whole chest vibrating. "When has *the* Catherine Babbitt failed?" he asked rhetorically. "Don't answer that question. Kitty Cat, you are going to do fine. We've seen all the other presentations. They have nothing on yours. Come on, you even saw mine. *Mine*, Kitty Cat. I wasn't as prepared as you are, and I still got a B-plus." His tone was soft, reassuring.

"But what if—"

"No buts. One more time, and then we're going out for dinner to get your mind off it." He shuffled through her flashcards. She looked at him, studying the way he lay on her bed like he had all the confidence in the world in her, believing she would not fail. She wanted to believe him. She wanted to feel as confident in herself as he seemed to be in her. But she knew she was going to mess up.

"Ready when you are," he said, not looking up. She sighed and presented to her audience of one, one final time. "See? That wasn't so bad. Now, on Tuesday, just pretend you're presenting only to me. You'll be fine." He stood up from the bed and walked to where she was sitting at her desk. "Now, shall we go eat? I'm starving." She looked up at him and nodded. He walked to the door and grabbed her jacket, helping her put it on. "What are we feeling?" he asked, placing his hands on her shoulders, tracing idle circles.

"Not pizza, please. We've had pizza twice this week already," she protested. He chuckled and bent down to kiss the top of her head.

She froze, and so did he. She panicked. This was the first time he had come so close to her. A warm feeling filling her chest.

"How about we go to that diner off campus and have some burgers and milkshakes?" he asked, breaking the awkward silence. She looked up at him, and he wiggled his eyebrows. She rolled her eyes at his antics, hiding a little smile. She stepped away and pushed him to the stairs. *Crisis averted.* The proximity and the action confused her. She didn't hate it, but she also didn't love it.

"You're driving," she warned him.

"How else are we going to get there?" he asked, chuckling. They got to his car, and he opened the door for her, bowing at the waist like a valet. "M'lady." She laughed, shoving him away.

"Let's go, I'm starving," she said, sitting in her side of the car. He smiled at her, his dimples appearing on his cheeks, and closed her door. He walked to his side and got in, turning on the car, and as usual, he had the 80s rock station playing.

"Any Way You Want It" by Journey came through the speakers. Devin started to drum his finger on the wheel, humming. She started to bob her head to the tune, singing softly. By the time they reached the diner, the song had changed to "Hit Me With Your Best Shot" by Pat Benatar. They entered the diner and sat at one of the back booths.

"Hello darlings, what can I get ya?" the server asked, placing two menus and two glasses of water on the table. She was a middle-aged woman, with blonde hair and streaks of gray on her temples. Her face looked soft, and her eyes kind.

"I—" Catherine started.

"We'll both have your greasiest burger with fries, as well as one strawberry milkshake for her and one chocolate milkshake for me," Devin said.

"Bacon?" the waitress asked.

"Yes, on both," he replied, shooting Catherine a wink.

"Alright, coming right up." She took the menus from them then walked toward the kitchen.

"You didn't even let me see the menu!" Catherine protested, crossing her arms over her chest and pouting.

"As if I don't know what you always order," Devin replied under his breath and taking a sip from his water.

"Right, I forgot you know me so well," she muttered, rolling her eyes.

"I do, Kitty Cat. More than you think."

"If you say so."

He placed his arms on the table, entwining his fingers, and looked at her. He was determined to prove her wrong. *And he did.*

"Your middle name is Elizabeth. Your favorite color is soft purple. Not quite lavender, not quite lilac. You love tulips. You love puppies. You are a perfectionist. When you are nervous about a class, you stay in your dorm room and don't go out. You eat, breathe, and drink the material until you perfect it. You are way ahead on all the homework. You love sunsets. You love winter weather. You hate seafood. You don't say it out loud, but you love Emily. She's the sister you never had, even though you haven't known her for that long. You worry about others more than you worry about yourself. You see the best in people. You don't open up easily or quickly to anyone. You wear your heart on your sleeve. You are sensitive. You love volunteering. Especially at animal shelters. You love to read in your free time. And you don't say it, but I know you want to change the world. Make it a better place for everyone. You wanna make a difference," he said, listing everything he knew about her. Describing her to a *t*. She recounted the past couple of months. From freshman orientation to now, and how, in such a little time, Devin had taken his time to get to know her.

Not just as Catherine, the next-door neighbor, but as Catherine. Just Catherine. He didn't list all those things to prove a point, he did it to let her know he cared about the little details, he cared about the things that made her, *her*. But it was the same for her. She knew him like he knew her. He hated injustices, fought for what was right, loved helping people, and always made sure she was fed, even when she was stressed with schoolwork. He was slowly becoming her safe space, and that scared her.

"Shall I go on?" he asked rhetorically.

"You knowing all of that is weird," she whispered. Something warm filled her chest. She looked down at her hands folded on her lap.

"I'm just very observant of the people I care about," he said, shrugging, confirming her thoughts. But there was something else there. Something shone in his eyes, fading too quickly for her to wrap her head around. Maybe he felt something for her. Maybe he liked her. That made her hesitate. Her experience of a boy liking her was nonexistent. The possibility of Devin feeling more than friendship for her terrified her because she enjoyed his company, she enjoyed having him around, and if all of that changed in the blink of an eye, she didn't know how to work through it.

When their food arrived, they ate in silence. The drive back to the dorm was quiet, with only the faint sound of music in the background. The silence was uncomfortable, leaving an elephant in the room neither of them acknowledged. Both were lost in thought. When they reached their doors, Devin wrapped a hand around the back of her neck and drew her forward to kiss her temple. And while it was only the second time he had kissed her, she liked it. She liked it a lot, and it confused her.

"Good night, Kitty Cat," he said before entering his apartment, the sound of his lock filling the silence. She looked back to his door, a small smile playing on her lips.

Tuesday rolled around faster than Catherine would have liked, and it was time for her to present. She sat in her usual chair, the one beside her still empty. She hadn't seen Devin since Saturday, his excuse being that he was busy with schoolwork. A lie she didn't believe at all but didn't want to press on. Rather than dwell on his absence, she dropped her bag into his seat, a habit she'd developed in order to save his chair for him.

"Okay class, settle down! We have two presentations today," the professor called from the podium. Catherine looked around. No sight of Devin. A pang of disappointment settled on her chest.

The other person, Whitney, presented first. A few minutes after she started, Catherine's backpack was placed at her feet. She looked up and Devin was there, holding a cardboard cup carrier. He smiled at her as he dropped into his seat. A wave of relief washed over her.

"I'm sorry I'm late. I stopped by the coffee shop to get you this," he whispered, handing her a cup of coffee and kissed her temple. She looked away, hiding her blush.

"I thought you weren't gonna make it," she whispered back, taking a sip from her coffee. Cappuccino, no sugar, oat milk, and a pinch of cinnamon—just how she liked it. Maybe he did know everything about her. She smiled into the cup.

"Are you kidding? I wouldn't miss it. I'll always be here for you." He flashed her a dimpled smile.

Chapter Three

Catherine - Summer, Present Day

"Maverick, what is the ETA on that Congress report I asked for?" Catherine asked, reading through the stack of papers in the folder in her hands.

"Boss, the draft on the energy resolution hasn't come out yet," Maverick said from his desk. Maverick was a young man in his late twenties, brilliant, with blonde wavy hair and piercing blue eyes.

"What do you mean the draft hasn't been posted yet?" she asked, gazing at the legislative aide.

"Exactly what you just heard, boss. My hands are tied. I can give you what I have, but without the resolution draft, mine is just useless points," he explained, sipping on his coffee.

She walked to his cubicle, placing an arm on the wall divider. "Kowalski," she said, turning to the office's legal counsel.

"Boss?" he said, popping his head from his cubicle. Kowalski was a man in his late fifties with a keen knack for small details.

"Damage control," she said, massaging her forehead. "We need this report before the boss flies out to the district for the rest of the week. I'm not about to have a pissed-off congressman on a plane throwing a tantrum."

"Cat, I will deal with him. Remember, I'm also on that plane back to Michigan," he pointed out.

"I forgot you're leaving with him. This is going to be a disaster," she whispered, cursing under her breath.

"Babbitt!" someone yelled from the office foyer. *Her boss.* She closed her eyes and gave a silent prayer, pinching the bridge of her nose.

"You got this, boss," Maverick said, giving her a thumbs up.

"Print what you have. And for the love of God, someone, please call the House Floor and ask for an ETA on the draft of the power grid funding resolution," she said, leaving the cubicles. "How bad is it, Isabela?" she whispered to the communications director outside the congressman's door.

"Bad," Isabela replied. Her dark curls moved as she shook her head.

"On a scale of losing the primary to being forced to forfeit on election day?" she asked.

"Impeachment."

"Shit." Catherine nodded, dismissing Isabela.

"Here," Maverick said, handing her a paper.

"Thanks," she whispered. She took a deep breath and opened the door.

"I don't give a flying rat's ass about your board of directors and how many issues your company has. My constituents don't have clean running water. I don't care if you have to get water from Antarctica. This issue has been going on for weeks now. And your inactivity and indifference are not something I will tolerate. And let's not talk about the millions of dollars for infrastructure you have wasted," the congressman said into the phone. Catherine stood by the door. The congressman was in his mid-forties with peppered hair, a full beard, and stood a good six-feet tall with an athletic body. "Fix this," he said, slamming down the phone. "I hope you don't have plans this upcoming week, Catherine," he said, sitting on his desk.

A knock on the door made her jump. Catherine turned to open it. Maggie, the scheduler, stood outside. She was a petite, curvy, half-Latina brunette with a sunshine and rainbows personality.

"What?" Catherine asked.

"I need him to sign this," she said, handing her a folder with a congressional logo. Catherine took it and nodded, closing the door. She opened the folder and saw a certificate for one of the departing summer interns of the office. She walked to the desk and placed the folder in front of him.

"Thanks," he said, grabbing his favorite fountain pen. "Is this the district office intern or the one here?" he asked, signing the bottom of the certificate.

"Here. She's the one who helped Isabela. We gave her a communications department internship, which is her degree," Catherine replied. Michael nodded, his eyes somber, tired. He gave her the certificate. She walked back to the door and handed the signed certificate to Maggie, who stood outside waiting. "Cancel his next meeting."

"But the next meeting—"

"Reschedule it," Catherine interrupted. Maggie nodded. "And get us some coffee please. We have a long afternoon."

"It's okay," he said.

"No, it's not, Michael," she said as she sat down in one of the chairs in front of the desk, crossing her arms on her chest, the folder hidden behind her arms.

"How is my favorite chief of staff handling the fort today?" he asked, looking at her.

"I'm your only chief of staff, Michael," she said, laughing.

"True," he said, smiling at her. "Still my favorite, though." He loosened his tie and unbuttoned his top button.

"You can't solve every problem, Michael."

"That's what they elected me to do."

"Yes, but sometimes there's only so much you can do. This is on the local officials. Not you," she assured him.

"But we need to escalate the matter, bring awareness, and I need to put pressure on the local officials," he said. "Or shit won't get done."

"Okay, what do we know?"

"Stella, one of the towns in our congressional district, has been without clean water for over a month, and the public-private company is responsible for it."

"What can we do?" she asked. "What's the solution?"

"I don't know. We need to figure out what's going on. Come to the district and help me solve this. You get shit done. You're quick and think fast on your feet. You see the small details nobody else sees. I need you down there with me."

"I'll cancel my meetings for next week," she said. "What happened on the Natural Resources committee? You were riled up when you got here."

"Nothing. Utterly nothing. No resolution was voted to be sent to the House Floor. Nobody could compromise. No one could find a middle ground," he said exasperated.

"Welcome to the dark side of politics."

A week later

"Let's plan a meeting with Senator Jenkins when we go back to Washington for the session. We need to solve this soon," Michael said. Catherine nodded, writing a new note in her phone.

"Anything else?" she asked. They had just left the water treatment plant responsible for the lack of clean running water, mainly due to bureaucracy and red tape, but mostly due to corruption.

"Go, I know you think you're late for the airport," Michael said. She laughed.

"I'll see you back in DC boss."

She arrived at the airport and passed security, leaving her with three hours before her flight. Some call her obsessive about her antics in wanting to be at the airport three to four hours before her flight. But she doesn't care. Shit happens. Better to be there early than late. She walked to a coffee shop in the terminal.

"Hi, what can I get you?" the cashier asked.

"I'll have a large hot cappuccino with oat milk, no sugar, and a sprinkle of cinnamon."

"Would that be all?" She eyed a cinnamon roll, and a pang of sadness hit her like a wave. Remembering how she always used to have a cinnamon roll with her coffee from the little coffee shop near campus with Devin. She looked back at the cashier.

"Yes," she replied and paid.

"Name?"

"Catherine." When her order was ready, she walked to her gate, but since she had two and a half hours to spare, she went into the convenience store and perused the book area while sipping on her cappuccino. She picked a book and read the back. Uninterested, she placed it back on the shelf. She tried reaching for one on top, but her five-foot-two body was unable to reach. "Dammit," she cursed under her breath. She fixed her glasses, trying to reach for the book again.

"Allow me," a man said as he reached for the book. The voice was familiar.

"Thanks."

The man stood a good foot taller than her. His t-shirt hugged his biceps, jeans accentuating his ass. He had short red hair styled back. Was she staring? Yes. Absolutely. Although maybe she shouldn't. She had a boyfriend back in DC who loved her very much. But a little peek never hurt anyone. The stranger handed her the book. Their fingers brushed when she grabbed it from his extended hand. She could have sworn she felt a shock when their skin touched.

"Here," he said. She looked up at him and met his eyes. Blue eyes she would recognize anywhere. "Catherine?"

"Satan?" she gasped, taking a minute to gather herself. "Shit, I mean Devin," she said, her voice surprisingly calm.

"It's okay, it's been so long." His eyes twinkled in amusement. "How have you been?" He made to hug her but decided against it. She looked around, hoping for a hole in the ground to open up and swallow her whole.

"I've been doing alright," she replied. "How about you?"

"I've been good," he said, putting a hand on his neck and rubbing it. She glanced around some more. The magnets on the other side of the wall looked interesting. Anything but seeing those piercing ocean-blue eyes. "You still have it," he said. She snapped her gaze back to him, furrowing her brows in confusion. He must have noticed her confusion because he added, "The necklace," he said, a hint of blush on his cheeks.

She didn't notice she was playing with it until he pointed it out.

Nine years ago - Christmas Break

"Okay, Kitty Cat. Ready for the exchange?" Devin asked from the floor in front of the Christmas tree. She nodded.

"I hope you like what I got you," she mumbled nervously.

"I'm sure I will," he reassured her. "Okay, here. Open it," he said, handing her a small box.

"Devin... I..." she stuttered.

"Oh, no, no Kitty Cat. It's not what you think," he reassured her, rubbing his neck nervously. She exhaled.

"Okay," she replied, opening the little box. Inside lay a silver chain, a small oval encrusted with a diamond pendant. "Devin..." she whispered. She looked up at him. He was gazing down at the floor—a bashful look on his face.

"Ugh, get a room, you two," Emily joked beside her. Catherine nudged her with her elbow.

"It's beautiful. But it must have cost you a fortune," she said, eying the necklace and passing a delicate finger over the pendant. "I can't accept this," she added, observing him. He looked offended.

"Bullshit," he admonished, kneeling, and taking the box from her. He got the necklace out. "Turn around." She did, gathering her hair in one hand. Devin clasped the necklace around her neck. She let her hair fall and looked down at the necklace. She turned and peered at him, wondering if he felt anything for her beyond friendship, just like she did.

"Thank you," she whispered and hugged him. He kissed the side of her head.

"Ah. Yeah," she whispered. "It was good to see you, Devin." She placed the book back on the shelf. Devin nodded. She turned around and left the store in a rush. She walked to her gate and sat at the far end.

Emotions she thought she was over resurfaced. Anger, nostalgia, hurt, sadness, confusion. All those mixed? A recipe for disaster. She put in her AirPods, opened her work computer, and caught up on some documents, hoping that work would help her forget those emotions. She called Maggie while typing.

"Mags, can you call Senator Jenkins' office and ask to schedule a meeting with the boss? He wants to meet with the Senator to discuss the water treatment plant problem. And it has to be ASAP," she said.

"I'll get right to it. Are you at the airport? Of course, you are. You're paranoid."

"Goodbye Mags, see you tomorrow at the office bright and early," she said, hanging up. She finished the final touches on the document and called Maverick. "Any news on the House Floor draft?"

"Yes. Just finished the report. I'm clicking send right about now," he said. Her phone pinged with the notification. She opened the attachment and read through it.

"This is good. Send it to the district so they can give it to the boss. I'll see you tomorrow."

An hour later, she was lining up on the plane, looking for her seat. She found it and sat down. Her phone rang with a call from her boyfriend, and she smiled at the screen.

"Hey, we'll have to make it quick, I only have a few minutes before take-off, how was work?" she asked him.

"It was busy, not the usual busy, but busy. We got some

new contracts from the Department of Defense. I might need to travel to Area 51 to train people there. That is all still on hold for the time being. They told me to have a bag ready in case I need to fly."

"Which means you are most definitely traveling."

"Yeah. Anyway, how was the district?"

"It was good. Sort of cold and wet," she replied. The stewardess announced they were waiting for one more passenger to take off. "Hey, we're taking off soon. I'll see you when I land. Remember, it's DCA, not Dulles."

"I know. I'll see you in a couple of hours," he said. "Love you."

"Love you," she replied and hung up.

"I'm so sorry I'm late. I got lost," a too-familiar voice said. The seat to her right was empty, but so were others on the plane. What were the odds that he would be seated next to her? "14A," he said, standing in the aisle. She was in 14B. Devin looked down at her, and he froze like a deer caught in headlights.

What were the odds?

Chapter Four

Devin - Fall, Sophomore Year

"You really need to learn to lock your door, Kitty Cat!" Devin exclaimed from the door of Catherine's new apartment, locking it behind him.

"Sorry, I came back in a hurry," she said in the distance.

"Can I come in?" he asked, knocking on her door.

"Well, duh."

He opened her door and found her standing in front of the mirror getting ready. She was wearing a miniskirt, a blouse, and her usual black Converse. Her hair was down, the soft waves loose. He frowned, confused by her outfit and why she looked nervous and self-conscious as she straightened the already straight hem of her shirt.

"What do you think?" she asked, turning around. She looked beautiful. He sucked in a breath. He opened his mouth to reply but closed it when nothing came out. He tilted his head to the side, gazing at her.

Why was she dressed up, and where was she going? It was unusual for her to dress like this when she was going to the bar to play pool with him and his friends.

"Where are you going?" he asked instead of answering

her question, sitting on the foot of her bed, leaning back on his hands, aiming for a nonchalant posture, trying to hide his confusion and jealousy.

"On a date," she replied, sounding excited. Too excited for his liking. He tried to hide the disappointment on his face. "Devin, be serious. How do I look?" she asked again, twirling around.

"You look fine. Who's the sucker?"

"His name is Miles. He's a defenseman and the captain of the lacrosse team."

"Miles Anderson?" he asked in what he hoped wasn't surprise.

"Yes. That Miles. I was surprised too. Who would've thought he, of all people, would ask a girl like me out."

"How did that happen?"

"I was in the student center, helping with the food and clothing donation drive for the shelter when he showed up to drop off a bag of clothes," she explained. "After introducing himself, he asked me out on the spot."

Devin nodded before standing and approaching her, throwing an arm around her shoulders, smiling fondly at her. Her angst melted away as she looked at his face through the mirror, and he felt her relax when he kissed the back of her head.

"Wear a jacket. It's kind of chilly out. And be careful. And call me if you need anything," he insisted, hugging her. He walked to her door but paused, turning back to her. "You look more than fine, Kitty Cat. You look beautiful."

The bar was full of students. He, Corbin, and Kyle were tucked away in their preferred corner, playing pool, some-

Political Affairs 35

thing they did more often than not. Catherine was usually by his side, as was Emily. Tonight, though, both were absent. Tonight, it was just him and the boys. Emily was out on a mission for the school's paper, and Catherine…

Well, Catherine was with that jerk he thought to himself.

"Where's Cat?" Kyle asked, chewing on his thumbnail, eyes on the pool table. He looked awfully nervous for a game of pool. Devin had been trying to hit the eleven ball, but at the mention of Catherine and thinking of where she was, he hit the white ball a little harder than needed, almost making him break his billiard cue. The ball, however, went into the pocket. He shot Kyle a smirk as he moved to the other ball.

"Yeah, where is she? It's weird she isn't here. You guys are always attached at the hip," Corbin added, a smirk on his face.

He met Corbin in his American Politics class when he got into an argument about politics and minorities with the professor. His witty comments and passion made the class less boring. Corbin was African American and the first generation in his family to go to college. He had a full-ride scholarship as the main defensive linebacker on the football team.

"She's on a date," Devin grumbled, taking his shot at the fourteen ball. The ball dropped into the pocket, again.

"How are you feeling about it?" Corbin asked.

"What d'you mean?" Devin replied, swallowing his anger. Was it truly anger that he felt? Or was it jealousy?

He tried for the twelve ball next but missed. He cursed under his breath.

"Oh please, don't play it with us. We know you have the fattest crush on Catherine," Corbin stated matter-of-factly. "Plus, what did the white ball and the billiard cue do to you? It's like you want to break them."

"It's not like that," Devin retorted, though deep down, he

knew Corbin was right. He took a sip from his soda, trying to appease the jealousy.

"Oh, but it is," Kyle retorted, taking aim, and hitting the nine ball.

Devin's phone rang, which was strange since it was past midnight. Catherine's name flashing on the screen. He shoved his billiard cue in Corbin's direction.

"Kitty Cat? What's wrong?" he asked.

"Simp," Corbin said. Devin flipped him off.

"Kitty Cat are you there?" He pushed through the crowd of people, heading for the exit, leaving Kyle and Corbin behind.

"Devin…" she cried, a sob breaking her voice.

"Catherine, tell me where you are!" he demanded, sliding into the driver's seat of his car.

"I don't know. Miles took me to this frat house for a party, and I don't know where it is. I'm locked in the bathroom. I don't want to go out. Please, help me. Please, come pick me up," she said in a whisper.

"I'm on my way, but you need to tell me where it is, Catherine," he said, starting his car and driving off.

"I think it's his frat house," she said. "Something Delta." There was only one frat that had Delta in its name.

"I know where you are. Stay locked in the bathroom and do not hang up," he ordered.

"Okay."

The drive to the frat house was longer than expected. He honked, making the people move out of his way. Once he reached the frat house, he parked on the curb, killing his engine and running inside. The music blasted, shaking the windows. Bodies grinding on bodies. The smell of sweat, nicotine, and alcohol mixed in the air. Going up the stairs two at a time, he started opening doors, not caring what or who was inside. He came up to a locked door.

"Kitty Cat?" Devin screamed, knocking. The door unlocked and inside stood a teary, scared Catherine. He ducked inside, locking them in. "Hey…" Catherine's arms slid around his waist, shaking, wrapping her arms around him. "Hey, I'm here. I got you," he said, kissing the top of her head. "What happened?"

"Get me out of here," she whispered. "Please."

"Catherine, did Miles hurt you in any way? Did Miles do something you didn't want to do? Did he put his hands on you?" Devin asked, cradling her face, and looking into her eyes, searching for an answer. She shook her head.

"No, god no. He didn't do any of what you are thinking Devin," she said. Her sincere gaze calmed the nerves and rage inside of him. Devin leaned in and kissed her forehead.

"Okay. Let's go." He shrugged off his jacket and wrapped it around her shoulders. Grabbing her hand, he entwined their fingers together and they left the bathroom. They made it out of the frat house and into his car. "Kitty Cat, what happened?" he asked a few minutes after they started driving. She was looking out the window. Devin reached for her hands that were folded in her lap. "Catherine, what happened?"

"I heard him say to his buddies he went on a date with me to try to get in my pants. That I'm just a boring goodie two-shoes overachiever," she said in a whisper. Devin cursed under his breath. He did a U-turn and drove back to the frat house. "Where are you going?" she asked, alarmed.

"Stay here. Do *not* leave this car, Catherine," he warned her as he parked and exited the car. He strode into the frat house, looking for him. Looking for Miles. He surveyed the dance floor and the upstairs spaces but didn't find him. He stalked to the kitchen. Nothing. "Excuse me, have you seen

Miles Anderson?" he asked someone who looked somewhat sober.

"Oh dude, he's hammered and high as a kite in the basement," the boy said, slurring his words. Devin nodded and bee-lined for the basement, where he found Miles and his buddies passing around a blunt, sitting in a circle on the floor, red cups everywhere.

"She's so uptight. I bet she's still a virgin man. Maybe this doofus was right. I swear, if he actually wins this bet, I will make him my right hand. I've never had a goodie two-shoes turn me down before," Miles said to his friends, passing the blunt, and Devin knew he was talking about Catherine. He got his phone out and started snapping pictures, the flash of his phone going off with each picture. "What the hell dude?" Miles asked, standing up and reaching for his phone. Devin smirked, lifting the phone in the air. He was a good three inches taller than Miles, rendering him unable to reach his phone.

"You and your buddies better stay the fuck away from Catherine. If you as much as breathe in her direction, you can kiss your lacrosse career goodbye. Do you understand me?" Devin said, showing them the phone. "I have proof that you guys are stoned, and I'm sure the coach and the university wouldn't like a scandal about their lacrosse team using drugs, right Miles?"

Devin smiled at Miles and walked back to the car. Catherine's frantic face looking at him.

"What did you do?" Catherine asked on the drive back.

"Nothing," Devin replied, squeezing her hand. "You are not boring, and there's nothing to be ashamed of with being a goodie two-shoes overachiever girl, Catherine." He turned to her, adding, "Miles won't be bothering you anymore. I promise." Devin put the car in park, and they got out. He walked Catherine to her apartment.

"Thank you," she whispered, unlocking her door. He tucked a piece of hair behind her ear.

"I'll always be there for you. I told you that," he said, hugging her and kissing the crown of her head. "Get some rest, Kitty Cat."

"Good night, Satan," she said, walking inside.

"Good night, Kitty Cat." He waited until she locked her door to go to his apartment.

Chapter Five

Devin – Summer, Present Day

"**D**evin, my favorite chief," Senator Jenkins exclaimed, patting him on the shoulder.

"I'm your only chief, Brian," he replied, smiling.

"Very true. My office."

"Get me that social media report stat," Devin said to the press secretary. He nodded. Devin walked to the Senator's office and closed the door.

"Give me the rundown," Jenkins commanded, drinking from his water bottle, and sitting on his desk chair. "How bad is it?"

"A town in the state, *our* senatorial state, has been without clean water for weeks now," Devin explained, handing Jenkins a folder with all the information.

Jenkins perused the information. Without lifting his gaze, he asked, "When was this reported?".

"Two weeks ago." Devin paused. Jenkins lifted his gaze from the report and looked at him. "To local authorities"

"And to us?"

"This morning."

"What?" Jenkins exploded. "Who reported this?"

"A constituent. They called this morning when they asked for a follow-up yesterday from the local authorities, and they got no answers. I called the local government, but you know, red tape, bureaucracy."

"Fuck. These are living and breathing people, kids without clean water," Jenkins muttered. "How can they be so indifferent?"

"Which is why, later today, we're heading to the district to figure out what's going on," Devin explained. "Everything is ready to go. We have a meeting with the local government tomorrow afternoon."

"You haven't packed."

"Oh, boss. Three years as your chief, and you still don't know me. I feel offended," Devin said, feigning hurt. "I always have a packed suitcase in my trunk for cases like this."

"When are we leaving?" Jenkins asked.

"Soon. You have one more meeting," Devin handed him the other folder. "With Politico." Jenkins nodded.

"We need to fix this. It's not fair to the people," Jenkins said to Devin while walking out of the treatment plant. Devin nodded.

"I know," Devin replied.

"Is this representative Johns' district?" he asked. Devin nodded. "Call his office. Schedule a meeting with him. We need to figure this out."

"I'll work on it. I'm going back to DC later today," Devin said, looking at his watch. "As a matter of fact, can I leave early boss? That way I can shower and change before my flight. I hate traveling in a suit," Devin said, walking to the rental car. Jenkins gave him a dismissive flick of the hand.

He drove back to the hotel and showered, changing into a T-shirt and jeans. He finished packing and checked out. His phone rang in his pocket. The ringtone, one he knew well.

"Emily, I can't talk right now, I'm on my way to the airport to go back to DC," Devin said, placing the phone between his shoulder and ear while loading the suitcase into the car.

"Daffodils," she said excitedly.

"What?" he asked, confused.

"Daffodils. Those are the flowers for the wedding," she said. "The colors go so well with the decorations. White and yellow," she replied. He laughed.

"What happened to the yellow roses?" he asked, walking to the driver's side and jumping inside.

"Too expensive. We're on a budget."

"Gotcha. Well, I'm on my way to the airport. So, I'll see you later."

"Alrighty. I can't wait to see you and show you all I came up with for the wedding," she said enthusiastically.

"You sound excited. Anything I should prepare for?" he asked, driving to the airport.

"Nope," she replied, emphasizing the 'p'. "It's a surprise."

"Alright. I guess I'll find out," he said. "Gotta go now. Love you."

"Love you."

"She looks the same," he said to the phone. Corbin was on the other side of the line. "Same hair, same smile. Same beautiful green eyes, Corbin. The same eyes I fell in love with," he said. "Are you listening to me?"

Seeing Catherine stirred up emotions he didn't know were still there. He wanted to tell her so many things, but nothing came out. Starting with asking her why she disappeared. And why the hell did she keep the necklace he gave her after all these years? After the encounter with Catherine, he needed to clear his head. So, he wandered in circles, heading off to the other side of the airport.

"Yeah, yeah. Hey Deion, stop running around. Aiyden, stop jumping on the couch," Corbin said on the other side of the line. "I'm sorry, what did you say, Devin?"

"That she—" he started to say but got interrupted again.

"Aiyden do not eat Play-Doh. Man, I'm gonna have to call you back. Brianna got the night shift at the hospital today, and I got the boys."

"Alright man. Do what you gotta do," Devin replied. "Say hi to the boys for me."

"I will. Hey Deion, stop drinking from the dog's bowl," was the last thing he said before hanging up. Devin laughed. Deion and Aiyden were two little rascals, the same as their father.

He walked through the terminal and looked for his gate. It wasn't even the same airline. Did he wander off to another terminal? He looked at his flight ticket. Terminal A, Gate 16. He looked around. He saw Gate 16, but it was for a completely different airline. He walked to a desk.

"Excuse me, can you tell me which terminal I'm in?" he asked the clerk there. The clerk looked at Devin as if he had grown another head.

"This is terminal F."

"How far is terminal A?"

"Far," was all he said, and he turned back to his computer.

"*Shit*," he cursed under his breath. He looked at his watch. Now, he only had half an hour to get to his gate, or he would miss his flight to DC. "Good one, Devin. Good one," he muttered to himself.

He hurried back through the terminal and made it just in time after all the boarding was done.

"I'm so sorry I'm late. I got lost," he said to the stewardess.

"You almost didn't make it," the stewardess said. He laughed, walking down to his seat.

"14A," he said, standing in the aisle. He looked down, and there she was. The seat next to him. In row 14, seat B. She was looking at him. He placed his carry-on in the overhead bin and sat down. She put her headphones on and turned away from him as the plane took off. She was there. Beside him. On a plane to Washington, DC.

What the hell was she doing on this plane? What was her business in DC? Was this a layover for her? A connecting flight?

Half an hour after takeoff, the stewardesses were asking if anyone wanted a complimentary drink.

"Miss, do you want anything?" she asked Catherine, but Catherine didn't hear, too invested in her work.

"She'll have a ginger ale. And I'll have a diet coke," he said. The stewardess frowned but nodded and moved on.

"Was that the stewardess?" Catherine asked, reaching for the call button. He extended his hand and brought hers down. Still as perfectly small as he remembered. He dropped it.

"It was. I got you a ginger ale."

"How do you even know I wanted that?" He looked at her. Something flashed in her eyes, but it was gone before he could decipher what it was.

"Catherine, I—"

"Don't," she said, turning back to her work. "Thanks for ordering my drink." He sighed. He found it vaguely disturbing that after nine years, this is where he crossed paths with her. Out of all places, an airport. He went into his backpack and got his notebook and pen out. He tore a piece of paper and scribbled something on it.

Timeout.

Timeout was something they came up with whenever they had a fight or were upset. *Timeout* was the safe word to sit down and talk about it. He still remembered the first time they had a big fight.

Thirteen years ago - Fall, Sophomore Year

"Catherine, can we please talk about this?" he pleaded, walking behind her in the hallway. They were leaving class together, but she had been giving him the silent treatment for two days now, and he missed her.

"There's nothing to talk about Devin," she replied. Devin, she called him Devin. Not Satan, not Dev. She called him Devin. She was angry.

"Kitty Cat..." he said, but she interrupted him.

"Don't call me that." He walked ahead and stopped in front of her. She stumbled into his chest.

"Talk to me. Let's call a timeout," he begged, crouching down to look her in the eyes. She diverted her gaze to the left.

"I don't want to talk about it, Devin," she mumbled, stepping sideways and walking away.

"No, no, no," he insisted, catching up to her and grabbing her arm. "You're upset with me."

She scoffed. "Understatement of the year."

"Timeout. I'm calling timeout," he voiced. "What did I do? Talk to me, Kitty Cat. I miss you. You have never been this upset with me. We haven't gone this long without talking. Ever. Talk to me. What did I do?" She looked up at him, her eyes misty.

"You forgot my birthday," she whispered. "You forgot my birthday, Devin. I had a small dinner party with Emily at the apartment, and you forgot about it. I don't expect you to remember everything about me, but the least you could've done as my best friend was say happy birthday to me on a two-minute phone call."

"Kitty Cat, your birthday is not until..." He started, but then it dawned on him. He closed his eyes, cursing himself. "Your birthday was two days ago. On Sunday," he whispered. "I went out of town this weekend with Corbin and Kyle." He passed a hand through his hair. "Fuck, I'm so sorry, Kitty Cat." Devin hugged her. She let him. "I'm such an asshole." He kissed the top of her head. "I'm the worst best friend. I feel awful. How can I make it up to you?" She shrugged.

"Maybe I'll let you sulk and grovel for a few days. Maybe you can be my little maid. Do all my chores so I can focus on my studies. Maybe you can be my little cook. I'll decide later. The possibilities are endless, Devin Mack," she said sarcastically. He chuckled.

"Deal," he said, kissing the top of her head again. "Can we do something? For the future?" he asked. She nodded. "Every time we do something that upsets the other, can we call a timeout and talk about it?"

"Okay."

Timeout. That's all it said. He folded the piece of paper and slid it to her. She looked at it and wrote on it.

No. That was all she wrote before she went back to her job.

Please, he wrote back. She heaved an exasperated sigh, took her headphones off, and looked at him.

"What?" she asked, taking off her glasses and dropping them on top of her computer.

"I just want to know how you've been, Cat. It's been so long," he said, looking down at his hands, suddenly feeling shy and vulnerable. This used to be his best friend. His everything. And now she was a stranger he hadn't seen or heard from in almost a decade.

"I've been fine. Great. Anything else?" she asked, exasperated.

"You're mad. I know you're upset," he said. She rolled her eyes.

"I'm busy, and you are interrupting me," she said, pointing to her computer. He nodded, looking down.

"I'm sorry, I didn't wanted to interrupt you," he apologized in a whisper, knowing better than anyone to not push her. He got his headphones out, shuffling through his music, and closed his eyes. It'd been almost a decade since they last saw each other. And he still didn't know what happened or why she cut all ties with him.

Nine years ago - Finals week, Senior Year

"Hey, so, what are you doing this summer? You want to take a trip to Canada?" Devin asked, entering her apartment. It was finals week of senior year. The last finals of

their undergraduate careers. She accepted a grad school offer, full-ride at Penn State. He was staying in Boston to do law. He found her hunched over the dinner table of her apartment that she shared with Emily. Her books were scattered around the table. He walked to her and bent down to kiss her head. She moved out of the way, leaving him in midair.

"I can't," she said, standing up. She gathered her stuff and looked at him. The bags under her eyes told him she hadn't slept in a day or two. Her eyes were puffy and red as if she had been crying. Her hair was limp and dull. Her normal rosy cheeks were devoid of color. He got worried. He had never seen her like this, so lifeless. Not even during her most stressful days.

"Hey, what's wrong? Are you sick?" He walked to her to check her temperature, but she moved her face, taking a step back.

"I'm fine. I'm just busy studying for finals. Can you please go?" she asked him, not meeting his gaze.

"We only have the final capstone and a couple of essays, which I'm sure you have finished already," he said.

She shrugged. "I still need to do the final revisions. And I need to start packing. I'm leaving the same day finals end."

"What about graduation?"

"I'm not going. So, as I said, I'm busy Devin. Emily isn't home. She's out with the school's newspaper covering her last story, interviewing seniors," she said, picking up her books.

"I didn't come here to see Emily, Kitty Cat."

"Don't call me that," she said in a whisper.

"Catherine, what's going on?" He took a step towards her, and she took a step back.

She shrugged. "Some people are in your life for just a period of time. Then they leave."

"What are you talking about?" he asked, confused but also worried. So worried. He didn't like her tone.

"I'm saying that I think our friendship has come to an end, Devin," she said, shrugging. Devin. She'd called him Devin for the second time in the last two minutes. *"I'm going to Penn State, and you're staying here. I think it's best if we say our goodbyes now. Thanks for keeping me sane these last four years,"* she continued, hugging the books to her. She turned around and walked to her bedroom. He just stood there, feeling as if someone had ripped his heart out and left him to die.

"Excuse me?" He heard the voice of someone bringing him out of his painful memories. He opened his eyes and saw the stewardess standing there.

"Oh, sorry." She smiled and handed him his diet coke. "Thanks." He smiled. The stewardess motioned for Catherine so she could give her the ginger ale, but Catherine was lost in thought. He nudged her arm, and she looked up.

"Oh, thanks," Catherine said. She looked at him briefly, and there was a sadness in her eyes that broke his heart. A sadness that he was responsible for, but he didn't know why. It shattered him.

After the longest three hours of his life, the plane landed in DCA. He stood and opened the overhead compartment, getting out his suitcase. He saw a lilac bag and knew who it belonged to. Without thinking, he lowered that suitcase into the aisle too.

"I... thanks," she whispered. He nodded and started walking, feeling her right behind him. Once out in the terminal, she walked past him.

He followed her with his gaze. When they were both out in the arrivals area, he saw her walk to a white car. A man got out of the driver's side. A blond-haired man he used to live with. A blond-haired man he didn't speak to anymore. Kyle walked to Catherine and kissed her, hugging her waist, and for the first time in almost ten years, Devin felt what he felt that night. As if someone had ripped his heart out and left him to die.

Chapter Six

Catherine – Summer, Present Day

"Hey, what's wrong?" Kyle asked from the driver's seat, bringing her back to the present. He placed a hand on the nape of her neck and squeezed softly.

"Uhm? What?" she asked, turning to him, fidgeting with her necklace. She dropped her hands, folding them in her lap.

"You've been quiet and distant since I picked you up. We're almost home, and you haven't told me about your airport adventures. What happened?" he asked, bringing his hand to her lap, grabbing one of hers, and kissing it softly. She smiled.

"Nothing happened. I'm just tired." She squeezed his fingers. "I need to be at the office early tomorrow," she said, looking back out the window.

"Okay," Kyle said, kissing her knuckles, keeping their hands in his lap, and running lazy circles on the back of her hand. They arrived at their apartment and went . "I know you ate coffee at the airport, so dinner is in the oven," he said to her. She smiled at him.

"Thanks, but I'm not hungry. I just want to shower and go to bed."

"*Corazón mío*, what happened?" Kyle asked worriedly. She sighed. She couldn't bring herself to tell Kyle. "Was it that bad in the district?" he asked. He had no idea, so she decided to roll with that. She nodded. He exhaled. "I'm sorry."

"It's fine," she said, nodding absentmindedly. "We're working on it."

"In other news, turns out I am leaving tomorrow for Nevada."

"I told you. For how long?" she asked.

"I don't know. The DOD doesn't have a time frame. We have to set up the equipment, install the software, create the encryption, and then train the people who work there. And until they master it, we can't leave."

"So, months maybe?"

"Six months, give or take," he replied.

She inhaled. "That's the longest you've been gone."

"I know."

"It's fine. I'll be busy anyway," she said.

He chuckled. "I know."

"Alright, we know the drill," she said, smiling. He nodded. "And it's not like they're sending you internationally this time. At least it is not Germany or Japan."

"Indeed," he agreed. "God, those thirteen hours of difference when they stationed me in Japan for two months were hell," he said, walking to her and hugging her, kissing her head. "I'll try to fly and visit whenever I can, I promise." He kissed her softly. She cupped his cheek and nodded, returning the kiss. His hands grasped her waist, bringing her closer. Her hands slid into his hair, pulling him to her. She needed to get her mind off Devin. He was ancient history. He was in the past. This was her present. Her hands slid down to Kyle's chest, toying with the buttons of his shirt. She undid the first one. He inhaled and pulled back. "Not tonight, *corazón*. You must be tired," he said, kissing her forehead. "You go shower, and I'll put the food in the fridge. You wanna take it for lunch tomorrow?" he asked, turning away and walking towards the kitchen. She exhaled.

"No, it's fine. I'll just get a salad in the cafeteria tomorrow. What time do you leave?" she asked.

"Seven in the morning," he said.

She nodded. "You want me to send you off?"

"Nah, it's okay. I'm a big boy," he teased.

She laughed. "Okay, big boy. Then I will retire and go shower and get under the sheets," she said, walking to where he stood and giving him a quick peck on the cheek.

She walked to the bathroom and locked herself in it, leaning against the door. She had been looking forward to Kyle helping her de-stress after today, but just like the last six months, it's never more than make-out sessions, with the occasional touching. Never reaching the end. No matter how many advances she made, he never returned them. It was exhausting for her to keep trying.

She exhaled, walking to the sink. She needed to de-stress. She had gone too long without satisfying her needs. She filled the tub with warm water. Stripping, she jumped in the tub, leaning against the tub walls. She closed her eyes and let her hand wander down her body to the area that needed the most care. Her fingers brushed lightly on her clit. She inhaled a deep breath, touching herself again. She bit her lip. Her fingers wandered lower to her entrance. She spread her legs wider as she pushed a finger inside, moaning quietly, feeling herself. She tentatively pushed in a second finger, pumping them slowly. Her other hand wandered down, doing small circles on her clit. She threw her head back. She felt herself, pleasured herself. She was close, so close. The pumping of her fingers picked up speed. Her moaning was low, her back arching off the tub wall. An image formed in the back of her mind. A man between her legs, feeling her out, feasting on her. She was so close. Just a few more strokes. The hand doing circles on her clit moved faster. The fingers pumping in and out of her at a faster pace. And then, a knock. She stilled, opening her eyes.

"Catherine? Are you okay?" Kyle asked on the other side of the door, rattling the doorknob.

"I'm fine," she said in a shaky voice.

"Why did you lock the door?" he asked, trying to open it.

"I'll be out in a couple of minutes," she said, ignoring his question.

"Okay," he replied. "Are you sure you're okay?"

"Yes, Kyle. I'm fine," she snapped, annoyed. She gave it a couple of minutes to make sure he was gone. She blew out a breath, and once again, she didn't reach the end. She showered quickly, and by the time she walked into the room, Kyle was on his side, snoring softly. She rolled her eyes, annoyed, turned his light off, and slid under the sheets.

Two months later – Fall

"Any alien sightings yet?" she asked Kyle on the other side of the line.

"They are shy to newcomers. So, I'm afraid not," he said, following her lead. "But soon. Is it cold there yet?"

"Yes. It was in the mid-fifties today."

"Just how you like it."

"Yes." There was a knock on her door. "Kyle, one sec," she said to Kyle. "Yes?" she said out loud. Maggie popped her head through her office door.

"They're here," Maggie said.

"Be there in a sec," Catherine replied. Maggie closed the door, and she returned to her conversation. "I have about two minutes before I hang up for a meeting."

"You're leaving me for a boring meeting?"

"Says the man who left me for aliens and the desert."

"Touché. You got me *corazón*," he said, laughing. "Alright, I'll call you tomorrow when I'm not chasing aliens."

"Sounds like a date."

"Alright. I love you. More than aliens."

"I know. I love you," she said and hung up.

She gathered her stuff and looked at herself in the mirror, adjusting her hair and retouching her makeup. She left her office and walked through the cubicles, passing Maverick.

"Boss! Here, this is for the meeting," he said while handing her a folder.

"Thanks," she said, offering him a smile. She walked to the foyer, it was empty except for Maggie and the new fall intern. "Where are they?"

"Outside, they had a call. The chief came into the office to say they arrived. He's hot," Maggie replied.

"Mags, focus," Catherine said to her. "Okay, I will go in, talk with the boss, and I'll tell you when we are ready." Maggie nodded. Catherine knocked on the door.

"Come in," Michael said.

"Boss, they're here. Jenkins, I mean. He brought his

chief," she said, walking to his desk and placing the folder in front of him.

"Thanks." She walked to the coat rack where his suit jacket was, picked it up, and walked to the desk to help him put it on. "Anything I should know?" he asked as he adjusted his tie.

"He also visited the treatment plant," she said. "Same day as us, but in the afternoon. Right after us. Something the treatment plant omitted. We could've toured it together."

"They've omitted a lot of things, and the longer this drags on, the more this people are left without clean water. It's been over two months now. I will not tolerate this a minute longer," Michael sighed. "Ready?"

"Ready when you are."

"Let them in," he said. She nodded and walked to the phone on one of the tables beside the couch. She pressed zero and dialed Maggie's desk.

"Yes, boss?" Maggie asked.

"We're ready for them," Catherine replied.

"Gotcha," Maggie said and hung up. Michael and Catherine walked to the couches and sat down, waiting on the Senator and his chief. A couple of minutes later, there was a knock on the door.

"We got this," she said to him. He nodded. The door opened, and they stood. The Senator walked in, and behind him, a face she had seen as recently as two months ago. At the airport. And on the plane back home.

"Michael!" the Senator said to her boss, walking inside the office.

"Brian, thanks for meeting with me," Michael said, shaking the Senator's hand. "This is my chief." Michael motioned to her. She extended her hand.

Political Affairs 57

"Senator, thank you so much for coming down here," she said, shaking the senator's hand.

"Of course, Miss…"

"Babbitt. Catherine Babbitt," she said, smiling.

"This is my chief, Devin Mack." Not that he needed an introduction when she knew exactly who he was. She extended her hand to him, pleading with her eyes for him to just go along with it. He understood and extended his hand to hers, his big hand engulfing her small one.

"Nice to meet you," he said.

"Likewise."

Their meeting went smoothly, and they agreed to work together to reach a solution. Not only for their constituents, but for every small town in America. When the meeting was over, she walked to her office and left Michael to get settled for his next meeting. A couple of minutes later, there was a knock on her door.

"Come in," she said, unlocking her computer. Piercing blue eyes looked back at her from the doorway.

"Timeout." Her hand instinctively went to her necklace. She motioned for the chair in front of her desk, and he briskly walked to it, sitting down. "I didn't know you worked in Congress," he said. She smiled nervously.

"Five years now." He nodded and looked around, his eyes settling on the bouquet with a *Happy Birthday* balloon.

"Happy birthday," he whispered. "I know it was yesterday, but happy birthday."

"You still remember?" she asked. He gave her a brief nod, looking down at the hand on her necklace.

"I do," he whispered. "Let's just put our issues aside and work together on this please. Can we do that?" he pleaded. She looked down, inclining her head.

"I know how to separate my personal life from my professional life, Devin."

"I know," he said, his voice distant. "Here's my business card."

"Here's mine." She removed one from her desk drawer and handed it to him. He took it and nodded once in acknowledgment, both of them falling in an awkward silence.

"Goodbye, Miss Babbitt."

"Goodbye, Mr. Mack."

Chapter Seven

Catherine

"Okay, let me get this straight. You used the funds the Environmental Protection Agency has given you, along with other private loans, to pay off a debt? Completely unrelated to what the funds were supposed to be used for? Why?" Catherine asked the CEO Stella Waterworks LLC, over the phone. It has been one week since her office and Senator Jenkins office have been working together on this issue.

"As I was saying, Miss Babbitt, in order to give the people a quality service..." the CEO started to explain again in a condescending tone.

"Mr. Thomas, with all due respect, I don't need you to mansplain your inability to run a company. I think we are seeing the results of it," Catherine interrupted. "The funds a federal agency granted the company were to be used solely on infrastructure to provide quality services to the people. You and your administration proved how incapable you are of managing federal funding. So, unless you and your board have a quick solution to provide quality service and the compensation of the funds provided in the past years, I will ask you to refrain from trying to salvage your asses. Quite frankly, your incompetence in running a company is showing, and your lack of accountability is not something I will tolerate. So, what is your plan for restoring the funding?" She looked around, and everyone in the room had their gaze on her, their mouths wide open, amusement and awe etched on their features. She looked at Devin across the room, and he was wearing a proud smile. The kind of smile he would often give her when they were back in Boston. That filled her chest with a warm feeling. One she didn't like.

"We don't have one," the CEO said. That brought her back to the task at hand, making the warm feeling in her chest turn into ice.

"What do you mean you don't have one? You spent the funds on something completely unrelated to their purpose, and you don't have a plan to restore said funds?" she asked, her anger rising. "I will be taking this into consideration. With how the situation is unfolding Mr. Thomas, I expect your and the board's resignation letters in my inbox in the next hour."

"You are not my boss. You're just a meaningless staffer. I do not answer to you," the CEO responded. She smirked, preparing herself for what was about to unfold.

"No actually, you do answer to her. She is the one in charge of this investigation, and I don't appreciate how you're talking to my right hand. So, I would reconsider your words if I were you," Michael, her boss, said. She gazed up at him. He had dark circles under his eyes from the lack of sleep these last couple of weeks trying to solve this mess. She glanced at the senator across the room, sitting beside Devin. He was looking at his phone, smirking after hearing Michael. She focused on Devin, a murderous look on his face and eyes. She had only seen that stare once, many years ago, after he rescued her from the frat house after her date with Miles. "I will be expecting your resignation letters within an hour as well. If the resignation letters are not on my desk in one hour, I will launch a full federal investigation for fund malversation. I also expect for you and your board to come up with a plan on how to restore the funding before the year ends. Are we understanding each other?" Michael asked. Jenkins smiled and looked at Devin, muttering something in his ear.

"Are you still there, Mr. Thomas?" she asked.

"We will be sending our letters shortly," the CEO said in a harsh tone and hung up.

"This is worse than we thought," Michael said, sighing, massaging his eyes with the heels of his hands.

"What do we do now?" Kowalski asked.

"This is what we're going to do," Catherine said, taking charge. Everyone looked at her. "First, we wait for the letters. Once we have those, we draft a plan." Everyone agreed. "In the meantime, go take a break. Take a walk around the block. Clear your head. Drink some coffee. Eat lunch. Once I have the letters, we'll reconvene."

Everyone looked at Michael. "You heard her. Go," he said, dismissing everyone. "Dismissed until we get the resignation letters." Everyone nodded and filed out. Catherine gathered her stuff and turned to Michael. "I'll be in my office. Good job."

Catherine looked up at him and smiled. "Thanks, boss." Nodding, she exited the room.

"Boss, we're going to order lunch from Good Stuff Eatery. Do you want anything?" Maverick asked as she passed him. She shook her head no and kept walking to her office. Once in her office, leaning against the door and sighing, closing her eyes. She walked to her desk, plopping down on her chair with a thud, dropping her papers and folders to the side, and burying her face in her arms on the desk. A couple of minutes passed, and there was a knock on her door.

"Come in." Her door opened and closed quickly. Catherine lifted her head. Someone placed a paper cup in front of her, the smell of coffee filling her nostrils. Catherine gazed up, and the ocean-blue eyes of a certain redhead were staring back at her.

"A cappuccino with oat milk, no sugar, and a pinch of cinnamon," he said, smiling down at her.

"How did you—" she started to ask but stopped. It was useless. Utterly useless. He knew her better than she knew herself. And nine years apart hadn't dimmed his knowledge of her habits. She hugged the paper cup with her hands. "Never mind. Thanks," she muttered, taking a sip, the warmth of it traveling through her body. "What are you doing here?"

"Coffee isn't a meal, Catherine. You are aware of that, right?"

"I'm not hungry, and I'm too stressed to eat," she responded with a shrug, taking another sip.

He studied her. His eyes lingered on her face a little too long.

"Some things never change," he muttered, his Tenerife Sea eyes scanning every inch of her face. He looked away and walked around the office, studying every book on the shelves. "What's the plan?" he asked, picking a book and opening it.

"What?" she asked, confused.

"The plan. What's the plan after we get the resignation letters?" he asked, not looking at her. He closed the book and placed it back on the shelf. He walked around more, looking at the pictures there.

"I don't know. I just got back to my office a couple of minutes ago. I was going to outline a potential plan," she responded, taking another sip of her coffee. He nodded, placing his hands in the pockets of his slacks.

"Do you want to work on it together?" She was too startled by his suggestion to offer any objection. He had taken off his suit jacket and rolled up the sleeves of his button-down shirt, undoing the top button as well. "So, do you?"

"Sure." She nodded, stunned. He smiled, sitting on one of the chairs in front of her desk.

"Okay, where should we start?" he asked, turning to look at her, his eyes a shade darker. His gaze was so intense she had to look away.

Gathering her wits, she turned to her computer, opened a new document, and started to brainstorm a convenient plan to present to their bosses. One that involved meeting with community leaders, townspeople, and hiring a completely new board of directors and CEO. As he took notes on a piece of paper, she realized two things. One, that he was one of the most competent and intelligent people she had ever worked with. Two, he matched her professional skills on a level that was unmatched. Conveniently so, her phone rang at that moment, startling her.

"One second," she said, placing the paper cup on the desk and picking up her cell phone. It was Kyle. She answered. "Hey, I'm kinda busy right now. Can I call you later?" she asked him.

"Oh, of course," he responded. "I'm sorry."

"No, it's okay. I'll call you when I get out of work."

"Of course, love you," he replied and hung up.

"Boyfriend?" Devin asked, an edge in his voice.

"Yes." He gave her a quiet nod, biting the inside of his cheek. Her email pinged, and she unlocked her computer. She opened her email app, and the most recent email was the resignation letters. She chuckled. "We just got the letters," she said, not looking at Devin. Devin walked over and stood behind her. He leaned in and looked at her email, his body heat engulfing her. His woodsy smell filled her nostrils. He was close, *too close*. Her heart began to hammer in her chest. Her breath became slightly agitated. His nearness was overwhelming.

"I'll call Brian," he said, his voice close to her ear, his breath tickling her temple. The hairs on the back of her neck rose. Goosebumps went off all over her body. His body heat left her too quickly.

Get it together, Catherine she told herself. *You have no business feeling like this. Your body has no business being this affected by him. He is ancient history. You moved on.*

"Catherine?" he asked, bringing her out of her mind.

"What?" she asked, her voice shaky. She cleared her throat. "You were saying?"

"Are you okay?" he asked. She waved a dismissive hand, taking another sip of coffee.

"I'm fine."

"Okay..." he said, not sounding convinced. "I asked if you wanted to reconvene in two hours."

She nodded. "Two hours should be enough," she replied, turning to her computer. Out of the corner of her eye, she watched him eyeing her.

"Alright," he concurred. She turned to him, and he nodded. "I'll let Brian know."

"I will send a confirmation email," she said, not looking at him while typing on her computer.

"Sounds like a plan," he uttered, turning around and leaving. She finished the email and sent it to all the staff from the previous meeting.

She took an hour break for lunch, and another one to catch up on emails and calls. She looked at the clock and she had twenty minutes left before the meeting. She went to Michael's office. Once outside his door, she heard giggles. She smiled to herself and knocked.

"Come in," Michael called from inside.

"It's that Heather's giggles I hear?" she asked, popping her head into the office, smiling.

"Auntie Cathy," a little girl with curly blonde hair screamed. Catherine walked inside, and Heather tackled her with a hug around her legs.

"How is my favorite future member of Congress?" she asked, dropping to the girl's level and engulfing her in a hug.

"Oh, no. We had a career change. Now she wants to be a dentist," Michael said.

"Oh, a dentist huh? Are you going to check my teeth?" Catherine asked, and Heather giggled. She kissed her cheek.

"I missed you," the little girl said to her.

"I missed you too, munchkin," Catherine replied, kissing the top of her head. She broke the embrace and stood up, sitting on the sofa. Heather climbed on her lap, leaning against her. She wrapped her arms around her. "Where's Olive?"

Olive was his wife, who had taken her under her wing as part of the family when she realized her and Michael were both workaholics, and that if she didn't feed them, they would live off coffee and candy. And so, Olive took it upon herself to make sure they didn't overwork themselves. Catherine was also one of the first to know about her pregnancy with Heather, and Olive named her Auntie Cathy.

"Oh, she went to the cafeteria. Heather wanted to spend some time with Papa."

"Auntie Cathy, guess what?" Heather asked, lifting her head. Catherine tucked a piece of hair behind her ear.

"What's up?" Heather made a motion for her to get closer

as if what she was about to say was a secret only for Catherine to hear. Catherine leaned closer, and Heather cupped her ear.

"I'm getting a puppy," Heather whispered. Catherine's eyes widened and found Michael smiling at his desk. She gasped.

"You are?" she whispered excitedly. Heather nodded. "Do you know what you're gonna name it?" Heather nodded enthusiastically.

"Trooper," she replied. Catherine laughed.

"I think that's a beautiful name, Heather."

"It's a black Labrador," Michael added from his desk.

"You're gonna have to come home to meet him," Heather said.

"I will."

"So, they didn't have chicken fingers, but they did have pizza," a female said, entering the office. "Catherine!"

"Hi Olive," Catherine greeted her.

"We missed you last night," Olive mentioned, walking to Michael's desk.

"Yeah, sorry about that. I got caught up with work." Heather hopped off Catherine's lap and walked to the desk to eat her lunch. Michael stood up and sat her in his chair, kissing her head before leaving his desk.

"What do you think he is discussing with the Senator that neither of the chiefs are inside?" Maggie asked Catherine, looking between her and Devin.

"I don't know Mags, something important. Deciding on our proposed plan. Who knows," Catherine replied.

The meeting to discuss the plan ended about an hour ago,

and ever since then, both the Senator and her boss closed themselves in Michael's office and haven't come out. Catherine chewed on her thumbnail nervously.

"Stop," she heard Devin say as he reached for her hand. She turned her head so fast it made her dizzy. He was as close as he had been in her office. His woodsy smell engulfed her. She turned around and closed her eyes, emptying her mind. Someone cleared their throat beside her. She opened her eyes and saw Maggie with a curious look on her face.

"Babbitt!" Michael yelled.

"Mack!" the Senator called in unison.

They both walked to the door. She reached for the door at the same time as him, their hands bumping.

"Sorry," she mumbled, removing her hand. He opened the door and let her in first. Both the Senator and Michael were sitting on the sofa. They moved into the room and stood in front of them.

"We've developed a plan," Michael started.

"That's good," she replied, nodding.

"Pack your bags. Both of you," Jenkins instructed. She frowned.

"I'm not following," Devin said.

"For the next three weeks, both of you will be handling the board, including finding replacements that we can trust to allocate the funding where it is due and meeting with the constituents and community leaders," Jenkins explained.

"What?" Catherine asked, confused.

"You are leaving for the district and staying there for three weeks. We talked with the EPA and they tasked us to take care of this," Michael replied. "It'll be a joint project of both offices," Michael continued, but his voice faded in the background. Suddenly, everything started to fall into place.

"You both clearly work great together, if the plan you

both came up with is any indication. And who better to work on this than the two that came up with the plan?" Jenkins continued.

Three weeks.

Just her.

And Devin.

Working together.

Chapter Eight

Devin

"So, how long are you leaving for?" Emily asked from the bed, her legs crossed.

"Three weeks. I'll be back before Thanksgiving," he said, folding some jeans and stuffing them in the suitcase. Emily nodded.

"How is she?" she inquired, looking down at her hands, her voice strained.

"She's good, Em. She's still a little firecracker. Still the same firecracker we knew in Boston," he added, giving her a lop-sided smile. Emily bobbed her head.

"And you? How are you? How are you feeling about this? Must be hard for you."

"I'm okay." She looked at him, skepticism in her eyes. "I'm fine."

"Whatever, Ross Geller," she replied, smirking. He threw the shirt he was folding at her. She caught it midair. She stood up and walked up to him, bumping him with her hip. "Move. Let the lady organize this," she said, folding the shirt he had just thrown at her. "I'm about to Marie Kondo this suitcase for you. I will give her a run for her money." He laughed and kissed her temple. He walked to the bathroom and started gathering his toiletries. "So, it's only going to be you and her?"

"Yes. I think there will be staff from both district offices. But it will mostly be just me and her," he said, packing his razor into the toiletries bag.

"Ohhhh. Just you and her most of the time, huh?" Emily responded from the room with a humorous tone.

"Don't start, Emily Choi. She's dating Kyle," he said nonchalantly. Even though it killed him inside to say those three words. It felt like eating glass.

"Kyle?" Emily asked, confused. She popped her head in the bathroom. "Your old college roommate Kyle? Asshole Kyle? As in the-same-Kyle-we-all-hate Kyle?" He nodded, distracted, thinking about what Kyle had done and curious about how he ended up with Catherine. "Do I wanna know how you got that information?"

"He picked her up from the airport," he said, getting his aftershave and a few medicine bottles from the cabinet. She went to the walk-in closet and opened the drawers and came back to the room with his underwear.

"Ooooohhhh," Emily said, stuffing his underwear into the suitcase. "How did those two get together?"

"I don't know, and I don't care to find out," he retorted, walking back to the room. "Em, you don't have to do this."

"Yes, I do. You are a man, and you don't know how to pack. I, on the other hand, know how to pack and organize a suitcase. Something your pretty, intelligent brain doesn't know how to do," she replied, walking back to the closet and grabbing clothes off the hangers. He rolled his eyes.

"I'm going to order food," he announced, getting out his phone. "What do you want? Pizza?"

"Pizza," she said enthusiastically. She threw a shirt at him. He chuckled, catching the shirt before it hit the floor.

"So, talk to me. Wedding," he said, opening his browser. He walked to where she was standing, handing her the shirt.

"Oh, it's coming along great," she answered excitedly.

"Do you have the details of where I'm supposed to get my suit?" he asked, locking his phone and giving her his undivided attention.

"You are getting a custom-tailored suit," she said, folding clothes and putting them on the suitcase in a very organized, very Emily way. Her last words registered in his mind.

"What?" he asked, confused. "A tailored one?" She nodded.

"Mom insists on getting your suit made for you," she responded, shrugging.

"Why?" he questioned. "That's gonna be expensive."

"I know. I told her that, and she said, 'Only the best for the son I never had.' I swear, she's so annoying sometimes," she mumbled, turning to him. "Which brings me to my next point. When are you leaving? We need to get your measurements before you go."

"I leave tomorrow late afternoon. I can ask for a half day. And go get measured," he replied, reassuringly. "That way, the tailor can start my suit while I'm out of town, and then when I come back, he can do the final touches before the wedding."

Emily nodded. "That's good. That works. One less thing I have to worry about. I need this wedding to happen already. Otherwise, I'll be turning into a bridezilla," she added with a sigh.

"You *will* turn into a bridezilla? Honey, you already are."

"You know what? Fuck you, Devin," she replied. He laughed.

"I'm kidding," he said, walking to her and hugging her, her shoulders melting into his chest. He placed his chin on top of her head. "Everything else is ready? Do you need me to go cake tasting with you?" She shook her head.

"Mom went with me."

"Okay, anything else you need help with? Anything else I should do when I come back?"

"Be more present," she answered in a whisper. He hugged her tighter.

"I'm sorry. I know I've failed you in that department," he blurted out, kissing the top of her head. "I promise I'll be more present when I come back."

"It's already enough that my nonexistent father and his family aren't coming. I need your support and presence."

"I'm sorry. I've been so busy. That's on me. I should've made more time for you," he apologized, hugging her tighter and kissing her head again. "I'm the worst, I know."

"It's okay, just promise you'll be more present."

He agreed. "I promise. Let's order the pizza. We'll finish packing later," he said, placing a soft kiss to her temple.

"Thanks." Catherine grabbed the coffee he got her at the coffee shop in the Baltimore airport. She took a sip and hummed. "Listen, we don't have to pretend we like each other. But let's be cordial," she voiced, taking her glasses off and cleaning them. "There's probably going to be people from the district offices there. We need to keep it professional." He gave her one simple nod. She put her glasses back on.

"I don't have to pretend to like you, Catherine, because I do like you," he murmured, sipping his coffee. He heard her inhale sharply.

They waited at the gate for a couple of hours, neither of them talking. She was concentrating on a document she needed to redact for her boss. And he, well, he was entertained watching the planes landing and taking off on the runway.

"It was nice our schedulers were able to find us flights leaving together," he said, breaking the silence that was killing him. Even though she was sitting next to him, she felt impossibly far away. There were so many things he wanted to tell her, ask her. But he couldn't bring himself to utter them. A million things ran through his mind, and not a single one of them rose to his lips. They all died in his throat.

"So much easier," she said, nodding. She turned briefly to him, her eyes lingering a little longer than usual on his. She smiled, but it was a sad smile. She turned her attention back to her task, bringing them back to the silence.

"So, no contacts today?" he asked.

"No. I didn't want to put my contacts in," she replied. Seeing her wear glasses brought back memories from their undergraduate years.

"They suit you," he added, smiling. She looked away and smiled.

"Thanks," she whispered, sitting back on the chair, and snuggling a little closer to him. They fell into a comfortable silence after that.

"I'm sorry, but all flights have been canceled due to the unexpected snowstorm," the clerk at the service desk at their layover airport said. Their flight had been delayed for four hours, only to find out it was canceled, delaying their arrival in the district.

"A snowstorm? In October?" Catherine asked the clerk in disbelief.

"Global warming, ma'am," the clerk replied.

"Okay, preach. No lies detected. But there must be a way. We have to reach our destination tonight," she stated, exasperated.

"My hands are tied. I'm sorry. We are offering a hotel voucher for the night and a discount for a rental car if that helps," the clerk offered, handing Catherine some papers. Catherine heaved a heavy, exasperated sigh, massaging her temples. One Devin knew too well. Not good. She was about to go into mental lockdown mode. He had to do something.

"We'll take these," Devin said, stepping in and taking the papers from the clerk. He looked at Catherine, and she was looking back at him, her eyes fiery, the green in them a shade darker. "It's okay. The drive isn't long. We can stay the night in a hotel and then drive there. I'll drive. It'll be alright. Besides, driving in a snowstorm is dangerous. I will not risk us like that," he assured her. She sighed, giving up.

"Fine. Thanks. And sorry about the outburst," she apologized to the clerk and turned around, leaving. He walked behind her, his phone in hand.

"There's a hotel in the airport. Kinda expensive, but with the discount, we should be okay."

"Whatever. I just want to shower. I was looking forward to the hotel in the district," she replied, sounding exhausted.

"Come on," he said, leading the way. They arrived at the hotel, and the lobby was full of people with canceled flights.

"Oh god, this is going to be hell." They walked to the back of the long check-in line. Their time to check in came and made their way to the front desk.

"As you may see, we are full. So, the availability of

rooms might be limited. I hope you understand," the front desk attendant expressed.

"Absolutely. Completely understandable," Devin replied smiling back at her.

"Looks like we only have one more room available."

"We'll take it," Catherine blurted out. "We will take it." Catherine dropped her forehead on the front desk. "I just want to shower." He laughed at her antics, the never-changing drama queen.

"We'll take it," he said to the attendant. She chuckled and nodded. He handed her his credit card and discount voucher while she typed on her computer.

"Alright, you are all set," she replied, handing him their hotel keys. "The hotel kitchen is open 24 hrs but has a limited menu."

"We'll take what we can," he said, picking up the keys. "Come on, *Miss-I-need-a-shower*." He took the handle of her carry-on and dragged it along. She walked behind him and picked her suitcase from his hands.

"I can get my suitcase, thanks." She walked ahead of him, calling the elevator. "What floor?" she asked once inside. He looked down at the keys and the envelope they were in.

"Fifth," he said. She pressed the button, and they rode the elevator quietly. Once on their floor, they walked to the room. He unlocked the door and let her in first. He followed her inside, only to bump into her, almost making her fall. He grabbed her elbow and stilled her. "I'm sorry."

"Oh god, this is going to be a disaster," she murmured.

"What are you talking about?" he asked, following her gaze to the middle of the room.

Only one bed.

"Shit," he whispered.

"Why?" she uttered.

"What?" he asked her, turning to her. She had her eyes closed, looking at the ceiling.

"Why must you punish me like this?" she questioned no one in particular. He furrowed his eyebrows. "Did I do something to piss you off?"

"Who the hell are you talking to?" he asked, walking to the little desk in the room. She jumped, startled. "It sure as hell ain't me." He placed his suitcase on the luggage rack.

"Devin, there's two of us and one bed," she exclaimed matter-of-factly. He snorted.

"Right, I forgot we've never slept in the same bed. Like ever. The summer of junior year in the mountains of Nevada, a fever dream of mine," he replied, rolling his eyes. "You're still scared of getting the cooties." Opening his suitcase, he removed his toiletry bag.

"I am not," she protested, placing her hands on her hips and taking a defiant stance. "Need I remind you…"

"Look," he started, massaging his forehead. "There's a couch. And there's the floor. I will gladly take either if you're so traumatized and scared. It's late. I'm tired and hungry, and I don't have the energy to argue with you about who is taking the bed, Catherine. It's been a long day. You take the bed, and I'll take whatever is left," he continued, walking to the bathroom.

"What the hell does that even mean? I am not traumatized or scared," she stated in a high-pitched voice.

"Then stop acting like a child," he replied, exasperated. "It's not the end of the world, Catherine. It's just one night. Not the rest of the three weeks. You have your room in the district. So, just take the bed for tonight. You shower while I go find something to eat," he said, leaving the room. He exhaled and walked to the elevator.

"I am not a child," he heard Catherine say as she followed

him out of the room. He closed his eyes and shouted a prayer in his mind, just like Catherine had done in the room. Pinching the bridge of his nose, he exhaled.

"Didn't you say you wanted to shower?" he asked rhetorically, calling for the elevator.

"I'm also hungry."

"I was gonna bring you food," he said, pinching the bridge of his nose again. "Do you think I would have gone, bought something for myself and not for you? What kind of monster do you think I am, Catherine?"

With perfect timing, his phone rang. He got it out of his pocket. Emily's name flashed on the screen. "Hey, Em," he greeted, picking up. Something rushed into Catherine's eyes. But just as quickly as it came, it left her eyes. The elevator arrived, and he went inside. "Em, one sec," Devin said to the receiver, holding the elevator with his free hand. "Are you coming?" he asked Catherine who was standing in the hallway, staring at nothing. She shook her head. "You sure?" She nodded. "Anything in particular you want?"

"I'm not hungry," Catherine replied in a whisper.

"But you just said—"

"I'm fine," she interrupted, turning and leaving. He stood there confused.

"Devin?" Emily questioned on the other side of the line. "Was that Catherine?" He shook his head and pressed the lobby button.

"Yes. It was her. Em, this was a mistake. I don't know why my boss thought it was a good idea to send both of us together," he replied, massaging his forehead. "She hates me. Like really hates me, Em," he added, defeated. "I don't even know what I did."

"No one knows. I don't even know. I arrived at the apartment on the last day of finals, and she was packed and gone.

As if she had never lived there. As if we never spent four years living under the same roof. Not even a goodbye note. So, your guess is as good as mine," Emily stated. "She even blocked my number," Emily added. "I couldn't even call her. You know this."

"I know. She did the same to me," Devin said. The elevator arrived at the lobby, and he walked to the bar, sitting on one of the stools. He eyed the menu.

"What can I get you fella?" the bartender asked. He looked up at him.

"A whiskey, double," he ordered while resuming browsing the menu.

"Coming right up," the bartender replied.

"What happened Devin? Aren't you supposed to be in the district already?" Emily asked, worry in her tone. The bartender came back and placed the drink in front of him.

"Thanks. Can I get two cold club sandwiches, one of them without mustard. Both to-go and two water bottles?" he asked.

"Anything else?" Devin shook his head. "I'll bring those right out," he said and disappeared.

"We're stuck in our layover city. All flights canceled," Devin continued his conversation with Emily, taking a sip of his whiskey and swallowing. The burning sensation sliding down his throat, a welcome treat.

"Why?"

"Snowstorm."

"Yikes," Emily replied. "What are you going to do?"

"We're staying the night at the airport hotel, and then we are renting a car and driving to the district. It's only a couple of hours from here. Em, I don't think I can do this for three weeks. We've barely spoken, and I know she is keeping the conversation courteous because that's her professional self talking. She hates me. And there's only one bed in the room. And she freaked out and started talking nonsense to no one. Em, I don't know what to do. I wish I could fix things. I thought I was over her. I thought I had moved on. But I guess not," he babbled. The bartender came back with a bag.

"Here you go, sir. Would you like to pay now or charge it to the room?" the bartender inquired, setting the bag in front of him. Devin downed the rest of his whiskey.

"Charge it to the room," he answered. The bartender nodded and placed a receipt there. He signed and picked up the bag, walking back to the room. They didn't speak about Catherine after that. Instead, Emily rambled about her work and how one of her coworkers got a promotion she was sure was supposed to be for her. "So, anything new with the wedding preparations? Anything I should know?" he asked, entering the room. Catherine was exiting the bathroom, towel drying her hair. "Em, one sec. There's a club sandwich without mustard for you here," he said, walking to the desk and dropping the bag. "I went with a safe option." Catherine nodded. "There's one for me too, but I'll eat after showering." Catherine's eyes never left him. He turned to his suitcase. "Okay, Em, what were you saying?"

"It's going great. Tailor started your suit."

"What about the flower girl? Did you ask your friend to have her little girl be the flower girl?" he asked, rummaging through his suitcase. He got out his pajamas and a pair of underwear.

"Yes! She said yes," Emily replied excitedly.

"Great! One less thing to worry about. And one less thing to keep you from becoming a bridezilla," he muttered, walking to the bathroom and closing the door. "Okay, well, I'm going to shower and eat. Hopefully, I can catch some sleep before my drive tomorrow. So, I'll talk to you later, okay?"

"Yes sir."

"Alright, love you."

"Love you," she replied and hung up. He showered and exited the bathroom, finding Catherine in bed eating the sandwich.

"I'm sorry it's bar food. It's the only thing that was open."

"It's okay," she noted quietly. He nodded and opened his box, taking a bite of his sandwich. "Is Emily okay?" she asked in a whisper. The question made him stop chewing. He looked at her. She was looking down at the untouched half of the sandwich in her hands, her gaze not meeting his. He swallowed, cleaning his mouth with the napkin.

"She's okay. She's happy," he said, looking at her. Catherine bobbed her head once, packing the rest of her sandwich back into the box. She took a deep breath and looked at him, her eyes cloudy. *Sad.* Her eyes were sad, making something in his chest crack. Something in his soul chipped away. He wanted to reach out and hold her. He was confused. Confused about her, and the look on her face. He faltered in the silence that engulfed them. "Cat…" he started, but she shook her head.

"I'm going to bed," she stated, walking to the desk and placing her sandwich box there. She walked back to the bed and got under the covers. "The bed is big enough, Devin. You don't have to sleep on the couch if you don't want to," she whispered. But he couldn't. For the life of him, he couldn't. He finished eating, throwing away his box. He walked to the bed and got the pillows from his side, along with the top sheet Catherine had folded out for him. He walked to the couch and set up his bed. Looking at the ceiling with his mind running a million miles an hour, he drifted off to sleep.

Chapter Nine

Catherine

"So, anything new with the wedding preparations? Anything I should know?"

"What about the flower girl? Did you ask your friend to have her little girl be the flower girl?"

"Great! One less thing to worry about. And one less thing to keep you from becoming a bridezilla."

Those words kept going on a loop in her head. *Nonstop.* Devin decided to sleep on the couch despite her telling him it was okay to sleep in the bed. She heard his soft snores. She heaved a silent sigh, a tear escaping her eye. She wiped it away quickly.

"So, they're still together. They are getting married after all," she whispered to herself. She threw the sheets away from her and swung her legs off the bed, grabbing her glasses from the nightstand and putting them on, walking to the bathroom, her socked feet padding quietly. She turned the lights on and closed the door. "Get it together, Catherine. He is ancient history," she pepped talked herself in the mirror. "And you…" she admonish, pointing to her heart, "you also get it together. This heart doesn't belong to him. Not anymore."

She splashed cold water on her face. "Ugh... I need a drink." She fixed her hair and walked back to her suitcase, getting out a hoodie.

Grabbing her phone and the hotel key from the nightstand, she left the room. "God I hope the bar is open. I could use a glass of wine. Or two. Or the bottle." She got down to the bar and sat in one of the chairs. The bar was empty. She looked at the hour on her phone. It was almost three in the morning.

"What can I get you?" the bartender asked.

"Got any wine?" she asked.

"Yes, ma'am, red, white, and rosé."

"I'll take a Chardonnay, if you have any." The bartender nodded and turned around.

"Room or card?" the bartender asked, placing the wine glass in front of her.

"Room. Room 536," she murmured, taking a sip.

"So, did you have a fight?" the bartender asked. She looked at him, confused. "You're with the redhead, right? He came earlier and got two club sandwiches."

"How do you...?"

"He also charged the sandwiches to the room and ordered a whiskey double," the bartender explained.

"Ah," she murmured, taking a gulp from the wine, and finishing it. She tapped the glass. "We didn't have a fight," she replied as the bartender filled her glass again.

"It sure seems like you did. You are here at almost three in the morning. Alone," the bartender said matter-of-factly. She rolled her eyes, taking a sip of the wine.

"He and I are just coworkers. We don't even work in the same office. We just got paired up to do this job."

"Right," the bartender replied, cleaning a glass.

"What does that even mean?"

"Based on his phone call earlier, you two clearly have a past, and you definitely feel something more than *coworkers-stuck-in-the-same-hotel-room-for-the-night*," the bartender stated, walking to her, placing his elbows at the bar, and leaning in. She rolled her eyes, annoyed at his suggestion.

"You are wrong," she replied with easy defiance, finishing her second glass of wine.

"Am I?" he replied. "My degree in psychology tells me otherwise."

She snorted. "Psychology degree? Okay, Freud," she retorted in cold sarcasm.

"Yes, from *the* Johns Hopkins University School of Medicine," he replied, looking serious.

"Then why are you a bartender at an airport hotel?" He refilled her glass without her asking.

"The medical field didn't work for me," he said, shrugging.

"So, you ended up pouring one for everyone?"

"I help some of them. Sometimes, all they need is someone who listens," he said. "So, tell me, room 536, what's bothering you?" She looked around. The bar was empty except for her. She debated if she wanted to reply. Biting her lip, she looked away.

"Have you ever been in love?" she asked, playing with the rim of her glass.

He rolled his eyes. "A couple of times, yes."

"Do you remember your first love?" He nodded. "I fell in love for the first time… a long time ago. Thirteen years ago, to be exact, and got my heart broken by that very same person. Nine years ago, to be precise. And by my best friend as well," she said, taking a sip from her wine.

"I'm gonna go out on a limb and say it's the redhead

upstairs," the bartender assumed. She kept quiet. "I see. Do you still love him?"

Did she? Did she still have feelings for him after all this time? Her hand went to her necklace, playing with the pendant. Nine years. It had been nine years since she walked away. Yet, her body and heart somehow still reacted every time he looked at her. Every time he talked to her. These next three weeks were going to be hell on wheels.

"I don't know," she answered honestly. "You see," she started, coming closer, leaning her arms on the bar, "I thought I was… okay. I thought I was over him. I thought I had moved on. I've been in a wonderful relationship with an incredible man for the past four years."

"But do you love him? This man you are talking about?" the bartender asked. "Do you love him the way you loved redhead upstairs? Or were you just using this wonderful man you are with now to fill in the void redhead left?" She looked down, ashamed. Deep down, she knew that what he was saying had some truth to it. Truth be told, for the last six months, her relationship with Kyle had not been the same as it was a year ago. They had drifted apart. Maybe this time away from each other would help them.

"Okay, Freud, why are you attacking me?" she questioned, downing the rest of her wine. "I need something stronger if you're going to continue psychoanalyzing me." She slid her wine glass to him. The bartender turned around and got an expensive bottle of whiskey. He brought back two shot glasses. He poured the amber liquor into both glasses and placed the bottle between them.

"This one is on the house," he exclaimed, picking up his shot glass. She did the same, and they clinked them. She downed hers in one sip.

"So, my Freudian friend, go on, tell me. Finish the psychoanalysis."

"Deep down, you still love redhead upstairs." She played with her glass. "And it's pretty obvious to me," he continued, "he still loves you too."

She scoffed. "Doubtful." Picking up the whiskey bottle, she filled her shot glass. She downed it in one go. "He's engaged," she continued, "and very much in love. Still with the same girl he was with when he broke my heart."

"Have you ever talked about whatever made you distance yourself? Have you guys talked about what happened?" She looked down at her empty shot glass, playing with the rim. She refused to open that wound. She refused to acknowledge that event.

"The past is the past," she said. "We can't change it." She stood up, and the bartender gave her an apprehensive look. "Thanks for the therapy session. I'll make sure to leave a wonderful tip tomorrow at check out."

She walked back to the room, throwing herself in bed. The world was starting to spin. Maybe mixing Chardonnay with whiskey wasn't the best idea after all.

"Everything okay?" a deep, sleepy voice said beside her.

"Fuck." She jumped and looked to her side. Devin's back greeted her. "You fucking scared me," she replied, setting her arms on her eyes. "What happened to the couch?"

"It was uncomfortable as fuck. I can go back to it if you want."

"No, it's fine. You can stay." She sighed, giving up. Hotel couches were indeed uncomfortable as fuck, and she wasn't that cruel.

"Are you okay?"

"I'm fine, Satan. Go back to sleep," she said, turning to

her side. The nickname didn't register right away. "Fuck," she whispered as he chuckled.

"Where did you go?"

"None of your business. Good night." Closing her eyes, she prayed the alcohol helped her sleep.

As it turns out, the alcohol did help her fall asleep. Followed by a killer headache she woke up with the next morning. However, what she didn't see coming was the cup of water and two aspirins that were placed on her nightstand, a note placed on the side.

Drink me. I went to get coffee and breakfast.

- Satan

She looked down at the note as a tear slowly found its way down her cheek. The act bringing back memories she didn't want to relive. She took the two aspirins and downed them in one gulp. She shrank back to bed and pulled the covers on top of her, blocking the small beam of sunshine leaking through the cracks of the heavy curtains. The handle of the door rattled, and the door opened and closed quickly.

"Phew, it's hell downstairs. Everyone is checking out to try to catch flights. I feel sorry for the airlines," Devin announced. "Come on, sleepy drunken head. Coffee is here. The magic cure for a hangover." She removed the covers and looked at him. "Good morning. Sleep well?" She looked at him through slit eyes. "Tough crowd? It's okay. Nothing coffee can't fix. Here," he said, taking one from the cardboard cup carrier and walking to her. She sat on the bed, her back resting against the headboard. "Just how you like it." Handing it to her, he dropped down on the bed, kissing the top of her head. She froze, and so did he, his lips still on the crown of her head. That warm fuzzy feeling started to grow in her chest again. She did not like that feeling one bit. He moved back quickly and looked around. She let go of a deep breath.

"So, breakfast?" she asked nonchalantly, breaking the tension, ignoring what had just happened and how it made her feel. It was better that way.

"Ah, yes. I got you a sausage croissant with egg and cheese. Hope that's okay. I also bought some dairy-free yogurt. With granola and strawberry," he said, walking back to the paper bag. "You know, in case you've become a health obsessed person or something." He chuckled nervously. She laughed quietly.

"Where did you get this coffee?" she asked, taking another sip. Between the coffee and the aspirin, her hangover was subsiding.

"There's a local coffee shop in the lobby," he said, bringing her—what she assumed was— the foil-wrapped croissant.

Extending her hand and picking up the foil-wrapped sandwich, their fingers brushed, and a little shock zapped at her. He recoiled, feeling it too. He nodded absentmindedly.

"How's the head?" he asked, poking his temple and walking to where his breakfast and coffee were.

"Thanks for the aspirin. It's helping," she replied, placing her coffee on the nightstand and opening the wrapped croissant. She took a bite and hummed, closing her eyes.

"What was the culprit?" he wondered as he took a bite from his sandwich.

"A very expensive whiskey the bartender brought out. Mixed with Chardonnay." The reminder made her feel sick. "Definitely don't recommend it," she added, taking another bite.

"Well, I'm glad that still hasn't changed," he laughed. She smiled. For the first time in a while their interactions felt natural and genuine. How the kiss he accidentally gave her didn't feel forced. How the more time they spent together things were, in a way, starting to feel like old times, and that terrified her. There was too much unfinished business, a lot hanging over their heads, an elephant in the room she was not ready to acknowledge. She thought about what the bartender said last night.

"Deep down, you still love redhead upstairs. And it's pretty obvious to me, he still loves you too."

Those were the words the bartender said to her. Was her body still affected by him after all these years? Yes. But did she still love him? Absolutely not. That was a closed wound. And she was not about to reopen the wound just to address the obvious. Not now. Not after all these years. Not when he was happily engaged to the same girl that caught his heart senior year. Her former best friend, Emily.

"Hey, where did you go?" he asked softly, bringing her out of her mind. She shook her head.

"Nowhere. I'm gonna shower quickly," she announced, finishing her sandwich and standing from the bed. Going to her suitcase, she picked out a pair of jeans, a long-sleeve turtleneck shirt, and some underwear. She walked to the nightstand and picked up her coffee, bringing it with her to the bathroom. She showered and dressed. When she walked to the room, Devin was all packed and ready to go.

"So, it's a four-hour drive from here to the district area," he explained, looking at his phone. "I packed all my stuff and the rest of the food. I also placed your sandwich from last night in the paper bag for the road in case you get hungry," he continued, not looking at her. She walked to her suitcase and placed the neatly folded clothes there along with her toiletry bag, closing the zipper. She put her shoes on and gathered her stuff on the nightstand, dumping it in her purse. "We have another rental in the district. So, we will pick out one here to get us to the district, and then I'll drop it off and pick the new one." He finally looked at her, and she assented.

"Then we better hit the road soon. It's going to be a long day," she replied, placing her suitcase on the floor. "Since I'm getting reimbursed after the trip, lunch and road snacks are on me." She put on her jacket.

"It's not necessary, Kitty Cat," he replied. She froze in the middle of pulling the zipper of her jacket up. Something inside of her cracked at the nickname. Something shifted inside of her. Something she couldn't quite place. She looked at him, and he had his eyes closed, a pained expression plastered on his face. "I'm sorry, Catherine," he whispered. "It just… it just slipped." Opening his eyes, he looked at her, a cloud of emotions brewing in the ocean of his gaze.

"Mistakes happen. It's okay," she whispered, turning around and looking away from his intense gaze. She took a deep breath and picked up the handle of her suitcase, slid the straps of her purse on her shoulder, and walked to the door.

"Calling you Kitty Cat is never a mistake," he replied in a whisper as she placed her hand on the doorknob. She inhaled and exhaled a shaky breath, opening the door. She walked to the elevator. She heard the door close and the sound of wheels behind her. She called the elevator, and the rest of the ride was an awkward silence. He checked them out of the hotel and walked to the airport car rental area. They picked out their keys and walked to where the car was in the parking lot. "I got it," he said, grabbing the handle of her suitcase.

"Thanks," she whispered, taking the paper bag he was handing to her. She walked to the passenger's side and slid into the seat. He followed suit a couple of seconds later, placing his backpack in the back seat. He started driving out of the airport, the roads covered in snow.

"I meant what I said in the room. Calling you Kitty Cat is never a mistake, Catherine. I don't know what I did to make you hate me but—"She put a hand up, stopping him.

"Don't," she said, looking out the window. "The past is in the past." She rummaged through her purse, getting out her headphones. Repeating the same words she said to the bartender, she added, "No need to bring it back. We agreed to be cordial. Let's forget what happened. The kiss and the nickname. Let's pretend it never happened." Putting her headphones on and looking out the window, she shuffled her music on and closed her eyes.

As much as it affected her when he called her *the* nickname, the one he used to call her, it brought up memories she didn't want to think of, memories she had worked hard to forget, because once upon a time, that nickname had meant something to her. Once upon a time, that nickname brought her happiness just hearing it come out of his lips. Once upon a time, she *loved* that nickname. Now, it only brought bitter memories. A tear escaped her eye, and she wiped it away quickly, praying he didn't notice. She leaned her head back and turned her body to the window, closing her eyes and praying these four hours passed quickly.

Chapter Ten

Devin

He fucked up. He utterly, masterfully, royally fucked up.

"It's not necessary, Kitty Cat."

He tightened his grip on the steering wheel, his knuckles going white. He shouldn't have said that. He should have kept quiet. Every minute that passed by, he just kept embarrassing himself.

Get your shit together Devin. She is in a relationship. You have no right. She's the past, he chastised himself.

He glanced at her, and she looked so peaceful he would dare say she was asleep. He looked at the road ahead. When he snuck a glimpse at her earlier today, he watched her wipe a tear from her face, and something inside him broke. He cursed himself, frustrated. Why couldn't he read her like before? What made her distance herself? He seethed with anger. He focused back on her and kept his eyes on her for a little too long. When he returned his gaze back to the road, a car swerved into his lane, no blinkers on, in the middle of the highway, making Devin swerve his car to the other lane, his arm instinctively going to Catherine's chest, protecting her. She stirred awake. He honked at the person.

"Fucking asshole!" he yelled. "Blinkers are there for a reason, asshole. Use them." He turned to her. "Are you okay?" Her eyes were wide open, assessing what had happened. He removed his arm from her, drove to the emergency lane, and parked, turning his on hazards.

"What happened?" she asked, confused and sleepy. *She was asleep.* She was asleep, and he'd woken her up. His carelessness had woken her up.

"An asshole swerved into my lane with no blinker. Are you okay? Are you hurt?" he questioned, inspecting her.

"I'm okay," she answered, looking around. She rubbed the sleep out of her eyes. "Where the hell are we?"

"Halfway there. You dozed off. I've only been driving for a little over two hours," he replied. "Are you hungry?" She shook her head. "There's a rest stop half a mile up. We can stop there. Take a break," he suggested. She nodded. "Alright. On we go then."

When they arrived at the rest area, she got out and went to the restroom. He took that opportunity to walk to the trees and get his pack of cigarettes out of his pocket, lighting one and taking one long drag from it. He was almost finished with the cigarette when he heard her voice.

"Since when do you smoke? That's going to kill you," she said, walking to him furiously and snatching the pack of cigarettes from him. He just shrugged. She looked at the box in her hands.

"Since a couple of years ago." She walked to the trash can and threw them away. "Hey!" he exclaimed, walking to the trash can, but she blocked his way.

"Don't," she said, looking up at him. Her green eyes were a fierce shade, a brew of emotions in them.

"Those are mine," he protested, trying to reach inside the trash can. She stopped him with her hands on his chest and pushed him back. She was stronger than he remembered. He looked at her, his nostrils flared in anger.

"Not anymore. Turn around, Mack. Leave them," she commanded, her voice breaking. "I won't let you dig your grave so young." He stopped fighting her. He studied her face, her eyes. She turned her face away.

"Cat…" he mumbled, his tone a shade softer. She cared. She still cared.

"Those things will kill you, Devin. And I'll be damned if I let you dig your grave like this," she replied in a whisper. She closed her eyes, taking a deep breath and composing herself. "We can go now," she said, walking back to the car. He kicked the ground, looking down in frustration, frowning at the ground. She was already seated in the car when he got there. He walked to his side and jumped in, putting on his seatbelt. He was starting the car when she spoke again. "I know I have no right to what I'm about to ask of you, but please, Devin, quit smoking," she whispered, looking down at her hands on her lap. "If not for you, do it for me. Do it as a last favor for me." Something inside of him chipped away.

"Okay, Catherine. I will quit. I'll do it for you if you tell me why you left nine years ago," he continued, turning to her. "What happened to us, Catherine? We used to be best friends. Inseparable. What did I do, Catherine?" he asked, studying her. She shook her head, a hand going up to her face to wipe away a tear that had fallen.

"Whatever happened is in the past."

"It doesn't matter. I want to know. I want to know what happened. I want to know what I did. Why did you change so much? Why did you leave without saying goodbye? Did those years mean nothing to you?"

"Devin, please, leave it. I don't want to talk about it." Her phone started to ring. She fumbled in her bag and got it out. "I have to take this," she said, unbuckling her seatbelt and exiting the car. "Kyle, hey," she answered as she closed the door. Devin looked out his window, and sighing. His phone buzzed. He got it out of his pocket, seeing it was a text from Emily.

> How's the road?

He didn't have the energy to reply to her. He locked his phone and decided he would reply later. He thought back to the interaction and how rattled Catherine looked when she saw him smoking. Her reaction was not normal. He couldn't stop himself from wondering what triggered her. Catherine was coming back, her phone still in her ear. She hung up and got inside the car again, buckling her seatbelt.

"I'll quit Catherine," he vowed, reaching for her hands folded on her lap, engulfing them in his massive hand and squeezing them. "Ready?" He saw her nod. "Just know that whenever you're ready to talk about it, I will always be here."

"Since you guys will be staying here for a while, we figured we would give you rooms beside each other. Breakfast is served from 7 am until 10 am. And here is the Wi-Fi password," the owner of the bed and breakfast they were staying at for the next three weeks said. "These are also the recently renovated rooms. We are in the middle of remodeling some areas, hence why the garden is closed down. We are fixing the gazebo area, and we are also doing some landscaping to the garden," she explained, walking out of the front desk.

"Derek, please help the young lady with her bag," she instructed the scrawny teenager sitting on one of the sofas, playing with his phone.

"It's okay, I got it, Mrs. Mattis," Devin reassured her. He gave Catherine a side look. He picked up her suitcase along with his, and this time she didn't protest.

"Oh please, call me Gloria. Alright, let's get you guys settled," she exclaimed, walking to some stairs. She stopped on the first step and turned back to them. "I'm hopeful you guys can find a solution to our water problem. We are blessed, and we have been using our well, but it is starting to run out. The rest of the town is not as lucky. Some businesses are operating for limited hours. For us, if the problem isn't fixed in a couple of weeks, we might need to ration, or worse close down until it's resolved. This, like most of the town's people, is the only source of income we have. This is Charlie's and my legacy, you know?" she mused looking to the distance. Gloria turned back around and ascended the stairs. He and Catherine looked at each other.

"We got this," he said for only her to hear. She nodded. "After you." He motioned for her to go up first. She did. He picked up both suitcases and started climbing the stairs.

"Here's the lady's room. And here's yours sir," Gloria said, stopping between two rooms. She handed both keys to Catherine. "I'll let you get settled," she exclaimed and disappeared. He put Catherine's bag down. She handed him a key.

"Alright. I guess I'll see you tomorrow for our first town hall meeting with the residents and community leaders," Catherine mentioned, turning to the door of her room and inserting the key into the lock. "Do you need me to go with you to get the other rental car?"

"No, it's okay. You get some rest."

"Okay. I'll see you tomorrow then."

"Bright and early, Babbitt," he chirped, unlocking his room door and ducking inside.

"You ready?" he asked, exiting the B&B and walking to the car. Catherine was already waiting there, leaning against her door, sunglasses on. One look at her and he knew something was wrong. "What happened? What's wrong?" he interrogated worriedly. She waved a dismissive hand in the air.

"I had to drink my coffee black. They don't have oat milk," she explained. "It tasted awful. I had to add sugar to it. It's fine. I'll go to a convenience store later," she continued. He sighed and chuckled, finding her adorable. "Ready?" He unlocked the car, and she got in.

They drove in silence to where the town hall meeting was happening.

They were in a small town in central Michigan called *Stella*. The sign on the edge of town mentioned something about fireflies he didn't get to read. The town didn't have a big population, just a little over a thousand residents. It was the kind of small town where everyone knew everyone. It reminded him a lot of his hometown. The space where the town hall was happening was in the middle of downtown, an adjacent makeshift theater of the church in the middle of the town square.

The square had small businesses surrounding it consisting of one hardware store, one supermarket that also doubled as a farmer's market, one barber shop, a hair salon, a small bakery, and a family doctor. He parked the car on the side road, and they walked around the town square. While the town was small, the buildings and the town spaces were well-kept. They passed by the bakery, and it had a sign that read

Operating on limited hours due to the water crisis. Devin glanced at Catherine who looked concerned. The despair on her face was heartbreaking.

They walked inside to where the people were gathering. Both his boss and the representative were also going to be there. They opened the door, a couple of people turned their way and smiled as they walked to the front. Catherine smiled back. He glanced around and saw Catherine's boss but not his. He shot him a quick message asking his whereabouts.

"Auntie Cathy!" a little girl screamed, running to Catherine.

"Munchkin!" Catherine said, kneeling and opening her arms. The little girl jumped, nuzzling her face in Catherine's neck, wrapping herself around Catherine, koala bear style. Catherine engulfed her in a hug, kissing her head. "You're here!" she stated, her voice muffled by the girl's hair. Catherine stood up and carried her.

"Papa said you would be here," the little girl replied, lifting her head.

"Of course, I'm here. I'm helping Papa," Catherine replied, tucking a loose curl behind her ear. All the dots were connecting. If his assumptions were right, this must be Catherine's boss' daughter.

"Auntie Cathy…" the little girl whispered.

"Yes, sweetie?"

"Who's that?" she asked, pointing at him. Catherine turned to where her little finger was pointing, looking at him.

"Oh, him. He is my coworker," Catherine explained. "His name is Devin." He waved at her. The girl giggled and shied away into Catherine's arms.

"He is pretty," she whispered. He chuckled. Catherine looked at him and then back at the girl.

"He is, isn't he?" she agreed with her. She walked to

where the stage was, and he was left in a daze.

'He is, isn't he?'

Did he hear her right? He shook his head and caught up with her.

"Devin, this is Heather, Michael's little munchkin. Heather, this is Devin. Say hi," Catherine said to Heather. Heather waved a shy hand at him. He smiled at her.

"Hi, Heather," he greeted, smiling. "Nice to meet you." Heather giggled.

"Catherine, you are here, good," Michael acknowledged. "Heather, let Auntie Cathy work," he said, reaching for the little girl, but she tightened her grip on Catherine.

"It's fine. I don't mind her," Catherine replied, hugging Heather tighter. "What's up, boss?"

"We are about to start. Just waiting on two community leaders." Catherine nodded. Dropping her purse on the stage, she sat down, adjusting Heather on her lap. "I'm going to do the rounds again and greet the other constituents that have arrived," Michael announced and disappeared.

"You two seem close," he pointed out, sitting beside Catherine on the stage. She nodded.

"I helped with raising her too," she stated, lovingly kissing Heather's head. "I've been part of her life since before she was born."

"Auntie Cathy?" Heather asked.

"Yes, munchkin?"

"Are you going to have dinner with us tonight? Mom said she had a surprise she wanted to give everyone."

"Of course, I am. Papa told me about it," Catherine replied, and the little girl's face illuminated.

"So, you get to meet Trooper," Heather exclaimed enthusiastically.

"Who?" Devin asked.

"Trooper. My new dog," Heather said like it was obvious. "Wait, Papa has pictures of him." Heather jumped out of Catherine's lap, running to her dad. Catherine smiled fondly at her.

"You really love her," Devin observed.

"Yes, I do. I really do. I lost count of how many times I have babysat her. My guest room is full of her toys, and she has her own drawer of clothes for when she comes over."

"She's lucky to have you." Catherine looked at him. "Everyone is lucky to have you in their life. I felt lucky to have you in my life, even when things changed so drastically," he said. She looked into his eyes, a storm of emotions there. Emotions he couldn't decipher. He used to be able to read her like a book, but now, it was like she had put these iron walls up, rendering him unable to read her.

"Here he is," Heather said, jumping on Catherine's lap again. Catherine turned her attention back to the little golden locks girl.

"Oh, my goodness, look at this precious boy," Catherine exclaimed, looking at the pictures. "Do you know what color his collar is going to be?"

"Red," Heather replied.

"Of course, it'll be red. That's your favorite color," Catherine retorted matter-of-factly, tickling her. Heather giggled. Catherine kissed her cheek. "Okay, so red. Are you also getting his toys in red too? His bed?" Heather nodded enthusiastically. "Well, now I know I need to ask Santa to add red dog toys to my Christmas gifts."

"Santa is going to bring him toys?" Heather asked, surprised.

"Oh yes. Santa and I are close. He will definitely bring Trooper toys."

Devin was mesmerized by their interactions. Catherine

was very fond of Heather. She really loved her. She adored her. She was so delicate with her, so loving. And in that moment, an image as clear as a sunny day passed through his mind. Catherine as a mother. As her loving, maternal self. Because he knew, he just knew, that Catherine would be an amazing mom. Just like he imagined, at one point, raising a family with her. She had all the great qualities of a mom. She was delicate, compassionate, loving, and understanding. Her future kids will be so lucky to have her. If she ever decided she wanted to experience motherhood.

"Okay, the last two community leaders have arrived," Michael said, bringing him out of his mind. He looked at Catherine's boss. Catherine nodded. She placed a soft kiss on the back of Heather's head and sat her on the stage. Heather was playing a game on her father's phone and didn't pay much attention to what was happening around her. Michael turned around and walked to the little podium.

Devin's phone buzzed in his pocket. It was a text from his boss.

> Running a bit behind. Heavy traffic on the highway. I should be there in the next ten minutes. Start without me.

He stood up and walked to Michael.

"Sir?" he spoke, bringing Michael's attention to him. "My boss is running behind because of traffic. He said we can start without him." Michael nodded.

"Where's your boss?" Catherine asked in a whisper by his side. He showed her the text. "Ah. Okay."

"Ready?" Michael asked, turning to them.

"Ready when you are boss," Catherine said. Michael nodded and turned around, starting what was possibly going to be the loudest town hall meeting Devin had ever attended.

Chapter Eleven

Catherine

"So, what's the plan? What happens now?" one of the community leaders asked.

"We will ensure that this situation gets resolved as soon as possible. We have already contacted the U.S Army Corps of Engineers to help with the situation in the meantime. They are sending brigades as we speak," Brian, Devin's boss, replied. "We can assure you we are doing everything we can to resolve this, and we will be working hard back in the Capitol," he promised them.

"In the meantime, we will leave our most trusted employees and our right hands. This is my chief of staff, Catherine Babbitt," Michael explained, looking at her. Every pair of eyes turned to her. She gave them a shy wave.

"Hello everyone," she addressed the people present. "I'm happy to be here and happy to be able to help find a solution as soon as possible."

"And this is my chief of staff, Devin Mack," Brian introduced him.

"Hello. Just like Catherine mentioned, happy to be here to try to find a solution as soon as possible," Devin added, smiling, making his dimples pop out. A few ladies in the audience swooned at the sight of them. She looked down in an attempt to hide a smile.

"What's your plan?" one of the residents asked. "You still haven't answered that question."

"Like I mentioned—"

Catherine interrupted her boss. "Well, firstly…" Michael glanced at her, a puzzled look in his eyes. He nodded, giving her the green light to keep talking. "Firstly, we sincerely apologize for how this situation went down. You guys should not be paying the consequences of incompetent people. Secondly, we need to hire a new board of directors, as well as hire a new CEO. For the public-private company, I mean. We had lengthy meetings with them, and they admitted they misused the funding assigned to them. As soon as we identified this, we asked them to resign. That's the main reason why Devin and I are here, to ensure that the new board of directors and CEO of the company are trustworthy with the best interests of the community in mind."

"What did they use the funding for?" someone in the back questioned. "Did they use it for themselves?"

"No. They used the funding assigned for maintenance and repairs of the infrastructure to pay off the debt the company is in," Devin replied. A lot of people sighed, and the rest looked pissed.

"Are they going to be prosecuted? Or is this going to be swept under the rug?" someone asked.

"There will be consequences other than the resignation we asked for," Catherine answered.

"Good. I had to close down my flower shop because my plants and flowers withered since I couldn't water them. I hope they all rot in jail," a woman on the front row said. The townsfolk agreed.

"We will review applications as we receive them to fill the vacant seats. And we will make sure they are trustworthy people," Devin said. "We promise we will make the right choices."

Catherine glanced around at the townspeople. Some looked convinced, some had a pensive gaze, and the rest looked relentless. This was a situation that was costing them energy, time, and effort. She needed to help them. They needed to help the town and ensure this never happened again.

"We would love to have all of you involved in the process. This is your town, and this is something that shouldn't have happened in the first place. If anyone wants to volunteer and help us by meeting with us on a roundtable so we can come up with solutions to avoid this happening again in the future, we would love to hear your opinions," she suggested. The townsfolk looked taken aback but started to smile and nod at her.

"Well, if that is all the questions we have from you folks, let's adjourn this meeting until we have more news," Brian concurred. People nodded and filed out. When it was just the four of them and Heather, they reconvened.

"Do we have applications?" Michael asked.

"No, but they needed reassurance that we are working on it and doing everything possible to fix this," Devin said.

"I agree. They need to have or feel some sort of reassurance. Otherwise, they'll be relentless and anxious until we tell them there are applications. Either way, they needed some sort of white lie. I know it sounds bad and something we don't usually do, but they needed something to calm their nerves. We should be getting applications soon," Catherine added, looking around.

Devin nodded. "Correct. We will open the applications

today. The mayor's office is also going to send us possible qualified people that can fill out those positions. We got this," he promised. Both Michael and Brian nodded in agreement.

"I don't doubt it for a second," Brian voiced, patting Devin on the back. Devin smiled at his boss.

"I like that part you added about getting them involved," Michael mused.

"Yes, I feel they will be less weary and on edge if they can be involved. Good job, Miss Babbitt," Brian responded. She beamed.

"Thanks. And since they are such a closed community, it'll be good to have their input as this is a problem that affects them directly, and they can make the decision on who should lead the company that provides them with water," she replied.

"Well, I have to go and run some errands. I'll see you tonight, right?" Michael asked her, walking to where Heather was seated. She nodded. "Great, Devin and Brian, please feel free to come. It's just a small dinner at my house, nothing big. Just Olive and us," Michael added, gesturing to him and Heather while gathering his stuff. "Come on Heats," he mumbled, taking Heather's little hand in his. Catherine bent down and kissed the top of her head.

"Of course, just text me the address. Devin, I'll see you tonight then," Brian replied. Devin looked at Catherine, and she shrugged.

"You got it, boss," Devin retorted. They both left. Catherine and Devin stood alone in the town hall. "Let's go to the office and see what we are left with." She nodded.

They left and drove to Stella Waterworks offices. Only one car was there. They walked inside, and an older woman greeted them. She appeared to be in her seventies, her hair mostly white, with piercing brown eyes.

"Good morning, how can I help you today?" she asked, smiling.

"We're the folks that are going to be working here. The ones sent from Congress," Devin explained.

"Who?" she inquired, confused.

"The new ones in charge..." Devin said.

"Did Mr. Thomas send you?" she asked. "I haven't seen him in a couple of days," she explained, confused.

"Mrs..." Catherine started but stopped. There was no name plaque or anything at her desk that could identify her.

"You can call me Helen."

"Helen, did Mr. Thomas not tell you?" Catherine asked.

"Tell me what dear?"

"Helen, Mr. Thomas no longer works for the company," Catherine explained softly, afraid of her reaction.

"Impossible, there's a board meeting today at 2 pm," Helen answered, showing her a desk calendar, pointing to a scribble of letters on the date. Catherine rubbed her hands together.

"Helen, Mr. Thomas and the board got fired. They were asked to resign," Catherine spoke softly. "A few days ago. By us," she continued, pointing between herself and Devin.

"But the meeting..."

"We are the meeting," Devin added, an apologetic smile on his face. "We are the board. Momentarily."

"So, everyone..." she started to say, looking at both of them.

"Gone," Catherine replied.

"Well, that is just great. Why couldn't they tell me?"

Helen argued, standing up. "Making me wake up early every day and be here all for nothing," she said, gathering her jacket and putting it on.

"Where are you going, Helen?" Catherine asked her.

"To Mr. Thomas' house to teach him a lesson."

"Helen, are you related to Mr. Thomas?" Devin asked Helen, who was cursing under her breath.

"He is my son," she replied, gathering her purse. "And the biggest disappointment my family has ever seen. Running his father's company to the ground. A company and legacy his father spent years building with the community. Tell me, why did you ask for his resignation?" Helen questioned them.

"He and his board of directors used the federal allocation money on other things," Catherine explained.

"What other things?"

"Instead of using it for maintenance and repairs of the infrastructure like it was supposed to be, he used it to pay off the debt of the company," Devin continued Catherine's sentence.

"I'm going to kill him," Helen retorted. "Is that why all the townsfolk have been calling nonstop?" she asked. They looked at each other.

"He didn't inform you of the problem?" Devin asked.

"No. Enlighten me."

"Helen, the town has been living without clean water for over two months now, and the problem reached Congress, as in Washington DC. I work for Representative Johns, and he works for Senator Jenkins," Catherine explained. Helen closed her eyes and pinched the bridge of her nose. "We have a meeting today with USACE, who are going to be taking over the repairs of the treatment plant and provide clean water to the townsfolk in the meantime," she continued. "They are supposed to be arriving any minute now."

"Do you guys need my help? Do you need me to stay? Oh god, why am I even asking? Of course, you do," Helen replied, shrugging off her jacket.

The meeting with USACE went better than they anticipated. USACE agreed to help provide the necessary equipment to supply the town with water until they figured out how to navigate the situation. Before they knew it, they were heading back to the B&B. Devin parked by the door and looked at her.

"What?" she asked, confused, reaching for the door handle.

"I need to run an errand. Off you go."

"Oh," she said, a little disappointed as she gathered her things and got out of the car. He rolled down the window.

"I'll be back before the dinner, then we can head there together," he replied and drove away, leaving her standing there alone.

A couple of hours later, they were on their way to Michael's house. The drive was quiet except for the faint radio music. They arrived at Michael's house, and Heather opened the door, jumping on Catherine again, along with a small black hairball.

"Oh goodness, hello, Trooper," she greeted, picking up the little Labrador in her arms and smothering it in kisses. Heather giggled. The Labrador started licking her face.

"Auntie Cathy, he likes you," Heather pointed out, giggling.

"I think he does," Catherine said, placing the dog back down. "Where are your parents?" she asked, taking Heather's hand.

"At the grill in the backyard," Heather replied, dragging her through the house. She turned around and saw Devin playing with the dog. She smiled to herself. They made their way to the backyard, and everyone was there, seated on chairs arranged in a semicircle.

"Ah, there you are," Michael said. "Thank you for being here." He gave her two beers.

"Thanks," she muttered, sitting in one of the chairs, Heather hopping on her lap.

"Devin, thanks for coming," Michael saluted, shaking Devin's hand.

"Thanks for the invitation," he replied, smiling. He walked to where she was and sat down on the chair next to her. He picked one of the beers from her hands, winking at her.

What in the hell is going on? she asked herself. She looked away, praying he didn't see the blush on her cheeks and taking a sip from her beer.

"So, Olive and I have an announcement to make," Michael declared from the grill. Everyone looked at the two of them, waiting. "We are expecting baby number two," he said excitedly. Catherine smiled and clapped.

"Congratulations guys!" she cheered from her chair. "You hear that Heats? You're going to be a big sister," she exclaimed, hugging Heather. Heather smiled.

"Really? Papa, you're not joking, right? I'm going to be a big sister?" Heather asked excitedly.

"Yes, munchkin, you are," Michael said. Heather jumped off her lap and ran to her father, tackling him with a hug. Catherine looked at her and smiled. "So, Devin, how long have you known Catherine?" Michael asked after a few minutes.

"What?" Devin asked, confused, choking on his sip of beer.

"You heard me. How long have you known her?" Michael questioned, smirking. "Don't think I haven't noticed the way you look at her like you've known her your whole life."

"We've all noticed kiddo," Brian added.

"I—" Devin looked at her for guidance.

"We went to college together," she explained. "We are both Harvard alumni. Same class and all."

"Ohhh. That makes sense. I had my suspicions about it the first time we all met together. She might be good at her job, but she is terrible at hiding her facial expressions," Michael said.

"What is that supposed to mean?" she asked.

"You speak with your face," Devin and Michael said at the same time.

"I do not."

"You do," everyone minus Heather retorted.

"Everyone knows how you are feeling because you, for the love of God, cannot control your facial expressions. Which would make you a terrible politician if you ever decided to run for office," Michael explained, chuckling. "It's okay. We can't all be perfect."

She looked down at her hands folded in her lap. Devin's hands came to rest on top of hers, squeezing hers. He withdrew and took another sip of his beer.

"Well... Yeah, we met in college. But then, after graduation, we hadn't seen each other until that day at the office," Devin lied, opting to omit their brief meet up at airport a few months ago. "It was refreshing to see a familiar face."

And that was the end of that conversation. The rest of the

dinner was spent talking about everything else. Michael and Olive, giving her and Devin recommendations of places to visit and things to do in their free time. Not that they would have much free time. After that, they had dinner, then Devin and Catherine left.

"You are going to be a great mom someday. You do know that, right?" Devin expressed on their way back to the B&B. She knew he was referring to how she treated Heather. She looked down at her hands folded on her lap. "Can we make a deal?"

"What?" she whispered, half afraid of what he was about to ask her.

"Can we try to be friends again? I really miss you, Catherine."

"I can't promise that, Devin."

Deep down, she knew she was lying to herself. Because she missed him too, no matter how much she denied it to herself, she missed him. She missed having him around and missed having him in her life. But most importantly, she missed the person who knew her the most.

"But can we try? Can we try this for the next three weeks? If it doesn't work after these three weeks, we can just forget about it. Like it never happened. But can we at least try?" he pleaded. She exhaled. "I promise I won't ask what happened or what I did again."

"I'll think about it," was all she said.

"Oh, you have oat milk today!" she exclaimed, looking at the little carton of milk in the mini fridge beside the espresso machine.

"Yes. Pretty boy went and got you some. He really is a

keeper. And he definitely has a thing for you," Gloria exclaimed, bumping her with her elbow.

"He does not. We're just coworkers," she said, pouring the milk into a stainless-steel container and turning the espresso machine milk heater on. "He's engaged."

"With the way he looks at you, I doubt it. He is definitely, most likely, single," Gloria added, arranging a bowl of cereal for herself.

"He doesn't look at me in any way."

"Uhm… whatever helps you sleep at night, my love," Gloria chirped and left the kitchen. She frothed her milk and poured it in her mug along with coffee and a pinch of cinnamon. She took a sip of her coffee and hummed.

"Someone is happy," Devin exclaimed.

"A little guardian angel went and got me oat milk for my coffee," she replied, walking past him to head out of the kitchen.

"That little guardian angel must really care for you then," he said in a whisper, but she heard him. That made her stop. "It's not a big deal." He shrugged. "I'd just rather not have you angry every morning for the next three weeks. You don't have to thank me," he added close to her ear, his breath caressing her cheek, as he walked past her, exiting the kitchen. She just stood there, her coffee mug in her hands, frozen to the spot.

"You okay over there, honey?" Gloria asked, entering the kitchen. She shook the haze out of her mind.

"Yes, sorry, just savoring my coffee," Catherine replied, her voice shaky as if being caught doing something she shouldn't be doing. She smiled at Gloria as she passed her by. She walked out of the kitchen and into the dining room. Most of the seats were free, but where Devin was seated, there were two plates. He looked up from his phone and pulled out the chair next to him, gesturing for her to sit there. For some reason beyond her, her body obeyed the command. She placed her coffee mug on the table and looked at the contents on the plate in front of her. It was filled with eggs, bacon, and fruits. Another smaller plate was beside it with toast. Jams and butter on a smaller pile in the middle of the table.

"Eat. We have a big morning ahead. We're meeting the USACE engineers again." Once again, her body reacted before she registered his words. He gave her a satisfied smile.

"Thank you," she said once she swallowed her first spoonful.

"For what?" he asked without looking at her.

"The oat milk… and this," she replied, pointing at the plate with her fork. She looked at his side of the table. A plate of toast was there, half-eaten. "You're not going to eat?"

"I'm waiting for the coffee to hit my system," he replied, still looking at his phone.

She nodded and kept eating. She'd given thought to his proposal all night and barely slept. She knew the answer to his question, but deep down, she was scared. What if it didn't work out for them? What if she ended with her heart broken all over again? She couldn't take it. But, at the same time, she wanted to try because she missed him. *Terribly*. So once again, her body reacted faster than she could register.

"Yes," she whispered, taking a sip of her coffee.

"Huh?" Devin asked, confused, looking up at her.

"Yes, we can *try* being friends again," she replied, emphasizing the try. He put his phone down and gave her his undivided attention, beaming. His smile was so big his dimples were showing, the same dimples she had missed.

"Are you serious? You're not joking with me? You really wanna try and be friends again?" he asked. She nodded. He stood up, reaching for her and kissed the top of her head.

"But no nicknames," she said. That was her one condition. She couldn't take it.

"But—"

"No. That is my one condition," she stated, shaking her head and looking up at him, his ocean-blue eyes looking at her. "No nicknames, Devin," she pleaded. "Just Devin and Catherine. If you can't accept my condition, then the deal is off."

He bent down and kissed her forehead softly. "No nicknames. Got it," he said and sat down again.

"No nicknames," she repeated.

And oh boy was this a mistake.

Chapter Twelve

Devin

"Stop stressing over the numbers," Devin argued, throwing a paper ball at her, landing beside her. She pursed her lips and returned to her work. She rubbed her hands together to warm them. The truth was, the office was cold, and the old heater wasn't the best. He walked to her side, shrugged off his suit jacket, and placed it around her arms, bending down to kiss the top of her head. She looked up at him and smiled softly.

It'd been a week since they made a deal to try and be friends again, and to be honest, it had been the best week he'd had in a while, nine years to be precise. He was getting his best friend, his everything, back. Little by little. Piece by piece. Even if it didn't work out in the end, at least he had her back for a short time. Who knows, maybe she would open up and talk about what happened. Or at least, he was hopeful she would. He was praying to all the mighty forces that she would so they could have closure and move on.

"Thanks," she whispered. He walked back to his chair across from her. "These numbers are awful. The logbooks are all over the place," she continued, massaging her forehead and taking off her glasses. Her phone buzzed on the desk, and she picked it up, stress and fury crossing her features. He wanted to ask what happened, but they weren't there yet. She threw her phone on the table, exhaling loudly. Putting her glasses back on, she returned to the logbooks, scratching and scribbling angrily with her pen. "We may have to hire a CPA to look at these."

He groaned. "Okay, enough numbers and enough logbooks. I want to go. It's past six on a Friday, Catherine." He stood up, walked to her side, and closed the logbooks along with her work computer. "Pack it up, and let's go" he ordered, looking down at her.

"But…" she protested, but he silenced her by putting a finger to her lips. His mind went back to that first day of freshman orientation when he met her, only this time, she didn't jerk his hand away.

"No buts. Pack it up, and let's go. And don't you dare take the logbooks with you. Leave them here, Catherine," he warned her. "I'll be waiting in the car." Taking his winter jacket from the back of his chair, he walked out. Helen was already gone. He walked to the car and unlocked it, putting his backpack on the backseat, undoing his tie, and unbuttoning the first button of his shirt.

"No, I don't understand, Kyle. This is the third time you have canceled on me," Catherine said as she walked to the car. She looked furious. She handed him his suit jacket, and he took it, his fingers brushing hers briefly. She looked up at him as if she too had felt the little electric shock. "Okay, well since you're so busy, I guess we'll talk later," she replied, hanging up. She inhaled a deep breath. It was night already, the half-moon shining down on the empty parking lot. She turned around and hopped in her seat, slamming the door. He got in and turned on the car.

"You wanna talk about it?" he asked as he put on his seatbelt. She shook her head. "Okay." He put the car in drive and left the parking lot.

"You know what is more infuriating?" she asked, sounding furious. He looked at her through his peripheral vision. She was gazing out the window, her arms crossed on her chest. "It's our fucking anniversary. *Tomorrow*. I don't even think he remembers. We were supposed to spend time together, after like two and a half months apart. Honestly, they should've shipped him to an international military base," she continued, uncrossing her arms and looking annoyed. He just nodded. She turned on her seat and gazed at him. He came to a stop at a red light and turned his head to look at her. "What's worse is this is the second time he's canceled on me. Third, if we count the time he asked me to cancel going to Nevada," she explained, exasperated, turning back to glance out the windshield. Her face illuminated green, and he turned his eyes back to the road. "Sometimes, I wonder if he really sees a future for us."

He counted to ten in his head. *Pissed*. He was pissed.

"Nevada?" he asked, confused.

"Yeah, he's in Area 51, working with the DOD, installing some equipment and shit. I don't know, Devin. He works in cybersecurity. I really have no clue what he does. Everything is so secret with him," she replied, sighing. He nodded, not wanting to press her further.

"How did you guys get together?" he asked after a few minutes of silence, in what he hoped was a nonchalant way, with his eyes on the road.

"He also went to Penn State," she replied, a dry laugh coming out of her throat. "He did one semester there, and we reconnected. Turns out we had one class together. We kept in contact after he went back to Stanford. He got a job in DC at the same time as me." She shrugged. "One thing led to another, and tomorrow is our fourth anniversary."

His hands on the steering wheel tightened, his knuckles white. "Oh," was all he could say, hoping it didn't give away his anger. The little motherfucker was playing her. After all Kyle did.

"Oh? What's that supposed to mean?" she questioned, turning to him. He looked at her briefly.

"Nothing. It's just an '*oh*' no hidden meaning behind it."

"No, that '*oh*' had a tone."

"What tone?" he asked, turning to her. They arrived at the B&B and got out of the car.

"I don't know. It had a tone," she said, exiting the car and walking to the front of it, waiting for him.

"Cat, I promise, it didn't have a tone. It was just an '*oh*'," he replied, walking with her to the B&B entrance.

"No, it definitely had…" she started to say but stopped mid-sentence, halting in the middle of the lobby, his front colliding with her back.

"Finally!" someone exclaimed from the lobby, jumping to her feet and walking to Catherine. He recognized her. Maggie, Catherine's boss's scheduler. Maggie hugged Catherine.

"Mags, what are you doing here?" Catherine asked, returning the hug. "Maverick?" Catherine looked at the young man standing behind Maggie.

"Hey, handsome," Maggie greeted, looking at him. "Remember me?"

"Hey, Maggie," he replied, giving her a lopsided smile.

"Oh, you remember my name," she exclaimed.

He chuckled. "Of course, I do. I have a great memory for names."

"What are you guys doing here?" Catherine asked them.

"Boss said you might need reinforcements. So, he sent the calvary," Maggie said, extending her arms and looking at Maverick. "Did you know Maverick grew up here? In this very town?" Maggie asked, placing a hand on his shoulder and smiling. Maverick's face reddened.

"Yes, I did know that," Catherine said.

"Oh, and guess what?" Maggie asked, excited, jumping on the balls of her feet.

"What?" Catherine questioned.

"The owner of the B&B is his aunt," Maggie whispered conspiratorially, excitement oozing out of her.

"She is? Gloria is your aunt?" Catherine asked, looking at him. "I didn't know that."

"Yes," Maggie replied. "Small world, huh?" she continued. "Oh, hello…" Maggie said, glancing at the door. There stood a tall man in a plaid shirt, with big arms and a full beard.

"Well, the rumors are true. The prodigal son returns," the man exclaimed.

"Hey, Luke," Maverick greeted shyly. "Everyone, this is my big brother, Luke. He's the town's carpenter. Luke, this is one of my bosses Catherine, this is Maggie, and this is Devin," Maverick introduced. Maggie gave Luke a toothy smile and a wave of her fingers. Luke looked around smiling, his eyes landing on Catherine.

"Luke. Nice to meet you," he greeted, extending his hand to Catherine. "Catherine was it?" Catherine smiled and took his hand. Instead of shaking it, he brought it to his lips and kissed her knuckles. She smiled, a hint of blush tinting her cheeks. Devin's blood boiled. He saw Maverick roll his eyes, and Maggie's smile dropped.

"Dude, back off. She has a boyfriend. And she's my boss," Maverick reprimanded, stepping in front of him and snatching Catherine's hand from his. Luke smiled. "I am so sorry about his behavior. His social skills are a bit rough. His only friends are an axe and wood logs."

Devin tried really hard to hide the smirk forming on his lips.

"Is Maggie short for Margarette?" Luke asked, turning around to Maggie, who now was uninterested, inspecting her nails. He extended his hand, and Maggie gazed at it, then at his face, giving him a once over. Rolling her eyes, she turned around and went up the stairs. "Oh, I like that one," Luke exclaimed, following Maggie. Maverick rolled his eyes, pinching the bridge of his nose.

"He is such an embarrassment," Maverick muttered. Devin laughed. "Anyway, I'm going to my room."

"It had a tone," Catherine said, turning to him and picking up the argument they were having five minutes ago. He sighed, glancing up at the ceiling.

"For the last time, it did not have a tone," he replied.

"It did."

"No, it didn't."

"What's going on here?" Gloria asked, appearing out of thin air. Catherine jumped and landed against his chest. He wrapped a protective arm around her shoulders, steadying her, her warmth searing through his clothes.

"My goodness, Gloria, you almost gave me a heart attack," Catherine exclaimed, stepping out of his arms, a coldness settling over him.

"I'm sorry," Gloria apologized. "Any plans for tonight?"

"Not really. I am kinda tired tonight," Catherine replied.

"Well, if you guys need anything, let me know," Gloria said and left.

"I'm going to go change and grab something to eat. You wanna come?" he asked her as he walked to the stairs.

"Come on, man. Mom was waiting for you to have dinner," Luke said as he came down the stairs with Maverick in tow. He looked at Catherine and smiled. "Miss Catherine." He saluted as he walked past. They both left, leaving him and Catherine standing at the foot of the stairs, looking at each other.

"So, do you want to join me for dinner or not?"

"Yes, I'm starving," she answered, walking to the stairs.

Twenty minutes later, they were driving around town, trying to find somewhere to eat. They found a bar and went inside. It wasn't packed, but it wasn't empty either, just your typical small-town bar full of locals. They sat in one of the booths in the far back. A waitress came by, placing menus on the table.

"What can I get you two lovebirds started with?" she asked.

"Oh. No, we are not..." Catherine started to say, but he interrupted her.

"We'll have two of your greasiest burgers, add bacon if you have it, and fries," he ordered, sliding the menus back to her. "And I'll take a large lager, and she'll take a Chardonnay," he finished, knowing her order by heart.

"Coming right up," she said, smiling, and disappeared to place their order. He looked around the bar, which was full of middle-aged people drinking, smoking, and playing pool.

"Why didn't you correct her?" Catherine questioned. He turned his gaze back to her and shrugged.

"They won't remember us in a month, Catherine. There's no need to do so." He shrugged. "Just loosen up a little," he added, winking at her. She scoffed, rolling her eyes. He used to love it whenever he riled her up and she would roll her eyes at him in annoyance.

"We need to start interviewing candidates for the board positions," she commented after a few minutes of comfortable silence. He groaned.

"Catherine, for fucks sake, it's Friday, and it's currently almost 9 pm. No work talk," he chastised, looking at her. "Do you even remember how to have fun? When was the last time you went out after work and had fun?" he asked rhetorically. "And no, I'm not talking about networking receptions or work-related activities after work. I'm talking about actual fun stuff. You know what? That changes tonight." He stood up, extending his hand. "Come on. Don't fight me on this. I will throw you over my shoulder and carry you to the pool tables. You know I will." She rolled her eyes and took his hand because she knew he would do just that. And he knew the last thing she wanted was a scene.

His fingers wrapped around hers, still as soft as he remembered them. He dragged her to one of the empty pool tables, setting their stuff on a high table near it. "Take a billiard cue," he instructed her, taking one himself. "You do remember how to play pool, right?" he teased, smirking. She gave him the middle finger, and he laughed. He remembered the first time he took her to the college bar he used to go to and taught her how to play.

"Of course, I do. I had an incredible instructor," she reminisced, smiling at the floor. He smiled.

"Here are your drinks. Your food should be out soon. Do you guys wanna eat here?" the waitress asked, placing their drinks on the table. Devin nodded. He slid Catherine her wine. She took a sip from it and made a face, making him laugh.

"This is awful," she uttered, placing her wine glass down.

He offered her his beer, and she took it. She took a sip from it and hummed. "Much better. I'll get one of these," she said, handing him the glass.

He shook his head and slid it back to her. "Keep it. I'll get another one," he mumbled, kissing her temple and going to the bar. He ordered his beer and waited, leaning one arm on the bar and looking at Catherine, who was dusting the end of her cue with chalk, the low lights hanging above her creating a halo on her head.

"Here you go sir," the bartender said, handing him a glass full of beer.

"Thanks." He walked back to Catherine. She had arranged the triangle and the balls in the middle of the pool table. "Ready?" he asked her, dusting his cue.

"Ready when you are Mack," she smirked, calling him by his last name. That only meant one thing.

This just turned into a competition.

Chapter Thirteen

Catherine

"You either lost your touch, or you really suck." She laughed at him, walking back to the table and sitting down on her stool. They had just finished their second game in which she had won again. She had a feeling he was letting her win. Devin had his back to her, rearranging the balls for a third game. "Two to zero," she smirked, taking a bite of her burger. He turned around and walked to her, his eyes never leaving hers. He came to stop in front of her, his hand reaching up to her face, his thumb brushing the corner of her mouth. She held her breath, looking into his eyes. He cleaned a blob of ketchup from her mouth, his thumb going to his mouth, cleaning his finger, giving her a mischievous smirk. A million butterflies erupted in her stomach at that smile that meant trouble. He walked back to the pool table, busying himself with chalking up his cue. She felt a blush creep up her face to her cheeks, warming her skin. She released a breath she'd been holding, returning to her food, picking a French fry, and dipping it in ketchup.

"I haven't lost my touch, and I do *not* suck, Babbitt," he said, turning to her.

"Oh, but you do," she replied in a shaky voice, taking a gulp of her beer, washing down the knot in her throat and the emotions she was feeling, drowning the butterflies in her stomach.

"I have not. And I will prove it to you," he protested, pointing at her. "Come on, Babbitt. Afraid of a little competition? That was just a warm-up for me." She finished the rest of her beer and walked to the pool table.

They lost track of how long they played, down to their fourth and fifth beers.

"Five to three. In my favor. Who sucks now?" Devin asked in a competitive tone.

She discreetly gave him the middle finger. He laughed, and she smiled down at the floor. She sat down on the stool and looked at him, rearranging the billiard balls on the triangle. She observed the way his muscles contracted with his movements under his shirt. After all these years, even with the angry feelings and hurt she held in her heart, even after all that happened, he still affected her. He still affected her body. A warmth spread through her as she fixated on his hands, the veins protruding from them. She gulped, a blush going up her neck and into her cheeks. She needed to get laid. The fight with Kyle earlier had left her all riled up. He hadn't even called back or texted her. Maybe this time apart would serve to set priorities and see where their relationship stood. They haven't been the same for quite some time. She turned to grab her beer glass to drown her feelings, good ones and bad ones, but it was empty.

"You want another?" Devin asked, coming to stand beside her. She looked up at him, and his ocean-blue eyes were already staring back at her. She gulped and nodded. He smiled, ruffling her hair on his way to the bar. He came back a couple of minutes later with two new glasses filled to the brim. "Here you go," he said, placing the glass in front of her and taking a sip from his beer.

"Thank you," she muttered, taking a big gulp from it, downing half of it, praying the alcohol would numb her feelings. "Another round?" she asked, pointing at the table.

"Would you do the honors?" he asked, bowing at the waist.

"My pleasure," she replied, walking to the table. Her mind felt fuzzy, her body tingly. She positioned herself to hit the white ball to break up the triangle, swaying on her feet.

"Wrong," he said, coming to stand behind her. Her mind went back to the first time he taught her how to play pool and how it made her feel all tingly and giddy inside. She took a sharp breath, her heart beating out of her chest. The butterflies resurfaced at the memory. His hands came to rest on top of hers, correctly positioning them. "You have to hold them like this," he said in her ear. Her whole body felt warm, his breath caressed her cheek. She aimed and hit the white ball. "Good girl," he whispered in her ear, kissing her temple. She felt the heat rush to her cheeks. A shudder went down her spine. Heat traveled all over her body. His words and lips made her feel things all over her skin, a tight pressure coiling in her middle. Something she hadn't felt in a while.

It has to be the alcohol, she told herself.

They played a few more rounds, and she won once, but he won the rest. She walked back to the table and downed the rest of her beer. She lost count of how many beers she had had after the sixth one. She turned around to rearrange the balls but swayed, stumbling over her feet. She grabbed onto the table and resumed walking.

"And now you are tipsy," Devin announced, noticing how she struggled to walk. He grabbed her arm and dragged her back to the table. "Enough beer for you," he added, steadying her, taking the empty beer glass from her hand that she didn't notice she was holding, and placing it on the table. He turned to her, placing his hands on her hips.

"Devin, this is not very '*just friends*' of you," she slurred, looking up into his eyes.

"Would you prefer if I let you fall on the germ-ridden floor?" he asked, his breath caressing her temple. She dropped her forehead to his chest, taking a deep breath. He still smelled like citrus and cedar, with a touch of vanilla. The way he used to smell. The smell that used to bring her comfort.

"You still use the same cologne," she murmured against his chest.

"What?"

"Your cologne, it's still the same," she repeated. He chuckled.

"Are you smelling me?" he asked with a hint of humor in his tone.

"Can I not smell my best friend?" she questioned, the phrase 'best friend' sliding off her tongue with no trouble. She gasped, closing her eyes and chastising herself for the slip-up. He dropped his chin on top of her head, his arms wrapping around her, bringing her closer to his chest. "I missed you," she whispered after a few minutes of silence, a few minutes of him just holding her like old times. "But you broke my heart, Devin." He held her tighter. "I really miss my best friend." She felt him kiss the top of her head, his lips lingering there, taking a deep breath.

"What did I do Cat?" he asked in a whisper. "Please, tell me so I can make it better. I hate that I hurt you," he pleaded. She shook her head, his arms crushing her to him, his fingers digging into her arms.

"You promised you wouldn't ask. It's in the past, but I'm

not ready to talk about it." She broke away from his embrace, grabbing her coat from the back of the chair and putting it on as she walked outside. The cold northern October air hit her face.

"Stop," he said, grabbing her elbow and steadying her. She shook off his hand.

"I can walk on my own," she argued, stumbling, almost tripping and kissing the pavement in the parking lot. Devin wrapped an arm around her waist, steadying her again.

"No, you can't," he said as he slid an arm under her knees and the other around her waist, carrying her. Her arms automatically went around his shoulders to hold herself upright.

"Devin put me down," she yelled, struggling to get out of his arms. He shifted her and threw her over his shoulder. "For fuck's sake, Devin," she argued, sobering up. "I'm sober. I can walk on my own." He didn't listen. "Put me down," she demanded. The grip of his hand on her upper thighs tightened. "Devin Mack, put me down this very instant," she yelled. He did, opening the car door for her. "You had no right," she seethed. He thrusted her purse in her arms.

"Next time, I'll let you kiss the pavement then," he said, walking to his side. He was seated inside, car on, when he spoke again. "Are you going to get in or not?"

She woke up the next day with a killer hangover. The brightness leaking through the curtains aggravated her pain. She got out of bed and showered quickly, going down to grab her coffee and two aspirins. When she entered the dining room, Devin was already there, scrolling through his phone, two plates and two steaming cups of coffee on the table, just like the past week. The domesticity of it all made her insides curdle. It was starting to feel an awful lot like old times. Flashbacks of last night played in the front of her mind like a movie. Devin looked up and smiled as his eyes landed on her, dropping his phone on the table. He moved the chair out for her. She walked over and sat down.

"Good morning," he said, his voice too loud.

"Shhh," she said, massaging her temples. A glass of water and two aspirins were waiting for her as well, making the sinking feeling in her chest deepen. She'd worry about that later. She took the aspirin as she drank a sip of her coffee and closed her eyes.

"Feeling better?" he asked, his voice softer. She shook her head.

"I will be once this coffee hits my bloodstream," she answered, taking another sip.

"It's Saturday, so you can go back to bed. If you want, of course. Sleep off the hangover," he said, looking at his phone again.

"I can't, I need to look over the logs," she replied, taking another sip from her coffee. He dropped his phone on the table with a thud, and she flinched, the noise making her head hurt. He turned to her, his face serious.

"You are going to do what?" he asked, furious, pinching the bridge of his nose and closing his eyes.

"We only have two weeks left, Devin. I want to audit as much as possible before we hand it over to the new board. I want to prevent this situation from happening again in the future. It's not fair to the people that live here. It's not fair that they have to suffer the consequences of something they are not at fault for. I know this is the dark side of politics I have to deal with, but I refuse to leave without properly handling this situation. I need to do a roundtable with community leaders to find ways to prevent this from happening again. See if we can help back in DC to make this a national issue, not just for Stella, but for every small town in the country, that way they don't go through the same situation that is happening right now in this town," she refuted, looking at him. "I'm also going to write a report for your boss and mine, detailing what has happened recently," she continued, placing her coffee down and grabbing the fork. She spooned eggs onto it and took a bite.

"Not today, you won't."

"Why not?" she asked, her fork clattering on her plate. She leaned back on her chair and crossed her arms.

"We're taking a little road trip."

"A road trip to the office, of course. I'll work better there. Zero distractions," she replied, taking a bite of her bacon.

"No. There's a little park near where I wanna hike. And you're coming with me," he continued. "Sweating the hangover off will help you," he pointed out, taking a sip from his coffee.

"You still hike?" she asked, remembering how that used to be his favorite pastime during their time in college. He had always tried for her to share that hobby with him, but she preferred staying inside, away from bugs. She shuddered at the thought of spiders and snakes while hiking. He nodded, taking a bite of his toast. "I'm not hiking, Devin."

"And you are also not going to work. It's Saturday, Catherine, for fuck's sake. I meant it last night. You are young, and you need to have more fun. I'm talking about actual fun stuff. Something you have to start doing, like getting a hobby and such. I know your boyfriend is boring, but that doesn't mean you should be too."

"Kyle is not boring," she protested, frowning.

"Oh really? When was the last time he took you out to do something fun? When was the last time he took you out on a date?" he asked, lifting a brow. "And I mean take you out on a date, the kind where you get dressed up."

She stayed quiet. She didn't argue because he was right. She had been feeling it for a while. Her and Kyle's relationship wasn't the same in the last months. The last six months, to be precise, and she could go as far back as the last year of their relationship. She looked down at her hands, the sinking feeling in her chest widening. It was astounding how well he still knew her, even after nine years apart. It was like his mind and soul never forgot her.

"That's what I thought. You keep forgetting I lived with Kyle and was his roommate for four years, Catherine. I know him. Just like I know you. Nine years apart have not dimmed that I know everything about you," he said, voicing her thoughts as if he read her mind. He took another bite of his toast. "So, you are not going to be working today. You and I are doing something fun. You are young, and you deserve it. You work extra hard, harder than anyone I know. We are going on a hike, a picnic, or whatever you want, but we are doing something fun. Not everything involving your life has to be *political affairs*," he added. "Since he isn't here to celebrate *your* anniversary, you might as well have some fun, even if it's without him since he didn't deem your anniversary important enough to come and celebrate with you," he spat, rage lacing his tone.

"Whatever Kyle and I have is none of your business, Devin." She glowered at him. He scoffed.

"I'll be in the car in an hour. Feel free to join if you want," he said, picking up his plate and standing up, leaving her to overturn his last words in her head like a loop. She looked at his receding back until he disappeared up the stairs. She felt suddenly weak and vulnerable in the face of his anger.

"Since he didn't deem your anniversary important enough to come and celebrate with you."

That is exactly what Kyle had done. She hated admitting that he was right, but Kyle not acknowledging their anniversary cemented the fact that something had changed between them.

"He's right, you know?" the voice of Maggie brought her back. She had sat down in the chair Devin just occupied. "You are young, and you deserve to have some fun. Your life shouldn't revolve around work only. Where is your idiot of a boyfriend? Still chasing aliens? Did he cancel on you again? On your anniversary? Shameless. Why are you still with this idiot? You deserve so much better, Cathy," Maggie said, reaching for her hands. Catherine looked down at her lap, Maggie's hand squeezing hers, a warm pressure forming at the back of her eyes. Maggie exhaled, letting her hand go. "Devin clearly has a thing for you, Cat. Your asshole of a boyfriend is not it. Devin cares, and from what I've seen, he *really* does care," she pointed out, emphasizing the '*really*'. She decided to ignore her last statement.

"You know, I've known Devin for longer than you probably think," Catherine started, feeling the need to confess. "We went to college together," she continued, playing with a loose thread on the tablecloth. "We were best friends in college. For four years," she added softly.

"What happened?" Maggie asked. Catherine shrugged.

"I left for Penn State, and he stayed at Harvard," she replied, not ready to talk about it.

"Yeah. Try telling that lie to someone else, not me, Catherine. That can't be it. There has to be another reason why both of you fell apart," Maggie stated. Catherine shrugged again. She lifted her gaze to Maggie, and Maggie's face softened, reading her and understanding what she was unable to convey with words. "Catherine…" Maggie started, her voice soft. Catherine shook her head.

"Anyways, reuniting after nine years has been a blessing and a curse, but I can assure you, Devin doesn't care. Not in the way you're thinking," Catherine expressed, drinking from her coffee. "He cares for me as a friend, like a little sister. You're young. You'll understand someday." She shrugged, placing her finished cup of coffee down and sliding her plate away, her appetite gone.

"Right, because I keep forgetting you are as old as the wind. Oh, wise old gentlewoman," Maggie teased. Catherine laughed a little. "Whatever happened, you will need to sit down and address it someday, Catherine."

"I hope that day never comes," Catherine replied, standing up.

"Catherine…" Maggie added, but Catherine walked out of the dining room. She went up the stairs and stared at his door for a moment longer than she should.

A sense of longing burned in her chest, making her eyes tear up, her vision getting hazy. She hated how vulnerable he made her feel. Hated how, no matter what, she still loved him, deeply. As much as she wanted to deny it, as much as she wanted it to not be true, she loved him. The wound was still there, fresh. Seeing him was like pouring salt on that wound. Most importantly, she missed him. She missed her best friend, missed the person who knew her and understood her the most. Missed the person who loved her unconditionally. She also missed the person she used to be when she was around him. A single tear slid down her face, and she didn't bother to clean it up.

The handle of his door rattled, and it opened suddenly. His ocean-blue eyes stared back at her emerald ones. They both stood there, looking at each other. He was dressed in hiking attire. He looked at her, his eyes longing, sad even. A little red, like he was holding back tears.

He took a tentative step towards her, unsure. Her feet felt like cement, unable to move, rooting her to the spot, her hand on her doorknob. He took another cautious step towards her, just two feet separating them.

He reached for her face, wiping the tear stain from her cheek. She leaned into his touch, closing her eyes. His thumb caressed her face. He walked the remaining distance, placing his other hand on her other side, and cupping her face. He leaned down and kissed her forehead softly. His lips lingered there.

"Catherine..." he whispered against her forehead, his arms engulfing her to his chest, a feeling of safety enveloping her.

"Please, don't ask again," she choked out. "I'm not ready to talk about it yet," she whispered. The realization that she misconstrued his feelings for her, when he was clearly in love with her former best friend, filled her with shame. His hands reached for her face again. He dropped his forehead on top of her head, his thumbs tracing small circles on her cheeks, wiping away the tears as they fell.

She was suddenly reminded of a very important detail. He was engaged, and the way he was treating her felt nothing like friends. The way she was starting to feel felt nothing like just friends. The way *he* made her feel with his actions was nothing like just friends. Confusing her to levels she couldn't understand. Confusing her because she remembered another important detail, *Kyle*. She had been so caught up in how Devin was making her feel that she'd completely forgotten about Kyle.

At that moment, she made a painful decision. One that she knew was the right choice, even if it hurt like hell. Even if it made her feel like the last piece of her heart and soul were being ripped apart.

"I don't think I can try Devin," she whispered. He exhaled a shaky breath. "I don't think we should. We should stick to just being coworkers. Nothing else. The deal is off. I'm sorry," she said, leaving his embrace and going into her room, closing the door behind her. She leaned her forehead on the door, softly sobbing. The same scene that happened nine years ago, all over again. After all, it's true what they say. History repeats itself.

Once again, she felt like her heart had been ripped out of her chest, leaving a gaping wound. Just like she did that night nine years ago.

Chapter Fourteen

Devin

"*I don't think I can try Devin. I don't think we should. We should stick to just being coworkers. Nothing else. The deal is off. I'm sorry.*"

That was all she said. That simple statement. Those simple words had been looping around his head since Saturday and had widened the gap in his chest. He tried. He tried not to think about them, but it had been the only thing circling his mind. He didn't see her today. She had some official business and meetings to attend in the district office, so today he took a day off and went fishing with Charlie, Gloria's husband, enjoying the peace and quiet of the lake.

"I don't think I'm strong enough," he groaned on Monday evening while video chatting with Corbin. He was lying in bed, his laptop propped on the nightstand, while Corbin was in the kitchen, bouncing Aiyden on his knee. Brianna was putting Deion to bed. Emily was running late, as usual.

"You were the one who suggested to make a deal and try to be friends again, and you knew where it would lead. This one is on you," Corbin said with a frown on his face.

"I know Corbin, it's just—" Devin started to say but

stopped. "I missed her, and I thought there would be a possibility of being normal again."

"Nothing was ever normal with the both of you, Devin. Never. Nothing will ever be normal until both of you talk about what happened. Until *she* explains what happened," he said, switching Aiyden to his other knee. "The two of you were always... Something out of the ordinary. You treated her like your girlfriend, but you were always too chicken to confess your feelings for her. And I think that is the root of the problem. That you waited too long to confess, and when you decided it was time, it all went down the drain. And that, my friend and godfather to my children, is on you. Right, Aiyden? Tell Uncle Dev how this is his fault," Corbin said in a baby voice, looking at Aiyden.

He sighed because Corbin was right. This was all his fault. If he had gotten the guts to be upfront the minute he knew he had feelings for her, maybe the story would have been different. Maybe they would've been married now. He sat against the headboard and placed the laptop on his lap.

"I bet you started treating her like you did back in college, didn't you? Kissing her forehead, bringing her coffee? You did, didn't you?" Corbin asked. Devin rolled his eyes, crossing his arms on his chest. "Admit it, you still love her, Devin. There's nothing wrong with that," Corbin added softly. "The question is, what are you going to do now?" He hated how Corbin was right. He still loved her. A girl like her was unforgettable, and he knew that. Nine years apart, and his feelings were still the same. It was like they went into a deep sleep, and once she showed up again, they awoke and crashed into him like a tidal wave. He exhaled, running a hand through his hair.

"I don't know, man. It's not like I can barge into her life

like that. I can't. There's also Emily and their history, and Catherine is dating Kyle and—"

"Whoa, whoa, back it up, buddy. What do you mean Catherine is dating Kyle? Kyle, as in the same Kyle we both know? Kyle, as in your old roommate Kyle? Kyle, as in asshole Kyle?" Corbin asked, scoffing, disgust coating his voice whenever he said his name.

"Catherine is dating Kyle. *The* Kyle you are thinking of. That's exactly what I mean. She's been dating him for four years now," Devin explained. "I thought I told you."

"No, you did not. How the fuck—"

"Corbin, language," Brianna reprimanded in the background.

"Sorry," he apologized, ashamed. He covered Aiyden's ears. "How the fuck did those two get together?" he asked in a whisper, letting Aiyden's ears go.

"From what she told me, in the week that we tried to mend our *friendship*, he did a semester at Penn State and reconnected with her. When he got a job in DC at the same time as her, it just happened."

"That little piece of…" Corbin started to say but stopped, looking to his side. "That little piece of useless human garbage," Corbin said, turning to look back at the camera.

"I can't believe he would do something like that. After what he did. He has guts. I bet he hasn't even told her. That little coward," Brianna muttered, popping her head on the screen. "How is she?" Brianna asked. She was dressed in her scrubs. Probably coming back from a long shift at the hospital. It's a miracle she made the call. Her cardiothoracic career as a surgeon kept her busy.

"She's great. She's still that little firecracker we knew in college," he replied, nodding and giving her a sad smile.

"Oh, he still loves her, like *loves her*, loves her. He's so gone," Corbin teased. "You are so screwed, bro."

"I know," Devin admitted, looking down.

"So, she's dating the little piece of human garbage. So what? Once she learns what he did, she's going to hate him. It's just a shocker we didn't find out about what he did sooner," Corbin added. "I'm sure you wouldn't have wasted three years living under the same roof as him." Brianna squeezed his neck.

"There's nothing I can do now," Devin mumbled.

"You could tell her," Corbin retorted. Devin snorted.

"Yeah, right. No. That's not for me to tell," he spat, anger filling him up as he thought about what Kyle did. Another person entered the chat. He let Emily into the call. She was seated on her kitchen island. Her hair and clothes were a mess.

"So sorry about my lateness. I was finishing some final touches on the design of the menus and name cards for the wedding. And then I went to get dinner with Nathalie, and we just lost track of time," she explained, adjusting her shirt, buttoning the last of the buttons, and fixing her hair.

"Dinner, of course. More like dessert," Corbin retorted. Devin chuckled.

"Hi, Brianna. How's my precious nephew Deion?" Emily said in a baby voice, ignoring Corbin.

"That's Aiyden," Devin corrected, laughing.

"They are almost two Em. You should be able to tell them apart. They're identical twins but not that identical," Corbin scoffed.

"How's my precious nephew Aiyden?" Emily spoke again in a baby voice, ignoring Corbin again. "What are we talking about?" she asked, going straight to business.

"About how Devin is still very much in love with

Catherine and how Devin should tell Catherine about Kyle and what he did," Corbin listed, handing a very restless Aiyden to Brianna.

"I agree with both statements," Emily concurred. "She deserves to know. As angry as I am at her, she can do better. He doesn't deserve her."

"Wait, you knew?" Corbin asked, shocked.

"Of course, I knew. Devin didn't tell you?"

"No, he didn't."

"I'm with Em on this," Brianna added, going back to the problem.

"I'm not telling her. It's not my job to tell her," Devin muttered.

"You have to Devin. She deserves to know," Emily said.

"No," Devin stated, his tone final.

"So, let me guess, the deal is off? She called it off?" Emily asked.

"She did," Corbin replied.

"Devin…" Emily mumbled in a soft tone, her gaze filled with pity. He groaned.

"I don't need nor want any of your pity. It's not a big deal," Devin replied. "She called it off. That's it. End of story. So, wedding? Anything new?" he asked Emily, changing the subject.

"Stop deflecting," Emily admonished.

"I'm not."

"You are," Corbin, Brianna, Emily, and the fourth voice on Emily's side, Nathalie, said in unison. He rolled his eyes.

"Am not."

"Listen, and I think I speak for all of us now. You need to stop being a bitch about this," Brianna said. They all looked at her. Brianna rarely cursed. For her to be dropping curse words was a shock no one was expecting. Corbin's hands went to Aiyden's ears.

"Honey, language," he reprimanded, but a glint of pride covered his face.

"I'm with her," Emily concluded.

"Me too," the distinct voice of Nathalie said from Emily's kitchen.

"You clearly miss her. Like, *really* miss her, Devin. You haven't been the same since she left," Brianna continued. "I know. I'm going to sound like a broken record, but you miss her. And you still love her, Devin. And that's okay. She was pretty special to you. But are you seriously going to let her go again? Let her walk away from your life just like that?" Brianna asked. "I don't think it's a coincidence that you reunited after so long. I don't think it is a coincidence the *way* you were reunited. This is your second chance, Devin. You need to take it."

"She doesn't want me anymore. She moved on. And I think it is time I do too," Devin replied, a sadness overcoming him. "She doesn't want anything to do with me. I will respect her wishes and just keep it professional between us for the rest of the time we have left. Do I miss her? Absolutely. Like crazy. But I am not going to force myself back into her life. I can't do that. I won't do that," he continued, shrugging. "Maybe it's time I finally pick me."

"I wish I could slap some sense into her right now," Emily exclaimed, defeated.

"I wish we knew what happened," Corbin added.

"Emily, violence is not always the answer," Brianna muttered. "Why are you so violent?"

"I'm an Aries. You do the math," Emily retorted.

"I think it's clear Devin has made his feelings about the situation final. He won't be telling her anything," Corbin interrupted. "Just being the same chicken he was back in college."

"Well, Devin is usually an idiot," Emily replied. Brianna snorted. He rolled his eyes.

"That's beside the point," Corbin said as he sighed, scratching his jaw. "Look man, we won't force you to do something you don't feel like doing, but just know this might be your last chance of keeping her in your life. *Forever*."

"And why do you think you are the most qualified person for the job, Mr. Adkins?" Catherine asked the male they were interviewing for the CEO position.

It was Friday, and they were in a time crunch now, with only one week left before they had to go back to DC. Most of the board positions were filled, with just a couple more left open and the CEO spot. They were going to have another meeting with USACE later that afternoon, in which they were going to discuss how to proceed. Catherine pored herself, along with a CPA, into the logs and audits all week, leaving Devin and Maverick, along with a few community leaders, to interview people for the board of directors. They had a couple of official meetings in between with townsfolk and other people in their respective offices. The last meeting was a joint meeting between the townsfolk and USACE, along with their bosses.

"As you can see on my resume, I have extensive experience managing and administering a company. Maybe not this type of company, but experience nonetheless," Adkins replied. "I also grew up in this very small town, so I experienced the struggle firsthand. I'm also very outspoken about the government not caring for small towns as they do with big towns or the metro area of the state," he added, passionate when saying that last statement. Catherine nodded, writing something down in her notebook. After a couple more questions, Catherine informed him they would be reaching a decision next week and would let him know. Maverick escorted Mr. Adkins out, leaving Devin and Catherine alone. Catherine took off her glasses, pinching the bridge of her nose and exhaling. She massaged her temples. She reached for her coffee and took a sip from it.

"Boss, the USACE people are here," Maggie announced, popping her head into the office. Catherine nodded, putting her coffee down and putting her glasses back on.

"Send them in," Catherine ordered, gathering the papers around her.

"Don't you wanna take a break?" he asked her once Maggie left.

"No, I'm fine," she stated, not looking at him. He clenched his jaw so hard it hurt.

"Catherine, you skipped lunch already. Coffee is not food," he said through gritted teeth.

"Devin, I said I'm fine. I don't need a babysitter. I'm a grown adult," she spat, looking up at him, her eyes furious. "I would appreciate it if you kept your opinions to yourself."

"Catherine, I get that you are a perfectionist and a workaholic, but—" he started to argue, but she interrupted him.

"But nothing. I didn't ask for your opinion or your advice on how to run my life. You're not my nutritionist or doctor, so like I said, you can keep your opinions to yourself because I don't remember asking for them. You are my coworker. That's it," she responded, standing up and leaving the office. He exhaled a long breath, closing his eyes. His phone buzzed in his pocket, and he got it out. It was a text from Maggie.

> Be patient with her. She is not having a good day.

> What happened?

> She will kill me if she finds out I told you. But she and Kyle had a fight. A big one. Last night. He canceled on her again.

> But you didn't hear it from me. She told me you guys used to be best friends in college. So, you should know better than me, to not press her when she is overwhelmed. So, go easy on her. I got her a sandwich when I went back to the B&B. She's currently eating it. Just be patient.

> Okay. Thank you.

He sighed, locking his phone, and placing it in his pocket again. Catherine walked in, sitting on the other side of the table, breadcrumbs on the corner of her lips, her lipstick smeared. He got his handkerchief out of his suit jacket pocket and walked to where she sat down, placing the handkerchief softly in front of her.

"You have crumbs in the corner, and your lipstick is a bit smeared," he murmured and turned around. He heard her gasp. "I'll stall them," he commented and left the office.

The meeting started well. Then the engineers came up with solutions. Solutions that were utterly out of reach. Solutions that would take years before the town saw a change. Solutions that were just not the ones they needed right now.

"The decay and lack of repair affected the whole

infrastructure system, down to the foundation. The whole thing needs to be rebuilt from the foundation up. That will take years. With the lack of budget, it's likely not going to happen anytime soon," the head engineer explained. "I wish I could tell you better news, but the truth is the treatment plant cannot be repaired."

Devin paced around the room. He had taken off his suit jacket and rolled up the sleeves of his button-down shirt, loosening the tie and undoing the top button. "Do we have any other solutions? Any other contingency plans?" he asked, placing his hands on the back of his chair.

"We have been providing water with our pumps and equipment directly from the river. But we cannot keep that there forever," the head engineer said shamefully, regret filling his eyes. "I hate to be the bearer of bad news, but USACE will need to remove their equipment by the end of November."

Devin heaved an exasperated sigh, hanging his head between his shoulders.

"So, there is absolutely nothing to be done about it?" Catherine asked. Devin lifted his head and looked at her. She was rubbing her forehead anxiously.

"Well…" the head engineer said. They both turned to look at him.

"Well, what?" Devin questioned.

"While we were there setting up, we found some old well equipment in semi-good condition. It looks like the town used to get clean water directly from the river through that old equipment. It has a built-in pump and filter. It's an old infrastructure. We did an assessment and found it's still usable."

"Okay, how can we fix it and make use of it again? I can't

go back to DC and leave these people fending for themselves without clean water," Catherine stated.

"We need to learn the history of it. The reason they stopped using it," he said.

"We'll call a town hall meeting," Devin replied, leaving the room. "Maggie, call Gloria and tell her to spread the word around. There's going to be an emergency town hall meeting tonight at 7 pm and call the town hall. Ask them to reserve the space for us," Devin ordered.

"On it, boss," Maggie said, taking out her phone. "I'll call Gloria so she can activate the spider web."

"The what?" Devin asked. Maggie ignored him.

"The spider web. It's the town's communication network," Maverick explained nonchalantly while taking a sip from his coffee. "I'll call my mom. She's the head of the spider web this season."

"This season? The spider web?" Devin asked, confused. "Just... just get the town in the know that there's going to be a meeting tonight," he commanded and walked back to the office. "So, it's arranged. Tonight, the town hall meeting is at 7 pm. The town's being informed as we speak," Devin mentioned, sitting down on his chair.

"That was fast," the head engineer said.

"Yeah, the spider web..." Devin stopped mid-sentence, realizing how crazy it sounded. "Never mind. I guess we'll see you at 7 pm," Devin proposed. The head engineer nodded and left.

"The spider web?" Catherine asked incredulously. "What the fuck is the spider web?"

"It's the town's communication network," Devin explained, standing up and putting his winter jacket on. "I need to run an errand. Can you hitch a ride with Maggie and

Maverick? If not, I can come pick you up after," he said, flinging his backpack on his shoulder. Catherine waved a dismissive hand in the air, looking at her computer. He gave her a silent nod and left. He drove to a gas station to fill up the tank. He went inside to get a snack. As he was paying, he glanced behind the cashier, looking at the packs of cigarettes. "Give me one box of the red ones," he said, exhaling, knowing full well he was about to break the promise he made her. But he really needed to smoke right now. He paid and left.

He drove to the town hall and got out of his car. He walked to the bench under the tree and got one of the cigarettes out. Thankfully, his lighter was still in the car. He took one long drag of the cigarette, keeping the smoke inside for a couple of seconds and releasing it, the white smoke swirling in the air. He finished the cigarette and went to the car, hiding them in the driver's door. He popped a mint into his mouth just as Maverick's car pulled up in the spot next to him with Maggie and Catherine inside. Maggie and Maverick got out of the car and walked inside the venue. He closed his door and went to retrieve his backpack from the backseat. Catherine got out of the car and looked at him. Her face dropped.

"You smoked." He shrugged because if there was one thing he wasn't going to do it was lie to her. "You promised you were going to quit," she whispered, almost inaudible.

"Yeah, well, we can't always get what we want, right? And it's like you said, you're not my doctor." He shrugged the backpack on his shoulders. "And just like you didn't ask, I didn't ask for your opinion nor your advice on how to run my life. We are just coworkers. That's it. We are not friends, and you said it loud and clear where we stand," he spat, slamming the door closed. "Isn't that what you said earlier today? So, what do you care if I smoke or not?" he asked rhetorically, walking away. The minute his back turned to her, his heart broke at the words he uttered. He regretted them. He stopped walking, turning around. She stood there, stiff, momentarily abashed. "Cat…" She brushed past him, bumping his shoulder with hers. He closed his eyes and cursed himself.

This meeting was going to be a long, agonizing one.

Chapter Fifteen

Catherine

"*We are just coworkers. That's it. We are not friends, and you said it loud and clear where we stand.*"

"*Isn't that what you said earlier today? So, what do you care if I smoke or not?*"

His words kept repeating in her mind like a broken record. He was right. She had said it loud and clear where they stood. So why were his words affecting her so much? Why did they hurt so much?

"Catherine!" Maggie yelled at her from across the table. She jumped at the mention of her name, shaking her head.

"What?" she asked, confused. "Did you ask me something?"

"Where did you go?" Maggie questioned.

"Nowhere. I'm right here," Catherine answered.

"You disassociated. Are you okay?" Maggie asked worriedly. She looked around the table, and everyone was looking at her. Devin included. She turned her face, unable to look at him.

"I'm fine," she whispered.

"You have barely touched your food, boss," Maverick added. She looked down to her half-eaten plate of pasta carbonara. She dropped her fork and picked the napkin from her lap, putting it on the table.

"Excuse me," she muttered, standing up, and picked up her jacket from the back of the chair, leaving the table. The cold October air hit her face.

They went to a little family-owned Italian restaurant on the outskirts of town. The townsfolk showed up for the last-minute town hall meeting. Turns out, the town did use that old equipment before the company was created thirty years ago. Once the company opened, the equipment was forgotten.

USACE estimated they needed fifty grand to fix it and make it usable until the treatment plant gets fully renovated. How they were going to raise that amount of money was a mystery. The company's account currently had close to ten grand in it, but taking government loans was not an option unless they wanted to put the company in more debt than it already was. No matter how much she looked at the books and numbers, the company was in the red.

The restaurant was on a little dock on the outskirts of a river. She walked down the dock, leaning against the railings, looking at the stars reflected on the dark waters of the river below. Footsteps, heavy ones she knew too well, resounded behind her. A jacket was placed on top of hers and a gentle kiss placed on the back of her head. She looked up, and the ocean-blue gaze of Devin was staring back at her.

"I'm sorry," he whispered. She knew what he was referring to. "I didn't mean it."

"You don't owe me an apology, Devin," she mumbled, turning back to the river. "You were right in everything you said."

"Yes, I do owe you one," he said. "I broke the promise I

made you, and I said things I didn't mean because I'm mad and frustrated. I'm calling *timeout*." He stood beside her, leaning against the railings. She watched his hand reach for hers, but he retracted it, lacing his fingers in front of him.

"I swear to God Devin, if you ask me again what happened, I will throw you in this freezing water," she threatened. He chuckled.

"I promised I wouldn't. You already established you aren't ready to talk about it, and I respect your boundaries. I know you will tell me when you feel ready. I'm not going to push you," he replied softly. "Why did you break the deal we made? We agreed to try and be friends again." He turned to her. She looked down at her hands.

"I can't, Devin. I just can't," she whispered. "It's too much. I'm too overwhelmed. I have too much on my plate right now to try and mend an old friendship. Our job here, my relationship with Kyle, I'm sorry. It's just too much. Maybe another time. But not right now." She looked up at him.

"Can I still treat you as a friend?" he asked quietly, biting the inside of his cheek nervously.

"You mean doing things friends don't usually do? Like you used to treat me in college?" she replied. He sighed. "No Devin, you can't. It's wrong." He nodded, pursing his lips.

"Okay. Coworkers then," he said, sounding disappointed but giving her a small nod.

"Coworkers," she repeated.

"Catherine, I..." He started but was interrupted by a phone ringing. "You're going to answer that?" he asked. She dug her phone out of the pocket of her jacket. It was Kyle. She felt her face drop and anger invaded her. After the fight they had the night before, she wasn't really sure where their relationship stood.

"I—"

Devin had already started to walk away. "You have to take that. I know," he said over his shoulder, leaving her alone. Her phone stopped ringing and resumed a couple of seconds later. It was Kyle again. She hugged Devin's jacket to her, his cologne invading her nostrils.

"Hello?" she answered the call in a shaky voice. She cleared her throat. "Hello?" she repeated, a little more composed.

"Hey," Kyle replied.

"What do you want?"

"I just wanted to know how you were," he murmured on the other end of the line. "I have a couple of minutes now." She scoffed. "I hate that you are mad at me," he added. She rolled her eyes even though he couldn't see her.

"I wouldn't be mad at you if you had put a little effort into seeing me. Fuck, Kyle, this is the fourth time you've canceled on me. I spent our anniversary alone for fuck's sake. Not even when you were sent to Japan did we fight this much. You didn't even call me on our anniversary," she spat, exasperated. He sighed on the other side of the line. There was something else going on. Something he wasn't telling her. She knew him too well. "What's really going on Kyle?" she asked. "Something is different between us. Something has changed. We haven't been the same the last six months."

"*Corazón...*" he sighed, calling her the pet name he gave her when they started dating. She didn't like the tone of his voice. He sounded defeated. "There's no easy way for me to say this. I... I think we have run our course. I think we need to break up."

"Are you seriously breaking up with me over the phone?" she asked incredulously.

"No... Well, kind of. I want to propose something to you.

Let's take some time. Let's use this time apart to do some introspection about us."

"You mean like a break?" she asked, scoffing.

"Yes. Oh my god, I'm so glad you understand," he said, relief in his tone. But she knew him too well. He was hiding something.

"Kyle, what is really going on?" she questioned.

He sighed. "You want me to be honest?" he asked softly, defeated.

"Always."

"I got offered a permanent position here, paying twice as much as what I earn back in DC, Catherine. This is the promotion I've been waiting for."

"Kyle, that's amazing. Why didn't you tell me?"

"Because there's more," he said, and he sounded guilty. She didn't like his tone. Anxiety rose in the back of her throat, choking her.

"What is it?"

"I met someone else here. We share a lot of common interests. And honestly, I don't know where that leaves us. You said something has changed between us. We aren't the same as we were six months ago. I thought I was the only one that noticed, but you are right. Something has changed with us," he added. "And I didn't want to accept it until I came here and met her."

"So what?" she asked. "You wanna take a break, fuck around, see if it works out with whatever it is that you found in Nevada, and if it doesn't work out, come back to me? You think I'm stupid Kyle?" she questioned. "Do you think I will be at your beck and call?"

"Well, it's not like you have a ton of men falling at your feet," Kyle refuted, his words cutting through her. She refused to give him the satisfaction of getting a reaction out of her.

"Let me make it easier for you then. Go chase whatever got your attention in Nevada. And don't ever call me again. We are done. I'm done being the one making an effort in this fucking relationship that clearly means so little to you. Did these past four years even mean anything at all to you? Or was I just someone keeping your bed warm? Did you ever love me?"

"Catherine..." he replied in a shameful voice.

"Don't try to salvage your ass. You meant exactly what you said," she said in a shaky breath. "Don't even bother coming back to DC. I'll pack your stuff, and I will ship it to your parents' house or put it in storage. Goodbye Kyle," she added and hung up.

She took a deep breath. Did he ever love her? But more importantly, did she ever love him? Was it fair of her to ask him that question? The bartender was right. Looking at the past four years, sure, Kyle had been an incredible partner and boyfriend. It was fun and romantic in the beginning. Then, they fell into a routine.

Looking deep inside herself, she knew the truth. She did love Kyle. She loved him, but not in the way he deserved. Not in the way she loved the redhead inside the restaurant. Not in the way she would ever love anyone again after Devin. Her hand went to the necklace hanging on her neck. The necklace he gifted her. The love she had for Kyle could never be measured up to the love she felt and, deep down, still feels for Devin. She loves him. She never stopped loving him. Despite everything that happened. Despite him breaking her heart. She loved him, and that was final. She sighed, the cold northern October air filling her lungs. She walked back to the foyer of the restaurant, texting Maggie to bring out her purse.

"What do you need this for?" Maggie asked as she gave her the purse. She shrugged Devin's jacket off and handed it to Maggie. Maggie frowned as she picked up the jacket.

"Give this to Devin," Catherine said, swinging her purse on her shoulder. "Y'all keep having fun without me. I'm going back to the B&B," she added, unlocking her phone.

"How are you getting back?" Maggie asked. "Wait for me. I'll drive us."

"Sweetheart, as much as I love you, I will never jeopardize my life like that," Catherine remarked, opening her browser and looking up taxi companies in the area.

"Okay, fair. I'm not the best driver. What happened? Did you and Devin have a fight again?" Maggie asked.

"How do you…"

"Everyone heard the fight outside the town hall, Catherine," she said. Catherine cursed under her breath, closing her eyes.

"No. We didn't fight again. I just want to go to sleep," she replied. "Fuck, no taxis."

"Cat, what happened?" Maggie asked softly.

"I wanna be alone, okay? I need to be alone," Catherine exploded, her voice shaky. Maggie's gaze darkened.

"What did the fucker do?" Maggie questioned, rage on her face and in her tone. Catherine looked at her with wide eyes. Maggie never cursed. "What did Kyle do?" Maggie asked again.

"We broke up."

"Over the phone?" Maggie screeched furiously.

"Shh, lower your voice," Catherine reprimanded, looking behind them to where Maverick and Devin were. Devin's eyes found hers, and she looked away quickly.

"Ugh, I'm going to cut his balls off if I ever see him again," Maggie threatened. "But wait, if you are single now, that means—" Maggie exclaimed, her whole face illuminating. She looked back at the restaurant. "That means you can date Mr. Hunk with the pretty red hair over there," she continued, pointing a thumb over her shoulder. Catherine placed both of her hands on Maggie's cheeks, cradling her face.

"Mags, listen to me because I will only say this once. Devin is engaged. And I am not interested. I'm not a homewrecker," Catherine said, dropping her face and looking down at her phone.

"But that's not—" Maggie started to say and stopped. A shadow appeared in her peripheral vision. A hand wrapped around the jacket that Maggie was holding. *Devin's hand.*

"Let's go," Devin spoke, putting the jacket on and walking past her, leaving the door open for her, her gaze following him. He tilted his head as he looked at her, motioning for her to follow. She frowned.

"What—" she started, but Maggie pushed her shoulders.

"Go," Maggie exclaimed. "She wants to go. She wants to be alone," she pressed. "Take her back to the B&B." Devin nodded, giving her a military salute.

"I already paid Catherine's and my share of the tab. Just you and Maverick are left since he said he wanted to get dessert." Maggie nodded, pushing Catherine outside and closing the door, waving at her. "Come on," Devin murmured, walking to the car. "I won't talk. I promise," he vowed. Her feet carried her automatically to the car. Her phone rang again. She looked down at the caller ID and saw it was Kyle. She rejected the call, sending it to voicemail. She turned the sound off. "You won't answer that?" Devin asked, unlocking the car.

"No," she responded. He nodded. She got in the car. Her phone buzzed in her hand. It was a text from Kyle.

> Please pick up. I didn't mean what I said. I'm sorry.

She ignored him. "Let him grovel," she murmured.

"What?" Devin asked as he turned the heater on.

"Nothing," she replied, shoving her phone in her purse.

The rest of the drive to the B&B was quiet, just like Devin promised, only the sound of the radio breaking the silence. It was on an old music station. "Separate Ways (Worlds Apart)" by Journey was playing. She started to hum it. This used to be their go-to song when singing karaoke. Everyone knew it was their song. The music grew louder, and she knew Devin turned the volume up. They both started singing like back in the day, as if they were back in Boston in the karaoke bar. The song ended, and Devin lowered the volume again.

"Do you ever miss it?" he asked, giving her a quick look. "Do you ever miss Boston? Do you ever miss those years?" he questioned, a sad smile on his face.

"Sometimes. I miss that little coffee shop we used to go to. I miss their cinnamon rolls," she said, mirroring his sad smile.

"Ah, yes, the cinnamon rolls," Devin replied dreamily. "Have you gone back to Boston at all?" She tensed at the question.

"No. I've never had the time after I left," she said, shrugging. *Liar*. She was a liar. She hadn't gone back because it was too painful and bittersweet. "I went to Penn State, then Washington. I haven't been there in nine years."

"I went there last year for vacation with Em—" he started but stopped. Pain shot through her chest. She swallowed the lump in her throat.

"It's okay. You can talk about her," she said, looking out

the window. "She's a part of your life now," she whispered. He cleared his throat.

"The coffee shop is still in the same place, and the cinnamon rolls are still the best," he added. She chuckled. "But I am biased, so don't take it to heart."

"Well, I am biased too, and I agree they are the best," she said. They arrived at the B&B, and she walked up to her room, Devin following suit.

"Well, Catherine, good night," he said, unlocking his room.

"Goodnight Devin."

Chapter Sixteen

Catherine

"I got it!" Maggie exclaimed excitedly, barging into the room and dropping her purse on the table. "The Fireflies Festival," she mentioned enthusiastically as if it was the obvious answer. Catherine frowned.

"The what?" Catherine asked, confused, looking up from her work computer.

"The annual Fireflies Festival," she repeated. Catherine gave her a puzzled look. Her smile dropped. "You don't know?" she asked, disappointed.

"Does it look like I know what you are talking about?"

"Ugh, okay. Every year on November 1st, the town celebrates the Fireflies Festival," Maggie explained. She was still confused. "Ugh, come on, you can't be that dense Cat. Okay, let me explain it like you are five. It's a town tradition that celebrates fireflies. They do a little fair in the town center, with music and food, and the whole town celebrates. They invited us. And this year, they asked me to help them coordinate it. They want the office involved. One community leader posed the idea that we could use the fair to raise the money for the old water equipment. I think this will be a great opportunity to bring people together and raise the money to fix the town's old equipment since USACE refuses to fix the pumps on the treatment plant in a timely manner," Maggie said, rolling her eyes.

"Are we talking about the Fireflies Festival?" Devin asked, entering the room, a cardboard cup holder in his right hand, his suit jacket in the other. His shirt hugged his muscles as they flexed, and he set down the coffees, shrugging his backpack off his shoulder. Her gaze lingered on his arms, on the way his shirt was hugging them.

"Yes! See? Even redhead over there knows what I'm talking about," Maggie exclaimed. That brought Catherine back to the present. She looked at Maggie, who had a mischievous smile on her face. Catherine rolled her eyes.

"Only against my will and because Gloria ambushed me and told me she would kick me out if I didn't go," he said, looking between both of them, chuckling.

"Anyway, I already cleared it with the boss. He said it was okay. So, I just wanted to let you know that I was going to be remote from now on, but I'll be one hundred percent reachable on my work phone if you need me. We don't have a lot of time left to help them," Maggie said, shrugging. Catherine scratched her forehead, taking her glasses off, and proceeded to massage her temples.

"But I need you here. We're still picking the people for the board and the CEO position," Catherine explained, looking at Devin for backup.

"Don't look at me," he replied, lifting his hands in surrender.

"You have Devin and Maverick. You'll be fine," Maggie said, taking her purse with her. Devin took a cup from the cupholder.

"Iced matcha latte with almond milk," he said, giving her

the cup.

"You are an angel," she stated as she took a sip from her latte. Her phone went off, and she looked down. "Okay, I gotta go now. The carpenter hunk, aka Maverick's big brother, is taking me around town to start talking with folks about the festival and planning," she said, checking her phone again. She blew them air kisses as goodbyes.

"Margarette…" Catherine called after her, but Maggie had already left. She pinched the bridge of her nose, closing her eyes. Taking a deep breath, she let it go, putting her glasses back on.

"Your coffee. Cappuccino, oat milk, no sugar, and a pinch of cinnamon," Devin said, placing the cup in front of her, one of his hands cupping the back of her head, his lips placing a gentle kiss to the crown of her head. She tensed.

The kiss shouldn't have made her feel anything, but a whole kaleidoscope of crazy butterflies erupted in her stomach, and she liked the feeling, more than she liked to admit. She hated how affected she was by him, by his presence and how he made her feel. He dropped his forehead on top of her head.

"Sorry. Old habits are hard to break. Or whatever the saying is," he mumbled against her hair. His hand brushed her hair, his fingers detangling the soft curls. He took a deep breath. "Lavender and chamomile." He knew her favorite smell, which was also how her soap and shampoo smelled. "You really are a creature of habit," he murmured. She chuckled lightly.

"I think you meant *old habits die hard*," she whispered, correcting him, deciding to ignore his last comments. He chuckled. "It's okay," she muttered. He let go of her and walked to the other side of the room, sitting down and picking his coffee, taking a sip from it. She took a sip of her coffee, welcoming the distraction. Hoping the caffeine rush would calm the butterflies still running wild in her stomach. "Thanks for the coffee." He nodded.

"This is good. Let her go. It shows that Michael and the office care about the townsfolk," he said, pinning her with a look of '*I know what I'm doing*' as if the last two minutes never happened. She rolled her eyes.

"Michael cares about his people," she retorted.

"I know he does. As does Brian. As do you and I. It's the whole reason we're here. We aren't even in session. I'm sure his district scheduler can handle a bit of this heat while she does this little side project. She's not going to be fully off the grid. Besides, she is going to be representing the office. This will be good in the long run," he said. "And this will look good for the campaign." He shrugged.

She dropped her coffee with a thud on the table. "The misfortunes of people should not be used as campaign tactics. Or to '*win over*' the people and their vote," she said, making air quotes. "Michael knows this. He stands by this principle," she refuted, examining the papers in front of her.

"I know," he whispered. "Then how about this? This is a good way to raise that forty grand we still need."

"Devin, look around. This town has a population of one thousand. They won't be able to raise forty grand with one activity," she said, pained. He looked down at his hands, defeat written all over his face. He knew, as much as she did, that they needed a miracle to raise that amount of money. She looked out the tiny window of the office. She heaved an exasperated sigh. "I just wish there was more we could do. Now, we are really running against the clock," she said, throwing her head back and closing her eyes.

"Hey, it'll work out. I promise. I'll make some calls," he replied. She felt his gaze on her. She turned to look at him.

"Once Maggie gives me more info, I'll make some calls. Can you trust me on this?" he asked, almost pleading. She looked at him, and his eyes held all the hope in the world. She heaved a defeated sigh because she knew that no matter what, a part of her would always trust him. Truth be told, they were running out of ideas. If he had some, it was worth a shot. This was their last chance.

He looked into her eyes and knew the answer to his question without her having to voice it. He nodded once and looked down at his hands folded in front of him. This was their only chance.

"I won't let you down. I promise. I know how much this means to you. I won't let you down again," he promised, reassuring her. *Again*. Something in her chest broke, and she looked away. The pressure built behind her eyes, a fresh set of tears burning on her eyelids. A knot formed in her throat. She wondered if he, deep down, knew why they had a fallout all those years ago. But that would be impossible. She left before either of them could sit her down. She left before he even thought to call a *timeout*. She needed this week and a half to fly by. This whole working together was messing with her mind and heart.

"I trust you," she whispered, not sure he heard her. He exhaled. *He had*. Those words meant more to her than what she cared to account for. They were heavy words. But something about his reassurance, about the way he said he wasn't going to fail her, she felt he was being sincere.

"Thank you," he whispered. She nodded, stood up, and grabbed her coat.

"I'm going to take a walk," she mumbled and left the room. She needed space. She needed to be far away from him, and not in the same room as him. Thankfully, he didn't follow her. She left the office, as Maverick jumped out of his car.

"Hey, boss. You okay?" he asked when he looked at her, his expression worried. She turned to him and gave him a smile that didn't reach her eyes.

"Yes, I just need some fresh air. And a walk," she replied, turning to where the tree line was, walking in that direction, the crunch of the leaves under her feet sounding with every step. Another set of steps sounded behind her. She turned and found Maverick with his hands in his pockets, walking a couple of steps behind her. She stopped walking. He caught up with her. "I'm fine," she told him. He looked at her as if he didn't believe her. She rolled her eyes and smiled.

"You don't look fine," he said. "What's happening, boss? What's bothering you? You haven't looked this bothered since the 2018 elections." She chuckled and sighed.

"Why are you and Mags so good at reading me?" she asked, linking her arm with his and walking.

"You're kidding me? Trust me, boss. You are very readable."

"What do you mean?"

"You talk with your face," he said, pointing to his face. She rolled her eyes, exasperated. "See? Exasperated. Everyone knows how you feel because of your expression."

"I thought Michael said that just to taunt me," she protested. Maverick frowned, confused. "A couple of weeks ago, Michael mentioned the same thing. That even if I don't voice it, my face speaks for me," she explained. Maverick smiled a little, nodding. She sighed.

"What's going on with the senate boy?" Maverick asked, making her laugh.

"Nothing is going on," she said, a sad smile on her face. She took a deep breath.

"Tell that to your face," Maverick pointed out. She bumped her shoulder with his. "I know I'm not Mags, but you can talk to me, you know? I won't gossip about it around the office," he said. "Not that Maggie goes around telling your business to anyone," he added, nervous.

"Please, Maggie is the queen of gossip in the office," she laughed.

"I will plead the fifth," Maverick answered with a smile. "But just between you and me, she told me there's a history with senate boy. Do I have to rearrange his pretty face?" Maverick asked.

"Oh, god no, I don't want you to commit a felony Mav," she said, stopping in her tracks. "Damn, she really is the queen of gossip. What did she tell you?"

Maverick shrugged. "That the two of you went to college together and were best friends. But I'm guessing she left something out, or you did," he replied. "But I am going to go with the latter," he guessed.

She chuckled. "And that is why you are my favorite."

"So, what really happened?"

She exhaled. "He was my first heartbreak."

"Ouch."

"It's fine. I'm over it. I'm over him," she lied, her voice shaking.

"Are you? Are you really?" he asked her softly. "You seem anything but fine, Catherine," he continued, calling her by her name. He never called her by her name unless he was trying to make a statement. "Look, I'm going to speak freely because you've given me your trust over the years, and I appreciate you in a big sister way. Catherine, you aren't over him. You still love him. Stop denying the obvious. His presence clearly still affects you. You are still hurt by him, by what he did. Spending time with him has clearly reopened the wound you thought had healed. And that's okay. Your feelings are valid."

"When did you become so wise?" she asked him. "You're only twenty-seven."

"I've had my fair share of heartbreaks. I know a thing or two about them," he explained, shrugging. She laughed. "You want my advice?" She nodded, unsure, but she knew he was doing it because he cared. "You need to sit down and speak freely to him. Bare your soul. You can't keep running away from this. You can't keep bottling up these feelings," he said, voicing exactly what she knew he was going to say. "Otherwise, you will never move on. Do you really want to be stuck in the past forever?"

"No," she said in a whisper.

"Then what are you waiting for?"

"It hurts to even think about it."

"What did he do that was so bad?"

"I love you. There I said it," the voice of her best friend and roommate, Emily, said.

The memory hit her like a train. She shook her head, clearing the image out of her mind.

"Can we change the subject?" she asked. "I don't want my depressing love life from the past to be the topic of conversation."

"You can't run away forever, Catherine," Maverick pointed out. She looked up and saw they were back on the office grounds.

"When did we pull a U-turn?" she asked. Maverick just shrugged.

"You don't have to worry about me, boss. I won't tell Mags about this," he said, stating the obvious.

"I know. You and Mags are two different people. Speaking of Maggie, she seems to have taken an interest in your brother. How do you feel about that?" Maverick shrugged. "Oh, come on Mav, you aren't the only observant one in the office. I've seen how you look at her."

"It's not like she would ever look at me in that light," he murmured.

"Oh, Mav," Catherine exclaimed. "You'll never know if you don't try. You are definitely worth it. Besides, Mags is not that air-headed or superficial. She's a good girl, a bit of a sunshine personality. Your rainy-day parade personality could definitely use her sunshine spark. Maybe create a rainbow," she muttered, bumping her shoulder into his. Maverick chuckled.

"You really think she would go out on a date with a guy like me?" he asked, hopeful.

"I know so."

"Thanks for the vote of confidence, boss. But I don't think she would. She likes men like my brother. All her other exes are built just like him," he said. They made it back to the parking lot. "We better get inside and start preparing. We have three people coming for interviews. It should be the final round. Then we can sit down and pick the ones we like." She nodded. The door opened, and Devin came outside.

"I have to run an errand," he mentioned, walking to the car.

"We have a couple of people coming for an interview," she replied.

"Can you do the interviews without me?" he asked. "Catherine, I really need to go."

"You're leaving me to conduct them alone?"

"I have to go into Jenkins' office. I need to go. I can't argue right now. I trust your judgment. I'll make it up to you," he said, opening the door of the car and jumping inside. "I owe you one."

"I guess it is just the two of us," she pointed out, looking at Maverick.

"Let's go inside," he replied, ushering both of them inside, finishing the day with the interviews.

Chapter Seventeen

Devin

"Where's the boss? And where is he meeting?" Devin asked, entering the senate district office.

"Hey Devin, good to see you. Yes, I am fine, thank you for asking," Rose, the old lady at the front desk, said to him, not lifting her gaze from her computer.

"Rose, the meeting, where is it?" he asked, leaning on her desk. She sighed.

"He's in his office, he is fine. Did he call you and say it was an emergency?"

"I forgot he was meeting with the mayor today about expanding funding for the construction of a new highway exit and renovation for a piece of the highway along with the rest stop in that area," he replied, exhaling. "But he said it was an emergency. Code red." Rose lifted her eyes and looked at him. "It's not an emergency, is it?" She shook her head, her eyes going back to her computer.

"Nope," she said, not looking at him.

"I'm going to kill him," Devin muttered, walking to his boss's office.

"Careful, Devin, I believe that could get you jail time. You're too pretty for jail."

"Hey Devin, good…" one staffer started to greet him, but he kept walking.

He walked into his boss's office, opening the door without knocking.

"Oh, Devin, good you're here," Brian greeted, standing up from his desk.

"You said it was an emergency. You said it was code red," Devin protested.

"Well, it is," Brian said matter-of-factly.

"Are you dying?" Devin asked him.

"Not particularly. Not today, at least. But we all will die in the end," Brian replied, waving a dismissive hand.

"Then this does not constitute an emergency. Nonetheless, a code red," Devin retorted. "You said it was an emergency."

"It is. My computer restarted, and I can't get into my profile or email. The mayor rescheduled the meeting, which I'm not going to be able to attend as I'm leaving for DC in the afternoon," Brian explained, pointing to his computer.

"Are you serious? Brian, that is not an emergency," Devin replied, frustrated. "We have the IT people for that! And you could've told me about the mayor rescheduling on a call or an email," he continued, pinching the bridge of his nose.

"Yeah, but IT doesn't know my password, and I couldn't email you the details because I'm logged out of my computer," Brian added. Devin rolled his eyes. "You, however, have my password."

"You made me drive an hour into your office, leaving Catherine to finish the last of the interviews alone, all because you couldn't remember your password?" Devin asked. "Did I miss anything?"

"Nope, you summarized it rather succinctly. Now, can

you log me in so I can send you the details for the mayor's meeting tomorrow?" Brian requested, looking at Devin. Devin scratched his forehead.

"I'm gonna drive back. Yeah. That's what I'm going to do," Devin mumbled to himself, leaving.

"Devin!" his boss called from inside his office, but he ignored him.

"I'm going to email you the boss's credentials. You or anyone here can log him in on his computer. I'm gonna go on my merry way before I commit first-degree murder," Devin said to Rose.

"I told you it wasn't an emergency," Rose replied without looking at him.

Once inside his car, he emailed Rose the credentials and left. He drove back to the office and arrived just as they finished the second interview. His phone pinged, and it was an email from Brian detailing the agenda and topics to discuss in the meeting with the mayor the next day. He gave the document a once over and locked his phone.

"You're back," Maverick noted as he walked to the door. Devin nodded. "Can we talk?" He sounded worried. Maverick motioned to follow him to the little forest behind the office.

"What's wrong?" Devin questioned. "Is Catherine okay?"

"Do you care about her?" Maverick asked him, straight to the point. Devin nodded, unsure. "You two need to talk. Both of you need to have *the* conversation. You are hurting her, even when you don't intend to. And it's also clearly hurting you as well. Listen, I care about her. She's like a sister to me," Maverick remarked. "Please, if you really care about her, talk to her. Help her heal and move on."

"What do you know?"

Maverick shrugged. "What I know or what I don't, is

not the point. That is not my place," Maverick replied. "That's between you and her. Just fix it, okay? She's hurting. I don't know what happened or what you did that hurt her so much that she's still hurting her today. But you better fix it."

"Your guess is as good as mine. She left our group the day finals ended. She didn't even go to graduation. I don't know what I did. Trust me, I've tried. I have tried talking to her. She refuses to tell me anything. She keeps saying 'the past is in the past' and that she isn't ready to talk about it. And I respect that. I respect her boundaries. And trust me, it's not for lack of trying because I have tried to get her to open up."

"Wait, so you don't know either?" Maverick asked, confused.

"No. I'm frustrated because I want to fix it. I want to apologize for what I did, but I can't apologize for something I don't know about. She refuses to tell me and shuts me down every time I bring it up," Devin explained, frustrated, passing a hand through his hair. "If I knew what I did, if I knew what happened, trust me, I would be serving penance for it." His phone rang at that moment. He got it out of his pocket. It was a call from Emily. "I have to take this," Devin mumbled, looking at Maverick. Maverick nodded and left. "Emily, hey, what's up?"

"It's a disaster, Devin," Emily sobbed.

"Emily, breathe. Just breathe. What happened?" Devin questioned in a comforting, calm tone.

"The venue. They canceled on me at the last minute. They double-booked. They just called me and refunded me the whole deposit and payments I have been making. They didn't even offer me a new date. Nothing. Devin, what are we going to do?" Emily asked, her voice shaky.

"Okay, Emily, sweetheart, listen to me, okay? Breathe. You have to breathe."

"Dev, it's too late to book a new place at a reasonable price. The invitations are already out. People have already started to send their RSVPs. The wedding is in less than two months. Devin, what are we going to do?" Emily asked, crying. "I bet this is my curse. From that one time we went to Salem, and I refused to enter that arcane shop with you and Catherine and decided to go to sleep. I decided sleep was more important, and I turned my back on fate, and now it's coming to bite me in the ass," Emily rambled. "Oh god, it has to be that."

"Em, you are making zero sense right now. Listen, we will figure this out, okay? Let me do some research at work. And I will help you figure it out. We got this. Together," Devin soothed. "Okay?"

He couldn't see her, but he knew she was nodding absent-mindedly like she usually does when she's stressed.

"Okay," she said. "I'll see what I can find, and we'll reconvene at night. Sounds good?"

"Sounds like a plan," he murmured. "Hey, we got this, okay?" he said in a comforting voice. He heard her exhale on the other side of the line. "I love you."

"I love you too," she replied and hung up.

He blew out a breath, walked back to the office, and plopped down on his chair. He opened his computer and started browsing.

"Wedding venues?" Catherine asked from behind him. He nodded, his eyes staying on the task at hand.

"Yeah. The place Emily reserved double booked on her date and canceled the reservation, refunding her. Now, I need to help her find a place on short notice. This is going to be a mess. Weddings are exhausting. This is the reason she is handling all of it with her mom. I'm just supposed to look pretty in my tux," he rambled, scratching his forehead.

"When's the wedding?" Catherine asked, walking to her chair.

"December 9th," he replied, still not looking at her. She picked up her phone and left the office. Around ten minutes passed when Catherine walked back inside and handed him a piece of paper with a number and a name scribbled on it. He looked up at her, confused.

"Tell Emily to call that number. They are expecting her call. It's a popular wedding venue in DC. The owner owes me a favor. They have the date open, and they're offering a discount too. Tell her to mention my name when she calls. If that doesn't work, I have another favor to call in from another venue. But that one is in Virginia. A bit far out of the city," Catherine said, shrugging. "Networking after work and not having fun has its perks."

"Catherine—"

"It's fine," Catherine replied as she walked back to her chair. "You don't have to thank me." She returned her attention to the papers in front of her. He stood up and walked over to her, cradling her face and kissing her forehead.

"Thank you. You just possibly saved my ass. Our asses," he mumbled against her skin. He gave her another kiss and walked out to send the number to Emily. He texted her a picture of the number and called her. She picked up in the first ring. "I sent you a number and a name. Don't ask questions. When you call, say Catherine sent you. Just trust me on this one, okay? Don't question it."

"Catherine?" she asked, confused.

"Just do as I say," Devin retorted and hung up. He walked back to the office. Half an hour later, he received a text from Emily.

> Just booked. How was she able to get this venue? The venue has a waitlist of three months just to get a consultation to see if the date you want is available?
>
> Tell her I say thanks but that I am still angry and pissed at her.

> I will tell her you say thanks. I will not tell her that last part.

"Thank you. She was able to book it," he said, looking at her.

"It's fine. Like I said, you don't have to thank me," she answered, waving a dismissive hand in the air, not looking at him.

"That's two that I owe you now."

"Devin, you don't owe me anything. Take it as—" she started but stopped to think. "—take it as your wedding gift," she finished, writing in her notebook.

"A wedding gift?" he asked, confused.

"Yes. A wedding gift," she emphasized. Maverick knocked on the door and popped his head inside the office.

"The last of the candidates is here," he announced.

"Great. One last person and we'll be good to finish picking the right candidates," she mused. She stood up and walked past him. He grabbed her wrist, stopping her.

"What do you mean wedding gift?" he questioned, looking up at her, but she was already looking down at him, her gaze drifting to where they were connected. His thumb traced her pulse, caressing her wrist softly.

"A wedding gift. When you give a gift to someone who is getting married. A wedding gift, Devin. It's not rocket science," she explained, removing his grip from her wrist. "Like I said, you don't have to thank me." She left the office conference room and walked to the waiting area. "Mr. Dall, so good to finally meet you. This way," she greeted the newcomer behind him.

"Your wedding gift." Why would she give him a wedding gift?

"Mr. Dall, this is my co-worker who will be helping me conduct your interview, Mr. Devin Mack," Catherine introduced, entering the room again. He shook out of his daze and stood up, extending a hand to the middle-aged man.

"Nice to meet you, Mr. Dall," Devin greeted, shaking his hand. "Please, sit down," Devin said, motioning to the chair in front of him.

"So, Mr. Dall, I had a chance to look at your resume. You have extensive knowledge and experience handling and managing a company like this one. Tell me, what do you bring to the table?" Catherine asked, her gaze focused on Mr. Dall. Devin observed her profile. She looked so composed right now. But he knew her more than she knew herself. This was all a facade. Everything faded in the background as he just stared at her.

"You are hurting her."

That's what Maverick had said. He knew his presence was hurting her. He knew it. But he didn't know what happened. He so desperately wanted to know what he did. He wanted to fix it. He wanted her to bare her heart and soul so he could fix it. So he could help her heal. So he could ease the burden on her shoulders. He has tried, but she'd been just as stubborn as she was back in college. She shut him and every attempt he made to get to the bottom of this problem down. She closed herself off. She refused to talk. Not only to him but also to Emily.

Emily had lost her best friend and sister. Emily was equally hurt by all of this. She'd lost someone that day too.

She lost her twin flame, as she used to refer to Catherine. It had taken a lot of strength for Emily to pull herself together after Catherine left. Just as much as he lost half of his heart, Emily also lost half of hers. Catherine left both of them like a thief in the night. Quietly and fast. Not even a note.

He knew she was stubborn, but if there was one thing he was good at it was knowing Catherine's triggers and getting past her defenses. If he had to use his knowledge and push her buttons to have her finally open up, so he could make it better, so he could help her, even if it was the last thing he did, he would. And there was no stopping him. He was determined. Just as much as Catherine was hard-headed and stubborn, he was equally or worse. And when he set his mind on something, nothing could stop him until he accomplished his goal. And he was set on doing it. He was going to do it before going back to DC. Before he lost her again.

Corbin was right, this might be his last chance to get her back into his life, and he sure as hell was going to fight for it.

Chapter Eighteen

Catherine

"Alright, so we have our picks," Catherine announced, looking at the whiteboard at the far end of the room with the pictures and names of the new CEO and the board of directors' members. They had spent the last week deciding, along with community leaders, and finally reached a consensus. They all nodded in agreement. Everyone was here. Brian, Michael, Helen, Maverick, and Maggie. Some staffers from Jenkins' office were also present.

"Good job everyone. And we still have five days left. Maggie, how is the fundraising event coming?" Michael asked.

"I'm pleased to say that with some calls and contacts from Mr. Redhead, we have almost thirty grand in donations," Maggie reported proudly.

Catherine turned to look at Devin, who was already staring back at her, and he gave her a smile that reeked of *I told you so*. She nodded slightly and turned back to Maggie.

"The events are coming along great. Isabela and I have extended an invitation to nationwide major news media, and she will be here for the festival to help with the coverage for our office."

"How many of those outlets have confirmed their attendance?" Brian questioned.

"I have—" Maggie started to say, pulling open her notebook, "—I have confirmed attendance from most major news outlets, newspapers, and major national television broadcasts. Oh, and also all the state and local newspapers and news stations. I'm still waiting for some of the bigger news outlets, but we are having great coverage through radio news stations on a local level and nationwide." She inspected her list, nodding with content, a smile adorning her face.

"Any decliners?" Devin asked.

"Yes. You take your guess because I won't be saying their name," she sighed.

"I can take a pretty good guess," Maverick mumbled.

"Anyways…" Michael exclaimed, diverting the conversation back to the topic at hand. "In five days, we will have the Fireflies Festival, with only a couple of grand left to be raised. Let me make some calls. We should be close to the goal by the time the festival rolls around, leaving the sales of tickets to cover for the rest of the fundraising. In the meantime, tomorrow we will have a jointed meeting with the new board and CEO in Brian's office, and we will also introduce them to the townsfolk in a town hall meeting," he continued. "Maverick, spread the word of the town hall meeting tomorrow at three in the afternoon to the townsfolk. Maggie, call all the people on this whiteboard and schedule the meeting with them for tomorrow at noon. Devin and Catherine…" he said, turning to them. They were seated beside each other.

"Boss?" Catherine asked, looking at Michael.

"Take the rest of the day off. You both deserve it. Especially you, Catherine," Michael remarked. Brian nodded. She frowned.

"Boss, I can't. There's too much to do and not enough time left. We have to get all of this set up and running before we leave," she protested.

"You can and you will," Maggie stated. "It was discussed by the boss and me. Maverick and I have it. We can hold down the fort for a day. You and Devin take the rest of the day off. Go sleep or read. Or do whatever it is you do in your free time," Maggie urged. "You haven't gotten a single day off since I don't know when. You *will* take the day off," she said, her tone final, leaving no room for discussion. Catherine stared at her with an incredulous look, her mouth agape. "It's not up for discussion."

"But—" Catherine started to argue, but Maggie put a hand up, stopping her.

"No buts. I have full authorization from our boss," Maggie smiled a toothy saccharine smile. She was enjoying this. Arguing with Maggie was useless. Catherine heaved a defeated sigh. "You're dismissed. You too Devin," Maggie said, leaving the office.

"Yes, ma'am," Devin nodded, standing up and putting his jacket on.

"I'll see you tomorrow, boss," Maverick said, leaving. Helen smiled at them and also left, along with Jenkins' staffers.

"I'll see you tomorrow at noon. Come on Brian, there's something I want to talk about for our next district project," Michael said, leaving with Jenkins, which left Devin and Catherine alone.

"You seem too calm about this," she said, accusation in her voice, narrowing her eyes at Devin. Devin was already packing his stuff into his backpack. He shrugged, looking at her.

"It's not like this is the first time Brian has pulled something like this on me," he said, swinging his backpack on his shoulder. "Plus, I've learned to never question or argue with women like Maggie." He smiled, his dimples popping on his cheeks. "I'm going back to the B&B. Are you coming?" he asked from the door, his hand on the doorknob. She hastily packed her stuff and walked out of the office. Maggie gave her a toothy smile and a finger wave as she passed by, exiting the building. She rolled her eyes and walked to the car, Devin unlocking it. She jumped in her side, crossing her arms over her chest and looking out the window.

"This feels like an intervention for my workaholic self," she murmured as Devin started the car. He chuckled.

"It is. And I wholeheartedly agree and support it," he concurred. She gave him a side-eyed glance and kept quiet the rest of the way. They arrived at the B&B, and Gloria was pacing in the lobby, exasperated.

"Oh, there you are," she exclaimed as soon as they walked in. "I need a favor from both of you."

"Of course," Devin replied.

"Wait, you guys are here early. It's barely mid-afternoon," she pointed out. "What happened?"

"We have the rest of the day off," Devin explained with a flick of his hand. "What's up? What's the favor you need help with?"

"It has to do with the Fireflies Festival. Charlie threw his back out this morning fixing the gazebo on the patio. We were supposed to go and buy the materials for our booth for the festival, but we can't go now. I would go by myself, but I don't want to leave him alone. He is a big man baby when he is sick or hurt," she explained. "Would the both of you mind going in our stead?" she asked nervously.

"Oh, we can't—"

"We can't imagine why not," Devin interrupted, looking at her with a frown. She sighed, giving up. Today was not her day. "We will go change, and we'll meet you down here in twenty minutes. That sounds good?" he asked, more to Catherine than to Gloria. She rolled her eyes so far back in her head that she was almost certain she saw her hypothalamus.

"Wonderful! I'll write down a list of things I need and stash some cash in an envelope," Gloria exclaimed and disappeared.

"Why would you volunteer me for this?" she asked him in a low voice, ascending the stairs, her shoulder brushing against Devin's.

"Because you keep forgetting a key detail, Catherine. I know you better than you know yourself. And I know you would have jumped into work the minute you closed your door. You're supposed to have the day off. So, no, you and I are going on this little shopping spree for Gloria," he said, unlocking his door. "Wear comfy shoes. I'll see you in the lobby in twenty minutes," he continued with a smile and disappeared into his room.

"Ugh," she whined, opening her door.

She dropped her work bag on the bed and stomped to the suitcase to look for a change of clothing. He was right. She'd been planning on getting back to work the minute she was left alone, but he'd outsmarted her. She walked to her bathroom and changed into more comfortable clothes, consisting of a pair of jeans, a long-sleeved shirt, and her trusty beat-up Converse. She put on her jacket, descended the stairs, and walked to the kitchen to grab a coffee to-go. Coffee in hand, she walked back to the lobby where Devin was reclined against the front desk, talking with Gloria. She was going over the list she had in her hands, his head nodding in attention whenever she mentioned something related to an item on the list. He turned to look at her and smiled.

"Alright. I got it. We'll see you in a couple of hours," Devin said, turning back to Gloria. She just took a sip of her coffee and walked to the counter. "Come on." He motioned with his head to walk, and her body followed. They walked to the car, and he handed her the list of things Gloria had asked for.

"It's mostly decorations and food ingredients," she muttered, taking another sip from her coffee.

"Yes, but we have to go to the city shops to get them. You know the big stores, and all those decorations stores. She also mentioned a couple of local shops in the city, mainly for her baking ingredients," he explained, starting the car. She nodded.

Two hours later, they were walking inside the nearest mega store looking for the first items on the list. Devin grabbed a shopping cart, and went to the produce area. She looked through the list to find what they needed. If Catherine was right, Gloria was going to bake apple pies and pumpkin pies, lots of them apparently.

"Three big pumpkins?" Catherine asked, confused. "Seems a bit excessive. We'll be eating pumpkin pie for the next week. I'm sure she'll send us with pie back to DC," she muttered, putting the last pumpkin in the shopping cart. Devin chuckled.

"Okay, now we need to head to the Halloween area decorations. See if we can find any fall related decorations," Devin said, guiding the cart.

"I keep forgetting Halloween is in a couple of days."

"It's in four days, actually."

"You go ahead. I need to go to the pharmacy area."

She bee-lined to the pharmacy area, and to the aisle she needed to go. She grabbed the items she was searching for and started to walk back to find Devin. Halfway there, she felt someone behind her. She discreetly turned around and saw a man looking at her and following her. She walked to the kid's clothing area and pretended to peruse the baby clothes. The man stood a couple of feet away. A wave of apprehension went through her, not even in a small town was she exempted from lurking men. She turned and kept walking, looking from aisle to aisle for Devin. The store was mostly empty. She looked back, and the man was still following her. She increased her pace and bumped into someone, dropping everything in her hands.

"I'm so sorry," she apologized in a shaky voice, dropping to the floor to pick up her stuff. A pair of familiar hands came into her line of vision. She looked up, and blue eyes were staring back at her. She sighed in relief, closing her eyes.

"What's wrong?" Devin asked worriedly, noting her anxiousness. She opened her eyes. He glanced behind her, and his stare turned icy. "Tell me you weren't being harassed, Cat," he demanded. She stayed quiet, hugging her stuff to her chest with one arm. He grabbed her free hand, lacing their fingers together and placing her behind him, shielding her. "Buddy, it's 2023. Harassing women is not okay. It never was. I suggest you walk away before I call the police," Devin stated, his voice furious. Her grip on his hand tightened. The man laughed sarcastically. She tensed. Devin stepped forward, but she pulled him back, tightening her hold on his hand.

"Dev, don't. I'm okay. Let's just finish up here and go," she whispered. She stared at the man, who gave Devin an up and down once over as he turned around and left. Devin turned to her, cradling her face.

"Are you okay?" he asked softly, searching her face for any sign of physical harm, his thumbs caressing her cheeks. She closed her eyes and sighed, basking in the feeling of his comforting touch. He placed a gentle kiss on her forehead. "Do not leave my sight again, please," he pleaded. She nodded, not wanting to argue with him. "Let's wrap up here and go." He traced small, soothing circles with his thumb on her cheeks while looking into her eyes. The motion left her cheeks inflamed everywhere his thumb touched. He wrapped an arm around her shoulders and hugged her. "Let's go." He grabbed the cart again, and she walked beside him. They kept shopping in silence.

After the incident, they visited three more stores and drove back to town. They stopped at a diner, sitting down in a far booth, and ordered. Devin stretched his hand and signaled for her to take it. She did. He laced their fingers together, squeezing her hand.

"Are you sure you are okay? That was pretty scary what happened," he said softly. She nodded.

"It's not the first time that has happened. It's happened a couple of times in DC. The only difference is this time is that it was in a store in a town I don't live in." She shrugged. She glanced up at him, and he was staring back at her with a soft look, almost a sad one. She released his hand and brought hers to her lap, lacing her fingers together.

"I'm sorry," he whispered. She gazed up at him, and his eyes were sad.

"Why are you sorry?" she asked. "It's not your fault."

Their food arrived, and they ate in silence. Devin refused to let her pay. The rest of the drive to the B&B was quiet, only the radio playing in the background.

"Catherine, please talk to me," Devin pleaded softly, breaking the silence between them.

"What do you mean?"

"Come on, don't play dumb with me Catherine. You know exactly what I'm talking about."

"You mean the deal?" she asked. "Devin, we already talked about it. Also, please stop. We're not in college anymore. You don't have to worry about me," she added, exasperated.

"That's the problem, Catherine. I will always worry and care about you," he said, frustrated.

She scoffed. "Yeah, right."

"What is that supposed to mean?" he asked furiously. "Catherine, for nine years, since you left with no explanation, the only thing that has been a constant in my mind has been the question of why you left. What I did. One minute, everything was fine, and the next thing I knew, you were gone with no explanation," he retorted, his voice rising in volume.

"I'm not going to do this. I've told you, stop bringing it up, Devin. I don't want to talk about it," she said, frustrated, rubbing her forehead. A streak of lightning appeared in the distant sky.

"No, Catherine, that's your problem. You don't wanna see *you* are the problem. You don't wanna see that your refusal to acknowledge this problem is hurting me, it's hurting you, and it's hurting *us*. *You* are the problem. Do you think I don't see right through you? Do you think that by burying this down and not talking about it, it will somehow disappear? No, Catherine, it won't. I think nine years is more than enough. I'm fucking tired of this. I'm fucking tired of wondering what the fuck I did that was so wrong, that nine years later, you are still hurting. Even after nine years have passed, every time you look at me, you are hurting. I hate myself because I don't know what I did wrong. So no, we are talking about it. This is going to be something we will talk about now. I miss you. I miss us. And I will be damned if I don't admit it. I miss *you*, Catherine," he shouted, his voice breaking. "Do you think I want this? Do you think I want to live like this? Walking on eggshells around you all the time? It's exhausting."

It was like a dam of emotion broke inside of her. Like a flood she couldn't contain. She couldn't take it. She needed to be away from him. She needed to get out of this vehicle.

"Stop shutting me out," he begged in a softer voice. "Please."

"Stop the car," she mumbled.

"What?" he asked, confused.

"Devin, stop the fucking car," she yelled, reaching for the handle and opening the door.

"Catherine, what the fuck?" he asked, parking in the emergency lane.

She jumped out into the emergency lane, heaving, throwing the door closed. She walked away from the car, away from him. Her chest felt heavy. Her head was pounding. She could hear her heart in her ears. Her eyes felt heavy and warm with unshed tears. She bent at the waist, hands on her knees. *An anxiety attack.* This was the beginning of an anxiety attack. Thunder rolled in the skies above.

"Catherine, get back in the car," Devin said in the distance, his voice muffled by her own heartbeat.

She started to pace. She could hear her pulse in her ears, louder now. It was too much.

Nine years of this was too much.

Chapter Nineteen

Catherine

"Catherine, get in the car," Devin yelled at her, getting out of the vehicle, furious. She heard the door slam. "It's about to rain. Get in the car, Catherine," he said, softer this time.

"Leave me alone," she retorted, walking away. She wrapped her arms around herself. The cold wind was not helping. Thunder rolled in the background. She scratched her forehead, pacing. This was not happening. Not now. Not when she'd been trying to avoid it all this time. Not now in the middle of the road when rain and thunder were about to make landfall. "This isn't happening," she whispered to herself, closing her eyes.

"Catherine Babbitt, get in the fucking car," he demanded. That made her stop in her tracks. "I don't know what the fuck happened nine years ago, I don't know what the fuck I did because I clearly did something to hurt you, but I'm sorry," he screamed, thunder sounding in the distance. The air grew colder. "Now stop being so stubborn and get in the fucking car, you're gonna catch pneumonia. You don't even have your jacket on," he pointed out, walking to her and shrugging his jacket on her. She shrugged it off, throwing it at him. "Catherine, for fuck's sake, it's about to rain. Get in the car, please," he pleaded, a little softer. "Let's talk in the car. I'm calling *timeout*."

"You don't get to call a *timeout* about this," she said in a whisper.

"What?" he asked. His voice was closer. She turned around, fuming.

"You don't get to call a fucking *timeout* about this, Devin," she said, looking at him. Her gaze blurred, tears pooling in her eyes. He stopped walking. "You don't get to waltz into my life like you have been doing for the past couple of weeks and brush off the past as if it was just a speck of dust on your shoulder," she yelled, a sob breaking out of her throat. She hated herself. She hated how affected she was by this. How it was eating her alive. She hated how vulnerable she became around him. How he made her feel. She hated that she was crying out of anger.

"Catherine, I don't know what I did!" he yelled. "You are blaming me for something that I have no fucking idea what it is. I've been trying to fix this since day one. And you have refused to talk about it because you said you weren't ready. And I understood, and I tried to be patient. I respected your boundaries, but enough is enough. So don't you fucking dare say I waltzed into your life as if I don't care. I care, and that's the whole fucking problem. I've been trying to fix this for weeks!" he screamed, walking closer. "So out with it, Kitty Cat," he said, calling her the nickname he used to call her back in college. That was it. This was the last drop. Everything came crashing down around her, choking her. "What evil thing did I do for you to hate me so much?"

"You took me for granted!" she yelled, pushing at his chest. "You took my heart and crumpled it like it was a piece of paper. Both you and Emily did." The tears were falling freely now. He stepped back, looking as if he had just been slapped. "Both of you disregarded me and my feelings, Devin. And in a blink of an eye, I lost both of you," she said between sobs. Devin's demeanor softened. The rain started to pour.

"What are you talking about?" Devin asked, confused.

"I'm talking about you dating Emily senior year. I'm talking about Emily knowing about my feelings for you and still deciding to date you. I'm talking about having to watch you kiss her and watch her confess her feelings for you at the top of the stairs on the first day of finals," she yelled.

"What?"

Nine Years Ago - First day of Finals, Senior Year

"I love you. There I said it," she heard Emily say. "And I think we should kiss." She giggled, and Devin laughed. She went up one more step, seeing both of them at the top of the stairs, right in front of the door of the apartment she shared with her best friend. She saw Devin lean in, his hands going around her waist. She didn't wait around to see what happened after. She didn't. She turned around and ran. Slamming the door on her way out. She ran to the only place she knew would be safe for her. The last remnants of her heart turned into ash.

"I loved you, Devin. *I loved you.* You could have asked me to marry you, and I would have hopped on the first bus to Vegas and eloped with you. But you were never interested in the goody-two-shoes overachiever girl. Why did you think I never went on any other dates after Miles? Because I realized that no one would measure up to you. For three years, I was so helplessly in love with you, but you never noticed. You sent me mixed signals, and made me believe I had a chance," she said between sobs. "But you were so caught up with Emily you didn't even notice that I adored you. But what is worse is that Emily knew. Emily fucking knew. And she stabbed me in the back. She betrayed me and my trust," she said, wiping the tears away, but it was useless. "I created this notion in my head that we might stand a chance, that maybe I wasn't that crazy and maybe you had feelings for me, but I was wrong. You broke my heart, but even after all that, for some reason beyond me, I still love you. No matter how much I distance myself. No matter how much I try to deny it. I still love you," she yelled. "But you didn't even care all those years ago.

"And guess what? Emily ended up getting you in the end," she added. "She gets to marry you," she said, walking up to him. "You don't get to question how I put my heart back together. You don't get to question *me*," she stated, poking his chest. His hand wrapped around hers, squeezing it softly, his eyes never leaving her face. His eyes were red as if he was holding back tears. She tried to withdraw her hand, but he held her there, his hold on her hand tightening. "Let me go," she said, struggling. His other hand wrapped around the nape of her neck, stilling her.

"Stop," he whispered. She stopped struggling, melting to his touch.

"Let me go," she whispered, her voice shaky. He placed his forehead on hers.

"Oh, Catherine," he said in a whisper. He lifted his lips

and kissed her forehead, his lips lingering there. "My sweet Catherine," he whispered, shaking. Was he crying? "I'm so sorry you ever felt like that," he apologized, peppering kisses on her forehead. He wrapped his arms around her, burying his face in her neck, crying.

That was her undoing. His sobs. His pained sobs. She stopped fighting her mind. She stopped fighting and broke down, her legs giving out. He held her tight, sinking to the ground. He sat down and brought her to his lap, holding her, soothing her.

"I'm sorry," he said, kissing her head, his hands holding her tightly against him. He placed his hands on both sides of her face, making her look at him. "I never wanted to hurt you, Cat. I never meant to break your heart. You have to believe me, Catherine. You have it all wrong." He kissed her forehead. Everything in her told her to ignore him. To not believe him, because how could she be wrong when she saw it with her own eyes? But in her heart, she knew he was being sincere. In her heart, she knew he had meant every word. Her heart was beating a million miles an hour, and her chest was suddenly too small for it. She placed her hands on top of his.

"I believe you," she whispered. He opened his eyes, and clear ocean-blue eyes looked back at her.

"Catherine, if I had known you felt that way about how I was treating you—" Devin started to say, frustrated, but stopped, shaking his head. "Doesn't matter now," he added, kissing her forehead. "God, I'm such an idiot," he whispered.

"If you knew how I felt? What are you talking about Devin?"

"There was no one else, Catherine. You had my heart. You always had it. Since orientation day," he continued. "I was hopelessly in love with you too. No, scratch that. I *am* hopelessly in love with you," he whispered. He kissed her forehead. "You will always hold my heart in your hands," he said, caressing her cheeks, drawing small circles with his thumb.

"What?"

"Seeing you again after so many years, I realized my feelings never left."

"But you're marrying Emily," she said slowly, confused. He laughed. A full chest, vibrating, throwing his head back laugh. Her favorite laugh. He saw her eyes widen in shock and laughed again, his dimples appearing on his cheeks.

"Emily?" he asked. "Are you serious? You have it all wrong, Kitty Cat," he said, laughing some more. "Catherine, Emily is… it's complicated, but I promise, there's nothing between us. There never was anything between us except good friendship."

"What?" she asked, confused, moving back, landing on her ass on the wet pavement. Devin laughed.

"Yes. Emily… I'll let her explain it to you," he said. "That conversation you heard on the stairs—"

"Wait, wait," she said, standing up and pacing around. "But the conversation on the stairs—" she started, anger creeping back into her tone, but Devin laughed. "Every time you have talked to her during this trip, you always mention the wedding. And you are so invested in it. No, it's impossible. You kissed her on the stairs that night!" she swore.

"I have never kissed Emily, Kitty Cat. Well, maybe her cheek and her head, but that's about it," he replied, smiling. "She was confessing her love, yes. But she was recounting what she said to the one she is getting married to in December. Her college love. They've been together for nine years," he explained. "She was telling me how she professed her love on their date that she had just gotten back from. We never kissed. I thought you knew she was going on dates, and dipping her toes in the dating pool. She was your roommate after all," he said matter-of-factly. "And the wedding talk, I'm her best man. I'm also the one walking her down the aisle. I have to talk to her about the wedding," he continued. "I need to be invested."

"So, you're telling me all these years—" Realization dawned on her. "Oh my God!" she screamed. "I was heartbroken over nothing? I've been mad at the two of you over nothing? All of this was just a big misunderstanding?" she asked, emotions flying through her. But then, she remembered what happened three minutes before that moment nine years ago, and her heart shattered again.

"Most definitely," Devin responded, standing up. "Emily knew you liked me, and she knew I liked you," he said, smiling. "She tried playing Cupid a few times. I should've come clean back then when I figured out my feelings. I shouldn't have strung you along for so long. I should've been better. I'm sorry. We would have avoided all this heartbreak," he confessed. "Kyle also knew. He knew all along," Devin said, anger lacing his tone.

"Kyle knew?" she asked. Devin nodded. "And he still went for me...Ugh, what is wrong with him?" she groaned, throwing her hands in the air.

"What do you mean?"

"He and I broke up a week ago."

"You broke up with him?" She gave him a dismissive flicker of the hand.

"Yeah, we were fighting a lot. He didn't want to come visit, nor did he want me to visit him, and kept canceling on me. I felt he was hiding something from me, so I confronted him. He said he met someone and didn't know where we stood. He said he wanted to take a break to figure it out. So I told him I would make things easier for him and ended things. I should've seen it coming. Our relationship hasn't been the same for a while. It's fine. I'm fine. We were together for four years, and he was a good companion, but we weren't really compatible. I don't think he ever really loved me. Not like I deserve. And to be honest, I don't think I ever loved him in that sense either," she said. "God, I hate his guts."

"Then I don't feel remotely guilty for what I'm about to do."

Before she had a chance to ask him what he meant, he strode to her, cupped her face in his hands, and planted his lips on hers. Soft at first, the action taking her by surprise. It only took her a couple of seconds for her brain to connect and receive the commands, and she closed her eyes, lifting her hands to his hair, drawing him closer. His tongue swiped on her bottom lip. She parted her lips, and his tongue dove into her mouth, kissing her with force. His hands moved, trailing down her body, desperate, landing on her waist, bringing her closer. All that pent-up anger she felt towards him all these years faded away with every stroke of his tongue. All the mistakes and assumptions she made nine years ago, dissolving with each swipe of his tongue against hers. His kiss erased the guilt of nine years ago after she walked out on them, after the experience that changed her life forever. Every ounce of what she felt in the past for him came back to her like a tidal wave. Everything she had been feeling the last three weeks crashed on her like a meteor falling into earth, her heart hammering in her chest a million miles an hour. The kaleidoscope of butterflies, a frenzy on her stomach.

He drew her closer, and something hard pressed against her lower half, earning a moan from her. His warm hands slid under her shirt, caressing her back, his fingertips leaving little fires burning across her skin. The heat traveled all over her body, pooling in her lower belly. His hands stopped their roaming, stopping at her hips, bringing her closer still. The hands gripping her hips tightened their hold, sure to leave marks, claiming her. She moaned into his mouth. He groaned. His kiss felt possessive and territorial. Primal. Feral. Like he had been holding onto this moment since freshman year and was finally able to let go. Something hard hit the back of her thighs. The hood of the car. The rain around them kept falling, thunder rolling. He broke the kiss, both of their breaths agitated. He placed his forehead on hers.

"Catherine…" he groaned breathlessly. His hands caged her to the car, placed on either side of her hips.

"I know," she responded, cupping his face. His swollen lips turned into a smile. She passed her thumb across his bottom lip.

"Catherine… Please tell me this is finally happening. Please, tell me I'm not dreaming, Catherine," he whispered. "Please, don't let this be a dream," he prayed, closing his eyes and taking a deep breath.

"It's not," she mumbled back. He groaned. She shivered, and she didn't know if it was because of the way his groan made her feel warm in places she didn't know could get warm or because of the cold air around them.

"We should get back to the B&B before the rain becomes worse. But I promise we will return to this." She nodded. "Let's get you dried up. I don't want you to catch pneumonia." He cupped her cheek, leaning in and kissing her lips softly. "Come on," he said, breaking the kiss and taking her hand, entwining their fingers together. He walked to her side of the car and opened the door for her. He walked to his side and got in. He turned the heater to the max. "Ready?" he asked, looking at her, and gave her a lopsided smile. She nodded.

He reached for her hand and brought it to his lips, kissing the knuckles. He placed both hands on his lap and drove away. She looked at his profile as he drove, smiling. She felt a bottomless peace and happiness at this and at how natural it felt, like the final piece of the puzzle of who she was finally coming together.

Chapter Twenty

Devin - First day of Finals, Senior Year

He was walking back from the bar when he spotted Emily kissing someone who hopped in a cab. Frowning, he couldn't believe his eyes and what he just witnessed. Once the cab left, he walked over to her.

"I gather the date was a success?" he asked.

"Fuck! You scared the crap out of me," Emily said, jumping and shoving him away nervously. "What are you doing here?"

"I was on my way to your place. Significant other?" he asked, nodding in the direction of where the cab had left. Emily opened her eyes wide. He saw in the dim sidewalk light the color drain from her face.

"Don't tell, Catherine, please. She will hate me if she finds out you knew before her."

"Your secret is safe with me," he acknowledged with a nod. She exhaled. "Come on, I'll walk you back to your apartment. I need to ask Kitty Cat something," he said, throwing an arm around Emily's shoulders.

"What are you gonna ask her?" she asked, the past two minutes forgotten.

"I'm going to ask her if she wants to go to Canada with me," he mentioned. "Quebec City and Montreal to be exact."

"Oh my god, those are her—" Emily started to say, but he interrupted her.

"Her bucket list places. I know," he finished. "I'm gonna do it, Emily," he declared. "I'm gonna tell her how I feel. I'm gonna tell her how I've been feeling about her for the past four years. I'm finally going to confess that I am utterly, madly, deeply in love with her."

Emily squeaked. "Oh my God, Devin. I'm so happy for you," she said, getting her keys out and opening the main door of the building. "She's going to love it," she continued, climbing up the stairs.

"I should've come clean a long time ago. Hopefully, she'll take me. Hopefully, she'll forgive me for not coming clean sooner. Hopefully, she doesn't feel like I've been leading her on because she is so wrong Em. I love her so much," he declared.

"Oh my god, look at us. Finding love. Being in love," she said dreamingly.

"So, how did you confess?"

"So, we went out on a date to our favorite restaurant. The same one we went to on our first date. And once we were settled in, I just said it. I said 'I love you. There I said it.' and then I said, 'And I think we should kiss.'" He laughed because she looked happy. He had never seen her this happy. He leaned in and hugged her. He broke away when he heard the downstairs entrance door slam shut. He looked back at Emily, and she just shrugged. "Of course, we laughed, but then we leaned in and kissed. More like make-out in the middle of the restaurant, but you get the gist. We held hands the rest of the date," she continued, hugging him again.

His hand tightened around Catherine's fingers. He brought her hand to his lips and kissed it. He returned it to his lap, drawing lazy circles with his thumb. He laughed quietly to himself, remembering that night.

"What are you laughing about?" she asked, turning to him. He turned to her and smiled.

"You." She frowned. "I can't believe you thought I was dating Emily. And don't get me started on thinking I was engaged to her. I can't believe you thought we would do something like that," he said softly.

"God, I was so stupid. But it really looked that way," she replied, looking down. She removed her hand from his.

"Honestly, you broke my heart. When you left, I felt a piece of me die. I felt a piece of my soul leave my body. I was left with a gaping wound in my chest. I was never able to love anyone the way I loved, or rather love, you. You have to know that, but I'm partly at fault." He shrugged, looking briefly at her. He heard Catherine take a sharp breath. "I should've gone after you that night. I should've known it was utter bullshit what you said. I should've fought for you. I should've called for a *timeout*. But I was too much of a coward. Just like I was too much of a coward back then for not telling you about my feelings sooner, but that changes tonight," he continued, parking the car and turning to Catherine who was shaking, one hand on her mouth, suppressing her sobs. He stretched his hand and cradled her face. He leaned in and kissed her head. "It's okay. You are here now. *We* are here now."

"I'm so sorry, Devin," she apologized. "I'm so sorry I hurt you. No amount of apologizing will be enough. No amount of excuses will be enough," she apologized again.

"We need ground rules," she added after a few minutes. He sighed.

"Agreed. What ground rules, Kitty Cat?"

"I don't want to go public yet. We have a lot of talking to do. A lot of catching up. A lot of things we need to get off our chests Dev, I don't want the world to intervene. I don't want the world telling us what we should or shouldn't do now that we are together. I hurt you. That's a fact. I hurt you and Emily. I need to atone for that. We need to heal first," she said. He looked down because as much as it pained him to admit it, he needed to heal from the nine years of agony. He nodded his agreement.

"I agree. We need time. We need to relearn each other. We are not the same people from nine years ago. We need to start from zero. We don't have to rush into this. We can take it slow. As slow as we want. As long as you are taking it slow with *me*. I don't want to let you go. These past nine years, Catherine, they've been hell. I'm not joking. Everyone knew I was never the same after you left."

"I'm so sorry, Dev," she said between sobs. His hand drew small circles on her back, soothing her. "I hated you for so long. I was so angry at you. And now I know it was for nothing. I've missed you so terribly these last nine years. So many accomplishments I had, and you were the first person I wanted to tell. But I couldn't. And then my—" She sobbed and stopped. It broke his heart to see her so broken. So vulnerable. He leaned in and kissed her forehead, urging her to keep going, to let it out. To rip the band aid off. He moved the hair out of her face, drying her tears with his thumb. "I couldn't bring myself to do it. I couldn't bring myself to call you. And now I know I should have," she explained. "And I loved you so much. God, I loved you so much it hurt walking away like that. I have never loved anyone that way. Not even

Kyle. I think partly that's why it was so easy to break it off with him. And these last couple of weeks, it has brought back so many memories. It made me realize I never stopped loving you, but I was still so mad at you. And then I felt like you were cheating on Emily because I had this notion that you were engaged to her. But it turns out you aren't, and she is marrying someone else. And God... I feel like a monster. We were best friends, and I left her with no warning. God, she must hate me so much," she said, her voice breaking. He brought her back to his chest.

"Something else happened that week, didn't it?" he asked. She nodded, wiping away a tear. He hugged her. "I don't know what it was. I really don't. And if you don't feel comfortable telling me yet, I understand," he said, kissing her head. "You don't have to tell me now. You can tell me when you feel most comfortable." He hugged her tighter. They stayed like that for a while.

"I'm not ready to talk about it," she said in a whisper once she calmed down. He kissed the top of her head. "It's something... personal. I'm not ready yet to talk about it."

"It's okay, I understand," he whispered back. He cradled her face, and kissed her lips softly. "Are you well enough to go inside? We have cold stuff in the trunk." She nodded. "I can take them inside and then come back and walk you in." She bobbed her head, her lip trembling. "Okay," he said, kissing her again. She got out of the car, and he followed. They walked to the trunk, and she leaned in.

"I meant what I said," she whispered.

"I know," he replied, throwing an arm around her shoulders and bringing her to his chest. He placed his chin on top of her head. She wrapped her arms around his waist. His phone decided to ring at that moment.

"You're gonna answer that?" she asked. He sighed. He

pulled out his phone, and Emily's name showed on the screen.

"Hey Em, right now is not a good time," he answered, looking down at Catherine. He nuzzled her nose with his and kissed it.

"This is an emergency. What color do you want your bowtie? You can pick navy, red, or golden colors. Where are you? What are you doing?" she asked.

"None of your business, Emily," he said, sighing.

"Is that Catherine you just kissed? I swear to God Devin, if it's her and you are hiding from me that you reconciled and that you found out what happened, I swear to God and everything that's holy, I will uninvite you from my wedding," she threatened.

"I'm walking you down the aisle. You can't uninvite me."

"Aha, so it is Catherine," she exclaimed. "You have to tell me exactly what happened. You guys talked about what happened nine years ago, right? Did she tell you what happened?" He looked down at Catherine and she gave him an anxious smile.

"Don't be mean to Emily. She's the only one that has been tolerating your ass for the last nine years," Catherine said.

"Put her on the phone, I wanna talk to her. I wanna know. I need to know."

"No, Emily, I won't put Catherine on the phone," he protested. "We are taking things slow, and that includes her talking to you." Catherine sighed. Catherine released herself from his embrace, extending her hand to him. He gave her a puzzled look.

"Rip off the band aid, right?" she whispered.

"Catherine, you don't have to."

"She deserves to know."

"Are you sure?" She nodded. "So much for keeping it in

our bubble, huh?" He smirked. "Em, someone wants to talk to you. Although I don't think this should be a conversation you guys should have over the phone."

"I need to hear her voice, Dev. Put her on the phone," Emily demanded. He sighed.

"You guys speak while I get these inside," he said, handing Catherine his phone. She nodded and walked to the patch of grass near the car, pacing around the wet grass. It has already stopped raining.

"Hey," he heard her say.

He turned around and started to busy himself with the stuff in the trunk, giving them some space. It took him a collective half an hour to walk most of the things inside. Thankfully, Gloria was awake and told him where to put everything. When he walked back to grab the last of the things, Catherine was sitting on the trunk of the car, his phone in her hands. She wiped her cheeks as he approached. He sat beside her.

"I gather it went... okay?" he asked.

"She hates me. And I don't blame her," she whispered. "I told her what happened, and she just laughed, told me I was out of my goddamn mind, and hung up. Then called again, crying, and told me she hated me, but that she also loved me and missed me like crazy."

"Sounds like Emily."

"God, I was so stupid. I should've known. She asked for my number and told me we were going to have another lengthy conversation about this. But I feel it won't be by phone, it'll be in person. She probably won't talk to me ever again after, but it's okay. I really can't blame her. I have only myself to blame." He leaned in and kissed her temple.

"Emily is a lot of things. But one thing I know for a fact is she is not a Catherine hater. She doesn't hate you, Kitty

Cat," he assured her, his lips lingering in her temple. "She's definitely mad. Pissed. Angry, but mostly, she was hurt. She *is* hurt. Give her some time." She nodded. "Let's go inside," he said, kissing her temple again. He helped her stand up and entwined their fingers together. They picked up the last of the things and Catherine's purse. They walked the length of the short parking lot in silence. He went to the kitchen and placed the last of the things there.

"Thanks a bunch, Devin. I hope Catherine is feeling better. Did she go up to her room? Maybe I can bring her some tea. Chamomile is really good for headaches. It will also help her sleep better. Maybe some lavender tea could help too," Gloria suggested, worriedly.

"No, it's okay. I got it. She had some ibuprofen on the way here," he lied. "She went back to her room. But thank you."

"Please, let me know if there's anything I can do to help," Gloria offered.

"That's very sweet of you, thank you," he said and left the kitchen. Catherine was seated on the first step of the stairs. "Come on," he mumbled, extending his hand. She took it, and they both went up the stairs. He walked her to her room. She unlocked her door and looked up at him. He leaned in and placed a gentle kiss on her lips. "I'll see you in the morning. Get some rest," he added and kissed her again. He went to walk away, but she tugged at his hand. He looked back at her, and her eyes were sad and tired. He sighed. He knew exactly what she wanted and needed. He nodded. "Let me shower and change into my pajamas. Give me twenty minutes, okay?" She nodded. She went into her room, and he did just that. Showered and put his pajamas on. He walked out and knocked on her door. She opened a second later, already in her pajamas, her hair wet. "You shouldn't sleep with your hair wet. You'll get sick," he chastised, walking in and closing the door.

"There's no hairdryer. I always sleep with my hair wet. It's okay," she replied, walking to the bed. She got under the covers and patted the spot beside her. He walked to it and got under the covers, wrapping an arm around her and bringing her closer to his chest. He kissed the top of her head, inhaling her scent. *Lavender*. He felt her breathing slow and her body go limp in his arms, and he knew she'd fallen asleep. He kissed her head again.

"I love you so much Catherine," he whispered before succumbing to sleep.

Chapter Twenty-One

Catherine

"Hey," Catherine whispered, sitting down on the bench. She took a deep breath, a lump forming in the back of her throat.

"Hey? HEY?" Emily yelled on the other side of the line. "Fucking hey? Are you serious right now, Catherine Elizabeth Babbitt? After nine fucking years, you just say hey?" she screeched incredulously.

"I'm sorry," Catherine muttered, a tear falling from her eye. She wiped it away. She swallowed the lump in her throat.

"What the hell happened to you? Why the hell did you run off on us like that, Catherine?" Emily asked, her voice softer. Catherine stopped pacing and looked down at her feet, another tear escaping her eye. She didn't wipe it away this time, letting it run down her cheek. She took a deep breath.

"I thought you were dating Devin," Catherine mumbled, biting her lip.

"*WHAT?*" Emily shrieked, laughing in disbelief. "You thought I was dating that doofus? Seriously?" Emily said.

"You better say sike right now, Catherine. You better say you are joking."

"I saw the two of you on the top of the stairs on the first day of finals. You said '*I love you, and I think we should kiss*'. And it looked like you were confessing to him. I put two and two together. I'm sorry. Now, I know it was a big misunderstanding. I have been hating you and been angry at the both of you for nine years over nothing," Catherine answered softly.

"You thought—" Emily started and groaned. "You are out of your goddamn mind." The line went dead.

"Hello?" Catherine asked, looking at the screen. Emily hung up. Another tear slipped from Catherine's eye. Devin's phone began to ring, Emily's caller ID on the screen. She picked it up and stayed quiet.

"I hate you," Emily sobbed. "Seriously? Me? Dating Devin? When you were hopelessly in love with him? Did you really think I was that crappy of a friend? Did you honestly think I was capable of doing that to you? Stabbing you in the back like that? Catherine, you were like a sister to me. Why would you think I would do something as terrible as that? Why would you even entertain the idea?"

"I'm sorry," Catherine whispered, whipping away another tear.

"Catherine, I'm a lesbian, be serious. Me and Devin?"

"Wait, what?" Catherine asked, shocked.

"Oh my god, he didn't tell you. God, I love him so much," Emily said proudly. "I don't bat for his team, Catherine. Gosh, you never even suspected it?"

"No," Catherine replied. "During the four years we lived together, I never saw you with anyone or going out on dates. You never mentioned anything either. I just assumed you weren't interested in dating. That you were invested in your studies and the school paper."

"It was a different time. People weren't as accepting. Society still isn't totally accepting. Devin knew. He caught me sending off my girlfriend back then, fiancée now," she explained. "What you saw—"

"I know. Devin explained that you were telling him about your date. He also explained that it's the person you are marrying. Congratulations," Catherine said. "All this time, every time he would call you or pick up your call and you guys would talk about wedding stuff, I thought it was yours and Devin's wedding," she explained. A gagging sound came from the other side of the line. She chuckled.

"Dumbass. Thanks for the venue, by the way. It helped a lot. You literally saved my ass. And my wedding," Emily replied. Catherine chuckled quietly.

"Consider it reparations for the last nine years. I know it's not enough, but it's a start," Catherine whispered. Emotions choked her, her eyes hot with tears. "God, I'm so sorry, Em," Catherine sobbed. "I was so selfish. I should've gone to you. I should've talked it out. I should've confronted you. I'm so sorry." She heard a sniffle on the other side of the line.

"You were selfish and broke so many hearts along the way. Mine included."

"I know," Catherine acknowledged.

"When are you guys coming back?"

"In about a week. Maybe less. We can meet up for coffee or something if you want."

The line went quiet, and she looked to see if Emily had hung up, but she didn't. The silence stretched on for a couple of minutes, neither of them saying anything. The silence spoke volumes.

"I missed you so much, Cat," Emily whispered, breaking the silence.

"I missed you too, Em."

"I loved you, you know? Like the sister I never had," Emily said. "I still do."

"Me too," Catherine replied. She looked up and saw Devin. "Em, Dev is coming back."

"Tell him to send me your number. And thank him for not outing me, letting me have that choice in telling you."

"I will."

"We'll talk later," Emily added.

"Yes," Catherine answered and hung up.

"I love you so much, Catherine."

She heard him whisper as she drifted off to sleep the night before. She woke up tangled in his arms, her head cradled on his chest, listening to his heartbeat. He was softly snoring. She tilted her head and looked at his peaceful face. She lifted her hand, tracing his nose, eyebrows, and lips with her pointer finger. He placed a soft kiss on her finger.

"Now, this is the perfect way to wake up. I could wake up like this every morning for the rest of my life," he mumbled, his voice deep with sleep, his eyes still closed. He tightened his grip on her, placing a kiss on top of her head. "Good morning," he said, opening his eyes, his blue eyes bright.

"Good morning," she whispered.

"We have to leave this little cocoon today."

"I know."

"I don't want to."

"Me either."

"We don't have to," he replied, matter-of-factly, giving

her a toothy smile, his dimples making an appearance. She chuckled.

"We have to. We have the announcement today. And the town hall meeting," she replied, moving away from his embrace. He tightened his hold on her.

"Where do you think you are going?" he asked, rolling on top of her. She squealed. His hand caressed her face, his knuckles softly tracing her cheek. He did the same thing she did when he woke. He traced her face with his pointer finger. His finger diverted its path down her jaw and to her collarbone, lingering on the necklace she wore, the same one he gave her for Christmas all those years ago. A look of longing crossed his eyes. His eyes studied her like he couldn't believe this was happening. His gaze softened, and he smiled. Her hands cradled his face bringing him down for a kiss. "I'm not going to kiss you until I brush my teeth," he said, rolling away from her. She suddenly felt cold. "I'll be right back." Leaving the bed, he walked to the door. She walked to her bathroom, and brushed her teeth. She felt a pair of hands on her hips when she was spitting the toothpaste and rinsing her mouth. "Good morning again," Devin said in a low voice, kissing her neck, wrapping his arms around her waist, bringing her closer. She snuggled into his chest and looked at him through the mirror.

"Good morning," she greeted, caressing his forearms. He spun her around and kissed her softly, his hands cupping her face. He kissed her lips, then her nose, and finally her forehead.

"We are in trouble," he murmured against her forehead, his tone serious.

"What?" she asked worriedly.

"Maggie saw me enter your room," he said, stepping back. "And I'm guessing she'll be knocking on your door soon," he mentioned as there was a knock on the door. She sighed.

"So much for keeping it secret. I bet the whole office knows by now. Probably the whole town," she surmised, walking to the door. She opened it, and Maggie stood in the hallway, her hands on her hips. She opened the door wider, letting her in, and leaned against it as she closed it. She looked in the bathroom's direction, and Devin was leaning against the doorframe. Maggie moved her gaze between the two of them.

"What's going on here?" she asked, pointing between them. "Did you guys finally figure it out?"

"We did," she concurred.

"About damn time. Did y'all bang already?" Maggie asked.

"Maggie!" Catherine exclaimed.

"Oh, come on, the sexual tension between the two of you is nauseating," Maggie stated, gagging. "You're telling me you guys haven't noticed it? Felt it?" Maggie questioned, rolling her eyes. "My goodness, you really are that oblivious. Well, whatever happens, I hope you guys work on it fast. We have a big day ahead," she continued, walking to the door. "Move, I need to have breakfast," she ordered, moving Catherine.

"Wait, Mags…" Catherine said, grabbing her arm and stopping her. "Please don't tell anyone. Not even Maverick or the boss," Catherine pleaded. "We still have a lot to figure out, and we won't be going public anytime soon. Not yet." Maggie nodded in understanding. "Thank you," she mouthed as Maggie left. She closed the door and sighed.

"Well, that went well," Devin stated, walking towards her from the bathroom doorway. She turned around and walked to him, wrapping her arms around his waist. He wrapped his arms around her and kissed the crown of her head. "We need to get ready to have breakfast."

"Can we go back to bed for a little longer?"

For the first time in nine years, she felt complete. She felt at ease. She felt happy. And that was a feeling she did not want to let go. Not yet. She needed a few more minutes of their little bubble.

"Oh my sweet Catherine, how can I put it into words? There's nothing you could ask me that I would deny you," he declared, walking them back to the bed.

They were in the Jenkins district office. Maggie was outside, along with Maverick, doing some last-minute paperwork, and both of their bosses were on their way. They had an hour to burn before the new board members and CEO arrived. She was going over last-minute papers when she felt his intense gaze on her. Like burning coal.

"Stop looking at me," she scolded, not looking at him. He chuckled. She heard the scraping of his chair and his heavy footsteps. Her heart started to beat a million miles an hour. He walked behind her and placed his hands on both sides of her, caging her.

"I refuse to do anything else that is not admiring you," he murmured in her ear, his breath caressing her cheek. He kissed her temple, making her shudder. The doorknob rattled, and the door opened. Brian and Michael walked in. "So, are these part of the people's profiles and paperwork?" Devin asked from beside her and picked up a stack of papers from her side.

"Yes," she said in a shaky voice. How in the hell he managed to move so fast was beyond her. He looked at her and winked, walking away. She let out a breath she didn't know she was holding. She lifted her gaze, and Michael was already looking at her, giving her a conspiratory smile. "Don't," she mouthed just for him to see. He grinned, shaking his head.

"Catherine. How did you spend your day off?" Brian asked her, not paying much attention to the elephant in the room. "Did Devin treat you well? I hope he took you out of town," he said, sitting down. She chuckled nervously.

"He did. We went shopping as Gloria's proxy. She needed some things for the Fireflies Festival and couldn't go buy them herself, so she asked us."

"Look at you," Michael said. "Using your free day to the max." He smirked. She gave him a scowling gaze.

"Really?" she asked rhetorically. He chuckled.

"So, what do we have?" Brian asked, looking over Devin's shoulder to the papers he was reading. "Is this the paperwork of the folks we are meeting today?"

"Yep. These are all the people we are meeting in an hour. This is the CEO," Devin said, showing his boss a paper. "Cat picked him. His resume is impressive, and he comes from this very own small town, he's a resident. So he knows the struggle."

"He's the perfect man for the job," Brian said, reading the man's resume. "Impressive, young lady," Brian praised, looking at her. She gave him a nod.

"Good job, team. The town hall is reserved, and the spiderweb was informed," Michael mentioned. "And you did all of this in three weeks."

"That deserves a celebration," Brian proposed.

"We have the Fireflies Festival for that," Maggie expressed, entering the room with two packets of papers in both hands. "Plenty of activities happening there. No need to go out to celebrate anywhere else," she stated, placing one of the stacks of papers on the table. "These are the welcome packets." She placed the other stack on the table. "And these are the individual contracts." She pointed to them.

"You did all of this?" Michael asked her, perusing through the folders.

"With all due respect, boss, I'm not getting paid to be pretty," she retorted. "If I did, I would be in New York City with a modeling career."

"Yeah, but you are a scheduler," he pointed out.

"But I also have a degree in human resources. So you needed me," she answered, leaving the room.

"Remind me to give her a raise when we go back," Michael said.

"Yes, boss," Catherine replied.

They spent the remainder of the hour eating a small lunch and debating if the weather was too cold to go trick-or-treating and how Heather wanted to dress as a little fairy.

"I'm telling you, every week, she gets a new obsession. Last week, she was obsessed with bumblebees. This week, it's fairies. Next week? Probably ladybugs. Or the fireflies since I'm bringing her to the festival," Michael said, taking a sip from his coffee.

"You are?" Maggie asked excitedly. "Oh, she's going to have so much fun. There will be tons of kid-friendly rides and activities."

"Catherine, can you babysit her? I have to be around the townsfolk," Michael asked.

"Boss, you know you don't have to ask me to babysit Heats. You know I would do it in a heartbeat."

"What about you, Devin? You like kids?" Michael asked him. Devin looked around and everyone was looking at him, her included, awaiting his answer.

"I love kids," he replied, giving the room a shy smile. That smile warmed her heart and sent the kaleidoscope of butterflies into a frenzy inside her stomach. "I have two nieces and two godsons," he continued. She smiled.

"Then it's settled. You and Catherine will be on babysitting duties at the festival," Michael mentioned, giving Maggie a conspiratory smile. Maggie looked at Devin and then at her, wiggling her eyebrows when she looked at her. Catherine rolled her eyes.

"Whatever you both are planning, I don't want any part in it," Catherine said, returning her gaze to her computer.

"What are you talking about?" Maggie asked, feigning cluelessness.

"Mmmmhhhmm," Catherine replied. There was a knock on the door. Maverick popped his head inside.

"They are here," he announced. Michael nodded.

"Let's get this show on the road, shall we?" Michael said, looking at all of them.

Oh boy, what kind of show it would be.

Chapter Twenty-Two

Devin

A shitshow. That's what the town hall with the townsfolk was, a complete and utter shitshow. Everyone was talking above everyone. Not one single person let the other talk. A loud whistle reverberated around the room right beside him. He flinched and looked for the source, finding his petite girlfriend being the cause of it. *Girlfriend.* He liked the sound of it. He looked around the room. As if by a spell, everyone quieted down.

"I need you all to settle down folks," Catherine said in a booming voice. Everyone sat down, and silence reigned in the room. "I know it's hard to get used to change. I do. I really do. But rest assured, my team and I did extensive research, and we picked the best of the best," she continued, looking around.

"She is right. My team, along with Congressman Johns' team, picked the best of the best. I can assure you all, this situation won't happen again," Brian added in his best politician's voice. "Now, can we introduce the new CEO and board of the treatment company? So we can move to more pressing details, like the Fireflies Festival?" Some heads nodded. "Okay," he said and introduced the new board and CEO. The town erupted in cheers as they realized it was one of their own.

They spent the next hour and a half discussing and getting to know the new hires. The townsfolk all questioned them, making it seem like a third interview. The rest of the meeting went smoothly. They found new vendors and donors, bringing the fundraising to almost the goal. The rest, they expected, would be fulfilled with the sales of the tickets. The town hall ended, and the folks left, along with their bosses.

"Cat, can I leave?" Maggie asked in a hurry, handing Catherine some papers.

"What's the hurry?"

"I'm going on a date," she said, walking away. "Don't wait up, Mom," Maggie exclaimed, turning around and blowing a kiss to Catherine. Catherine rolled her eyes and chuckled. They were the only ones left in the space. Devin walked to her and wrapped his arms around her, burying his face in her neck.

"Maybe we should go on a date too," he mumbled, kissing her shoulder. "A proper one. Our first date. Maybe we can go to that restaurant with the deck," he said, kissing her temple, his lips lingering there. He inhaled, taking in her lavender scent. "What do you say, Kitty Cat?"

"I think I would like that."

Someone cleared their throat behind them, making both of them jump. They turned around and found Maverick standing there.

"I see you made up," he mentioned, his eyes looking everywhere but them. Catherine put distance between them.

"What do you need, Mav?" she asked him.

"My mom sent me to ask if you have any plans for Halloween. The neighborhood throws this Halloween bash, and she wants all of you to come. You too, Mack," Maverick explained.

"I was supposed to go trick-or-treating with Heats," she said. "But we can swing by after. You know she's an early bird." Maverick smiled and nodded.

"That works, boss," he stated, stuffing his hands in his pockets. "Okay, I'll let you guys get back to whatever you guys were doing. And don't worry, I won't be telling anyone. It's not my business to tell," he said, turning around and leaving.

"So…" Devin muttered, turning to her. She rolled her eyes and pushed him away, earning a chuckle from him.

"You are going to lose, Mack," she challenged, pointing a finger at him. They ended up going back to the same bar they went to a couple of weeks ago. She turned to the table and grabbed her beer, taking a long gulp from it. She turned back to the pool table and positioned herself to hit the white ball. He walked behind her and slid his hands up her waist. He felt her shudder. He leaned in, nibbling on her earlobe.

"Are you sure about that?" he whispered, running his nose down her jaw. She shot and missed, groaning, all the blood rushing to the front of his jeans.

"That's foul play."

"All is fair in this game," Devin said, smirking. He picked up his billiard cue and walked to where the white ball was, leaning in, and aiming. Devin felt her hand sliding down his back. He shot, hitting the white ball and scoring one. Devin turned around, smirking. "It's going to take more than a soft hand down my back, sweetheart." He winked, walking to the white ball and leaning in.

"Oh, something like this?" she asked innocently, hiking her hand up the front of his leg, skimming over his groin. He shot and missed. He groaned. "All is fair in this game, right sweetheart?" she whispered in his ear, walking back to the table to munch on a fry. He took out his wallet, fishing out a couple of bills and slapping them on the table, grabbing his jacket and hers in one hand, her arm in the other. "Hey, I wasn't finished with the game or my fries," she argued as he dragged her outside. He walked to the car, turned her, and caged her in. She looked into his eyes, a smirk on her lips. "Sore loser," she taunted. He chuckled. He pressed himself against her, her eyes opening wide.

"We have a situation. I'm not a sore loser, but I would rather not have a hard-on in the middle of the bar," he said, his voice deep.

"Well, that sounds like a *you* problem, Mack," she sassed back. He took a sharp breath in.

"Do not sass me now, baby girl."

"Or what?" His hand cupped her jaw, forcing her to look at him.

"Stop this. I'm not going to do this in the back of a rental car, and I certainly won't do it in the B&B," he stated. "Trust me, when I take you, we will definitely not leave the bed for days. In the meantime—" He leaned in and kissed her, the hand he had on her jaw going to the back of her neck, bringing her closer. She moaned, opening her mouth, and he took his chance, exploring her mouth with his tongue. She brought her hands to his hair, tugging lightly. He groaned and ground into her, his pants impossibly tight. He was going to take care of that back in the B&B, not now.

Now, he wanted to ravish her lips, taste and touch her, her

body heat a welcoming presence in the cold weather. His other hand went to her hip and brought her closer. His phone rang in his pocket, shaking him out of the bubble he'd created around them. He detached his lips from Catherine, dropping his forehead on hers, groaning.

"It better not be my boss," he rasped.

His phone stopped ringing. He detached himself from her, walking a couple of feet away. He got his phone out just as it started ringing again. It was Emily on a video call. He looked over to Catherine. She was putting on her jacket and fixing her hair. He picked up the call.

"You better be dying."

"No, I am not. But you look a little flustered over there. A little out of breath. Doing some cardio?" Emily asked, a knowing smile on her face.

"What do you want?" he asked, wringing out all the patience he could muster. Catherine was walking to him, his jacket opened in her hands. He shrugged it on. She walked back to the car, trying to open the door. He unlocked the car and walked to her, giving her the keys. "Turn it on and crank the heat up," he said, bending down to kiss the top of her head. "Emily Choi, you have three seconds to tell me why you called me, or I swear to God, you can find someone else to walk you down the aisle," he threatened. Emily chuckled.

"Please, you will walk me down the aisle no matter what. You know that. I'm sorry I interrupted though. I forget that you're basically a horny teenager around Cat," she teased, smirking. He hung up on her and walked to the driver's side of the car.

"Did you just hang up on Emily?" Catherine asked when he settled in. He gave her a wide smile.

"Absolutely. Well deserved," he replied and started

driving. She laughed, and it sounded like music to his ears. He placed a hand on her thigh, drawing small circles with his thumb. "I meant what I said, by the way. When we decide to go for a home run, it will not be in the back of the rental car or the B&B. I've waited fourteen years for it, and I intend for it to be special. Mind-blowing," he continued. She snorted. "What?" he asked, confused.

"Mind-blowing?"

He winked. "Yes. Mind-blowing."

"You have a lot of confidence," she argued.

"Oh baby, you have no idea," he said, squeezing her thigh.

She yelped. "Stop that," she whispered. He chuckled. They arrived at the B&B and made it to their rooms.

"Good night, Kitty Cat," he said, kissing her forehead, her nose, and then her lips. "I'll see you tomorrow," he whispered, tucking a piece of hair behind her ear. He kissed her forehead one more time and walked to his room. He closed the door, locking it, and leaned back against it, closing his eyes.

The pressure in front of his pants was impossibly tight. He unbuckled his belt and undid the button of his jeans, pulling the zipper down. He exhaled. He walked to the bathroom, turned the shower on, and undressed, stepping inside and letting the cool water roll down his back. He leaned his hands on the wall, closing his eyes. A certain black-haired woman appeared behind his eyelids. Her beautiful emerald green eyes looking at him.

One of his hands grabbed his already hard cock, pumping slowly up and down. He pictured what it would be like to be inside of her. How soft her skin would feel on his hands, on his mouth, on his tongue. What her mouth would feel like on him. Around him. Kissing him. Licking him. Sucking him. How she would moan underneath him. The hand on his cock grew faster in movement, his thumb caressing the tip, getting a moan out of him, bitting his lip. He was close, so close. His hand movements became erratic, faster. The pressure at the base of his spine strong, his vision going dark. The picture of Catherine, a moaning mess on top of him, riding him. He groaned, his fist hitting the wall, and he felt it. His orgasm hit him like a train. His knees buckled, and white spots formed in his vision. The hand on his cock kept pumping, riding his high as he emptied himself. Gasping, he opened his eyes. He needed to do something about this. About this wait. The need to feel her, hear her come undone underneath him, feel her naked skin around him was too strong. He needed to bury himself in her. But not here. Not now.

Devin stopped daydreaming about her, feeling his cock harden at the thought of her writhing under him in pleasure, and turned the water colder, letting the ice-cold water cool his body down. Showered quickly, he was walking to his bed, in nothing but his pajama pants, when a soft knock sounded. A smile formed on his lips, knowing who was on the other side of the door. He opened it and leaned against the frame.

"Miss me already?" Devin asked, looking at Catherine. She scoffed, rolling her eyes, and walked past him to the bed. She pulled the covers away and snuggled inside.

"Are you coming?" Devin smirked, closing the door and walking to the other side of the bed, getting under the covers. Snaking an arm under Catherine's head, the other circling her waist, he brought her closer to him, her back molding to his chest. He kissed her head and snuggled her. "Do you know how many nights I wished we did this back in college?" Catherine whispered after a couple of minutes. He kissed her head again, exhaling.

"Me too. Since the first day I saw you," Devin whispered back. "But we have now and the future. I never stopped loving you. Ever." He kissed her head again. "And I will forever love you." She snuggled closer to his body, and he tightened his hold on her. They both drifted into sleep.

"I did my little magic, and she is a princess," Maggie told him. Catherine decided she wanted to dress as a princess for Halloween to match the fairy costume Heather was wearing. "I went shopping yesterday and found the perfect princess dress and crown. I did her hair and makeup, and she looks stunning," she said, her glittery wings flinging around. As soon as she stopped bouncing around, Catherine appeared, standing at the top of the stairs. He looked at her, and his breath caught in his chest. She was wearing a short lilac puffy dress, a crown on top of her head, and her black hair in loose waves framing her face and running down her back. "What did I tell you?" Maggie asked, elbowing him. Someone whistled beside him. He peeled his gaze from Catherine and looked at Maverick.

"Damn boss, looking very Mia Thermopolis," Maverick mumbled. Devin looked back to the stairs, Catherine already at the foot of them.

"Well, thank you. I was aiming more for Queen Clarisse, but Mia Thermopolis works as well," Catherine replied. "Hello, my Prince Charming." she said, looking at Devin. "Ready to go trick-or-treating?"

"You look beautiful," he whispered, mesmerized by how she looked. Despite what happened, and that she hurt him, he knew it was all worth it, because in the end he got her. The woman he had been helplessly in love with for most of his life.

"And you look handsome," she winked. He smiled and kissed her forehead.

"Ready?" he asked. She nodded.

And boy was the night long.

Chapter Twenty-Three

Catherine - Halloween Night

"That's a lot of kids," Devin pointed out as he parked the car.

Michael's house was in the middle of a cul-de-sac. Fall and Halloween decorations adorning the houses around them. Kids with all sorts of outfits and costumes were prancing and running on the streets and sidewalks. It was fairly early, with the last bit of sunlight in the sky.

"Well, it's Halloween, Devin," she replied matter-of-factly. He parked right in front of Michael's house and turned the car off, reaching behind him for a bag with a pumpkin pattern.

"Don't sass me, Kitty Cat," he mused.

"Me? Never," she retorted, smirking. She opened the door and got out of the car, waiting for him on the sidewalk. "What's that?" she questioned, nodding towards the bag.

"You'll see. Ready, princess?" he asked, extending his elbow. She hooked her arm through his and nodded.

"Ready, Prince Charming." They walked to the door and knocked on it.

"You're late," Heather complained as she opened the

door. "Everyone else is already trick-or-treating. All the good candy is gone," she added as she walked inside the house, her little fairy wings flopping up and down.

"Heats, Halloween has barely started. You still have a chance," Catherine replied. "Where's Trooper?" she asked, looking around for the little hairball.

"Upstairs. Come on, we have to go now."

"I don't think all the good candy is gone," Devin mentioned as he stretched his arm with the bag on it. Heather looked at him suspiciously. "Go on," he added, smiling. Heather walked to him and reached for the bag. She picked it up and held it at arm's length, eyeing it warily. She opened it and squealed, sitting on the floor and turning the bag upside down, candy flying all over.

"I take it back, Auntie Cathy," she mentioned as she picked up a candy bar and broke the wrapper, popping it into her mouth. "I guess you are cool," Heather said, looking at Devin and shrugging. Devin laughed.

"What is this mess?" Olive questioned, putting her hands on her hips. Heather looked guilty, finishing her candy and swallowing.

"He gave them to me," she argued, pointing at Devin. Devin scoffed.

"Excuse me, I gave you candy. Why are you throwing me under the bus, missy?" he asked incredulously. Heather gave him a smirk.

"Clean it up, Heather Johns, or you won't be going out to trick-or-treat around the neighborhood," Olive ordered.

Heather groaned. "Fine," she protested as she started to stuff the candy back into the bag.

"Catherine, Devin, so good to see you both. Come on in," she gestured for them to go into the living room. "Michael is on a call with the mayor, but he is almost wrapped up. He should be out soon."

"I should probably go see if he needs help," Catherine mentioned as they walked to the living room.

"You will do no such thing," a deep voice reprimanded. She turned to find her boss in the doorway, Devin's candy bag in his hands. "Kowalski and I were able to manage. It's Halloween, Catherine Babbitt, live a little. Devin, thanks for coming," Michael said, extending his hand and shaking Devin's hand.

"Thanks for the invite," he replied. Heather appeared in the room carrying two orange Halloween pumpkin buckets. She gave Catherine one and the other to Devin.

"Can we go trick-or-treating now?" she asked, exasperated, grabbing her pumpkin from the coffee table.

"Aye, aye, captain," Devin replied, saluting her.

"Behave," Olive warned Heather.

"Yes, Mom," she said as she walked to the door.

"I'll take care of her," Devin added.

"Oh, we're not worried about her. We're worried about you," Michael murmured with a smile. Catherine chuckled.

"Come on, guys!" Heather exclaimed from outside.

"We're coming," Catherine replied, going down the porch stairs and walking to the sidewalk where she was. "Okay, Heats, where do you want to start?"

"Come on," she said as she grabbed Devin's hand and dragged him. They went to the first house and knocked, an old lady greeting them with a bowl of candy.

"Well, aren't you the cutest fairy," she cooed as she dropped a handful of candy in Heather's bucket. Heather smiled.

"Thanks," Heather replied. "They also want candy," she added, looking at them, tilting her head slightly.

"Well, of course, it's Halloween. Everyone gets candy," the lady said, motioning for them to bring their buckets closer. They did, and she dropped some candy in them.

"Thanks, Mrs. Wheeler." Heather smiled as she tugged Devin down the porch steps. Mrs. Wheeler waved at them and closed her door. Heather stopped in the middle of the sidewalk, looking at them. "So, you both will get candy along with me, but I will have dibs on which candies I get from your buckets at the end of the night."

"Heats, that's not how trick-or-treating works," Catherine protested.

"It does for me." She huffed. Catherine rolled her eyes.

"Fine with me," Devin replied.

"See? That's why I like you. Come on."

"You're trying too hard," Catherine pointed out.

"I don't know what you're talking about, Kitty Cat. I'm just practicing," Devin smirked and winked as he caught up to Heather, grabbing her tiny hand.

"Thanks for going with her," Olive said as she took the buckets from her. Catherine smiled. Michael pulled Heather into his arms. Trooper was scratching and whining at her feet.

"Hey, buddy," Catherine said as she bent down to scratch his ears.

"Come on, little lady, let's tuck you in bed," Michael cooed as he walked up the stairs, Trooper following close behind.

"She had fun, and she behaved," Catherine said. Olive nodded.

"Thank you, I'll make sure she gets her candy."

"I'll see you guys tomorrow," Catherine replied with a

smile. Olive nodded and waved, closing the door as they sped off to Maverick's party.

"This party is packed," Devin mentioned as he rounded the cul-de-sac where Maverick's mom's house was. He parked at the end and got out, walking to her side. The music from the party was loud, and people from the other houses were walking towards where the music was coming from. He grabbed her hand and they made their way inside. The door was wide open.

"Boss, Senate Boy, you guys made it," Maverick yelled from the top of the stairs. She looked up and smiled, waving at him. He was dressed in a makeshift bumble bee costume.

"Hey, you got a last-minute costume," Catherine mentioned as he came to stop in front of them. Maverick looked down at his costume and smiled.

"Oh yeah... I just put something together." Maggie came down the stairs, her hair tousled. "You guys want drinks? Come, they're this way," he said, motioning to the kitchen. Devin kissed Catherine's temple and followed Maverick. Maggie looked up, her gaze finding Catherine's. Her steps faltered, eyes going wide. She looked down at the floor and disappeared. Catherine frowned.

"No wine, but I mixed you some ginger ale and vodka," Devin said at her side a couple of minutes later, giving her a red cup.

"Thanks," she replied, looking up at him and smiling. He leaned in and kissed her lips softly.

"Have I told you that you look beautiful? Regal. Like a real princess," he murmured against her lips, his free arm wrapping around her waist and bringing her closer to him. She beamed, feeling warm inside.

"Yes, you have."

"Well, let me repeat myself. You look absolutely stunning," he mumbled as he nuzzled his nose on her cheek. His lips kissed her cheek and skimmed down her face to her jaw. His breath caressed her ear. "And this dress looks wonderful on you, but it would look better on the floor," he whispered as he nibbled on her lobe. A shudder made its way down her spine.

"Devin, please, can we just get a hotel? I'm starting to notice what Maggie means," she said in a shaky voice. Devin's hand moved down and cupped her ass.

"No, Kitty Cat. You made me wait nine years. You can wait a few more days," he purred in her ear. He suddenly moved, letting her go. He extended his hand and bowed at the waist. "A dance?"

"I hate you," she breathed out, taking a sip from her drink, welcoming the bitter taste of the vodka on her taste buds.

"No, you don't, baby girl." He smirked. She rolled her eyes, taking his hand. He guided her to the makeshift dance floor, wrapping his free hand around her waist and bringing her closer. She wrapped her arms around his shoulders, her fingers playing with the curls at the nape of his neck, the other hand holding her drink. They started to dance, grinding on each other. "Brings back memories, doesn't it?" he asked. She nodded. "Of course, we've never danced this closely, but you get the idea."

"Yeah," she said. They danced for a few songs, then went to the patio where most of the people were.

"Oh, my goodness, you guys made it," a woman in her fifties with a doctor's outfit said. *Maverick's mom.* She had the same smile as him with dirty blonde hair and blue eyes. She approached them and hugged Catherine. "I'm so glad you guys came. It's nothing big, just a neighborly party. Everyone in the cul-de-sac joins in planning, and every year, we alternate the house that is hosting. This year was me," she explained. Catherine nodded as she smiled at her.

"Thanks for inviting us, Mrs. James," Catherine replied.

"Please, call me Grace."

"Ma, we're running out of ice. I'll run to Mr. Tim's store and buy some more," Maverick's brother said. He was dressed in his usual lumberjack outfit.

"Catherine, Devin, have you met my other son, Luke?" Grace asked.

"We were briefly introduced. Hi," Catherine greeted him.

"Catherine, so good to see you again," he said as he picked up her hand and kissed it.

"Alright, buddy, this is not the nineteen-fifties," Devin interrupted as he grabbed her hand and moved it out of Luke's grasp.

"Oh, you *are* the boyfriend Maverick mentioned. My bad, *buddy*," Luke replied. Devin's nostrils flared, and he took a deep breath. "Anyways, I'll go get that ice, Ma. Catherine, save me a dance?" he asked as he retreated, winking at her. Devin's hold on her hand tightened, and she suppressed a laugh.

"Absolutely," she replied. Luke smiled and left.

"So, Maggie was telling the truth," Grace murmured, smiling.

"I'm going to need to have a conversation with Maggie," Catherine mumbled, looking at Devin, who was still looking at the spot Luke had just vacated.

"Oh, there's Gloria. If you'll excuse me, I need to finish some details for the festival tomorrow. Feel free to mingle.

The majority of the people here are the ones you've met during our meetings," Grace said as she smiled and left.

"You're cute," she mentioned, looking up at Devin and smiling, patting his cheek. "But jealousy doesn't suit you, Satan," she added, calling him the nickname she gave him in college, and kissing his cheek. That made him look at her.

"What did you just call me?"

"Satan. Come on, we still have some mingling to do, and I need to talk with Maggie," she said, tugging on his hand and walking around the patio. Now, it made sense why Maggie was avoiding her. She spotted Maggie mingling with some townsfolk. They walked to where she was. "Hey, Maggie," she greeted as she walked to stand beside her. "Sorry folks, I need to steal her for a few minutes," Catherine apologized as she grabbed Maggie's arm.

"She's all yours. We need to get some refills," one of the men in the group said as they left.

"Margarette Rivera, what did I tell you?" she asked, calling her by her full government name.

"Don't call me by my full name, babes. You know I don't like it. Makes me feel like I'm in trouble."

"You *are* in trouble."

"Listen, whatever they say I did, it's a lie. Nothing happened," Maggie argued, looking anxious.

"So, Grace saying out loud that you were telling the truth about me and Devin is not true? You're calling her a liar?" Catherine questioned.

"Oh, that!" Maggie exclaimed, giving her a nervous laugh. "Well, she asked Maverick and me if something was going on because of the last town hall and how you couldn't stop looking at each other." She shrugged. "I just confirmed her suspicions. I didn't lie."

"We asked you not to tell anyone."

"Catherine, babes, the whole town knows. It's not a secret. Even Michael knows," she added. "You guys did an awful job at keeping it a secret. Now, if you'll excuse me, I need to go save poor Maverick from a very unfortunate event," she mentioned as she walked away, her voice having an edge. Catherine pinched the bridge of her nose, taking a deep breath.

"She is right, you know? We have done an awful job at keeping this a secret," Devin added, his hands snaking around her waist, bringing her to him, her back melding to his chest. He kissed her neck. "But can they blame us?" he asked, trailing his lips up her throat to her jaw. "We have nine years to catch up on. Fourteen if we keep an exact count. I refuse to keep my hands off of you," he purred in her ear, his hand traveling up her leg to the hem of her skirt.

"Satan, we are in a party full of people," she whispered harshly, stopping his hand. He chuckled.

"No one is watching us, Kitty Cat," he breathed against her neck, his hand continuing its journey. He dove his hand inside her skirt, walking them behind a tree out of everyone's sight. He pinned her to the trunk, one of his hands on her hips, the other still making up-and-down patterns on her leg.

"Devin," she mumbled as his hand skimmed higher.

"Yes, Kitty Cat?" he asked as he leaned in and trailed kisses up her throat to her jaw. His lips kept their journey up her face to the corner of her lips. He placed a soft kiss there as his hand cupped her ass, bringing her closer, his hard, hot erection pressing against her. His lips engulfed hers, swallowing her moan.

"Devin, please," she pleaded, her arms wrapping around his shoulders. His lips trailed down her face, his hand caressing the inside of her thighs.

"When was the last time you had sex, Kitty Cat?" he

asked as his hand brushed the hem of her underwear, making her whimper. Her body had a mind of its own, moving her hips and seeking friction. He tsked. "Stop moving, Kitty Cat. You will only make it worse for yourself," he purred against her lips, his fingers brushing slightly against her. Her hands tightened around his neck.

"Devin, please," she pleaded. It had been too long since she'd been touched. Too much time since she felt cared for. It has been eons since someone, or something, other than her hand and battery operated objects made her feel something.

"Tell you what, I will give you a small taste, but you gotta keep quiet. Can you do that, Kitty Cat? Can you stay quiet?" he asked as his knees pried her legs open, his fingers finding the hem of her underwear with expertise, moving it to the side. His lips found their way down her throat, biting the spot where her shoulder meets her neck. "Can you stay quiet, Kitty Cat?" She nodded, closing her eyes. "Good girl," he praised as his fingers touched her. She bit her lower lip to keep from moaning as his fingers rubbed her clit. "So wet, Kitty Cat." He kissed her, plunging two fingers inside her, his thumb pressing against her clit, the sensation feeling like ecstasy. "So wet," he murmured against her lips.

She moaned as he found the exact spot inside her that made her see stars. "You like that?" He started to move his fingers inside of her. She whimpered, biting her lip to keep quiet. Her knees were weak, the trunk of the tree biting into her skin with how hard she was holding on for support. "Such a good girl, staying quiet," he praised, fingering her. She clenched around his fingers, gasping. Throwing her head back, seeing stars as his fingers expertly rubbed her G-spot over and over again, the tension building inside of her. "Such a good girl being wet for me. You like to be praised. Don't you, pretty girl? You like to be told how good of a girl you are?" he asked as his fingers inside of her picked up speed, his thumb rubbing circles on her clit, his lips kissing her throat. She was so close.

"Devin, please," she pleaded, clenching around him.

"Such a good girl," he said, taking her hand and placing it on his crotch, moving it up and down. "You feel that, pretty girl? That's how badly I want you," he rasped. Her hand tightened on him, making him groan. She rubbed her hand in an up-and-down movement. His lips found hers, biting her lower lip. His fingers picked up speed, and then they were gone as he took a step back. "But I said I was giving you a small taste, and that means no coming tonight," he said, his fingers going to his mouth, licking them clean. "Sweet," he murmured as he savored her on his tongue, fixing his pants.

"I hate you," she said breathlessly. He smirked.

"Come on, Kitty Cat."

Chapter Twenty-Four

Catherine

She woke up in a tangle of bed sheets and limbs, Devin's arm firmly wrapped around her waist, her back to his chest. For the first time in a long while, she felt safe. However, she was waiting for the other shoe to drop.

"Stop thinking," Devin's groggy, sleep-ridden voice said. He kissed the top of her head. "Your mind is going a million miles an hour, I can feel it."

"Today is the Fireflies Festival," she replied, snuggling closer to him. He groaned.

"Stop moving, Catherine," he mumbled. "We will have a situation on our hands that we will be unable to control. So I suggest you stop moving your pretty little ass."

"Sorry," she whispered, blushing. He kissed her head again and slipped out of bed, making her feel instantly cold.

"I need a cold shower," he muttered, standing up from the bed and walking to her side, sitting there. His arms caged her to the bed. "Good morning," he whispered, leaning down and placing a soft kiss on her forehead.

"Good morning." She smiled. Her hands cupped his face,

moving the long strands of hair away from his forehead. "Breakfast in half an hour?" she asked, her thumb tracing soft circles on his cheeks. He leaned into her palm, kissing it.

"Absolutely," he said. He kissed her forehead, nose, and lips and left, wandered to his bathroom. She stood up and walked silently to her room.

"Still no banging? I'm disappointed Cat," Maggie said from the top of the stairs. She looked like a mess. Her hair in a messy bun, her shoes in her hands, and a hoodie and sweatpants too big for her covered her body. Her makeup was smudged, and a bruise that looked like a hickey marred on her throat.

"Rough night?" Catherine asked, leaning into her closed door, crossing her arms, and smirking. Maggie's demeanor changed, a hint of shame behind her eyes, but it left as soon as it came.

"The good kind of rough. You should try it sometime," Maggie said, walking past her into her room.

"You better put makeup on that hickey," Catherine mumbled.

Maggie gasped. "What hickey?" Catherine pointed to a spot on her neck, signaling where the hickey was. Maggie covered the spot with her hand. "I'm going to kill him," Maggie whispered and closed her door. Catherine chuckled and ducked inside her room, bee-lining to the bathroom. She showered quickly and got ready. By the time she exited the bathroom, Devin was on her bed, against her headboard, looking at his phone.

"Hey, beautiful," Devin said, tossing his phone on the bed. He spread his legs and patted the spot between them. She walked to his side and crawled over, sitting in the spot he patted. He engulfed her in his arms, kissing her temple. "Today is our last day in the bubble," he whispered. "Then it's back to the city and work," he said, exhaling. "I don't want to go back. Not yet."

"Me either," she whispered.

"Which is why…".

"What'd you do?" she asked, spinning in his arms.

"A cabin. In the middle of the woods in West Virginia. Just us. For a week. I already talked with your boss. He approved your leave. The cabin is all ready to go," he said, reaching for his phone and unlocking it. He showed her his screen. A wood cabin picture was there. "It's a cabin from a friend. He lent it to me," he continued. She scrolled through the pictures. She smiled up at him, swooning over the gesture. "Remember when I said I wasn't going to take you in the back of a rental car or the B&B. I have a lot of things planned for that week." He kissed her behind her ear, nibbling on her earlobe. "The things I have planned…" She shuddered. "I promise, you won't be able to walk the next day," he vowed, and she squeezed her thighs closer. She felt a blush creep up her cheeks, the temperature in the room rising by a couple of degrees. He chuckled and kissed her temple. "Okay, breakfast," he added, removing his arms from around her. She gave him his phone and stood up.

"I just need to put my shoes on," she said in a shaky voice. He combed a loose piece of hair behind her ear.

"Take your time." He smirked. She gulped.

She turned and scrambled around for her shoes, putting them on and walking to the door. He chuckled behind her. She opened the door and exited the room, waiting for him. He exited, closing the door behind him. He wrapped an arm around her shoulders, bringing her closer.

"Come on, Kitty Cat, let's get you your oat milk cappuccino," he murmured, kissing her head.

"Good morning, lovebirds," Gloria greeted as they

walked inside the B&B breakfast room. She was beaming. Catherine made to move from Devin's grasp, but he held her tighter.

"Good morning, Gloria. Happy Fireflies Festival," he said, smiling at her.

"Happy Fireflies Festival. Are you two lovebirds excited to experience it?" she asked with a toothy smile.

"Absolutely, we wouldn't miss it for the world," Devin replied.

"I guess you guys worked it out?" Gloria inquired as Devin kissed Catherine's temple.

"We sure did."

"When are you guys leaving?"

"Tomorrow afternoon."

"Bummer. But I hope you guys come back."

"Oh, absolutely. Now, if you'll excuse us, someone here needs her caffeine intake," he mentioned, walking to the kitchen area.

"Oh, of course. I'm heading out to set up my booth at the festival."

"How's Charlie?" Catherine asked. Gloria's smile dropped a bit.

"He's better. His back is still a little thrown out. He can't do much lifting, but the doctor said with more rest he should be back to his normal activities in a couple of weeks."

"Do you need help setting up?"

"Oh no, don't worry, darling. Our son came over to help us. He and my daughter-in-law are already there setting up the tent. They came earlier to pick up the table and the heavy stuff. You guys enjoy your breakfast and the festival."

She turned around and left. They walked to the kitchen, and Devin fixed her coffee just how she liked it. She took a sip and let the caffeine hit her bloodstream. She hummed.

"Is it okay?" Devin asked, fixing his coffee.

"Yes," she replied, taking another sip. "It's perfect."

"Come on, Miss Oat Milk Cappuccino," he joked, taking her hand and lacing their fingers together. They walked to a table and settled down. "I'll get us both breakfast," he mumbled, kissing the top of her head and leaving.

"Man, he is *whipped* for you," Maggie exclaimed, sitting on the other empty chair across from her, no sign of the hickey in her neck. "Is this what *in love Catherine* looks like?"

"I'm going to choose to ignore you, Margarette," Catherine said, taking another sip from her coffee. Devin appeared a couple of seconds later with two plates filled to the top.

"They had French toast today," he mentioned, placing a plate in front of her.

"Good morning everyone," Maverick greeted, walking to them. Maggie froze, and an anxious look crossed her face, her eyes widening like two full moons. "Good morning, Mags."

"I... Um... Good morning, Mav," she stuttered nervously, standing up and walking away to get breakfast. Maverick looked at her departing figure.

"You know, Maverick, all of this would be solved if you actually talked to her," Catherine pointed out, taking a sip from her coffee. She looked at Maverick, then to Devin sitting beside her. Devin was looking between Maverick and Maggie, the pieces falling together in his mind. Maverick was looking longingly at Maggie. Maverick sighed and walked in the direction of the kitchen to get coffee.

"What was that?" Devin asked, still looking between them both. She shrugged, taking a bite from her bacon. Devin looked at her and smiled, going back to his breakfast and spreading jelly on his toast. She opened her mouth to him. He dramatically rolled his eyes and extended his wrist, giving her a piece of his toast. She chewed while smiling. She cut a piece of her French toast and dipped it in the maple syrup, extending her fork to him. "Oh, those are good," he said, standing up and walking to the breakfast buffet. Maggie came back and sat down where she had previously seated.

"Care to explain what happened between you and Mav?" Catherine questioned her with a conspiratory smile over the rim of her coffee cup. Though, she had a pretty good idea of what happened.

"No, because nothing happened," she replied nonchalantly.

"Oh, hi, Mav," Catherine said. Maggie tensed, straightening her back. Maggie looked around, realizing she was playing. She glared at Catherine. "Spill. Do I need to worry about our work environment?" Catherine inquired. Maggie sighed. She took a bite from her eggs, stabbing the plate a little forcefully. Maggie mumbled something barely audible. "Sorry, what?" Catherine asked, leaning closer. Maggie mumbled again, but she still didn't understand her. "What?" Catherine repeated.

"We hooked up in his childhood bedroom," Maggie said. "And I left before he woke up."

"You and Mav?" Catherine asked. Maggie looked down, shame clouding her gaze.

"It's so unprofessional. An office fling," Maggie mumbled.

Catherine laughed. "About damn time."

"What are you talking about?" Maggie questioned, confused, looking at her.

"Maybe that's a conversation you and Mav need to have. But I will only say this. Mav is a great guy. And definitely an upgrade from your previous relationship," Catherine uttered, taking another sip from her coffee and leaving Maggie perplexed. Devin returned and sat down, a small plate of French toast in his hands. They finished eating in silence.

"Did he say something to you?" Maggie asked, breaking the silence.

"He didn't have to," Catherine lied. "It's all about the way he looks at you." Devin looked between the two of them.

"Am I missing something?" he inquired, confused. Maggie stood up and left in the direction of the stairs.

"Either I just played cupid, or I'm going to have to build a cubicle wall between those two," she stated, sighing. Devin rubbed her arm.

"Come on, we need to leave now if we want to get a good parking spot," Devin said, gathering their plates and putting them on the dirty dishes pile.

"Let me go get my purse." She walked to her room, brushed her teeth quickly, and grabbed her purse.

"Ugh, you know what? Forget it," Maggie exclaimed. Seconds later, she left what she assumed was Maverick's room, slamming the door and getting inside her room, slamming that door too.

"Mags, come on, I didn't mean it like that," Maverick pleaded, knocking on her door. She tiptoed down the stairs, speed walking in the parking lot to the car.

"What happened?" Devin asked.

"Cubicle. I need to build a cubicle wall when I get back," she replied, rubbing her forehead. Devin blew a half whistle, half breath.

"That bad?" he asked, starting the car.

"Devin, there were door slams," she said, turning to him.

"Ouch," he mumbled, driving out of the parking lot.

"I know."

"I'm sure they will make up by the time they go back to

DC," he replied, reaching to her and placing his hand at the base of her neck, giving it a comforting squeeze.

"I hope."

God it's me. Can you fix those two? We have a good work-office dynamic. I promise I'll start cursing less, she prayed to no one in particular.

Chapter Twenty-Five

Catherine

They arrived at the festival, and there was already a crowd of people. It took them around twenty minutes to get there, half an hour to find parking, and another fifteen minutes to walk to where the fun stuff was. The smell of fried food was already wafting through the air. There was a small crowd gathered already at the ticketing booth.

They walked around it and saw Maggie crossing the street in a hurry, along with another town woman. If her memory served her well, it was the woman who owned the coffee shop where Devin usually bought from during the day. She looked at them and smiled.

"Hey, Mags. When did you get here?" Catherine asked. The last time she saw her, she was slamming the door of her B&B room, Mav close behind her, knocking on it. She looked up at Devin. He looked down at her, his eyes wide open. They followed Maggie to the ticketing booth, where four people were setting up. Maggie placed her purse on the table and went to peruse in a box under the table. She found what she was looking for and walked to them.

"I just got here. Put these on—" She handed them some lanyards that said *staff*. She looked tense, pissed even. "Be useful and go around checking the tents and booths before we open the doors to people," she said, walking back to the booth. "And make sure they pass this checklist," she continued, handing Catherine a clipboard. "Write the name of the business in the corner and the person in charge of the tent so I can cross-check later before opening."

"Got it," Catherine replied, looking at Devin, who had the lanyard already hanging from his neck. She put hers around her neck, Devin helping to fix her hair.

"Let's go," he said, taking the clipboard in one hand and entwining his fingers with hers with the other.

They walked around the area, making sure the tents and booths complied with the checklist Maggie had gathered, which all of them did. They went back to the ticketing booth and handed her the clipboard.

"Here," Catherine said. "All good to go."

Maggie took the clipboard, scanning through the pages, and nodded.

"All right, half an hour, and we will open for the festival activities, folks!" Maggie yelled excitedly to the people in line, earning her a wave of shouts and whistles of excitement.

"Auntie Cathy!" the voice of Heather carried through the crowd. She turned in time to see her running up to her. She crouched down and opened her arms, Heather hugging her koala bear style.

"Munchkin, hello!" she exclaimed, standing up, hugging Heather still.

"Hi, Uncle Dev," Heather greeted, reaching for Devin. Devin picked her up and hugged her.

"Hey, H," Devin mumbled, beaming. She looked at them, at their interaction, and suddenly she realized, she wouldn't mind raising a family with him. Just like she had once daydreamed. She gazed fondly at them, a smile tugging at her lips.

"I leave her in good hands," someone said. She turned and saw Michael looking at them, a fond smile on his face, Olive beside him. "She's all yours for the day."

"We are going to have lots of fun," Devin said, moving a piece of hair behind Heather's ear. Michael nodded and left. "Let me go get her ticket," he said, placing Heather back on the ground. Heather hugged her legs. Devin came back with the bracelets and helped them put them on.

"Okay, the ticket booth is up and running. I'm going to do my rounds," Maggie exclaimed beside them.

"Hi, Maggie," Heather greeted.

"Hi, baby cakes," Maggie said, booping Heather's nose and blowing her an air kiss. Heather giggled. "Are you guys good?" Catherine nodded. "Great. I will go do my rounds and see that everything is in order. We hit our goal with ticket sales." Maggie beamed.

"Oh good!" Catherine replied enthusiastically.

"Okay, I will go do my rounds. I'll see you guys around," Maggie repeated, pinching Heather's cheek and walking away.

"She repeated that she was going to do her rounds three times," Devin pointed out. Catherine sighed. "Alright, H, ready?" Devin inquired, looking down at Heather.

"Uncle Dev, are you going to marry Auntie Cathy?" Heather inquired out of the blue.

"Yes. Someday, Auntie Cathy and I are going to marry," Devin replied, looking at her. She looked away and blushed. She liked that idea, more than she cared to admit.

"Can I be your flower girl?" Heather asked excitedly.

"Absolutely," Catherine replied, turning to look at her.

"Awesome, but also, can I ride on your shoulders, Uncle Dev?" Heather questioned.

"Absolutely," Devin replied with a smile. He turned her around and lifted her by her armpits, seating her on his shoulders. Catherine tensed. "Kitty Cat, relax, I'm not going to drop her. I have two godsons and two nieces," he said, kissing her forehead. "Alright, H, what should we do first?" Devin asked.

"Bumper cars!" Heather squealed.

"Let's go!" Devin said, walking in the direction of the bumper cars. She smiled at both of them, at how close they had become, and once again, she pictured what it would be like to raise a family with him. How good of a father he would be.

They spent the rest of the night playing fair games, Devin winning Heather the big pink unicorn she wanted in the Balloon and Dart game. It wasn't until a couple of hours and another sugary drink later that Heather fell asleep while on Devin's back, her tiny arms wrapped around his neck. It was a little past eight when they came to the entrance to meet Michael.

"Oh, she's dead," Michael commented, referring to Heather.

"She crashed," Catherine replied. Michael walked to where Devin was standing and picked Heather up, cradling her in his arms. Catherine walked to Olive and handed her the unicorn. "Devin won her this. She literally begged him for it," Catherine said, smiling. Olive chuckled.

"She wrapped you around her little finger, didn't she?" Olive asked Devin.

"I'll be lying if I say no," Devin replied, smiling.

"We call it the Heather effect." Michael chuckled. "Thanks for looking after her."

"Anytime, boss," Catherine replied. They watched them go as she felt Devin's arm bring her closer to him.

"Time for the adults to have fun," he purred in her ear.

"We are in a public place, Devin Mack," she said, moving away from his grasp and shoving him. He laughed, putting an arm around her shoulders and bringing her closer, kissing her temple.

"Come on, Kitty Cat. Let's have some fun," he expressed, walking back to the fair, towards the food trucks. "Okay, let's get some alcohol first." He went to the makeshift bar and got them both beers that they chugged like they were back in Boston. "Damn, you almost gave me a run for my money."

"Let's go," she said, walking to the carnival games. They played all of them, but she was set on the water gun game.

"You want that puppy plushie, don't you?" She looked at him and smiled, nodding. He grasped her face in his hands and caressed her cheeks with his thumbs. "I will get it for you," he vowed and kissed her. Then he kissed her nose and forehead. He turned around and paid, getting a water gun. He turned around and pointed at her. "This one's for you." She laughed and walked to stand behind him. He got a perfect score, winning her the plushie. "Told you, baby," he mumbled, kissing her cheek.

"Look at it. It's so cute," she exclaimed, lifting it for him to see.

"Not as cute as you." She blushed. "The line to the Ferris wheel is semi-empty. Let's go." He grabbed her hand and dragged her to it. They stood in line, waiting. "You remember our junior year? That little fair we went to on the outskirts of Boston?" he asked. She snorted.

"How can I forget? Emily's twenty-first birthday. She got shit-faced at the fair," she replied, smiling at the memory.

"It was also the day I almost kissed you," he confessed,

caging her between his body and the wait-line fence. She looked up at his ocean-blue eyes. "All my resolution almost faded into the background on that Ferris wheel ride all those years ago. I should've kissed you then," he said, searching her face, his eyes longing. She wrapped her arms around his shoulders.

"*You* are here now. *I* am here now. *We* are here now. That's all that matters," she replied, standing on her tiptoes and kissing his lips softly. He returned the kiss.

Chapter Twenty-Six

Devin

"Hey man, are you going to move in the line?" a teenager behind them asked. They broke away and laughed. He placed his forehead on top of hers.

"You guys can go ahead," Devin replied, chuckling.

"Oops." Catherine giggled. He looked down at her and laughed. He kissed her forehead and grabbed her hand.

"Come on, you little heathen," he said, smiling. They got on the Ferris wheel, and she leaned into him. He wrapped his arms around her, kissing the top of her head. When they reached the top, she sighed dramatically.

"Isn't this the part where you are supposed to kiss me?" she asked playfully. He turned to her and cupped her cheek, moving a stray hair away from her face.

"Yes, Catherine Babbitt, this is the part where I kiss you," he answered, leaning down and kissing her.

Softly at first, then hungrily, as if his body and mouth couldn't get enough of her. He swiped his tongue on her bottom lip, and she opened, their tongues dancing around each other. Soft and warm. His hand moved to the nape of her neck, keeping her there. His other hand skimmed around her waist. He felt her hands come up to his shoulders. He moved away, biting and tugging at her bottom lip. His lips trailed down her jaw, to the little spot behind her ear, biting her earlobe. Her hand moved up to his hair, tugging at the little hairs on his nape. He groaned and felt her shudder. The blood traveled to his groin, making his pants impossibly tight.

"Dev…" she mumbled quietly.

"Say my name again, Catherine." He groaned, tugging her closer by the hips. Her response was another tug in his hair and a whimper.

"Devin…" she whispered. He kissed back up her neck to her mouth. When his lips covered hers again, the Ferris wheel shook. He stopped, cradling her to his side. She groaned, frustrated.

"Fuck these things," he said in a grave tone, dropping his forehead to hers. She laughed. "You okay?" he asked worriedly, searching her face.

"I'm fine. Are *you* okay?" she asked, glancing down at his pants. He looked down and closed his eyes. He was impossibly hard. He groaned, cursing under his breath. He gazed back at her, her eyes hazy.

"Just a little bit more love. Just one more day," he replied, nuzzling her cheek. He pecked her lips, her nose, and forehead, his lips lingering on the spot.

"I can't wait," she retorted sarcastically. He chuckled.

They got off the Ferris wheel and walked around, getting on all the other carnival attractions, her hand never leaving his.

He had an arm around her shoulders, and she was tucked to his side, one of her hands in his back pocket, the other holding the plushie.

"Catherine?" someone asked from behind them. They

turned and saw Catherine's coworker. Isabel, if memory serves him right.

"Isabela!" Catherine said, a little too enthusiastically.

Close enough, he thought. She removed herself from his side, and he frowned at her.

"Hey! What are you still doing around?" she asked nervously.

"Oh, I was checking the attractions after the boss left and lost track of time while hanging with Maggie and Mav, but I'm heading out now. Maggie and Mav are still somewhere in here. I swear those two are gonna end up marrying each other," Isabela said. She turned her dark gaze at him. "Hello, Mr. Mack. Fancy seeing you—" she mumbled, hesitant, "—around."

"Hey, Isabela. Devin is fine," Devin replied with a smile.

"Isabela, Devin and I—" Catherine started but stopped when Isabela put a hand out.

"None of my business," Isabela said with humor. "Although I might have heard something about it."

"I'm going to kill Maggie," Catherine exclaimed, exasperated. Isabela laughed.

"It's fine. She didn't say who. Just that you were in a predicament..." Isabela explained. "I see the predicament now. Loud and clear," she continued, smiling. "I'm happy. You look happy. You deserve to be happy. I'm guessing Kyle is out...?" she asked hesitantly. Catherine nodded, looking down. Devin wrapped his arm around her. "Good. He was an asshole."

"Why does everyone keep saying that? You, Maggie, Mav... was I not seeing something? Was I that oblivious?" Catherine asked. Devin looked between the two of them.

"Don't forget Catherine, I come from a long line of

brujas. My *abuela* was one, and her mom before her, and her mom before her. I'm very susceptible to people's auras. I read people like books, and Kyle is not a good man. He's not evil. He is just not good for you," Isabela explained. "Unlike him. He is good for you," she continued, pointing at Devin. He looked down, blushing. "Anyways, I'm going to take my *bruja* ass back to the hotel. I have an early flight to DC tomorrow. I'll see you when you come back. And for the love of everything that's holy, do not even look at your work phone this coming week. Take the time off. You need it. You earned it. You deserve it. We have it handled. We can survive without you for a week. Michael can survive without you for a week. We have Kowalski for a reason," Isabela chastised, turning around and leaving. He hugged her, pressing her back to his chest and kissing the back of her head.

"I am going to kill Maggie when I see her back in DC. A predicament? Really?" Catherine expressed, incredulous. "Does she even know what predicament means? And how do they even know I'm off for the week?" she scoffed. He chuckled.

"Come on, grumpy pants," he said, kissing her temple and dragging her with him. They kept walking around the festival. Music sounded from the town square. They walked over and saw there was a stage with a live band. "Would you like to dance?" he asked with a British accent, bowing.

She curtsied and giggled. "Why, yes, my brave knight. I would love to."

He grabbed her hand and dragged her where the couples were dancing. He placed her arms around his neck and moved his arms to engulf her waist, bringing her closer. He dropped his forehead to hers and sighed. They were dancing out of rhythm. The song was a fast pop one, and they were slow dancing. Her fingers played with the little hairs on his nape. His arms wrapped tighter around her.

"I dreamt about this moment for so long. Just us. No one else. I really prayed to whatever is out there to bring you back to me. And they did," he confessed in a whisper. Her hands wrapped tighter around him. "I really missed you. I missed us. I've been miserable for the last nine years, you have to know that," he said, looking into her emerald eyes. He tucked a loose piece of hair behind her ear and cupped her cheek. "There has been no one, Catherine. No one. I tried. I tried so hard to move on from you, but I just couldn't. I will always belong to you. My heart will always belong to you," he whispered, caressing her cheek. A lone tear fell from her eye, and he caught it with his thumb.

"I love you, Catherine Babbitt. And that's a fact," he kissed her nose. "I will always love you," he continued, kissing her lips softly. He kissed her nose again and then her forehead, his lips lingering there. He inhaled her smell. Lavender and chamomile. Addictive. Intoxicating. *Home*. She smelled like home. He was finally home. After being lost for nine years, he was finally where he belonged. In her arms. He dropped his forehead to hers again and closed his eyes. The song changed to a slow one, matching their dancing.

"I love you too, Devin. I always did. I don't think I ever stopped," she whispered in a shaky voice. "I'm so grateful life brought us back together. So grateful it gave us a second chance," she continued. "Nine years apart couldn't dim my feelings for you."

"I know that feeling. I know that feeling very deeply," he muttered. Her phone rang, and she jumped.

"Fuck. Way to ruin the mood," she mumbled and got her phone from her pocket.

She looked at the screen and frowned. He traced a thumb over her brows, smoothing away her frown. When that didn't work, he got worried.

"What's wrong?" he asked.

"It's Kyle."

"Why is he calling you?"

"I don't know." She handed him the plushie and answered the phone, placing a hand on his mouth, silencing him. "You better have a good fucking excuse for calling me," she spat. "Why do you need your W-2?" she asked him. "You idiot, I'm your accountant," she said, walking away. Devin followed her. "I filed your taxes," she said. "No. Why do you need it?" she asked. "Impossible. I triple-checked it before I sent them." A pause. "Well, you need to figure out what the fuck you did. Send me a picture of what they sent you," she said, putting the phone on speaker. She opened the message and looked at the picture frowning. "How are you a cybersecurity expert?" she asked rhetorically. "This is the IRS sending you a pin for your account for next year. Not that you owe them. Is this all?" she asked, taking the phone off of speaker. "Great. Then, I am hanging up now." She turned to Devin and frowned. "I'm sorry he ruined the mood," she mumbled, hugging his waist. He hugged her back.

"He didn't ruin anything baby." He kissed her head. "Are you ready to go?"

"One more dance," she replied, batting her eyelashes.

"Catherine, let me repeat myself. There's nothing you could ask me that I would deny you. I told you that before," he expressed, cupping her cheek and kissing her nose. "One more dance. Let's go," he said as he dragged her back to the middle of the town square. They danced until their feet gave out.

"Please, come back again in the future," Gloria said, hugging Catherine.

"Absolutely," Catherine replied, smiling. "We will definitely come back."

"Good. We will always have room for you both. Come back whenever. And thank you so much for all you did for us and our community," Gloria expressed, patting Catherine's cheek in a motherly way. "Oh, I almost forgot," Gloria said and disappeared. She came back with a box in her hands. "Here's an pumpkin pie for you both to take back home," she said, handing Catherine the box.

"Thank you," Catherine said, smiling. They walked to the car, and Devin opened the door for her.

"Thank you," she muttered, kissing his cheek. He walked to his side.

"Ready?" he asked her once he turned the car on. She nodded. He kissed her cheek and drove away.

It was a little past midnight when they made it to the cabin. It was huge. With forest all around it. He turned to look at Catherine, and she was fast asleep. He chuckled. He got out of the car and called his 'family friend'.

"What's up, man? You made it to the cabin okay?" Corbin asked on the other side of the line.

"We did. I just parked in the driveway. Just wondering where the key is."

"Okay, go to the right side of the house. There's going to be the hose's little shed or box. I put it inside. I also restocked the pantry and refrigerator like you asked me." Devin walked to where Corbin told him and found the hose box. He opened it and saw the keys inside. He grabbed them and walked back to the car.

"Alright, man, I got the keys. Thanks."

"Have fun," Corbin replied and hung up. Devin smiled to himself as he walked back to the car.

Chapter Twenty-Seven

Devin

He made his way back to the car, the shadow of Catherine sleeping inside making him smile. He touched his lips unconsciously, reminiscing on the memory of their make-out session the night before after the fair. One that gave him the most unendurable hard-on he has ever gotten. He was barely able to restrain himself from taking her then and there. He shook his head, clearing the image of her moaning and writhing underneath him last night from his mind. He needed to control himself. He walked to the trunk, getting their suitcases out, and went to the cabin to leave them in the room, turning on the heater.

"Alright, sleeping beauty," he whispered, unbuckling her seatbelt, sliding his arm under her knees and the other one across her waist, and carrying her. He kicked the door closed and pressed the lock button on the keys. She instinctively dropped her head on his shoulder. He walked up the steps to the porch. She stirred awake, looking around. "Welcome back, princess," he said, looking at her. She glanced around, her gaze landing on his. She smiled, throwing her arms around his neck, nestling her face there. Her warm breath tickled his skin.

"I can't wait to get a warm shower. I'm freezing," she murmured.

"There's a bathtub in the master bathroom. You can definitely run a bath," he said, kissing her head. She nestled further into his arms. "I already dropped our luggage inside," he mentioned as he opened the door. He walked inside, locking the door behind them.

"You know I can walk, right?" she mumbled, her lips featherlike on his neck.

"I know," he whispered, "but I'm scared." She lifted her head and looked at him.

"What?" she asked, frowning.

"I'm scared the minute I put you down, it'll all be a dream, and I will wake up," he confessed, looking into her eyes. Eyes the color of forests. Eyes that sparkled with such longing and love. She cupped his cheek, and he leaned into her touch, closing his eyes, engraving this moment into his memory forever. He turned his head and kissed her palm.

"Devin..."

"I know." He put her down, wrapping an arm around her shoulders, bringing her to him, placing his chin on the top of her head, and placing a soft kiss there. She looked around the cabin.

It was spacious, with an open floor concept and a big kitchen. To his right was the living room, a fireplace on the far wall. They walked down the hallway to the master bedroom. Once inside, he turned to her. She glanced around, entering the adjacent bathroom, groaning. He shifted from one leg to the other, walking to the bed and sitting down.

"I am definitely running a bath," she commented, walking

back into the room. She picked up her suitcase and placed it on the bed. She stared at him and smiled, walking to stand between his legs. He slipped his hands under her shirt, feeling her warm skin. She shuddered. "Devin… I need to shower. I'm freezing. We've been on the road all day. You must be tired."

"You promise this is not a dream?" he asked, looking into her eyes. She smiled.

"I promise it's not. My feelings never went away," she said, picking up his hand and placing it in her heart. "They are still here. I know it feels like a dream, but I promise you it is not," she whispered, leaning down and placing a soft kiss on his lips.

"I meant it, Catherine," he said against her lips. "You had, and you will always have, my heart. There has been no one else. Not before, not during, not now," he vowed, kissing her. He moved his hand up her back, cupping her neck. "It's you. It's always been you. It will always be you." She sat down, straddling his lap. He started kissing down her neck. "I promise I will make you the happiest woman alive," he said, kissing behind her ear. She shuddered. He stood up and shifted them, lowering her to the bed. He threw the suitcase to the floor. "I will worship you every day." He trailed kisses down her throat to her chest. Her fingers laced on his hair.

"Devin…"

"I promise I will always worship you, Catherine." His hands trailed down her body. "I will always make you feel like the only woman in the world," he promised, and he meant every single word of that oath. "You will never have to worry about me." He peppered kisses down her throat. He lifted her shirt. She raised herself off the bed enough to take it off. He rained down kisses on her bare skin. "I promise you this." He kissed her left breast through her bra, earning a moan out of her. "You are safe. You are loved. You are enough." Her fingers tightened on his hair. "You will always have someone loving you. Now, until my dying breath." Kissing down her chest, he fumbled with the button and zipper of her pants, tugging them down and taking them off. "You have me. All of me." He kissed her navel, then licked his way up, finding her lips. "Catherine, you will always have me and my heart. I am yours for eternity." Slipping his hand into her panties, he felt her. She bucked her hip to his touch. "So ready for me already, pretty girl." Rubbing her clit teasingly, he slipped a finger inside. "So wet and ready for me," he said, pumping his finger.

"Devin..." she moaned. He inserted a second finger. She squirmed, bucking her hips, seeking friction.

"Tell me what you want. Tonight is all about you." He pumped his fingers, drawing circles. She clenched on his fingers. "Tell me what you want, baby girl," he said, trailing kisses down her throat. "Tell me, baby girl." She rode his fingers. He made his way up her face, his fingers pumping slowly, his thumb drawing circles. He pressed down on her clit, and she whimpered, riding his hand.

"Devin... I..." she moaned, breathy.

"Yes," he said in her ear, biting it. "You wanna ride my hand? Just do it. Nothing is stopping you, and I certainly won't stop you," he added, pumping his fingers faster. She clenched around him.

"Devin... I'm—"

"You're what?" he purred, drawing faster circles on her. He inserted a third finger, making her squirm under him. "That's it, baby girl," he groaned. She was a moaning mess under him, riding his hand, rolling her hips to meet the thrust of his fingers. He bit her ear. "Come for me," he commanded. That was enough. That was all she needed.

"Oh god..." she moaned, spasming on his hand.

Once she was done, he removed his hand from her panties, bringing his fingers to his mouth, moaning at the taste of her. It wasn't enough. He took his shirt off and kissed her, fumbling with his belt and the button of his pants. He was so hard it hurt. She wrapped her arms around him, bringing him closer. He got off the bed, taking his pants and underwear off. She ogled him like he was a meal, and she was starving. She looked like a goddess, cheeks flushed and eyes half-lidded.

"Fuck, baby," he said, standing at the foot of the bed, skimming his hands up her legs, parting them, coming to a stop on the hem of her underwear. In one swift movement, he took them off, discarding them somewhere on the floor. He parted her legs as he trailed kisses all over her stomach. He grabbed her ankles and scooted her to the edge of the bed, kneeling in front of her. He kissed up her left leg, stopping in the middle and biting her upper thigh. He gave the same treatment to her right leg.

"Devin…" she pleaded. "Please…"

"Baby, you don't have to beg." That was all the confirmation he needed. Grabbing hold of her hips, he gave her one long and slow lick.

"Oh god, Devin…" she moaned, her hands flying to his hair, her back arching off the bed.

"You like that?" he asked, smirking. She bucked her hips. He licked her again. Her fingers tightened around his hair. He moved one of his hands from her hips, inserting two fingers inside her. She cried out. Her moans would be the end of him. He licked and pumped his fingers inside her until she became a shaking mess under his tongue and fingers, moaning his name. He gave her one last lick, kissing her inner right thigh. She groaned at the loss of contact.

"I was so close to coming again," she breathed out. He licked his fingers, groaning at the taste of her.

"I know. But not yet, baby girl." He stood and crawled up her body, his tongue exploring her skin from navel to neck. "We need to take this off," he pointed out, kissing her shoulder and playing with the strap of her bra. He slid one side down, leaving a trail of kisses down her arm. He snuck his hand under her, unclasping her bra and taking it off in one movement. "Tell me what you want, baby," he ordered, biting her neck. One of his hands grasped his already hard, throbbing cock, aligning the tip to her already aching entrance, the other one supporting him.

"I want to feel all of you tonight. All," she breathed out. "Nothing between us."

He groaned, inserting the tip inside, making her squirm. "Do you want it rough? Do you want it sweet and slow? Tell me what you want."

"I want you, Devin. I don't care," she responded, out of breath, bucking her hips for more contact. He looked into her eyes.

"I'm clean, baby girl," he said as he teased her entrance.

"Me too," she moaned, angling her hips to take more of him. That was all the confirmation he needed.

"Don't close your eyes," he ordered as he slammed into her to the hilt. He groaned, dropping his face into the crook of her neck. "Catherine, for fuck's sake, you feel better than I ever imagined. So much better than my hand," he moaned, stilling. He drew out and thrusted into her again, earning a moan from her. "Oh, good god, Catherine, I won't last long," he groaned, pounding in again. He fit perfectly. *They* fit perfectly. Like two pieces of a puzzle. Like they were made for each other. He slammed into her again, her walls clenching around him. "Oh no, baby, no, don't do that. Don't do that, please," he moaned. He thrusted again, harder. Rougher. She wrapped her arms around him, kissing his face. Her hands roamed his body, landing on his ass, pushing him forward, closer. "Oh, good God," he moaned, slamming inside her again. "Catherine," he groaned, picking up speed. She moaned, her nails digging into his back, leaving marks. He guided one of his hands to where their bodies connected, finding her clit and touching it. She clenched around him. He groaned. He made circles around it while slamming into her.

She moaned. "Devin, fuck, please—"

"Please, what?" he breathed out, thrusting harder, sloppier. He was close, so close. He could feel the pressure at the base of his spine, but he willed his body to wait. He willed his desire to wait until she found her release.

"Harder," she whispered, on the verge. She was close, so close. Her hands brought him closer. He did as she asked. Slamming ruthlessly into her, his fingers expertly caressing her clit. "Devin, I'm—" she moaned but stopped, bucking her hips to meet his thrusts, stilling mid-air, spasming while screaming his name. He groaned, stopping his hand and grabbing her hip. He felt his earth-shattering release, white spots forming on his vision field.

"Fuck, Catherine," he moaned, pumping into her, riding his high, emptying himself inside her. Panting, he dropped beside her. She was equally as breathless. They stayed like that for a couple of minutes, catching their breaths. Catherine rolled over, nuzzling herself to his side. He wrapped an arm around her, his hand tracing idle patterns on her back. Her hand caressed his chest, her nails scratching softly. She sighed.

"I hope it was mind-blowing."

She laughed softly. "Well, it's been a while since I had sex, so it was indeed mind-blowing."

He sighed and closed his eyes, relishing the feeling of her. Of her soft, warm skin against him. On her slightly agitated breathing. He felt her hand cupping his cheek. He opened his eyes and looked at her. She stretched out and kissed him, her hand grasping at his hair. He deepened the kiss, his other hand cupping her jaw. She bit his lower lip. He groaned as she smirked. Her hand wandered down his body, her nails scratching his abs. Her lips trailed down his jaw, to his throat, biting lightly. He groaned, the feeling making his blood hot. He felt his cock starting to harden.

"Catherine, what are you…"

She climbed into his lap. "Shhh…" she said, bending down and kissing him. "I've waited thirteen years for this moment," she said, lifting herself onto her knees and grabbing his member, placing it between her legs. "And it has been over six months since I last had sex. Real sex. This is far from over," she purred in his ear as she sank down on him, slowly, taking all of him deeper. He sat up, wrapping his arms around her waist. She peppered kisses down his face. "I love you, with my heart and soul, Devin. I'm not going anywhere. You have me," she murmured, making her way back to his lips, kissing them softly. "I'm all in," she whispered against his lips, biting his lower lip. He groaned. He kissed the middle of her chest. She wrapped her fingers in his hair, pulling his head back.

"Catherine…" he groaned. One of her hands grabbed his chin, making him look at her.

"Mine," she said as she rotated her hips. He moaned. "Say it," she commanded. He groaned, thrusting up as she lifted herself and sank down again.

"Yours," he vowed. "Forever." And he meant it. His hand trailed up her back, fisting her beautiful black hair and pulling her head back, exposing her neck. She moaned, closing her eyes. He nibbled there, sucking and biting. She whimpered in pleasure. The sound was music to his ears. "Mine," he growled, thrusting up, marking her. She moaned. He kissed her neck. "You are mine. You will always be mine, Catherine Babbitt." He thrusted up, meeting her hip movements. She whimpered. Before they knew it, they both found release again, collapsing on the bed, Catherine on top of him. He ran his hand up and down her back. An anxious feeling settled in his chest. It all felt too good to be true. Too good to be real. He wrapped his arms around her, kissing her head.

"I know I said I wanted all of you, but we are gonna need to find a drugstore," she mumbled against his skin.

"Why is that?" he asked, tracing lazy circles in her lower back with his pointer finger.

"I need a plan b pill."

"Why?"

"I'm not on birth control, and we didn't use protection."

"We won't need that," he replied, kissing her head. She lifted her head to look at him.

"Why not?" she questioned, frowning.

"I got a vasectomy two years ago."

"You what?" she asked, sitting up. He tucked a piece of hair behind her ear.

"I wasn't sure I wanted kids, so I just got one."

"Do you still feel that way?"

"Right now, I'm not sure. If it's with you, when the time is right, and *if* you want kids as well, I absolutely would love to," he stated. She bent down and kissed his chest. He wrapped his arms around her, bringing her closer. "Now, how about we preserve the earth and take a bath together?"

Chapter Twenty-Eight

Catherine

She woke up to the sunlight leaking through the shades, her naked body pressed into a bare chest. She snuggled closer to the warmth. Devin's arms automatically tightened around her, burying his face in her neck. Smiling, she closed her eyes and fell asleep again.

She stretched her arm to find the other side of the bed cold and empty. She opened her eyes and realized she was alone. She got off the bed and found Devin's discarded shirt on the floor. She picked it up and put it on, looking through her suitcase for clean underwear. She walked to the bathroom, washed her face, brushed her teeth, and gathered her hair in a messy bun. The door opened, and Devin walked in, wearing nothing but his boxer shorts.

"Good morning." He had a steaming cup of coffee in one of his hands. He walked to her, kissing her forehead. "This is for you," he said, handing her the mug. "You look absolutely ravishing in my shirt." He smirked. She took a sip from her coffee, humming. "What do you want for breakfast?" he asked, placing a strand of her hair behind her ear, caressing her earlobe.

"Pancakes," she replied. "Can we make pancakes?" He chuckled.

"I can absolutely make you pancakes." She smiled. "Come on," he said, kissing her cheek before walking out of the bathroom. She followed him. She glanced around the house. Now, in the daylight, the house looked bigger.

"Whose house is this?" she asked, sitting on one of the stools at the breakfast bar.

"Corbin's family cabin," he answered, gathering the ingredients for the pancakes. "I asked him to borrow it. He also restocked the food for us."

"I didn't know Corbin had a family cabin."

"It's his parents, but they don't use it much. Corbin and Brianna are usually the ones that use it the most. Emily and I always join them up here in January when they do their annual trip," he clarified, preparing the batter.

"I have really missed out on so much," she whispered. She watched him nod, not meeting her eyes.

"Yeah, you have, Kitty Cat. Brianna and Corbin's wedding three years ago, the birth of the twins two years ago, Emily's engagement, lots of things you missed out on, Kitty Cat," he mumbled, inhaling.

"I'm sorry," she muttered, looking down at her coffee mug. *Shame.* She felt shame. All over one stupid mistake.

"It's in the past. We can only heal and move on," he added, turning around.

"Dev..." she whispered. He inhaled.

"Catherine, it's fine," he replied, turning the stove on. He started to make the pancakes, and they settled into silence. An uncomfortable, awkward silence. She busied herself and set up the breakfast bar, getting plates and utensils. He finished making the pancakes and arranged them on the bar. He went to the fridge and got some juice. He got the maple syrup out of the cupboard and walked to the breakfast bar, sitting down beside her, avoiding her gaze. "Eat before they get cold," he uttered, scooping some pancakes onto her plate.

They ate in silence, only the sound of the scraping of the utensils on the plates filling the silence between them. Only a few inches separated them. Yet, it felt like miles. They finished eating, and she gathered their plates to wash them. Once she was done, she rested her hands on the sink, dropping her head.

"We should take this week to work things out," she said, looking out the window on top of the sink that overlooked the woods behind the house. "Hurting you is the biggest mistake I ever made, Devin, and I will carry that burden for the rest of my life. That stain will always be there. It will be a regret that I will never escape. No amount of apologies will ever make up for the nine years of hurt I inflicted on you. No amount of time will erase that wound I left. I know that. I just hope that one day, we can move past it. I have to atone for my sins. One of them was hurting you. The other was hurting Emily. I will carry those two mistakes in my soul until my last breath. I just hope one day you forgive me," she continued. Heavy footsteps padded behind her, and a pair of arms wrapped around her shoulders. He kissed the back of her head.

"I agree. We should talk about it."

"It's okay if you don't trust me. It's okay if you are hesitant of me and this, whatever this is between us," she added, looking down, a tear escaping her eye. "Earning your trust back is the thing I will work the hardest for."

"Come on, let's sit down and talk about this. I think it's time." She nodded. He kissed her head again and unfolded himself from her, walking away. He went to the living room, where the fireplace was. He had already started the fire, adding more logs to the roaring pit. She sat down on one of the sofas. He walked to her with a blanket in his hands, wrapping it around her legs. He bent down and kissed her forehead.

"Thanks," she whispered. She fidgeted with her hands on her lap. She was nervous and scared.

"I'm going to put some clothes on. I'll be back."

"Yeah, that would be a good idea," she replied, nodding.

Devin turned and left the room. He came back a couple of minutes later, dressed in sleepwear. His pajama pants hung low on his waist. Devin sat down on the floor in front of her sofa. He folded his arms on her legs, leaning his head on them.

"You're right. I am hesitant about this. Anxious even," he started after a few minutes of silence with his eyes closed. "It feels too good to be true," he continued, opening his eyes and looking at her. His eyes were red. "Catherine, I don't think I can let you go if something happens again. If there's a misunderstanding or we get into a fight, you can't just run away like you did back then. I won't be as strong as I was. The only reason I didn't sink into depression was because Emily needed me. I needed to be there for her. I really can't do this, Catherine. If we move past this, it's forever. It's until one of us dies. Catherine, I can't… I won't do this again. I won't go through this heartbreak again. You are either fully in or not. We can't do halfsies. *I* can't do halfsies.

"I already wasted nine years sulking over you, longing after you. If life decided to give us a second chance, we have to take it. But I need to know where you stand. I need to know if you see a future for us. We can heal together. This journey is for both of us. But I need to know if you are in or not. Yes, you broke my heart, and it still hurts. Every time I hold you, every time I wake up next to you, I feel it's all just a dream. That I'm going to wake up and you won't be there. That I imagined everything," he confessed, his voice breaking. "I can't do that again, Catherine. I won't do it again," he whispered, leaning his forehead on her legs and crying. She wrapped her arms around him, hugging him. "I need to know you are all in." She kissed his head.

"I'm all in, Devin. I promise, I'm all in," she whispered. "I'm so sorry I hurt you. I'm sorry you never got to feel your emotions because you became Emily's emotional fortress. I'm so sorry, Devin. If I had known what I know now, we would have avoided all this heartbreak. We would have avoided all of these tears. There's nothing I can say or do that would make the pain of the last nine years go away. I can only apologize and promise to do better. I can promise I will not shut you out again," she promised, her tears falling. She kissed his head again. "I'm so sorry, Devin. You were the last person I ever wanted to hurt. I'm so sorry I broke your heart. But I can promise I will do whatever it takes to mend it. I will do whatever it takes to make it better," she vowed, cradling his face in her hands and wiping his tears away. "If you give me one more chance, just one, I promise, I'll make it count. I promise I will not disappoint you, Devin," she pleaded, leaning her forehead on his and closing her eyes. "You are right. If life gave us a second chance, we have to take it." Devin's hands came to rest on the side of her head.

"It's okay, Kitty Cat. One step at a time." She moved from the sofa and sat on his lap, wrapping her arms around his neck.

"One step at a time," she said, looking into his eyes. His hand came to rest on her cheek, wiping away a stray tear. She leaned into his touch, kissing his palm.

"I love you so much, Catherine, it physically hurts. I think I've loved you since the day I met you. I feel like my heart is too big for my chest," he admitted, kissing her lips softly. He proceeded to kiss her nose, and then her forehead, his lips lingering there. They settled into a comfortable silence with her still on his lap, hugging him and playing with the little hairs at the nape of his neck. Her eyes burned with tears as she realized that the event that happened five minutes before she saw them at the top of the stairs was the reason for all this heartbreak. She couldn't keep running away from it. She needed to talk about it. She realized *that* is what led to all the heartbreak of the last nine years.

"My mom..." she choked out, her voice shaky. "My mom died during finals week of senior year," she murmured, a tear escaping. She wiped it away fast. Devin cradled her face.

"What?" he asked in a whisper. "You never mentioned anything." Catherine looked at him, tears brimming in her eyes. Realization dawned on Devin. "It happened that day, didn't it?" She looked down and nodded.

"It happened right before it," Catherine murmured, remembering that day like it was yesterday, forever engraved in her memory.

Nine Years Ago - First day of Finals, Senior Year

"So, Cathy, how are finals? Ready for them? I had my first one earlier today," Kyle asked. He was walking her back from the library where they'd met up by chance.

"It's going okay," she replied as her phone rang. It was Mrs. Turnil, the neighbor. She never called her unless it was an emergency. "I'm sorry, Kyle, I have to take this," she

apologized, answering her phone and walking away from him. "Mrs. Turnil, hi. It's odd to get a call from you. Everything okay?" *she asked, speeding up her walk back to her apartment.*

"Sweetie..." *Mrs. Turnil replied. That wasn't a good sign.* "Sweetie, I need you to sit down. What I'm about to tell you is a bit of a heavy thing."

"Mrs. Turnil, you're scaring me. What happened? Did something happen to my mom?" *she questioned, her voice breaking.*

"Oh, sweetie, I'm very sorry," *Mrs. Turnil answered.*

"Mrs. Turnil, what happened?"

"Sweetie, your mom has passed away," *Mrs. Turnil uttered, her words hitting her like a bucket of ice water. The books she was holding in her arms fell to the ground, and her knees gave out, hitting the concrete floor of the sidewalk.*

"No..." *she whispered, the first tear falling.*

"Sweetie, she died peacefully. The treatment was too much for her body," *Mrs. Turnil explained.*

"Treatment? What treatment? She was fine when I visited in February for her birthday. It's only been three months."

Mrs. Turnil gasped. "Oh, my goodness, she didn't tell you?" *Mrs. Turnil asked her.* "Of course, she didn't. She didn't want her baby girl to worry. For goodness sake, that woman was so hardheaded."

"Mrs. Turnil, what treatment?" *Catherine asked desperately.*

"My sweet child, your mom was diagnosed with lung cancer in March," *Mrs. Turnil explained softly.* "She started treatment right away. She wanted to make it to your graduation, but her cancer was too advanced."

"She what?" *Catherine asked in a whisper, shifting to a*

sitting position in the middle of a sidewalk. The tears were falling freely now.

"I'm so sorry, sweetheart. She didn't die alone. I was there with her, holding her hand. I can assure you she died without pain and in peace. I promised her I was going to look after you now. I know you must be in finals week, but it didn't feel right to wait until you finished them. I'm so sorry, darling," Mrs. Turnil apologized, but her mind muffled the words. She didn't know how she made it home or how long she sat on the sidewalk. She stood up and walked to a nearby bench, burying her face on her knees and crying, not giving a damn who saw her.

She needed to contact the family lawyer. She needed to go back home to deal with her mom's stuff, plan her funeral.

The house. What was she supposed to do with the house? Was she supposed to sell it? Keep it? Live in it? What about Penn State? Was she supposed to give up Penn State now and move back home?

Did she want to be buried or cremated? Should she do an open casket or not? Would people even show up to her funeral?

Graduation is next week. What am I supposed to do? Do I turn everything in early and go back home? Do I wait until graduation?

Oh my god, did she even leave a will?

Why didn't she tell me? Why did she keep this to herself? A sob escaped her throat as tears ran down her face. Why did this happen? Why to her?

All of these thoughts ran through her mind. Another sob ripped out of her throat as she realized she had lost both of her parents, but it hit her the hardest when she realized she lost her mom. The woman who sacrificed so much for her to be where she was right now, the woman who worked extra hard to make sure she succeeded, and she wasn't even going to be able to see her walk down the stage to get her diploma. She dried her tears and stood up.

She needed her best friend. She needed the safety of Devin's arms. She got her phone out, ready to dial his number. She was going up the stairs when she heard his laugh, a sob escaping her throat. He was there. He was going to make everything better. He was going to tell her it was all a bad dream.

And then, what was left of her heart got ripped out of her chest.

"I love you. There I said it," she heard the voice of her best friend and roommate, Emily, say. "And I think we should kiss," she said, Devin laughed. She ran away, slamming the door shut.

She didn't know when it happened, but she was sobbing, fisting his shirt. He was kissing her head, rocking her softly, and running a soothing hand through her hair.

"It's okay. You're okay," Devin's voice said in her ear, kissing her temple. "It's okay, I got you now, baby," he murmured in a comforting way that only made her sob harder. "Is that why you wanted me to quit smoking? Oh god." Devin's voice broke, and he hugged her tighter. She didn't know how long they sat there, but by the time she finished crying, her eyes were dry, and the heavy tightness on her chest that had been living there for almost a decade was gone. She lifted her head, and Devin's cheeks were tear-stained. She kissed his cheek. "I'm so sorry, Cat," he consoled her softly. She leaned her forehead on his, closing her eyes, her hand caressing his cheek.

"I know. I don't blame you," she replied. "You are right. That's why I wanted you to stop smoking. She got diagnosed a few months before graduation, but her cancer was too advanced. The treatment didn't work. She didn't tell me because I was graduating soon. She smoked for as long as I can remember, and she didn't take good care of her health. Always worrying about me and being able to provide for me. And she knew that if she told me, I would put a pause on my school to be there for her. So, I assume that's why she didn't tell me. She died on the first day of finals," Catherine continued. "And then I overheard you and Emily on the stairs, which now I know wasn't what I have been thinking all these years. In my defense, I learned about my mom minutes prior to that. My mind wasn't in the right place, so I assumed the worst." Catherine shrugged. "I still should have confronted both of you, but I didn't have the energy to do it. So I turned in my finals early, packed up, and was out by the last day of finals."

"Is that why you didn't go to graduation?" Devin asked. Catherine nodded.

"I had to go back home and plan her funeral service. Empty and clean out the house and sell it. I was her only child. My father died when I was little, so I had to do all of that." She shrugged. Devin leaned in and kissed her forehead, his lips lingering there. She leaned into the touch. She took a deep breath and let it go.

"You should've come to me," he mumbled.

"I didn't have the mental or the emotional energy to do that." Devin hugged her, kissing her head.

"Thank you for telling me," he whispered. They sat there, hugging and leaning on each other for who knows how long.

"Have you ever had s'mores made in a fireplace?" she

asked, breaking the silence and looking into his eyes. He smiled a little and shook his head.

"I have not," he replied. "But we have the ingredients. I'll go get them while you prepare the blanket bed in front of the fireplace, sounds good?" he proposed. She nodded. He kissed her forehead again and helped her stand. He kissed her lips softly.

As he gathered the ingredients, she placed a bunch of blankets and pillows on the floor. She was engulfed in one when he got back to the living room. They made the s'mores and settled, cuddling in front of the fireplace after eating them, Devin's arms around her, holding her close to him.

"Tell me about the last nine years. Tell me what happened to you," he said, playing with her hand. "What happened after you went to Penn State?" She lay on her back, looking up at Devin, who had his head propped on his fist, looking down at her. She smiled and dove into telling him about her life for the past nine years, all the accomplishments, all the milestones, all the struggles, and all the happy memories. She told him about how she came to DC, how she ended up in Michael's office, and how she climbed the ladder and ended up as his chief of staff. All the while, Devin's eyes never left her face.

"But enough about me. How about you? How was Harvard Law? How did you end up at the Hill?" she asked.

He told her about law school, how he was at the top of his class, how he graduated with honors and became class president, about Corbin and Brianna's wedding, and how he was the best man. He told her about Brianna going to med school and graduating at the top of her class, becoming a cardiothoracic surgeon, about the twins, about Emily and her fiancée. He told her about every single little detail about his life for the past nine years. They talked about everything and anything for hours. It felt like old friends catching up. And for once in nine years, she felt lighter.

They were snuggled in the blankets, night had already fallen.

"Do we have to move from this place?" she asked.

"Do you want to spend the night here?" She nodded. He kissed her shoulder. "Then we will sleep in the blankets tonight, Kitty Cat. We don't have to go anywhere." She nestled closer to him, and he tightened his grip on her.

"Satan?"

"Yes, Kitty Cat?"

"I missed you. I missed you so fucking much. I am so happy life brought you back to me. That it made us cross paths again," she confessed, kissing his arm. "I missed my best friend and the person who knew me the most."

"I missed you too. I missed us."

"I promise I will always call *timeout* when I'm upset."

"And I promise I will never let you walk away again. It's going to be you and me against all odds."

"You and me," she said, closing her eyes and falling asleep in his arms.

Chapter Twenty-Nine

Catherine

"No coming until I say so, baby girl," he ordered, slamming into her. He trailed his hand up her back, stopping at the back of her head and fisting her still-wet hair.

After they had sex that first night they arrived, more sex followed in the upcoming days. In the shower, in the bathtub, against the sink, by the fireplace. They were barely able to keep their hands off each other. There wasn't a single surface in the cabin they hadn't christened in the last five days. Today, they barely got cleaned up in the shower or dried off before Devin pushed her on the bed again, desperate to touch her. Desperate to feel her, to be inside her. For once in her life, she was happy to relinquish her power and authority if it meant she'd be rewarded in other ways, and Devin was more than happy to oblige, both of them having similar kinks.

This time, she was laying face down on the mattress, Devin pounding into her from behind. He thrusted harder this time, bringing her out of her mind. She clenched around him. He fisted her hair and pulled her head back, her back arching.

"I said no coming until I said so," he growled, biting her neck. She laughed.

"Make me," she challenged. His grip on her hair tightened.

"Baby girl don't provoke me," he said, slamming harder into her. She clenched again, knowing the simple movement drove him crazy. He growled in her ear. "You like that? You like getting a reaction out of me?" he asked, his free hand wrapping around her throat, squeezing. "Who would have thought that the little quiet girl from college was a freak," he added, biting her ear lobe. "It's always the quiet ones. Did Kyle know? Did he know how much of a freak you are? Or did he fuck you vanilla-style? Did he ever indulge in your fantasies? Answer me, Kitty Cat," he demanded, pulling her head back and tightening his grip on her throat. She was on the verge of coming, clenching around him. "You didn't answer, baby girl. Does Kyle know the type of woman who slept beside him?"

"No, fuck. No, Devin, he didn't," she panted. "He never did," she breathed out.

"That's what I thought," he retorted, pounding harder, deeper.

"Devin, please, I can't—"

"You can't what?" he asked. "Do you need to use your safe word?" he asked. She shook her head. "No coming until you use your words, Catherine." His grip on her throat tightened.

"Please, I can't hold off much longer," she breathed out. He stilled, and she whimpered.

"Use your words," he ordered, the hand on her throat traveling down her body, settling in her middle. His fingers pressed down on her clit just as he slammed into her again.

"Please—"

"Not what I wanted to hear."

"Please, let me come." He groaned, pressing harder in her clit, tracing erratic circles.

"Good girl," he said, kissing her neck while thrusting ruthlessly into her.

Before she could comprehend what happened, her knees buckled, her whole body spasming in an earth-shattering orgasm. He bit her shoulder softly while growling, one arm holding her up by the hips tightly, finding his own release. Her hands went to the bed, holding her there in shaky arms. He pulled out of her, leaving her feeling cold and empty as she laid down. She lost count of how many times he had made her come today, her whole body feeling achy and sore but deliciously so. She was panting, sweating. Devin lay sideways, looking at her. His eyes were heavy with emotions but also with exhaustion.

"You're tired," she said. He brushed the hair away from her face.

"You have to cut me some slack. The last time I had this much sex was never," he said. "Pardon me if I'm a bit rusty." She chuckled.

"Can I ask you something?" she asked, moving closer to him.

"Anything," he said, bringing her to rest on his chest.

"Were you seriously never in a relationship?" she questioned, tracing idle circles on his naked chest.

"Never. No one could fill the void you left," he replied. "When you left, when you said our friendship was over, I felt like a piece of my heart shattered, a piece of my soul left me, and when you blocked my number and I couldn't reach you, my whole heart was pulverized," he continued, kissing her head. She kissed his chest, and they fell into a comfortable silence. "So…" She looked up at him. "This week, we discovered you have a praise kink, you're into choking and hair pulling, and you are a brat. Anything else I should know?" he asked, listing most of her kinks. She nestled herself into his chest.

"I'm a masochist," she said, barely a whisper.

"I'm sorry, I didn't catch that."

"I'm a masochist," she repeated, a little louder this time.

"Oh?" he asked, intrigued. "So into spanking?"

"But it's okay if you aren't into that," she said, nodding. He flipped them and towered over her, her back on the mattress, his massive hands pinning her wrist down and his body caging her to the bed, one of his thighs between her legs, creating friction in her middle.

"Who said I'm not into that?" he asked in a low voice. "Who said one of my kinks isn't putting you across my knee and spanking some sense into you, like the little brat you are?" She smiled at him. "It's always the quiet ones. I should've known." He bent down and placed a soft kiss on her lips. "Would you be opposed to doing it slowly and romantically every once in a while? Or shall we always do it as kinky as possible?" he asked, kissing down her neck and releasing her wrists.

"There must be a balance to everything," she replied. He chuckled against her neck, kissing the spot behind her ear.

"I love a good balance," he whispered in her ear.

"Good," she replied, sliding her hands into his hair and gripping it, pulling his head back. "Because I'm a switch, and sometimes I like to be in control." He growled. "I hope that's okay," she said, batting her eyelashes at him.

"Like I said, I love a good balance." Her grip tightened in his hair, and he groaned.

"Not now, though. I'm spent, my body is sore, and I'm

not sure I will be able to walk tomorrow," she retorted, releasing his hair and cupping his face.

"Just like I wanted you."

"Get off," she said, pushing him off. She sat up and got out of the bed, groaning at the soreness everywhere, and waddled to the bathroom to pee. She looked at herself in the mirror. She had a small hickey on her neck. *A hickey*. He gave her a hickey like he was some hormonal teenager. "I'm going to fucking kill you, Devin Mack," she screeched, exiting the bathroom.

"That would be a good way to leave this world," he replied, smirking at her.

"You gave me a hickey? We are not hormonal teenagers. We are thirty years old, Devin Mack," she reproached, putting both hands on her hips. He got out of the bed and walked to her, grabbing her throat and slamming her softly into the wall behind her.

"I was marking what's mine. I was marking what has been mine for fourteen years. And I will mark you as I see fit," he growled. He gripped her chin, forcing her to look up at him. "This won't be the first or last time. Get used to them, baby girl," he continued, bending down and placing a rough kiss on her lips, biting her lower lip. Heat gathered in her lower stomach again, and she melted into his kiss. His free hand traveled down her body, cupping her middle and parting her legs. "This belongs to me now. No other man will ever have you, you hear me?" She moaned, his possessiveness making her feel things. Every single cell of willpower left her body at that instant. She nodded. He tightened his grip on her. "Mine. Don't you ever forget that," he said, kissing her again and letting her go, leaving her in a daze, her back against the wall, looking for anything to hold on to. The door of the bathroom closed, and she released a breath she didn't know she was holding. She evened her breaths and recomposed herself.

In all the four years she had been with Kyle, he had never made her feel this way. He was never up to try what she wanted to try. It was always the same boring way, missionary, and sometimes she even faked it. With Devin, she had no words. He knew what he was doing. She must have come at least a dozen times since they arrived at the cabin. She walked to her suitcase, pulling out a pair of underwear and putting them on. She walked to Devin's suitcase and opened it. Rummaging through it, she picked out one of his t-shirts and put it on. It was too big on her, landing mid-thigh.

"I have a shirt thief," he exclaimed behind her, wrapping his arms around her shoulders. She melted into his chest.

"I'm sorry, you mean *our* shirts?" she asked rhetorically. He snorted.

"I'm sorry, you are correct. I no longer have anything of mine. Everything I own is *ours* now." She chuckled and kissed his arm. He kissed the crown of her head. "I wanted to kill him," he confessed.

"Who? Kyle?" she asked, confused.

"God, yes, but he is not worth it," he replied, kissing her temple. "No. I wanted to kill Miles for what he said to you. About you," he whispered. "It killed me inside because I once called you that. I felt so ashamed," he confessed. "Kitty Cat, I know I already apologized for it, but I'm sorry." His grip on her tightened, and she rubbed his forearms.

"I know," she whispered. "You never told me why you call me Kitty Cat." He placed a hand on her cheek.

"When I first met you, you were so dismissive of me. Like a black cat. Proud, ambitious. You even rolled your eyes when I called you Kitty Cat the first time," he explained, and she chuckled. "And when you said your name was Catherine, calling you Kitty Cat just felt right. It just slipped off my tongue. And it felt so easy to call you that, because your personality is like a black cat. Plus, the nickname feels unique." She leaned into his touch. He kissed her cheek again. She moved and felt something poke her back. She widened her eyes. He closed his eyes and groaned. "It can't be normal to be this horny after coming over a dozen times," he said, dropping his forehead to hers.

"We have fourteen years to catch up on. I think it's normal," she replied, grinding her hips on his already hard cock. His hands slid to the back of her neck, tightening his grip.

"Stop," he commanded. She did it again, his hand fisting her hair and pulling her head back. "I said stop. We need to rest. We have a long day of driving tomorrow. Don't. As much as I want it, and as much as the thought of being inside of you again is very appealing, we can't. We need the rest," he continued as she ground her hips again. "Catherine—"

"Let me take care of the problem," she replied, one of her hands sliding down his chest. He grabbed her wrist before she made it past his collarbones.

"I said stop. That's an order." She pouted, batting her eyelashes at him. "Stop. Don't do that. Don't give me puppy eyes," he said, closing his eyes. Her free hand continued her journey down his chest, reaching his happy trail.

"Let me take care of the problem. I'll be a good girl," she purred, dragging her nail down his shaft. It twitched to her touch, springing to life. The hold on her wrist and hair loosened. He was at her mercy. Her other hand joined the other, cupping him in her hands, feeling like silk. He groaned. She jerked him off, her hands slow but rough. She peppered kisses down his chest, her tongue licking his abs. She kneeled in front of him, looking up at him through her eyelashes. She trailed kisses down his middle. Kissing his hip bones and down his navel. "I will take care of it," she murmured, giving him one long and slow lick. He groaned. She grazed her teeth along the tip, and his hips buckled.

"Cat—" he choked out. She took him fully in her mouth, sucking from tip to hilt. His hands went to her hair, fisting it, guiding her mouth. She scraped her teeth as she came up to the tip, feeling him twitch in her mouth, the tip covered in precum. She swirled her tongue on the head. Her tongue dragged against his underside vein. "Oh baby, that feels so good," he moaned. She hollowed her cheeks, increasing her pace, bobbing her head. His grip tightened on her hair. He stilled her, slamming into her mouth, fucking it. He thrust all the way down the back of her throat. She grabbed onto his hips, gripping hard. "Your mouth feels so good," he rasped. Her tongue swirling on the tip. His knees buckled. "Fuck, do that again," he demanded. She smirked and did it again while he fucked her mouth. "For fuck's sake, Catherine... what are you doing to me?" It wasn't long before he stilled and twitched, emptying his seed down her throat. She bobbed her head, sucking every ounce from him. Once she was done, he pulled her up by her hair, grasping her chin and kissing her aggressively, guiding her against the wall. His hands moved to her hips, ripping her panties in two. He grabbed hold of her knees, lifting her up against the wall. She wrapped her legs around his hips. "You started this, Babbitt. I guess we aren't sleeping tonight. Again."

Chapter Thirty

Devin

They'd been on the road for an hour. After the incredible week they had, there wasn't an inch of skin on Catherine's body that he hadn't tasted. Not an inch of skin he hadn't marked. Not an inch of skin he hadn't kissed. Taking his time to explore her skin, her soul. Her body and their time together were everything and more. Everything he had ever hoped for. Everything he had wished for.

The revelation of what happened moments before the disaster that took away nine years of their life together still shook him to his core. Any resentment or hurt he held over it was gone. His only goal moving forward was to love her the way he was always meant to do. That much was clear to him. It hurt him to think she shouldered all that pain alone. That she had carried that burden all alone. One of his hands was on her thighs, moving up and down in a slow motion, his other hand was on the steering wheel.

"So, how are your parents?" He turned briefly to her and smiled. "Goodness, I miss your mom's apple pie so much.

Remember that year I met her? When she gave me that whole pie to take home?" she recalled. He chuckled.

"Move-out day, freshman year," he said, the flashback clear in his mind.

Thirteen years ago - Move-out Day, Freshman year

"So, where is she?" his mom asked, walking behind him.

"Uh?" he replied, confused, looking around for her shining black hair.

"Where is she? The girl you're looking around for," his mom questioned, putting a box in the trunk and fumbling to arrange all his boxes.

"I don't know what you are talking about," he said, trailing his gaze around and spotting her black hair. He smiled. His mom smacked him on the head.

"Don't know what you're talking about my ass," his mom mocked and followed his eyesight. She inhaled. "Devin... she's beautiful," she whispered.

"I know. Her name is Catherine," he whispered, so low he didn't think his mom heard him.

"What? Her name is Catherine?" she asked, confused. He nodded.

"Yes. I call her Kitty Cat." Catherine looked around and found him. He waved, and she waved back, walking to where he was.

"Wait until I tell Josh about her."

"Please, don't. I don't need his big brother ass making comments about this."

"Hey, you," Catherine mumbled as she approached, hugging him. He threw an arm around her shoulders and

kissed the crown of her head, a habit he'd developed in the last couple of months and one he intended to keep.

"Hey, you," he said back. "Catherine, this is my mom, Sarah. Mom, this is Catherine." *Catherine moved out of his embrace and extended a hand to his mom.*

"My, my. Aren't you a pretty girl?" *his mom mumbled. She shook Catherine's hand.*

"Mom…" *Devin replied with a warning tone.*

"Oh hush, Devin," *his mom retorted, hugging Catherine.* "So, Catherine, do you like apple pie?" *Catherine nodded.*

"I love apple pie."

"Good, because we were about to drop these off at Devin's new apartment, and I was heading into the grocery store to get all the ingredients and make some. It would be lovely if you tagged along."

"I would love to tag along, but I'm dropping my stuff at my new place, and then I need to go pick up my badge and work computer at my new summer internship office," *Catherine replied.* "But if you guys want, I can join you guys for dinner."

"Wonderful. Are you allergic to anything?" *his mom asked.*

"No, but she doesn't eat seafood," *Devin added, busying himself with the boxes in the trunk.*

"I can make my famous lasagna," *his mom suggested.*

"That sounds yummy," *Catherine replied.*

"Then it's settled. Let's aim for seven. Does that sound good?" *He saw Catherine nod from his peripheral vision.*

"Yes, that's wonderful," *she replied as she flicked his arm.* "Be nice, Satan."

"What a lovely girl," *his mom commented as she sighed.* "Come on, let's finish up here and go buy the ingredients," *she added as she walked back to the dorms.*

A few hours later, and countless trips back and forth to the car, he was all unpacked in his new apartment. They were just coming back from the grocery store when his phone pinged with a new message from Catherine.

> Just finished all I needed to do today. Send me your address.

He sent her his address, and twenty minutes later, she was knocking on his door.

"Hello, Miss Internship," he greeted, leaning on the doorframe. She had a small bouquet of flowers in one hand, and a paper bag on the other.

"What's in the bag?" he asked.

"Just some chips and the artichoke and spinach dip you like."

"Catherine, I'm so glad you made it. You're here early. Come, you can help me make the apple pie," his mother said as she ushered Catherine inside.

"I'll take these," Devin said, taking the bag and the flowers from her hands. He closed the door and watched his mom connect with Catherine, treating her like the daughter she never had. He looked at them, and something clicked inside of him. Something he had been trying to figure out since January.

He was falling in love with Catherine.

"You know, I never told you, but I have something to confess about that day," he said. He felt her tense.

"What?" she asked softly, looking out the window.

"I was going to take you to Canada. Montreal and Quebec City. I was going to surprise you that night. I was going to confess in Quebec City. Had a whole thing planned. But shit happened," he admitted, shrugging. "Canada will always be there," he said, looking briefly at her. She was still looking out the window. "Hey…" he whispered, massaging the nape of her neck. "It's okay. Second chances, right?" She looked at him, her eyes misty and red.

"You were going to confess in Quebec City?" she asked in a shaky voice. He squeezed her neck and nodded, his eyes on the road. A sob escaped her lips.

"Hey, hey, hey. It's okay, Kitty Cat," he reassured her. He saw a highway pit stop and parked there. He undid his seatbelt and turned to her. "Come here," he murmured, hugging her. She sobbed on his shoulder, and he let her. She had nine years of regret and guilt on her shoulders over a misunderstanding. A misunderstanding that wasn't completely her fault. "It's okay. I got you," he mumbled, tracing circles on her back and kissing her head.

"I'm such a jerk," she whispered. He grabbed her face between his hands, drying the tears with his thumbs. He kissed her forehead.

"You made a mistake. You are human. You are allowed to make mistakes, Catherine. The important thing is that we are here. We are moving on, and we are working on it. That's what's important. Realizing you made a mistake didn't make me love you less. Didn't make me hate you," he continued, kissing her forehead again.

"How can you still love me even after this? After knowing everything."

"Because everyone deserves a second chance," he simply said. Another tear escaped her eyes, and he caught it with his thumb. He kissed her temple.

"Thank you," she muttered. He hugged her and kissed the top of her head.

"Do you want to take a break from the road? Should we stay here for a while? Sit down on those picnic tables and take a break?"

"Yes." He let her go and turned the car off.

"I'll get us some snacks. You go sit, okay?" he said, and she nodded. They got out of the car, and he walked her to the picnic tables. A cold breeze swooped in. "Okay, maybe it is a bit too cold to be out here," he mentioned. She chuckled. "Let's just get snacks and go sit in the car instead," he observed, throwing an arm around her shoulders.

"I love you, Devin. I mean it," she whispered. He hugged her tighter.

"I know, Kitty Cat. I love *you*." They bought snacks and walked back to the car.

An hour later, they started to drive again. Catherine leaned in on his arm and fell asleep. It was night by the time he saw the Washington Monument in the distance, shaking Catherine awake. She stirred but didn't open her eyes. He shook her again, and she squinted.

"Wake up, sleepy head. We are near," he announced.

"Five more minutes."

"Okay," he chuckled, squeezing her thigh.

"Can we go to your place?" she asked, her eyes closed.

"Of course, we can, Kitty Cat," he responded. "We have to return the car first. So, I'm going to head into the airport. Then we can take a taxi to my place. I left my car at home."

She nodded and exhaled. "I don't want to go back to my place tonight."

"Well, lucky for you, I have a king-size bed."

She chuckled. "Not like that," she said, lifting her head. She looked down at the hand in her lap. She placed hers on top of his, playing with his knuckles. "Kyle's stuff is there. And I don't want to deal with that now."

"You guys lived together?" he inquired, keeping his tone neutral. He saw her nod from his peripheral vision.

"For two years now. But it's my place. The lease is under my name. I'm the one who makes the most money. But his stuff is there, and I don't want to deal with it. Not now," she continued. "I'll deal with it tomorrow."

"You can stay with me as long as you want," he reassured her.

They drove the rest of the way to the airport in silence. He dropped the car off and called a taxi. The ride from the airport to his place was quiet. He kissed the top of her head, inhaling her scent.

"I'll help you with his stuff. You'll be okay," he whispered against the crown of her head. She nodded. They got to his place and stopped at his doorway. "You're not allergic to cats, right?" he asked. She frowned, confused.

"No, why?"

"Okay, that's good," he said, unlocking his door. "Just so you are aware—" he started to say, but a black fur ball curled itself around his legs. He crouched down and petted it. "Hey, pretty girl," he cooed, picking the cat up in his arms.

"Oh, my goodness, who is this?" Catherine asked, extending her hand to the cat. The cat smelled her and nudged her hand with her head, giving Catherine the green light to pet her.

"This is Ellie," he replied, a little embarrassed.

"Well, hello, Ellie. Aren't you the sweetest," Catherine cooed, petting the cat. "Wait, Ellie?" she questioned. "As in short for Elizabeth?" she asked, giving Ellie ear scratches. He looked down, a little embarrassed.

"In my defense, that was the only name she reacted to. I tried everything. Her original name was supposed to be Cinnamon. But she only responded to Ellie. And Kitty Cat is only reserved for you. So yes, Ellie is short for Elizabeth," he explained, feeling a blush creeping onto his cheeks. "She is five."

"Well, aren't you the cutest cat I have ever seen?" Catherine cooed. Ellie purred. "Oh yeah, you like that?" Catherine asked, giving Ellie chin scratches. "I feel you and I are going to be best friends, Ellie." She looked up at him. "So, are we going to stay in the threshold, or are you going to let me in?" she asked. He chuckled, making space for her to walk inside. She looked around. "It's very you," she said, taking in the decor.

His space was simple, yet his style. White walls with black decorations. He laughed quietly and nodded. He dropped Ellie on the floor, and Ellie ran to Catherine's legs, demanding attention. Catherine picked her up in her arms, kissing the top of her head and giving her ear scratches. Ellie purred.

"The room is this way," he said, wheeling both of their luggage to his room. He turned the light on and let her in. She walked to it and threw herself on it. "Comfortable?" he asked. She nodded.

They showered and jumped under the covers, Ellie curling herself by Catherine's feet. He brought her closer to him, tucking her in his arms, and kissed her forehead, falling asleep.

Chapter Thirty-One

Catherine

"You think these are enough boxes?" Devin asked behind her. She nodded.

They had woken up and finally decided to leave the bed after spending the morning between the sheets. They went to a hardware store to get boxes for Kyle's stuff. Devin refused to let her do this alone.

"Yes. When we moved in together, he sold most of his stuff, or donated it. He is very minimalist," she explained, unlocking the door to her apartment. "Sorry, let me turn the heater on. I turned it off when we left," she said, walking to the thermostat, setting it to 72 degrees.

"Some things never changed. He was the same in college," Devin replied, walking inside. He looked around, his eyes lingering on the pictures hanging on the wall. "He hasn't really changed much," he whispered, taking his jacket off and hanging it in the coat closet. He helped her take hers off.

"Why did you guys stop talking?" she asked. "You used to be friends."

"He never said anything?" She shook her head.

"I only asked him once, and he changed the subject." She shrugged. "In a way, I also did the same. Do you know what happened?"

"Of course I know, but that is something *he* needs to be the one to tell you," he said, looking away. "For what it's worth, it was something bad, and no one from the inner circle talks to him at all." She nodded and sighed.

"Should we start packing?" she asked, folding up the sleeves of her sweater. He followed her lead. She walked to the room and turned the lights on.

"You really are a creature of habit," Devin mumbled, looking around. She smiled.

Her room was simple, with no astounding decorations. Her walls were white, and she had a lavender sheet set on her bed. She walked to the closet and stared at Kyle's side. She picked up a bunch of hangers with his clothes and walked back to the room, dropping them on the bed. They spent the next hour packing all his clothes in the boxes and labeling them.

"I'll just put these in a storage room and tell him to pick them up after he comes back from his trip," she mentioned, picking up the last of his clothes. She came back to the room. "This is the last of his clothing and stuff from the room," she added, dumping the clothes in the box. Devin was leaning against the doorframe, nodding.

"I'll help you take them. Also, I will run to the grocery store down the block. Get some food for you, is that okay?" She nodded. "I'll buy the ingredients to make my mom's lasagna. I know how much you love it. I'll be back in a few," he said, walking to her and kissing her temple.

Her phone vibrated in her pocket. She got it out, and it was a text from Emily.

> What are you doing for Thanksgiving?
>
> Please say nothing.
>
> Please come over for Thanksgiving.

>> I'm sensing that you really want me to come over for Thanksgiving.
>>
>> No, I am not doing anything. Yes, I would love to come over.

> Then it's settled. You will be Devin's plus one.

Emily replied with a bunch of emojis, and Catherine replied with a purple heart emoji and locked her phone.

She looked around, and the apartment felt empty. Placing the box on the floor beside the others, she took that moment to take all of Kyle's stuff from around the apartment and put it in a box. By the time she was done, Devin was opening the front door. He looked at the wall again. All the picture frames were in the box she was closing.

"You took them down?" he asked, shutting the door. She hummed in agreement. He walked to the kitchen and placed the groceries on the counter.

"All of his stuff is packed away," she said matter-of-factly. "Also, I'm your plus one to the Thanksgiving dinner at Emily's house."

"Whoa, whoa, whoa. What?" Devin asked enthusiastically.

"Yeah, Emily texted me earlier today and asked me what my plans were. Since I didn't have any, she said she would put me down as your plus one for Thanksgiving dinner."

"Are you sure you want to? It's okay if you aren't ready," he mentioned, looking at her from the kitchen. She nodded.

"I think it's time. We've been communicating these past

weeks," she replied. He walked to her and embraced her, kissing her head. They stayed like that for a while.

"I talked to my mom," he said, breaking the silence. "Told her about you. About us," he continued. "She said you better show up for Christmas and that it was about damn time." She chuckled.

"Christmas?" she asked, confused.

"They are coming up for Christmas. Shoot, you might have plans already. I'm sorry, I don't want to impose," he apologized. "Don't stress about it. If it's too soon, it's okay," he added, cradling her face and kissing her forehead. "Don't feel obligated to come."

"It's fine. I don't have plans."

"Okay."

"So, food," she commented, smiling at him. He smirked, walking past her into the kitchen. Her mouth watered at the thought of him making lasagna. She used to love it back in college. He made it at least once a week just for her.

Fall - Midterms week, Sophomore Year

"There she is," Devin cheered from the kitchen. "How did your Statistics exam go?" he asked, turning around from the stove. She walked to the kitchen island, dumping her bookbag on the floor.

"Awful. I think I flunked it," she said, placing her arms on the kitchen island and dropping her head.

"You always say that and end up acing the exam." She glared at him, and he chuckled, turning around to the stove and putting oven mittens on. "And your volunteering? Any new donation drives happening?"

"Yes, we started planning the winter clothes donation drive and food bank," she explained. *"What are you doing?"*

"Using the kitchen, since you and Emily don't," he replied. She walked to him and smacked him on the arm.

"Hey, I heard that," Emily protested, wandering into the kitchen. Catherine chuckled, glancing back at Devin.

"I know you did. Did I lie?" he asked, turning to look at her. She twirled around to look at Emily.

"For your information, I do use the kitchen," Emily retorted, giving him the middle finger.

"Making sandwiches or fixing a bowl of cereal does not count Emily."

"Yes, it does," Emily replied, picking utensils and walking out of the kitchen to set the table. She turned to him.

"Smells great," she muttered.

"It's my mom's lasagna."

"You know how to cook?"

"Contrary to popular belief, Kitty Cat... I do. My mom made sure I knew how to cook. This was the first recipe she taught me," he said, opening the oven and getting out a ceramic dish. *"Close your mouth, you're drooling."* He placed the lasagna on the countertop.

"I hope it tastes like hers."

"Sit. I'll bring you a plate," he ordered, taking the mittens off and ushering her to the table. *"Out of my kitchen."*

"This is my kitchen," Catherine protested, crossing her arms.

"Not now. Now it's mine. Out."

"Okay, okay," she conceded and walked to the table. A couple of minutes later, Devin placed a plate and a glass of water in front of her.

"Compliments from the chef," he announced and kissed

the top of her head. She blushed. He sat opposite her and dug into his plate. Emily did the same.

"My god, this is delicious," Emily said, her mouth full. Catherine ignored her and kept looking at Devin. He caught her staring.

"What? Do I have sauce on my face?" he asked, wiping his face. She shook her head.

"Thank you," she uttered softly.

"What for?" he questioned, downing half his water.

"Everything," she replied, looking down at her plate.

"Ugh, get a room, you two. I think I'm gonna throw up," Emily teased, taking another mouthful of her dinner.

She looked at him and smiled. After the disastrous date with Miles, she decided not to go out with anyone else because she realized one thing. No one would ever compare to Devin. Because she realized she was falling in love with him.

"You don't have to do all of this."

"I want to. I want to take care of you, Catherine. Let me."

"Okay," she whispered. "How can I help?"

"Oh, no, no. Out of my kitchen," he said, ushering her out. "Go unpack your suitcase."

"Okay, okay," she said. "Jeez," she protested, walking to her room.

She started to unpack her suitcase, putting everything away. The smell of food reached her, and she shuffled out of the room. Devin was facing away from her, stirring a pot on the stove. She walked up to him and wrapped her arms around him, placing her ear to his back, listening to his heartbeat.

"You finished unpacking?" he asked softly, and she nodded against his body. "Well, the lasagna is going to take a while, so why don't you freshen up? I'll be right here."

"Showering in my own bathroom for the first time in a month sounds like a good idea right now," she mumbled, kissing his back. "Is it too soon if I ask you to stay the night?"

Devin chuckled. "It will never be too soon for us, Catherine. Never," he said. "After dinner, I'll go home and grab an overnight bag and come back. Sounds good?" She nodded and walked to his side, kissing his cheek.

"I'll be in the shower. The one who's naked," she purred in his ear. He inhaled a shaky breath.

"If we want to eat today, I can't join you in the shower, Catherine," he said. She kissed down his jaw to his shoulder.

"Are you sure about that?" she asked in a low tone. He inhaled.

"Catherine—" he breathed out. "Don't test me."

"Oops, sorry," she said. She kissed his cheek once more and walked away. She closed the door and stripped. The door opened, and someone grabbed her hair and tugged it. She smirked, her back meeting Devin's chest.

"That 'oops, sorry' it's going to cost you, baby girl," Devin growled in her ear, kissing her jaw. She moaned. He turned them, their eyes meeting in the mirror on top of the sink.

"What about the lasagna?" she inquired innocently.

"The lasagna can wait. I would much rather eat something else at the moment," he replied, kissing down her neck. One of his hands slid down her body, letting go of her hair, the other one grabbing her chin. "Eyes on yourself," he said, sliding a finger inside her. She moaned. He pumped his finger. "So wet." He kissed her jaw. "Look at yourself. Do *not* close your eyes," he commanded as he inserted a second finger inside. She clenched, grinding into his hand. "You like that?" he asked, kissing her shoulder while pumping his fingers. "What if I add a third one? Look at yourself." He took his fingers out, and she whimpered at the loss of contact. "Open your mouth, Catherine," he ordered. She did as she was told and he inserted his fingers in her mouth. "Taste yourself," he ordered. She closed her mouth around his fingers and sucked them clean, tasting herself, pleasure traveling down her spine. "Good girl," he praised, bringing his fingers out of her mouth. "Now, touch yourself." He kissed down her neck to her back and the nape of her neck, his lips leaving a trail of little fires that ignited her whole skin. "Don't make me repeat myself, Catherine." He bit down on her shoulder, making her whimper.

"I've never done this in front of anyone," she confessed, a tint of blush creeping in her cheeks.

"It's easy. All you gotta do is this," he explained, taking her hand and sliding it down her body. Placing her hand at her navel, he guided her wrist down. Her fingers brushed her clit. She inhaled. "Just like that. Just as if you were touching yourself with no one in the room. I'm sure you have done it before, no?" he said breathlessly, guiding two of her fingers down and splitting her lips. She was drenched. "Now insert two fingers inside and fuck yourself like the good girl that you are," he purred in her ear, fisting her hair and pulling her head back. She did as she was told, her fingers sliding inside easily. She pumped her fingers in and out. "Good girl, now look at yourself," he said, guiding her chin to make her look. His other hand joined hers, circling her clit. She moaned, feeling herself clench around her fingers. "A goddess." He kissed down her back. "A literal goddess." He kneeled and turned her around, taking her fingers out and sucking them into his mouth. He moaned. Before she could register what happened, he parted her legs and gave her a long, slow lick from the bottom to top, her knees buckling. She grabbed onto the sink, willing her arms to hold her. Her legs parted farther. His hands traveled up her legs to her hips, holding her in place. His tongue paid careful attention to her clit. He bit it gently, making her whimper. His tongue slid inside of her.

"Devin, please," she pleaded breathlessly.

"Please, what, Catherine?" he asked, inserting two fingers inside her. "Use your words," he ordered. She whimpered, the air knocking out of her lungs.

"More, I need more," she begged.

"My pleasure," he said, standing up and turning her. She heard the buckle of his belt and the zipper. "Eyes on yourself." Before she could register anything, he slammed into her. He braced his hands on the mirror. "Catherine, fuck's sake," he groaned, thrusting in and out of her. He kissed her back, her neck, her jaw. She held onto the sink, her hips hitting the marble countertops. He slammed mercilessly into her, making her clench and close her eyes in ecstasy. A hard slap on her ass made her gasp and open her eyes. "I said, eyes on yourself. Don't make me repeat myself, Kitty Cat," he ordered. She shuddered and clenched at his command, making him groan. "If you keep doing that, I will come. Hard." His hand reached around her, his fingers finding her clit. She moaned.

"Harder," she pleaded. He obeyed, the sink counter rattling on the wall. She was definitely going to bruise. His thrusts became erratic, sloppy, and she knew he was close. So was she, her orgasm was building up like vapor. "I'm so close," she breathed out, closing her eyes. Another hard slap on her ass made her bucked her hips, meeting his thrusts. Another slap was all it took. It was like a snap, her orgasm rattling her body. She didn't have time to register it. She was breathless, dots appearing in her vision. His fist slammed into the countertop as he growled. He wrapped an arm around her waist and dropped his forehead on the back of her head, breathing hard as he rode his high. He pulled out of her, a slickness traveling down her leg. When her breathing came down, she lifted her gaze to the mirror. Devin was already staring back at her, his arm around her shoulders.

"A goddess," he breathed out.

Chapter Thirty-Two

Catherine - Thanksgiving Day

"What if she hates me?" she asked, stopping mid-walk. It was Thanksgiving, and they were walking to Emily's apartment. "I can't just waltz back into her life. Not after how I left nine years ago. No. She hates me, Devin. This was a bad idea," she said, the idea of reuniting with the one she once considered a sister creeping in. Texting non-stop was one thing. Seeing her after all that happened was another. She threw an anxious look at Devin, who was smiling. "Why are you smiling? It's not funny Devin," she exclaimed furiously. "I think I'd better go. I don't wanna ruin her Thanksgiving."

"I swear to God, Catherine Babbitt, that if you as much as take a fucking step towards the elevator, I will fucking kill you. You hear me? Kill you," she heard a distinctly familiar voice say beside her. She turned around, and in the doorway to her left stood her former best friend looking almost exactly the same as she had looked nine years ago, her hair longer, the bangs on her face framing her eyes. "You have five seconds to give me a hug, or I will strangle you with the extension cord of the Christmas tree," Emily threatened.

Catherine dropped the plastic bag she had in her arms and ran to her, engulfing her in a hug. Emily hugged her back. Catherine started crying. Emily hugged her tighter, running a soothing hand up and down her back.

"I'm so sorry, Em. I'm so sorry," Catherine sobbed. "I missed you so much. You have no idea how much I missed you all these years," she choked out. "How much I needed you all these years," she continued, sobbing.

"You are back. That's all that matters. You are here," Emily replied in a comforting way. "You're back," she repeated. "I missed you too, babe." She broke the hug and grabbed her face between her hands, wiping away the tears on her cheeks. "If you ever leave like that again, I swear to everything that you believe in, Catherine Babbitt, I will hunt you down, kill you, chop your body into tiny pieces, and feed the fishes in the Potomac River with your body parts," Emily threatened. Catherine smiled.

"Okay," Catherine replied. Emily nodded and let go of her face, punching her arm. "Ouch, what was that for?" she asked, rubbing her arm.

"That's for leaving without an explanation or saying goodbye nine years ago," Emily retorted. Catherine looked down at the floor.

"I'm sorry."

"I can't believe you thought I liked that doofus," Emily retorted. "Or that I would do something like that. For fuck's sake, Catherine, if anything, I had a crush on you." Catherine laughed, cleaning under her eyes. "But enough, come in. Dinner is almost ready," Emily said, ushering them inside. Devin bent down and kissed Emily's cheek. Emily disappeared, and she turned around, watching Devin close the door. He looked at her with a fond smile.

"She doesn't hate me," she pointed out. He walked to her and kissed her forehead.

"She never did," he replied. "She was really hurt when you left, a mess. Cried for like three whole weeks that summer." He shrugged. "Come on," he mumbled, grabbing her hand and entwining their fingers together.

"My favorite son is here," Mrs. Martin greeted him.

"Hello, Ma," Devin said to Emily's mom, leaning down and kissing her cheek.

"Oh goodness, Catherine, look at you! You haven't changed a bit," Mrs. Martin added, looking at her and pulling her into a hug.

"Hello, Mrs. Martin. You look exactly the same as well," she said into the hug. Mrs. Martin was about to say something when Emily appeared with a woman by her side.

"Cathy, let me introduce you to the love of my life, my fiancée, Nathalie." Nathalie was a tall, athletic girl with short blonde hair, a myriad of freckles adorning her face, and piercing hazel eyes. Her face was familiar. Catherine racked her brain on where she had seen her before. Then it clicked.

"Hey, I remember you! You were in Emily's newspaper association," Catherine commented.

"The school paper, yes. Nice to finally meet you. I have heard *so* much about you in the last nine years," she answered with a hint of humor in her voice. Catherine laughed. "And you asshole, you owe me a big explanation," she admonished with an accusatory finger pointing at Devin. Catherine watched the interaction. It looked like all three of them were close.

"What did I do?" he asked, his hands going up defensively.

"Why didn't you tell me she was the woman you loved?"

Nathalie questioned him. "All these years, and I had to find out through Em that Catherine was your one true love."

"I didn't think you would be interested in my love life like that."

"You are my fiancée's best friend. Of course, I care."

"I'm sorry," he replied, walking to her and kissing her head. She pushed him away.

"No kisses. I'm mad at you." He hugged her and planted another kiss on her head. "Stop. I'm mad at you," she protested, pushing him away. Emily just smiled at them.

"You love me. I'm one of the only straight men you love. Admit it."

"Never," she declared. "I love Corbin more." Devin laughed.

"Okay, whatever helps you sleep at night, Nat," he retorted and let her go. "She loves me, Catherine. Don't let her fool you," he added, looking at her.

"Corbin called. He said he, Brianna, and the boys won't be able to make it this year," Emily uttered.

"Aw, why?" Devin asked, walking back to her side.

"Aiyden is down with the flu," Emily replied.

"Aw, man. Poor little guy," Devin said, pouting.

"Corbin and Brianna were coming for Thanksgiving dinner?" Catherine asked.

"Yep, they were, but not anymore," Emily mentioned. "Anyways, dinner is ready. Devin, would you do the honors of carving the turkey?"

"Absolutely." He smiled, and they both walked into the kitchen.

"So, Catherine, tell me, what do you do?" Mrs. Martin asked as they sat down at the table.

"Oh, I do the same work as Devin," Catherine explained.

"Oh, so you work on the Senate too?" Nathalie inquired, placing a bowl of mashed potatoes in the middle of the table.

"Not in the Senate but in the House. Do you guys need help?" Catherine asked, standing up.

"No, no. You sit down," Devin said, walking into the dining room, the turkey in his hands. He placed it on the table and bent down to kiss the top of her head. They finished setting up, and Devin sat down to her right, Emily to her left. They started eating, the conversation revolving around Catherine and what she'd been up to in the last nine years.

"So, Cathy, how's your mom? God, I used to love the chocolate chip cookies she would bake for us every time she came to visit," Emily asked. Catherine's smile dropped, realizing she needed to tell Emily. "What happened? What's wrong?" Emily questioned worriedly. Devin's hand wrapped around hers.

"Let's talk later, yeah?" Catherine said as she kept eating.

She was in the kitchen helping Emily with the dishes, but it was just an excuse so she could get some time alone with her to address the elephant in the room. She was looking out of the doorway to the living room where Nathalie, Mrs. Martin, and Devin were seated. They were laughing.

"Nathalie loves him," Emily mentioned beside her. She turned to her. Emily was finishing up drying some dishes. She knew she couldn't delay it anymore.

"Em..." Catherine whispered. Emily looked up to her, her eyes misty. She took a deep breath and dived into telling her about her mom dying. Emily's face dropped, and she rushed to her side to hug her as she recounted that night. "I'm so sorry I walked away nine years ago. I'm so sorry I assumed the worst. That is something I will carry with me for the rest of my life," Catherine mumbled, looking down. "I feel like a monster. I shouldn't have shut either of you out. But I really didn't have the energy nor the will to do it," she said, a tear escaping her eye. "Finding out my mom was sick and hadn't told me, and on top of it that she had passed away, it was an emotional burden that felt like a brick wall fell on me. I really don't have an excuse, but that's my explanation. And I will understand if you don't want to be my friend ever again. But at least I got to apologize in person." She looked up to see Emily wiping tears away.

"You're not a monster, Catherine," Emily whispered, looking into her eyes. "Am I still hurt? Absolutely. Did I hate you? No, I could never bring myself to hate you, Catherine. You were my sister. You *are* my sister," she said, taking her hand and intertwining their fingers together. "It will take some time for me to heal, but you are here now. We can heal together. We don't have to do it alone. We will have each other. Just promise you won't do it again. Promise me we will talk about it. Promise me you will not shut me out again."

She nodded. "Devin made me promise the same thing. I think I can do that. I would love that," Catherine replied. She felt Emily kiss her knuckles. "So, wedding, huh?" Catherine asked, wiping her face. "Who proposed to whom?" Emily laughed.

"I did. We went on a trip to Switzerland, and I proposed in the Swiss Alps."

"I'm happy for you. You look the happiest I've ever seen you."

"I am happy. I really can't envision a life where Nathalie is not in it," Emily said, looking out the doorway to where her fiancée was seated. Catherine ran a soothing hand across her back. "So, tomorrow. Are you doing anything tomorrow?"

Emily asked, looking up at her. Catherine frowned. "Devin's final fitting for his tux is tomorrow, and I want you to come. And we need to find you a dress," Emily added. "So, do you want to be one of my bridesmaids?"

"I am going to respectfully decline. I don't think I deserve such a title," Catherine replied. Emily looked down and nodded. "I will, however, compromise and let you pick my dress," Catherine said. Emily beamed.

"Deal," she replied, hugging her.

"How did the talk with Em go?"

"It went okay. We are far from being close or for her to trust me again, but we'll get there," she answered as she nodded. "So, do you wanna come inside? I have a great wine bottle that I haven't opened."

"I can never say no to you. We've been through this already," he said smiling, his dimples appearing. She lifted herself on her tiptoes and kissed his cheek. Fumbling with the keys, she opened her apartment. The lights were on. She stopped in the doorway, Devin bumping into her back, steadying her by wrapping an arm around her waist.

"Catherine." A man stood from the sofa and looked at her, his gaze going to the hand on her waist, trailing up to meet the eyes of the man behind her.

"*Kyle.*"

Chapter Thirty-Three

Devin

"Kyle." The hand Devin had on her waist tightened protectively. "What are you doing here?" she questioned. He moved in front of her and shielded her.

"Devin," Kyle spat as he sized him up.

"You really have some guts showing your face after what you did. What are you doing here?" Devin asked him.

"I'm here to see my girlfriend. Ex-girlfriend," he corrected. "Although, it looks like she is busy with you. What are *you* doing here? I thought you guys weren't friends anymore," he replied. Devin scoffed. He felt Catherine walk to his side, gripping his arm. "When did this little reunion happen, *corazón*?" he inquired, his hands in his pockets.

"Kyle, what do you want?"

"It's Thanksgiving," he said matter-of-factly.

"So?" she asked, confused. "You broke up with me… you wanted a break."

"And I see how you have been spending your break," he replied. Devin's blood boiled.

"Says the one who met someone with '*a lot of things in*

common'," Catherine scoffed. "Kyle, I'm not going to ask you again. What do you want?" She paused. "You know what? No, answer this instead. What did you do that everyone hates you?"

"It's not relevant nor important," he answered with a dismissive shrug. Devin scoffed. "Have something to add, Devin?"

"Plenty," Devin replied. "But let's start with the fact that you have the guts to sleep in the same bed as her after what you did," Devin spat, taking a step towards him. "Why?"

"None of your business," Kyle replied.

"Enough!" Catherine yelled.

"You really are the lowest of scum. Tell her Kyle. Tell her how you played her," Devin said. "Tell her, or I will." Kyle snorted. "He lied to you, Catherine. All this time, he has lied to you," Devin explained, turning to her. "He lied to you and has been doing it for years. I still remember that day like it was yesterday. I will never forgive you for what you did," Devin spat. "Miles. Remember Miles? Kyle made a bet with him the day you went on a date with Miles. A bet that Miles was going to get in your pants. And if Miles was unsuccessful, Kyle was going to try. All because he wanted in at the frat house," Devin said, the memory of a drunk Kyle blatantly admitting it hitting him like a train.

Nine Years Ago - Graduation Day

"Congratulations, everyone. We made it," Emily said, finishing her shot. "We are adults. Dysfunctional, but adults."

They were shitfaced drunk. Graduation had been earlier

that day. The absence of Catherine was felt throughout the whole day. Hell through the whole week.

"*She should have been here,*" *Emily sobbed. Brianna passed a hand across Emily's back.*

"*Oh please, stop crying over her. She was just an overachiever goody two-shoes. Did y'all seriously think she would take any of y'all into consideration after graduation? She left. She's not dead. Move on,*" *Kyle slurred.* "*I knew it the minute I made that bet with Miles,*" *he said, drunk, a hiccup escaping his lips. He took another swig from his whiskey.*

"*Did you say you made a bet with Miles about Cathy?*" *Corbin asked, sobering up.*

"*What bet?*" *Devin questioned. Kyle waved a dismissive hand in the air.*

"*It was back in sophomore year. I wanted to get into the frat house, and the only way he would allow me in was by making a bet with him. We bet that one of us was going to get into her pants. I told him she was a goody-two-shoes, but he didn't care. He said those kinds of girls were the easiest and fastest ones that fell for the trap. He told me that if he didn't succeed, but I did, he'd consider letting me in. Safe to say neither of us succeeded, and I never got in,*" *Kyle replied, shrugging.*

Devin's vision went red. He didn't register what happened. It was as if something had taken over his body. He swung his fist back and punched him, making him fall on the floor. He shook his hand.

"*Fuck,*" *he groaned in pain. He looked at his hands, his knuckles red. Kyle stood up and wiped blood off his lip. Devin grabbed him by the collar and dragged him away from their table.* "*You're the lowest. Don't you ever come near any of us again.*"

"You did what?" Catherine asked, clutching Devin's arm, eyes wide with tears as she looked at Kyle.

"That was a long time ago. We were nineteen," Kyle replied.

"It doesn't matter. You lied to me. You keep lying to me." Her voice broke. It took Devin all the self-restraint he had to not punch Kyle as he did that night at the bar. "When you came to Penn State, did you think you were winning some unfinished bet?" she questioned, a tear escaping her eye. She wiped it away fast.

"No, it was different then," he answered. "Contrary to popular belief, I do care about you, Catherine," he mumbled. "Once I actually got to know you, I realized why everyone loved you and why Devin cared so much for you. I just stopped loving you in that way. Not in the way Devin did. Or rather, do, should I say. You were more like a roommate," he said in a guilty tone.

"A roommate? Then why stay with me?" she inquired, her voice sounding defeated. Kyle just looked at her. "Why did you lie? Why didn't you come clean?" she asked, furious. "Did you feel I would leave you after I found out? After all this time? Really?" Kyle looked down. "Get out of my house." He looked up.

"Catherine—"

"Get out," she ordered, walking to the door and opening it.

"Catherine, please, I just want to talk."

"Leave, or I'll call the police."

"Can you at least let me know where my stuff is?" he asked, frustrated. She grabbed a key from the plate on the table in the foyer.

"In a storage room. I'll text you the details." He walked to her and grabbed the key.

"I'm sorry."

"Don't you ever contact me again, Kyle," she replied, looking away from him. He nodded. He looked back at Devin. His eyes conveyed something Devin never thought he would see. *Regret*. Devin gave him a simple bob of his head. It didn't erase the fact that he wanted to rearrange his face. Kyle nodded once and left. Catherine closed the door, leaning her forehead on it.

"You knew," she whispered so low he almost didn't catch what she said. He stayed quiet. "You all knew." He knew her. She was shutting herself off.

"I know what you are doing. We are going to talk about this. You promised, Catherine. You promised you wouldn't close yourself from me. You promised we were going to talk through the tough stuff. I'm not leaving you," he said, walking to her. "I'm not letting you shut yourself away like that again. I made the mistake of walking away and not talking about it once, and it cost me nine years without you. I am not making that same mistake again. I'm calling *timeout*," he mumbled softly. He cradled her head. "Talk to me," he whispered. A tear escaped her eyes, and he wiped it away with his thumb.

"Why didn't you tell me, Dev?" she asked, defeated, looking into his eyes. "You could have told me."

"Trust me, I wanted to tell you since that day we met in the airport after I saw him picking you up. The next time I saw you, I wanted to tell you so badly. But it wasn't my place to say. He fucked up, and he was the one who needed to tell you, not me. He was the one who needed to come clean. It was his responsibility," he continued. "Don't shut me out, Kitty Cat, please, don't shut me out," he pleaded. "I'm sorry I didn't tell you," he said, kissing her forehead again. She inhaled and nodded.

"Okay. I won't," she whispered, "but I need time to gather my thoughts." He exhaled a shaky breath, feeling light. All his worries left his mind.

"Okay," he said, kissing her head. He let her face go and grabbed the doorknob. Her hand stopped him.

"Don't go," she said softly. She hugged him, pressing her chest to his back. "I don't want you to leave. I don't want to be alone. Thank you for sticking around," she whispered. He inhaled. "Is there anything else that I need to know?" she asked. "Be honest."

"I punched him," he confessed in a low voice.

"You what?"

"After he admitted what he did, I punched him, but I made sure he bled," he said, turning around in her arms. He wrapped his around her and kissed the top of her head. "I told you I was always going to be there for you." Her hold on him grew tighter.

"Thank you," she said, looking up at him. He kissed her nose.

"Always," he murmured, kissing her forehead.

"But next time, let's not punch anyone," she stated, and he chuckled. "We should go to bed. You have an early day tomorrow. *We* have an early day tomorrow. You have your final fitting for your tux, and I have to go dress shopping." He looked at her, confused.

"How do you know I have my final fitting tomorrow?" he asked, baffled.

"Emily told me. When I was helping her do the dishes." She shrugged. "She asked me to be her bridesmaid, but I said no."

"Why?"

"I don't feel I deserve it. I'm letting her pick my dress, though. I don't know if that's a good idea, but it's a start." He chuckled.

"Okay, missy, time for bed," he said, kissing her lips. "Because you are right, we have an early day tomorrow." He let her go. "Come on." He turned to lock the door and entwined his fingers with hers. He walked to the closet and to the single drawer he had made his own and changed into his pajamas. Catherine emerged from the bathroom and flopped down on the bed. He lay next to her, bringing her closer, and they both drifted off to sleep.

"So, on a scale of one to ten, how hot do you think he will look?" he heard Emily ask Catherine outside.

"I heard that," Devin yelled from the fitting room, adjusting the vest.

"We know," Emily and Catherine said in unison, followed by their giggles.

"Maybe the two of you reuniting was a bad idea. I already had Emily and Nathalie roasting me. Now, it's Emily, Nathalie, *and* Catherine. It's like the Powerpuff Girls," he said, adjusting the bowtie.

"Oh, I'm just getting—" Catherine started to say and stopped as soon as she saw him. Her emerald-green eyes were bright as they took him in. She swallowed. "Eleven. Definitely eleven," she said, nodding.

"Agreed," Emily concurred, equally baffled.

"It's just a tux," he replied, looking in the mirror.

"It's not just a tux, Devin. It's *the* tux for my one and only wedding. I don't think we need to make any other adjustments," Emily said to the tailor.

"Agreed," the tailor answered.

"Great. Now, take it off. We need to get it dry-cleaned. We are in the final countdown now. One week," Emily ordered, pushing him back to the fitting rooms.

They finished at the tailor's shop and dropped the tux at the dry cleaners. They had lunch and then headed over to a dress shop for Catherine's dress.

"This is a bridal shop," Catherine pointed out.

"I know," Emily replied.

"Why are you taking me to a bridal shop?"

"Because, the kind of dress I have in mind for you requires you to buy it at a bridal shop, Catherine Elizabeth. Now, can you please enter with me so we can find your dress?"

"I already declined being your bridesmaid, Emily."

"I know. You are not one. But I want you to have a pretty dress for my wedding. Come on." Emily dragged Catherine inside the shop.

"What are you planning, Emily?" Devin muttered under his breath.

"Okay, we are looking for a light-yellow dress," Emily said, eyeing Catherine. She left with the store clerk, leaving Devin and Catherine alone. She was looking around at the wedding dresses.

"One day, this will be you," he mumbled. She gave him a side smile.

"Not anytime soon, though," she said, perusing around. He opened his mouth to reply, but Emily interrupted him.

"Come on now," Emily said, ushering Catherine away. Once Catherine was out of earshot, Emily turned to him. "She is one of my bridesmaids. She doesn't know it, but she is."

"I thought I was your bridesmaids," he replied, pouting, feigning sadness.

"Don't get me wrong, I love you, but you are not a girl," Emily said. "The dresses I got her are for bridesmaids. The clerk isn't going to say anything, though."

"I know you had something up your sleeve."

Emily smirked. "Everything is good to go?" Emily asked him. He smiled and nodded. "Good, good."

"I look like a little easter chicken," Catherine complained, walking out of the fitting rooms. His mouth gaped.

"No, you don't. You look hot, babe," Emily retorted. "Close your mouth, or you will drool all over the floor, Mack," Emily teased. He shoved her playfully. He smiled back at Catherine. The dress was floor length, with a top cut like a Greek toga, one shoulder exposed and the other draped in a long train. The skirt had a slit that ran up to mid-thigh.

"You look beautiful," he said because she did. The light-yellow color went so well with her skin and green eyes.

"And it fits her perfectly. No need to make any adjustments," the store clerk commented.

"Great. We'll take it."

"Em…" Catherine started to protest.

"Shush it," Emily said, walking away with the clerk to pay for the dress. "Wait, what about the other dresses?" Emily asked. Catherine shook her head. "Why?"

"I didn't like the designs."

"Okay, then this one it is," Emily declared, walking to the front of the store.

"Stop her," Catherine pleaded. He pointed his finger at himself. "Yes, idiot. You," she said, exasperated. He chuckled.

"Oh, I learned the hard way to not get in her way where the wedding is concerned." She groaned and turned around, looking at herself in the mirrors. "You look beautiful, Kitty

Cat," he complimented, walking to stand behind her. "And the dress color goes with my bow tie." She sighed.

"I do like the dress, though," she noted. He smiled.

"Go take it off," he ordered, kissing her exposed shoulder. "I can't wait until I take it off of you next week," he purred in her ear. She went red.

"We are in public, Satan. Behave," she scolded, walking away. He laughed. And he was indeed not going to behave that night.

Chapter Thirty-Four

Catherine - One week later, Rehearsal Dinner

"Okay, everyone places again so we can have the official rehearsal," Emily called from the back. Catherine was sitting in one of the chairs at the front, looking back. "Jesus, I'm so ready to get this wedding over with. Alright, we are ready to start," she said to the wedding planner at the front.

The wedding planner gave the cue to the pianist, and music started to float through the air. They practiced the entrance and the exit three more times and then headed to the official rehearsal dinner. Everyone close to Emily and Nathalie was there. She was seated with Devin to Emily's right after her mom. Brianna and Corbin were to her left with Aiyden and Deion. Their reunion was filled with tears and hugs.

"Aiyden, do you want to play with Auntie Cat?" Brianna cooed to Aiyden, who was seated on her lap.

"Catherine is really good with kids," Devin said from beside her. "I've seen her in action," he commented, looking at her and winking. She smiled, blushing.

Aiyden looked at her with his beautiful big dark brown

eyes. She booped his nose, and he laughed. She booped it again, and he grabbed her finger, squeezing it. At some point during the night, Deion ended up on her lap, fast asleep on her chest, while she rocked him softly. She played with the little curls on his head.

"Wow, she really *is* good. Usually, Deion is the one that gives us trouble to put him to sleep," Corbin mentioned, looking at Devin. She smiled and kissed the top of his head softly. The rest of the dinner went smoothly, and close to midnight, everyone started to leave. "I'll take him," Corbin said from beside her.

"It's okay. I have plenty of experience with sleepy toddlers," she replied, arranging Deion on her shoulder as carefully as she could to not wake him up. "I'll follow you." Corbin smiled and nodded, walking to the door and opening it for her. She walked to the car, and he opened the door, and she placed him in his car seat, securing his seatbelt.

"Thank you. It's nice to have you back, Cathy," he said, hugging her. She smiled, returning the hug.

"It feels nice to be back," she mumbled. "I'll see you tomorrow," she said, walking to the restaurant. When she walked inside, Devin was waiting for her at the door with her jacket, helping her put it on and kissing the back of her head. He gave her her purse.

"Ready?" he asked. She nodded. They went back to his place where she unpacked her dress and everything she needed for tomorrow. They went to bed, and she cuddled to his side.

"Make sure you don't trip tomorrow," she joked, giggling. He squeezed her. "Devin, I can't breathe." He pinned her to the bed with his body, pinning her wrist to the mattress with his hands, lowering his head to her jaw, and kissing his way down to her collarbones. "Dev, it's late, and tomorrow is going to be a long day. We both need our beauty sleep. Plus, you said you were going to peel my dress from my body. I *will* hold you to that promise." He stiffened.

"I *hate* when you make good points," he muttered, kissing her throat. She laughed.

"What can I say, I'm incredible at being right," she replied. He settled beside her and spooned her, wrapping her in his arms.

"Good night, Kitty Cat," he said, kissing her shoulder. She snuggled closer to him, kissing his arm.

The morning after was a blur. They woke up late, and Devin didn't have breakfast before he burst out the door, kissing her in a rush. She went and started to get ready. When she got out of the shower, her phone rang. It was Emily.

"Do I need to get the getaway car?" she asked.

"I need you. Like yesterday," Emily pleaded through the phone. She sounded desperate.

"Em, are you having second thoughts?" she questioned, worried.

"No, but I need you here while I get ready."

"Em, I'm getting ready."

"You can get ready here. You have twenty minutes to get here," Emily demanded and hung up. She blew out a breath and packed everything in her little carry-on, getting in a taxi. She arrived at the place, Emily's mom met her at the front door and took her to the room where Emily was. "There she is," Emily exclaimed when she passed through the doorway.

"You're not in a crisis, Emily Choi. What the hell?" Catherine asked. Emily walked to her with a small bouquet in her hands.

"No, I'm not, but I can't do this without my other bridesmaid," Emily stated, placing the bouquet in her hands. "I can't do this without you, Cat. You are my sister. It feels wrong not having you here after all we went through. It's just you, Brianna, and Devin. I lost a lot of friends and family when I came out. And I stopped trying to make friends because most people don't understand," she explained, looking down. "So it's just us. That's it. We can continue our healing journey tomorrow. Today is all about happiness and love," she added, squeezing her hand.

"Is this her?" someone asked beside her. Emily nodded. "Great. Let's go. We have much to do and not a lot of time," the woman said, ushering her to a chair beside Emily.

"Em…" Catherine started to protest but then saw Emily's face. So full of hope and love. "Ugh, fine," she groaned. "But I am not giving a speech," she conceded. Emily beamed.

"It's okay. Nathalie's brother and Devin are the ones that are going to give the speech," Emily said, sitting down where they were fixing her hair.

"You picked my dress on purpose, didn't you?" Catherine asked, looking over at where Brianna was, noticing the dress hanging in the background was the same color as the one Emily picked for her. Emily chuckled. "I should've known." Emily extended her hand to her, and she took it, entwining their fingers and squeezing Emily's hand.

"I missed you," Emily muttered softly. Catherine gave her hand another squeeze.

They finished getting ready an hour before the wedding and were on their way to take pictures of the first look. Emily had opted for a simple strapless princess dress with a heart-shaped neckline.

"Stop touching your hair," Catherine chided, snapping her hand out. "You are going to ruin it. You look fine."

"Okay, so Nathalie is—" she heard Devin say. She turned to where the sound of his voice was coming from, and he stopped talking, looking at her.

"What?" Catherine questioned. "Do I have something on my face?" she asked, touching her face. Devin walked to her and grabbed her wrist.

"Stop, it's not that. You look absolutely stunning," he said. She blushed. He kissed her forehead softly.

"Nathalie is what?" Emily inquired from behind them, worried.

"Oh, she's coming."

"Oh god," Emily replied, nervous.

"Okay, Em. Let's get you over here," Brianna said.

"So, I gather she made you another bridesmaid?" Devin asked, smirking. She nodded.

"I was left with no choice," she said. "You knew, didn't you?"

"I plead the fifth," he vowed, winking. Someone cleared their throat behind them. They both turned and saw Nathalie in a white suit with black lapels.

"Is she—" Nathalie started.

"Losing it. And super nervous," Catherine replied. Nathalie blew out a breath.

"There you are," the photographer exclaimed, spotting Nathalie. He ushered her away to take the pictures.

"We are walking to where the ceremony is going to be," Devin said. She nodded. He extended his arm, and she grabbed it, walking to where everyone else was. Devin kissed her hand and walked to stand beside Emily.

"Okay. Positions, everyone. We will start in five minutes," the wedding planner ordered.

Five minutes later, they were walking down the aisle. The rest of the ceremony went smoothly and was tear-jerking. Nathalie and Emily exchanged vows and kissed.

They walked hand in hand down the aisle, and Devin escorted Catherine to his car to go to the reception.

"Your suitcase with your stuff is in my trunk, by the way," he mentioned.

"Thank you." As she sat down, the slit of her dress revealed her legs. Devin took a deep breath beside her. "Don't even think about it," she warned. He chuckled.

They arrived at the reception and got seated with the rest of the bridal party. The rest of the night was spent drinking, eating, and dancing. She danced until her feet hurt. Everyone was happy and together. She was surrounded by friends and the people who loved her, and she felt genuinely happy. She stood by the open bar while Devin danced with Emily and looked around. While their lives were vastly different, Catherine realized she was happy that they were all happy. She knew there was always a missing piece in her she couldn't fill, and she found out this was the piece that was missing. She was happy they were back in her life. She went back to the table to finish her wine. A slow song started to play, and Devin turned to her.

"May I have this dance?"

"Absolutely," she replied, taking his hand. She placed her arms around his shoulders, and he grabbed her waist, bringing her closer, nuzzling his nose in her neck. They danced in circles until someone interrupted.

"Ugh, get a room, you two," they heard Emily say beside them. She was dancing with Nathalie. They chuckled. "Are you guys having fun?"

Catherine nodded.

"Yes," Devin answered.

"Good," Emily said, looking at Devin and winking. She swirled and disappeared. Catherine looked at Devin, and he rolled his eyes.

"Ignore her," he mumbled and kept dancing.

For the rest of the night, they didn't leave the dance floor.

The bouquet toss came, and Emily pushed her to the crowd, right in the middle, along with another dozen girls. She made to throw it, faking it twice. On the third try, she just turned around and walked to her. Emily smiled as she handed her the bouquet.

"I think it should go to you," Emily said, smiling. She looked at her, confused.

"Em, I'm not getting married any time soon," Catherine replied. Emily just shrugged. She turned around and looked at where Devin was seated with Brianna and Corbin.

All of them were smiling at her. Devin shook his head and looked down. After that, Devin and Catherine went back to the dance floor, where they switched partners between Corbin, Brianna, Nathalie, and Emily. The cake-cutting came, and the time to say goodbye to the couple suddenly arrived. They left for their honeymoon, and everyone else began to filter out as well. As they were leaving, Devin stopped short.

"I left my suit jacket, and your purse is still inside," he said, walking back to the reception room.

"I'll wait for you here," she said. He turned around and disappeared inside. "Lover" by Taylor Swift started to play. She walked back into the reception room, and Devin was standing in the middle of the dance floor, his back to her, his hands in his pockets. "What are you doing?" she asked, stepping inside the reception room. He turned and looked at her and smiled.

"I may have asked the DJ to play your favorite song so we can have one more dance. I may have also bribed him to play it. The world may never know," he explained, extending his hand. "Care for one more dance?" She smiled and nodded, walking in his direction. He shook his head. "Take your shoes off," he ordered. She looked at him, frowning in confusion. "Just trust me," he said, smiling, his dimples showing. She took her shoes off and walked to him. He took her hand. "Now stand on my feet." She did as she was told and placed her feet on top of his, her arms automatically going to his neck. His arms engulfed her waist, keeping her closer and from falling. He started to dance, guiding both of them. "You know I love you, right?" he asked, nuzzling her cheek with his nose. She played with the little hairs on the nape of his neck. "And you know there is nothing I wouldn't do for you, right?" he asked in a whisper. "You have me, Catherine Babbitt. You have me for life. You have had me for the last fourteen years.

"And there is not a single day where I regret meeting you. You are the best thing that has ever happened to me," he said. He placed his forehead on top of hers. "I love you so much. The last nine years without you were hell for me. I don't ever want to feel like that again, Catherine," he lifted her gently off his feet, setting her on the floor.

He kissed her forehead softly. He moved back, cradling her face. He kissed her lips, claiming them. He kissed her as if there was no tomorrow. A promise that he was hers, that he was here to stay. A promise that she would always have him. He kissed her cheeks and down her jaw. His touch left her, and she opened her eyes to find him down on one knee.

"This is by far the easiest decision I have ever made, and I don't want to wait any longer," he said as he got a little velvet box out of his pocket. Her eyes started to water. "Catherine Babbitt, it will never be too soon for us. I don't care how long I've had you back, but I will never let you go again. I don't ever want to be in a world where Catherine Babbitt is not a part of it," he continued, opening the box and revealing the most beautiful ring she had ever seen. The first tear fell from her eyes. "I have never been more sure in my life than in this moment, Catherine. It's you and me for the rest of our lives.

Say yes. Say yes to the rest of our lives. Say yes, and I will make you the happiest woman alive," he promised, his voice shaky. She smiled and knelt, cradling his face, wiping away the few tears that fell from his eyes.

"This is going to be the easiest yes I have ever said in my life, Devin Mack. A thousand times yes," she answered, kissing him. He engulfed her waist and kissed her back. Cheers exploded from behind them. She broke the kiss, looking in the direction of the cheers and seeing Nathalie and Emily beaming, along with Brianna and Corbin. Emily wiped a tear from her face.

"About damn time," Emily yelled, running to them. She tackled both of them in a hug.

"You knew?" Catherine asked.

"Baby girl, I'm the one that came up with the idea," Emily replied. She smiled and kissed her cheek. "God knows you deserve each other." They both giggled. "Okay, let me see the ring!" Catherine looked at Devin. He smiled at her. Taking the ring out of the little box, he grabbed her left hand and placed the ring on her ring finger. Lifting her hand to his mouth, he placed a soft kiss there.

"You and me," he said. She kissed his cheek.

"You and me."

Chapter Thirty-Five

Catherine - Christmas Eve

"Okay. So, I will come and pick you up around 6 pm. Remember, don't forget to—" Devin started to say on the other side of the line.

"Bring the cookies. I know. I'm going to bake them soon. Did you hide the gifts?" she asked. He chuckled.

"I don't have a lot of places to hide them, so they are under my bed."

"Okay," she mumbled, looking up at the ceiling from her bed. "How are they? How was the trip? I know their flight got in late last night." Sitting up, she picked up her coffee from the nightstand, taking a sip and putting it back.

"They are still sleeping," he replied. "I already started preheating the oven. And I have all the ingredients out so Mom can start making her famous potato casserole."

"Did you tell them?" she inquired, looking down at her hand where the ring Devin gave her sparkled. She smiled at the memory.

"No, I was thinking we can do it together," he suggested.

"I like that idea."

"Give me a second, Kitty Cat." She heard the lock of his

door click. "Josh, hey, what are you doing here? Weren't you supposed to arrive later tonight?" Devin asked. "Cat, I need to go. Josh just got here. I'll see you tonight. I love you."

"Alright, I'll see you tonight. Love you," she said, picking up her coffee mug and hanging up. Tonight, she was finally meeting Josh, Devin's older brother, for the first time. She decided to do some cleaning around the house while finishing her mom's chocolate chip cookies. She was getting the cookies out of the oven when a knock on her door sounded. She didn't believe her eyes as she saw Kyle standing outside. She opened the door. "What are you doing here?" she questioned. He looked up and smiled a little.

"Can I come in?" he asked. "I swear, I come in peace." She walked away and left the door open for him to come in.

"Do you want anything to drink?" she inquired. He shook his head.

"I just came to talk. We left too much unfinished business, *corazón*," he answered, sitting on the sofa, patting the spot beside him. She sighed and walked to the sofa, sitting far away from him. He looked at her left hand as she played with the ring. "I guess congratulations are in order."

"Kyle, why are you here?" she asked, fidgeting with the sleeve of her sweater.

"I'm here to talk, Cat. We left things on a bad note, and I don't like that," he replied, looking down, ashamed. "I'm sorry," he apologized in a whisper. "I should've come clean. I should've told you when we reconnected." He looked into her eyes. "I swear, I never wanted to hurt you, Catherine. I didn't know you that well back when I made the bet. I didn't get why everyone loved you and protected you so much. Especially Devin. I think I understand him now. I understand his infatuation with you all those years ago."

"Why did you even make the bet then?" she asked, looking down at her fingers.

"Because I wanted to be someone. In school, I was always the shadow, a '*sitting in the back*' kid, the punching bag of the bullies. When I got to Boston, I promised myself I was going to become someone. Miles took advantage of that. He asked if I knew any girl he could—" he started to say but stopped.

"Use? Fuck? Get her hopes up?" she asked. He looked down, nodding.

"At the moment, it didn't click just how fucked up the situation was. I was getting in with the cool crowd, and I was desperate to fit in. No longer being the shadow kid. No longer the punching bag. So, I didn't think it through when I said your name. Then he asked who you were, and I told him about you. Then we made the bet. If you were as gullible as I said, and he was successful in getting into your pants, I was going to get into the frat house, and I'd finally have what I wanted. If he wasn't successful, but I was, there would be a probability of being considered. I didn't even ponder on it. I just said yes. Then he asked you out on a date, and everything unfolded. Devin took those pictures and threatened him. He knew Devin was my roommate, so he automatically called the bet off after. If I could go back and tell nineteen-year-old me to not do it, that it's not worth it, I would."

"Is that the reason why you didn't interact much with me every time we would hang out together?" she asked. He nodded.

"I was mad at you. I should've realized that Devin would come to your rescue if anything ever happened to you. He adored you even back then. He was so pissed that you went on that date with Miles," he said, looking at her. "The kid has worshiped you all this time," he added, a smile forming on his lips.

"Why didn't you tell me about the bet? Why did you evade the question when I asked you about Boston?" she asked him.

"I was ashamed that nineteen-year-old me would do such a stupid and horrible thing. When I saw you at Penn State during my semester there, I felt ashamed. You treated me so nicely, yet you had no idea I did such a horrible thing to you years before. I did befriend you to apologize at some point."

"Why didn't you?"

"I fell in love with you," he confessed with a sad smile. "I did love you, *corazón*. Once I got to know you, the real you, I realized why Devin loved you so much. I thought that if I *did* apologize and came clean, you would break what we had as friends. That terrified me," he admitted, looking down at his hands. "I would have deserved it, but it terrified me to lose you," he whispered. "So I promised myself I was going to be better for you. We started this long-distance friendship after I left. Then, we both got jobs in DC. And four years ago, I finally got the guts to tell you I was in love with you. But I was never brave enough to tell you about the bet." He shrugged. "But a year ago, I started to feel myself drifting away from you. I still loved you, but not like I used to. Call me selfish, but you were the only constant thing in my life, and I didn't want to let you go. So, we fell into a routine. And I loved our routines. But six months ago, the routines were starting to become tiresome. Monotonous. I don't think it's either of our fault. These things happen. And I still love you. God, I do, Catherine. I love and care for you deeply, but not in that way anymore, and not like you deserve to be loved."

"What changed? Was it something I did?" she asked, looking at him. He reached for her hands.

"*Corazón*, this is not on you. I should've ended it a year ago when my feelings changed. This is completely on me," he said, leaning in and kissing her temple. "You did nothing wrong," he assured her, squeezing her hands. "I love you, I really do. But not romantically. Not anymore. I'm sorry. I wish I could tell you why I stopped loving you that way. But I just can't. I don't have an answer," he continued, giving her a sad smile. "You are a wonderful woman, Catherine. You have a golden heart, you are selfless, and you always see the best in people," he said, tucking a piece of hair behind her ear. "You are, by far, one of the best things that has ever happened to me. It just isn't the same for me." He shrugged. "Devin is one lucky son of a bitch. He is taking the winning prize."

"So, when you said it felt more like roommates…" she said, and he nodded.

"I promise, there was nothing you ever did that made me love you less, *corazón*," he said, leaning in and kissing her forehead.

"You said you met someone back in Nevada. Someone you share the same interests with. How is that going?" she asked. He smiled, looking down, a hint of blush on his cheeks.

"She… She is something else," he answered. "I think she might be the one."

"Are you accepting the job? Are you moving to Nevada?" He nodded.

"I accepted the job. They are just finishing my paperwork. I officially start the new job after New Year's. I already found a place, and all my stuff is packed and ready for the movers. You did half of the job," he said. She chuckled. "Which brings me to this," he added, standing up and looking for something in his pants pocket. He got a little silver chain out. *A bracelet.*

"This was your Christmas present," he mumbled. He took her hand, palm up, and placed the silver chain on it, closing her fingers around it. "Merry Christmas, *corazón*," he murmured. She opened her palm and saw it was the same silver chain bracelet she had looked at from outside the window of a shop a few months back.

"Kyle…" she whispered. He leaned in and kissed her head.

"You never get yourself nice things, *corazón*," he said. "You liked it. You actually debated on buying it and then decided not to. So, I decided to buy it for you. And no, I won't accept it back. It's yours. I got it for you."

"Thank you," she muttered, extending her arm. "Can you put it on me?" He smiled, picking the bracelet from her palm and clasping it on her wrist. He sat down next to her and threw an arm around her shoulders. She hugged him back. "I don't hate you, Kyle. I really don't. You deserve to be happy." He kissed her head.

"I'm glad you found Devin again, and I'm happy he is making you happy," he replied, picking up her left hand. "He finally did it," he uttered. "How did you guys reunite after all these years?"

"Remember my work trip to the district?" she asked. He nodded. "He was part of the other office."

"From the senate side? Small world," he added. "So all this time—" he started to say, and she nodded. He sighed. "You're still my closest friend. You know that, right? And you know I will always love and appreciate you, right?" She hugged him tighter.

"I know."

"Be happy, *corazón*. I want you to be happy and live," he mentioned, kissing her head. "I should go. My flight leaves in a couple of hours."

"Flight?" she questioned, breaking the hug. He nodded.

"I'm going back to Nevada," he answered, standing up. "I'm one call away if you ever need me, *corazón*." He continued bending down, kissing her forehead.

"Goodbye, Kyle."

"Goodbye, *corazón*," he replied as he turned around and left.

"That's a nice bracelet," Devin mentioned when he picked her up. She looked down at her wrist, where the bracelet was. She played with it and smiled.

"Kyle stopped by earlier," she said. He inhaled. "He apologized. We parted as friends, Devin," she whispered. "He accepted the job in Nevada. The girl he met there… he thinks it's serious. We moved on. It's fine. This was supposed to be his Christmas gift to me."

"I'm glad you worked it out. I still dislike him," he retorted. She chuckled.

"You'll survive." He laughed. They arrived at his place, and they walked to his apartment, stopping by the door.

"Ready?" he asked. She nodded. "I'm home," he yelled to no one in particular. His mom's face popped up from the living room. She gave him the bowl with the cookies.

"Oh, my goodness, Catherine, look at you," his mom exclaimed and walked to her, engulfing her in a hug.

"Hi, Sarah," she greeted.

"How are you? How's your mom?" Sarah asked.

"Ma…" Devin warned.

"She passed away," Catherine replied, giving his mom a sad smile.

"Oh dear…" Sarah said, placing a hand on her cheek.

"Come here, sweet child," she comforted, giving her another hug.

"It's okay. It was a long time ago."

"Catherine, long time no see," Devin's father, Richard, remarked.

"Come on, sweetheart. Dinner is ready," Sarah announced, linking her arm with hers. They walked to the dining room, where the table was set.

"I'll put this in my room. Be right back," Devin mentioned beside her, kissing her temple. He gave her the cookie bowl and carried her overnight bag to his room.

"Here, Catherine, you can sit here," Sarah said, gesturing to a chair. A man with dark reddish-brown hair walked into the room. She looked at him and smiled.

"You must be the famous Catherine," he assumed, his voice deep. He looked like Devin but older. "I've heard so much about you for the past fourteen years," he added, sitting across from her.

"Josh, leave her alone," Devin admonished, walking into the room. Josh smirked at Devin. "Catherine, meet my older brother, Josh. Josh, meet… never mind, you know who she is," Devin introduced them, sitting beside her.

"Nice to finally meet you," she replied. He nodded, smiling at her. He had the same dimples as Devin.

"I feel like I've known you for a better part of my life," Josh teased.

"Oh, fuck off, Josh. You're annoying," Devin replied.

"Richard, do the honors?" Sarah said to her husband, dissipating the argument between the two brothers.

"My pleasure," Richard replied, cutting into the turkey. Dinner was lively. Full of laughter and smiles.

"I have some news," Josh announced, taking a sip from his whiskey. "Emma and I are divorcing," he continued. "We sat down and talked about it. We've been fighting a lot lately. The girls were catching on to our fights. They kept asking why Mom and Dad were yelling at each other the night before during breakfast. We decided we would work better as friends and co-parents," he explained, looking down.

"Well, this is a damper on my news," Devin murmured.

"What are you talking about?" Josh asked.

"Catherine and I are engaged," Devin said, smiling down at her.

"What?" Sarah asked enthusiastically. Devin nodded, looking at his mom.

"Dude, this is great news. Congratulations. You finally got the girl," his brother exclaimed.

"I did, didn't I?" Devin replied. "I'm sorry about you and Emma." His brother shrugged.

"I'll be fine. It was amicable and mutual. We haven't told the girls. The girls think I'm on a business trip. They went skiing with Emma and her parents. They are having a blast in Reno," he said.

The rest of dinner went smoothly. Midnight rolled around, and they all went to bed. They were both cuddling in bed when Devin kissed her shoulder.

"You and me," he whispered, kissing her head. She snuggled closer to him.

"You and me."

Epilogue

Catherine - January 2024

"Are you sure you want to do this?" Emily asked. "There's no turning back. Once you sign those papers, that's it," she said. "Trust me, I would know. I've been married for over a month now," Emily continued. She shoved her.

"I'm sure. I don't even want the whole big wedding thing," Catherine replied, looking at the dress in the mirror. They were at a bridal shop, buying her dress.

In a spur of the moment decision the previous night, Devin suggested they go to city hall to elope, and she agreed. So now, here she was, with Emily as her maid of honor, picking a simple dress for the elopement ceremony in two days.

"I suggested we go to Vegas, but tickets were expensive," Catherine added.

"That's what happens with last-minute decisions, babe," Emily pointed out. "Try the other one," she uttered, ushering her inside the dressing room again. Three dresses later, she settled on the perfect one, her face illuminating with a beaming smile.

Two days later

"Nervous?" Emily asked her.

"I have never been this nervous in my life," she confessed. Emily laughed.

"Pretty boy is pissing his pants over there too, don't worry."

"The judge is ready," Nathalie announced, coming out of the courtroom. Emily linked her arm with hers.

"Ready?" she asked, smiling. Catherine nodded nervously.

"Ready, Heats?" Catherine asked her flower girl.

"Auntie Cathy, I was born ready," she answered, straightening her back. Catherine laughed. They walked inside, where everyone from their inner circle turned to look. Her boss with his very pregnant wife Olive, Maverick, and Maggie. Brianna and Corbin with the twins, Nathalie holding one of them. Devin's parents and brother were also there, along with his boss and his wife. Emily walked her to where Devin was, and Devin took her hand.

"Here's to forever with you," he whispered, kissing her cheek.

"Do you have vows?" the judge asked.

"Yes," they both said in unison.

"You first," Devin muttered. She inhaled and nodded.

"I love you to infinity and back. You annoyed the hell out of me when we first met, but you were also my fiercest protector from the beginning. I didn't know what falling in love was until you. You're my best friend. My soulmate. My forever, Devin Mack. I promise to always love, cherish, and protect you. I promise to never shut you out again," she vowed. He laughed. "I promise that I will always come to you first. You're my favorite person in the whole world. This started fourteen years ago and will conclude with forever. I love you, and I can't wait to see what the future holds for us," she finished, smiling. "Your turn." He laughed, squeezing her hands.

"My sweet Catherine," he started, looking into her eyes. "You had my heart from day one. It has always been yours, and it will be yours for eternity. I promise I will always love you. You will always have someone in your corner cheering for you. I promise to never let you walk away. You're stuck with me for life now. There's no escaping me. I will always make you feel like the only woman in the world. You will never have to worry about me. You're safe and cherished. You will always have someone loving you. You will always have my heart, body, and soul. It will always be us against all odds and the world," he promised, his voice breaking. He kissed her forehead. "Forever and always, you and me," he whispered, looking into her eyes.

"You and me," she replied. He dropped his forehead to hers.

"The rings," the judge said. Maggie stepped forward and gave them the rings.

"Ready?" Devin asked her, and she nodded. He looked at the judge and nodded.

"Do you, Devin Mack, take Catherine Elizabeth Babbitt to be your wife, to have and to hold from this day forward, for better, for worse, for richer, for poorer, in sickness and in health, to love and to cherish till death do you apart?" the judge asked.

"I do," Devin vowed, placing the ring on her finger.

"And do you, Catherine Elizabeth Babbitt, take Devin Mack to be your husband, to have and to hold from this day forward, for better, for worse, for richer, for poorer, in sickness and in health, to love and to cherish till death do you apart?" the judge asked.

"I do," she said, placing the ring on Devin's finger.

"Witnesses, please come forward and sign here," the judge said. Emily and Corbin stepped forward and signed. Devin and Catherine signed after. "By the power and authority given to me by the District of Columbia, I now pronounce you husband and wife. You may kiss the bride." Devin smiled, wrapping his arms around her waist, bringing her closer, and kissed her. He kissed her like there was no tomorrow.

"You and me," he whispered against her lips.

Bonus Epilogue

A year and a half later - Summer 2025

The beeping of the heart monitor brought her out of her sleep. She blinked her eyes, letting them get used to the bright hospital lights. The room was quiet. She turned her head to the side until she spotted the red hair she was looking for. He was all curled up on the sofa beside her bed.

"Your neck and back are going to suffer so much," she mumbled as she smiled. She stirred, and he was up in a heartbeat.

"Oh goodness, you're awake," he said, groggy. He walked to her and smiled. "Hello, Kitty Cat," he whispered, kissing her forehead. She smiled, glazing around the room and spotting lots of flower bouquets and balloons. She looked around for the one thing missing.

"Where is she?" she asked. He smiled.

"She's in the nursery. Kitty Cat, she's perfect. She has your hair," he answered, kissing her forehead again. "And she's healthy. Ten toes, ten fingers, perfect hearing. Everything is okay. You, on the other hand…" he said, brushing a piece of hair out of her face. "You are my role model. You are a goddess. You created a whole human being and then brought it into this world. You deserve all the worship in the world," he praised, kissing her nose. "And I would happily oblige." She smiled. "Are you hungry? Thirsty? Do you want to take a walk to the nursery to see her?" he asked. She shook her head.

"Everything hurts," she mumbled. "And I'm tired. Pushing a human being the size of a watermelon out of me was hard," she said, closing her eyes. She heard him chuckle. He kissed her head.

"Okay. Then we'll just stay here until they bring her." She opened her eyes and looked at him.

"We are parents," she whispered incredulously.

In the year and a half since Emily's wedding and their engagement night, a lot had happened. After they decided to elope and have a city hall wedding, they took a month-long honeymoon across Canada. In December, a year after Emily's wedding, they found out they were three months pregnant. Of course, they were through the roof with excitement. When Devin had asked earlier in the year if she wanted children, and she'd said yes, the second easiest yes in her life, he'd booked the next appointment available to get his vasectomy reversed.

"We are parents," he uttered, beaming. He kissed her lips softly. "You are going to be the best mom. Our little girl is going to be so loved. She is so lucky to have you as her mother. I am one lucky motherfucker to have you as the mother of my children," he said. There was a knock outside, and they looked at the door. A nurse walked in.

"I'm bringing a little something that is yours," he announced, rolling in a little bassinet with a bundle inside. Devin helped her get the bed into a sitting position. "Alright, Momma, do you need help? Are you going to nurse her?" the nurse asked, picking the baby from the bassinet.

"Yes."

"Alright. I will get the nursing expert here to guide you and help you," he said, walking to her side of the bed and handing the baby to her.

"We got it from here," Devin said to the nurse, but she tuned them out. Her focus was solely on the little bundle in her arms. She took the little hat off, a mop of black hair springing out to life. She chuckled, wiping a tear away. She passed her pointer finger delicately down the little girl's nose, tracing her eyebrows and cheeks.

"You are perfect," she whispered, leaning down and kissing her head softly, inhaling her baby scent. The baby stirred.

"Did you guys pick a name already?" the nurse asked, checking her monitors.

"No, we haven't," she replied as Devin said, "Leonora." She looked at him, another tear escaping her eye. He wiped it away with his thumb.

"It's your mom's name. It was on the list. At the top of *your* list," he said, smiling. She turned back to the baby.

"Leonora," she repeated. She felt his arm come around her. He kissed her temple.

"She has a lot of hair, doesn't she?" he asked, taking her little hand in his finger. Baby Nora squeezed it.

"She's perfect. We got this, right? You and me?" she asked, looking at him. He glanced down at her and kissed her forehead.

"You and me, Kitty Cat. You and me."

Another knock sounded on the door. The door opened, and Emily and Nathalie walked in.

"The fairy godmother is here," she whispered. Emily

looked at her and smiled when she noticed the baby. "Let me see my baby," she said, walking to her side. "Oh, my goodness, look at all that hair," Emily whispered. "She's so beautiful. Babe, maybe we should make one," Emily added, gazing at Nathalie.

"We'll talk about that later," Nathalie replied, grinning happily at Emily. Emily smiled back and nodded. Emily turned her attention back on baby Nora, her eyes twinkling with happiness.

"I'm so proud of you, babe," she praised, kissing her head. "How are you feeling?" she asked, brushing a loose piece of hair behind her ear.

"Sore, and not in the good way," she admitted. Emily chuckled.

"Did you pick a name?" Nathalie asked from the foot of the bed.

"Leonora," Catherine and Devin said at the same time.

"Like your mom," Emily pointed out. She nodded.

"Any middle names?" Nathalie asked.

"Still debating," Devin said.

"Baby Nora. It suits her. Can I hold her?" Emily asked. Catherine nodded.

"Go wash your hands first," Catherine commanded, looking at her. Emily gave her a military salute and went to the bathroom to wash her hands. Nathalie walked to her side and peered down to baby Nora, passing a delicate finger through her hair.

"She does have a lot of hair," Nathalie pointed out. Catherine laughed. Emily and Nathalie stayed for a while and then left. Devin was holding baby Leonora on his chest, giving her skin-to-skin contact while she looked on from the bed. She smiled to herself at the image.

If you had told her three years ago that she was going to

end up with her college crush and the man she was so hopelessly in love with back then after not seeing him for almost a decade, she would have laughed in your face. But here she was, married to the love of her life with a newborn. She chuckled. He turned to her and smiled.

"What?" he asked softly. She shook her head and smiled at him. He kissed the top of baby Nora's head.

"You and me, right?" she asked.

"You and me," he replied, smiling at her.

And she knew that it was, indeed, him and her against the world and all odds.

Acknowledgments

First and foremost, I want to hug 14 year-old Carolina, for never giving up on her dreams and persevering. We did girlie. We got this.

Secondly, to BTS, for believing in me and encouraging me to follow my dreams. Apobangpo!

To Anna, my favorite Gemini and the one that reads everything I write first, the one I come to with my crazy ideas and future projects and cheers on me. Thank you for everything girlie pop! You shall keep being the one that reads everything I write first.

To M.S Murphy, my absolute partner in crime through this adventure. Here's to more trips, more stories, more FaceTime writing sessions and more crazy conversations about our future projects! Thank you for helping me and guiding me on this journey!

To Teralyn, thank you for your guidance, and answering all the questions of this newbie author!

To Brandi, my copy editor, thank you for helping me polish this and make its best version!

To my alpha readers Anne, Brenda, Andrea, Sabrina and Denise. Y'all are the realest for reading this when it was nothing but scraps and helping me develop it into what it is now. Your feedback is greatly appreciated.

To Kimbo, my amazing illustrator. Thank you for helping me bring the cover to life exactly how I pictured it!

To all my friends and family who were cheering on me

and were excitedly waiting for this! Thank you for all your encouraging words.

And last, but not least, the reader. Thank you for giving this hopeless romantic following her dream a chance. Don't worry, there's more to come. Everyone is getting a book. Can you guess who the next couple is? - I'll give you a hint, both of their names start with M ;)

About the Author

Pen-named author Carolina Guzman is a 27 years old, proud Latina/Hispanic, born and raised in Puerto Rico with a hopeless romantic heart. She has been avid reader since the age of 7. She's been writing since she was 13 years old, and it has been her dream to publish her work since as long as she can remember.

She has always been a bookworm, a passion instilled in her by her godmother, who was a kindergarten teacher. She is a fangirl. When she is not writing, you can find her devouring books or collecting BTS photocards and crying over them. She currently lives in the Nation's Capital (Washington, DC), the place who inspired her to write books about romance in the politics world with her never-ending TBR.

You can find her on her socials:
- IG: CarolinaBetweenStems
- TikTok: CarolinaBetweenStems
- Facebook Page: Author Carolina Guzman
- Goodreads: Carolina Guzman

- instagram.com/carolinabetweenstems
- tiktok.com/@carolinabetweenstems
- goodreads.com/carolina_guzman
- amazon.com/author/carolina_guzman